SECOND CHANCE

AN ENDWORLD EVERLASTING SAGA

A BATTLE MAGE REBORN (BOOK 1)

R. BRADY FROST

PERMAFROST
PRESS

ISBN: 979-8-7820-8452-3 (Paperback - Second Edition)

Published by PermaFrost Press, LLC.
2637 N. Washington Blvd STE 306
North Ogden, UT 84414

permafrostpress.com

__To my wife, Tara.__ Thanks for sharing my dream with me for all these years. I know it hasn't always been easy, and there are so many words I've yet to publish.
I love you.

__To my kids...__
Dreams can come true if you work hard
and never give up.
This book is proof.
Now, go clean your rooms... (ya hooligans!)

__Stephen Murray.__ You know why.

__And special thanks to Tyler Joseph.__
Thank you for entertaining your faith when you could have walked away.
Your music has been an inspiration.

There is a magical place that exists beyond memory and reason. Somewhere between dreams and reality, this world awaits the steadfast dreamers. Only those who act on their dreams and persist through self-doubt and the temptation to abandon their quest may find purchase within its boundaries.

1

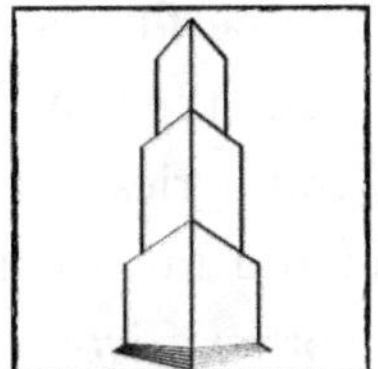

Cyberternal Industries, Inc. wasn't housed in one of the newest-generation mega skyscrapers that had reshaped the American skylines. It wasn't hidden in a super-secret mega bunker. The elusive headquarters wasn't even operated out of a lunar base, as some rumors might suggest.

I took one labored step. Then another.

No. The company behind EndWorld Everlasting, a game for the dead, had a story of far humbler origins.

At least according to Roger, the Assistant Vice-President of Something-or-Other at the world's newest and fastest growing gaming conglomerate.

Roger was also my ex-wife's new husband.

And, as he told it, EndWorld Everlasting was the biggest breakthrough science had ever achieved. It wasn't just a game. It was a man-made afterlife.

For that reason alone, it scared me.

Yet, people all around the world paid Cyberternal Industries a subscription fee, all hoping to live forever in their world of make-believe.

Their headquarters, Roger was more than happy to inform me, was located right here in the middle of Dallas, Texas.

How horribly convenient.

It still didn't change my mind. If that's what he thought would happen, he was a bigger fool than I'd taken him for.

The heart of the company was no further than a stone's throw away, he'd said, in the newly renovated glass spire once associated with one of the largest banks in North America.

It seemed like such a superfluous detail at the time, but it reminded me now of how much the world was changing. He told me it was because Cyberternal Industries wanted to invest in technology, to grow the capabilities of the human mind and even save lives, rather than getting mired in other, frivolous pursuits. Like fighting for real estate above the clouds.

I looked up at the once-familiar glass building in front of me and let out an exasperated sigh.

So much for my sense of progress.

There were still twenty more steps before we reached the entrance and my legs were already wobbly. Perhaps I shouldn't have been as bullheaded about walking in on my own. It didn't help that, despite all I seemed to have forgotten in recent months, I could still remember a time when I wouldn't have batted an eye at climbing twenty steps.

I could also recall a time when this building didn't have nearly as many. So much had changed but, I had to admit, despite the building's old bones, the new renovations looked amazing.

"You doing okay, Daddy?" My oldest daughter, Eliza, asked as she walked with her elbow linked in mine. "We can stop for a minute if you need to."

At seventeen years old, she'd only recently started calling me Daddy again. It was something she hadn't done since she was small. I wondered if she even noticed she was doing it.

My guess: probably not.

Maybe it was her way of grasping at the past. Whatever it was, it was my first real tip-off that she'd discovered the secret I tried so hard to keep from her.

I was sick.

Okay, I wasn't just sick.

I was dying.

Though I hated to give in to my weakness, I agreed.

"For a minute, if you don't mind," I huffed, placing my hands on my hips and leaning forward to catch my breath.

I wanted to be stronger.

And not just in some game. That was just it, wasn't it? With all the promises this company made its prospective customers, they couldn't give me the one thing I wanted most.

Time.

I wanted to be around to watch Eliza get married and have children of her own. I wanted so much to be a part of that experience. And not just for her, but for all three of my children.

It didn't take much to wear me out these days, what with the heavy doses of medication they forced me to take as a part of my government health plan. If it were up to me, I would have stopped taking them altogether, but things weren't that simple.

Even though there was no hope for a positive outcome, abandoning my treatment meant giving up any death benefits that might go to my kids.

Not that they needed it, what with a high roller like Roger in the picture, but a man has to stick with his principles. At least, that's what my father used to say.

"We'll go at your pace." Eliza smiled again. "There's nothing wrong with taking our time."

I wanted to take more than just my time. I wanted to turn around and walk right back to the light rail station. I wanted to get on the next train and leave the whole idea of Cyberternal and the reminder of my sickness behind.

I just wanted to enjoy what I had left before it was too late. I'd already lost so much.

But a promise was a promise. So, I stayed and let my mind wander where my body couldn't.

After the initial shock about the location of the Cyberternal home office wore off, I guess it sort of made sense. The financial sector had exploded in recent years, especially with the global monetization of in-game currencies for the latest online games, fully immersive virtual reality MMORPG's.

Once, long ago, there were only a few games dominating the Massively Multiplayer Online Role-Playing Game scene with smaller titles scrambling for the scraps. Things were different now.

For the first time in a nearly a whole generation, business was booming. The emerging virtual markets reinvigorated a stagnant economy. People could go to work inside their favorite game worlds, outside the over-saturated and highly mechanized manufacturing and consumer goods industries that had failed them.

With the widespread shift in fortunes, many financial institutions moved their headquarters into the new generation of skyscrapers, ones that truly contended with the clouds for dominion of the horizon. This left their old real estate empires up for grabs at better prices than new startups could ignore.

For those of us used to the old speed of progress and construction, it seemed as though entire cityscapes changed almost overnight. It was now apparent that companies like Cyberternal had capitalized on that change. Even as I stared at the new heart of Dallas, I realized that the future was here.

"I used to work over there," I said, pointing across the street, "in the old Earle Cabell Federal Building, before they tore it down. It was a lot different back then. You could actually see the sky from street level, believe it or not."

Eliza nodded and smiled. I'd told her this before.

"Right," I added. "Mentioned that already, didn't I?"

"It must have been a whole different world back then," she said without skipping a beat.

"It was." I returned her smile and started walking again. "Ten years ago, these fancy, endless steps weren't even here."

"Oh?"

"Believe it or not—" I turned and surveyed the area we'd come from. "Where we're standing now would have been in the middle of the street. And that over there," I pointed diagonally to the spot in front of where the federal building once stood, "was a park."

Eliza laughed. "A park. In the middle of the city?"

I nodded. "Complete with water features and squirrels, if you can imagine that. Of course, the buildings weren't as big back then. The folks who lived in the high rises needed a place to walk their dogs and, as far as I know, there weren't any of the indoor facilities like they have now."

Eliza had grown up in the once-rural townships, about an hour to the east, and well outside the booming Dallas-Fort Worth megaplex. I silently wished I could see the world around us with her eyes instead of mine. Everywhere I looked, there were ghosts of a city I once knew.

I stretched my back and glanced at my watch.

"I suppose we have an appointment to get to," I said, doing my best to keep the resistance I felt out of my voice. "Enough reminiscing for now, we better get a move on."

Climbing the final steps leading up to the grand entryway was like hiking a mountain. Each successive foothold was a triumph, but it was also one step closer to an experience I had no desire to endure.

"It was nice of Roger to arrange this," Eliza said.

"Eliza—"

She stopped and looked at me in earnest. "Daddy—"

There it was again. The regression. The desire to hold on to something that was rapidly slipping away. But there was also stubborn obstinance. I knew how she felt, but I didn't have the luxury of hope. I was certain there was nothing Roger or Cyberternal Industries could do for me.

Some things couldn't be changed, no matter how badly you wanted it or how hard you tried. If only she knew that I'd already been down that road.

"You said you would keep an open mind," she reminded me.

"I did, didn't I?" I asked, allowing her to help me up the steps.

"And I suppose you won't be letting an old man off the hook, will you?"

She laughed. "You're not that old."

Her laughter faded, leaving in its place an unmistakable note of sadness. "Anyway, no. I won't let you off the hook. Besides, we're already here. Would you really want to turn back now?"

"Yes?" I answered.

She rolled her eyes.

The door in front of us swished open, sending a blast of cold air out into the hot, Texas day. It felt good. More than that, it felt almost heavenly.

"Oh, wow," I muttered. "On second thought, maybe we can go inside. Just for a little while."

Together we walked through the threshold and into a beautiful lobby. The door swished closed behind us, the lights dimmed, and we heard the unmistakable sound of falling rain.

A clap of thunder rumbled through the air, sending a shiver down my spine. Eliza and I exchanged glances and looked around for the source of the sounds.

"What is real?" a disembodied voice asked.

A flash of lightning lit up the area, followed by a second, and then another.

"What is reality?" the voice emphasized the last word.

Tiny raindrops stung my skin before another reverberation of thunder and lightning unleashed a downpour. Eliza grabbed my hand and huddled close.

"Is this real?" the voice whispered.

Just as quickly as it had begun, the storm faded, and the sun seemed to break out from whatever cloud it had been hiding behind. The rest of the lobby, once enshrouded in shadow, was now far too bright.

The fresh scent of rain receded, and the dry smell of desert heat infused the surrounding air. I shielded my eyes against the glare with my hand.

"How about this? Is this real?"

An impossibly large lizard scampered around Eliza's legs and then faded into the glare. Startled, she screamed and jumped before insisting, "It touched me. It really did."

"Imagine a world full of possibilities."

The light receded, and I blinked in an effort to return my vision back to normal.

"Cyberternal Industries, Incorporated, proudly presents the biggest revolution in gaming history. EndWorld Everlasting. What comes next? You decide."

When I surveyed the lobby, I saw two guards in crisp uniforms standing to the side, eying us with a sense of casual amusement. An attractive woman with platinum blonde hair sat behind an immaculate glass desk.

She adjusted in her seat as the program dissipated and she flashed us a warm smile. Her piercing green eyes seemed to take in every detail and she stood as we approached.

"How did you enjoy the VIP treatment? You must be Mr. Wade, and—" she cast a thoughtful glance toward my daughter, "Eliza, I presume?"

"That's us, and it was amazing." Eliza beamed.

"Roger has told me so much about you both," the woman said, reaching out her hand.

I looked for a badge or name tag but couldn't spot one. I didn't want her to think I was staring at her chest, so I promptly shook her hand and averted my eyes.

A quick look to the side confirmed both guards wore building access badges, reinforcing the feeling that something was a little off.

"It's an embedded chip," she said, as if reading my thoughts.

"I see," I murmured.

"All high-level employees have them instead of the normal badges. It's a much more secure way of tracking our movements inside the facility. The chip works with biometrics to grant access to certain restricted areas. It also monitors our vitals, and a few other things we don't disclose to the public."

Then she added, "My name is Krysta."

My mind was reeling. I tried in vain to process all the implications of what Krysta had so casually explained.

Chipping employees wasn't exactly groundbreaking territory by any means, but the idea still evoked a certain sense of apprehension that bordered on superstition.

I swallowed hard and forced a smile.

"It's nice to meet you, Krysta," Eliza said and shook the woman's hand.

Just then, a young man with a building badge approached from an area behind the desk and took a seat where the woman had been sitting only moments before.

Krysta nodded at him and smiled. "Thank you, Harvey," she said.

"My pleasure, Ms. Peterson."

She looked back at me before giving us both a disarming wink. "Shall we?"

Then she walked toward the elevator without waiting for a reply.

2

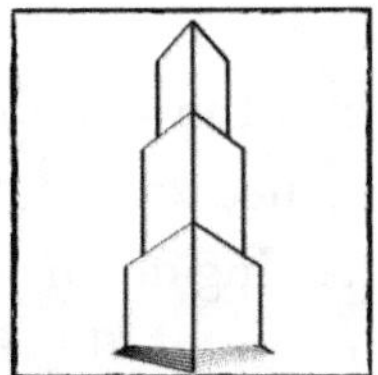

Eliza stepped inside the elevator and shot me a backwards glance. The meaning of her wordless gesture was clear. She was excited, but she recognized my hesitation.

The slightest squint around her eyes silenced any protest I might have made.

A promise was a promise.

I let out another sigh and shook my head before following her lead. Roger had pulled some strings to get us here, but he and I both knew this wasn't about me. This was for Helen and the kids.

I had to give it to the man.

He had class.

Even at seventeen, Eliza was still young enough to have hope. She always seemed to see the best in everyone. While I had wracked myself over all the possible ulterior motives Roger might have had up his sleeve, she instantly clung to the idea that somehow Cyberternal Industries could do the impossible.

In some respects, they already had. To say the creation of EndWorld Everlasting was revolutionary would be a gross under-statement. It was a game-changer, literally.

Beyond the metal exterior doors, the small chamber was made of glass. Afraid to look down, I stared up through the transparent ceiling. Small LED lights appeared to mark the stories within the elevator shaft, extending somewhere past the vertical horizon.

The metal doors of the lobby swished closed, followed by a thin inner glass pane a few seconds later. I looked at the new front wall, then the sides, and finally caught Krysta's eyes in the reflection. I raised my eyebrows.

"No buttons, Mr. Wade," she explained before her smile and the look in her eyes hinted at something almost sinister.

The elevator plunged into the unknown without so much as a warning and my stomach lurched as we fell. Despite my best efforts, I couldn't keep myself from looking down. The same LED lights faded into oblivion, racing toward us as the transparent chamber sped through the darkness.

Twenty.

Thirty.

Forty floors?

My mind struggled to keep up while simultaneously wrestling with the utter impossibility of the plunge. I had been amazed that a city like Dallas could have such an extensive, interconnected underground when I'd first moved to the area for work. It made me wonder if something similar existed in other parts of the world. But this? This was something else.

I was no geologist, but I hadn't thought something of this scale could be done in this area. I immediately pictured the shifting clay soil and low water tables I thought might have plagued the old underground.

Even now I could remember how some sections had been closed off for years due to neglect.

Or maybe it wasn't neglect. Maybe it was this? The question threatened to dismantle everything I thought I knew about the city I'd worked in for years before getting sick.

Eighty.

One-hundred.

One-twenty.

Finally, the elevator slowed and came to an easy stop at sub-level 126. The pane slid back and another set of metal doors retracted into the wall-space.

Eliza let out her held breath and clasped her shaking hands. "That. Was. Awesome," she exclaimed.

Krysta's devilish smile did nothing to hide her pleasure.

"Ms. Peterson?" I breathed.

"Yes, Mr. Wade?"

"That was pretty cool." Then, after considering the show in the lobby, I added, "But was it real?"

That same self-satisfied smile played about Krysta's lips before she answered. "Unofficially?"

"Sure." I shrugged my indifference.

Officially. Unofficially. It made no difference to me. We'd already signed full non-disclosure forms and, really, who was I going to tell?

"It's the full one-hundred." Krysta beamed.

"That means it's one-hundred percent real," Eliza explained.

I rolled my eyes and smiled at her helpful innocence. "I got that." I laughed.

Eliza frowned but when Krysta started laughing as well, she couldn't help but join us.

"This way," Krysta said before leading us down a sterile-looking hallway.

From the sparse out-of-date motivational posters framed on the otherwise barren walls to the perfectly polished floors, it was clear that sub-floor 126 didn't get much in the way of human traffic.

I almost reached out to pinch Krysta to see if she was real but managed to catch the impulse before it turned into action. For all I knew, the real Krysta could be sitting in the comfort of her office in one of the top floor suites.

Wouldn't that be a mind trip, two meat-suits following a cybernetic unit or a haptic-enabled hologram into the depths of the earth for a medical examination that could have been done over the phone with even the briefest review of my charts?

"You undoubtedly have questions," Krysta said, breaking into my chaotic stream of thoughts. "What lies ahead? Why this far under-ground? Why would Cyberternal Industries take an interest in your case or go to such lengths? What's in it for us?"

While all of those questions were fair assumptions for someone in her position, I felt conflicted as to whether I really wanted the answers she was offering. Really, what reasonable person wouldn't want to know?

It all seemed straight-forward enough, but I wasn't here for any of it. Certainly not for a miracle cure. There was no real hope for that anymore. I was just a man spending one of the few remaining days he had on this world with his oldest daughter.

The setting wasn't perfect, and the activity probably less-so, but where else could Eliza begin her journey of coming to terms with my decision? What was left for a man like me?

EndWorld?

I wasn't interested.

Before I had a chance to protest, however; Krysta stopped and turned to face a recessed door in the side of the hallway. A gentle voice intoned, "Biometrics confirmed. Welcome, Krysta Peterson. I see you are accompanied by two guests. Please allow me a moment to verify access."

If the security system could be believed, it seemed Krysta really was here. In the flesh. I was suddenly very happy I hadn't given in to the temptation to pinch her earlier.

"Identity confirmed: Denton Wade and daughter, Eliza Wade. Access granted."

"Thank you, Miriam," Krysta said and walked through the now-open doorway. Once inside, she turned and beckoned us forward.

The immediate area inside the door was smaller than I expected. I crossed the threshold and my eyes were drawn toward a large, upright pod standing directly across from the entrance.

Eliza turned to me and put a steadying hand on my shoulder, but I could see the fear in her eyes.

"What's with the pod?" Eliza turned and asked, speaking for both of us. "I thought this was just a medical evaluation."

It was in that moment that I realized how brave she must have been. Perhaps I was mistaken in my previous assumptions, superimposing on her my own childish hope when I was her age. In truth, I wasn't certain how well I really knew my daughter. I thought I did, but things were slipping. Kids grew up so fast, especially in this crazy, new world.

Maybe things weren't that simple.

She was becoming such a strong young woman, someone I was very proud of. But maybe she was both strong and blissfully hopeful; a complex creature built from her own unique experiences, and so much more than any one particular emotion.

I put my arm around her neck and turned my gaze toward Krysta. Her eyes were soft and she had a sort of half-smile that said so much more than I expected from a complete stranger.

Compassion.

"As you must know, Mr. Wade, traditional medical procedures are out of the question for someone in your... situation."

"Daddy," Eliza said. "Daddy?"

I bit my lip and nodded. "That's right."

It was the best answer I could give. It killed me to break it down to the cold, hard truth in front of Eliza, but if she didn't know by now, maybe it was time to fess up.

"And yet you're here," Krysta went on. "Roger has informed me that you have some reservations toward the idea of what EndWorld represents. Is that correct?"

"To put it lightly," I admitted.

Krysta nodded.

"What you see before you isn't a standard immersion pod. As you can probably tell, there's something a bit different about this one. We've been experimenting with a new technological breakthrough. It's truly the stuff of science fiction.

"We've already been able to achieve incredible things, things not yet thought possible by the medical community at-large. With the aid of Artificial Intelligence and our patented nano-helpers, we've been quietly saving lives while the rest of the world struggles with accepting the existence of sentient machines."

"You aren't planning on turning me into a machine, are you?" I asked. "That doesn't even come close to what I signed up for."

My arm was still around Eliza's shoulders and her grip on my wrist tightened.

"Of course not." Krysta laughed. "If you choose to move forward with this, your physicians will be the sentient machines," she said. "Millions of them, coursing through your bloodstream to attack the cancer at the source. Actively rewriting the DNA code to eradicate the mutations and put your body back on track one sequence at a time."

"You're right," I agreed. "That is some serious science fiction shit."

"Dad," Eliza exclaimed in classic teenage fashion, then let out an embarrassed giggle.

Krysta smiled before continuing.

"That said, you must understand, nothing is guaranteed. We've made incredible breakthroughs, but we're not quite there yet. There are still some things even the machines aren't capable of fixing. Maybe some day. They're learning at an incredible rate, doing things I never would have dreamed. But, as always, we have to take things one step at a time."

"You're saying there's a chance you might be able to save my dad?" Eliza asked, her jaw now firm.

"I'm not in a position to make promises," Krysta answered. "But, yes, there is a chance."

3

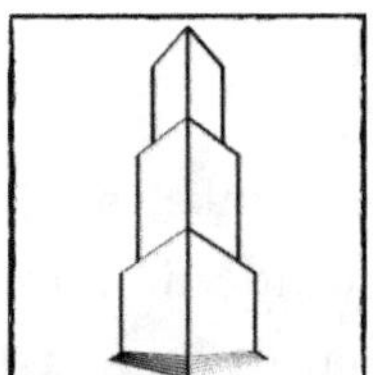

"**D**addy, you have to do this," Eliza breathed, stepping out from under my arm and turning to look me square in the eyes. She had her mother's determination. "There's no question about it. You have to."

Krysta's intense gaze softened, and her eager smile faded slightly, vanquishing any doubt I might have had. There was no denying it, she'd seen this play out a few times before.

"Let's slow down for a moment," Krysta said, putting a gentle hand on Eliza's shoulder. "You have to understand, this might be a lot for your dad to process all at once."

"You're offering him a new lease on life. What could he possibly need to process? It's a no-brainer."

Krysta offered a sympathetic smile and took a step backward.

"Say yes, Daddy."

I couldn't bring myself to look at her. Not yet. There was so much to consider.

"Say yes."

I stared straight ahead, allowing my eyes to drift in and out of focus as I looked at the pod. It had a red glass front that wasn't quite see-through and an alarming number of tubes that trailed up into the high ceiling. I wondered what millions of nano-helpers looked like.

Would I feel them in my veins?

Would they slip through my bloodstream like quicksilver on their quest to hunt and kill my offending cells? What would fill the space where the tumors had been? I had so many questions, but lacked the fortitude to ask.

Eliza's fingers intertwined with mine and when I looked down, our eyes met.

"Dad?"

"It's common in situations like this," Krysta explained, "for our potential patients to take a little time to come to terms with other, unexpected options. You have to understand, your father probably started his grieving process months ago."

"I don't understand. What difference would that make?"

"You'd be surprised. The process of letting go is a spiritual one for many people. Not everyone who's entered this room has opted to undergo the procedure, though all have been equally vetted. There are different reasons, of course."

"Like what?" Eliza pressed.

"Some considered the odds and even the slightest chance of failure was too much to bear," Krysa went on.

"Some held tight to their fear of the machines, even in the face of salvation. Some had simply let go of their desire to fight. They had already progressed too far through the stages of grief."

"You mean they chose to just... to just die?" Eliza asked, sounding small.

"While no two people who have crossed this threshold have been the same, one thing remains a constant similarity: they are all very complex creatures with their own unique versions of logic and reason," Krysta said.

"Why are the machines sentient?" I asked, hoping to take away some of the pressure to keep fighting Eliza must have been feeling. "Wouldn't simple, directed nano-tech be sufficient?"

"I think you already know the answer to that question, Mr.

Wade," Krysta answered. "Directed technology can't save you because we lack the ability to assess and act with the speed and precision with which these machines can. With the speed the cancer took hold, we're looking at a very complex series of procedures and gene therapy. It's beyond current human capabilities."

"But they're not perfect. The machines. They can make mistakes?"

Krysta remained silent, allowing me time to process.

"Why?" I asked. "Why would Cyberternal Industries, the makers of EndWorld, be concerned with this?"

"Saving lives, you mean?" Krysta asked.

"Underground operating rooms. Scary looking medical pods. Tiny sentient robot doctors? All of those would work, but sure. Let's go with saving lives."

"Do you know why our company was founded?"

I shook my head and shrugged. "The same reason as any other company, I imagine."

"Well, yes. And also, no," Krysta said. "You won't see it in any of the advertisements, but Cyberternal Industries was born from a father's love for his dying son."

"How so?" I asked, allowing myself to take the obvious bait.

"Even with the rate technology has grown and the boom we've seen in the past few years, especially in the Biotech industries, our founder and CEO was unable to save his only child. Instead, he was forced to watch him waste away as the disease ran its course."

She paused a moment before continuing.

"No matter what he tried, he couldn't change the reality of this world. So, he had a vision to create a new one. One where his son and countless others could have a second chance to live. That was how EndWorld was born, but the focus has always been here. Secretly, we've always been about saving lives so that other families don't have to watch as their loved ones are taken from them before their time."

Silent tears fell down Eliza's cheeks as she turned from Krysta to look at me once again.

I let out a breath I hadn't realized I was holding, then I looked from Eliza to the machine and back again.

"What if it doesn't work?" I asked.

"I'd rather take the risk." Her voice was quiet and small. "And even though I don't understand your hesitation, I love you. That won't change, no matter what you decide." She wrapped her arms around me and sobbed into my chest.

I reached up and put my hand on her head, doing my best to comfort her. Then I looked at Krysta and nodded. "I'll do it."

"Great," Krysta said with what appeared to be a genuine smile. "If you're prepared to undergo the first of your procedures this afternoon, we're all ready on this side."

I stared at her in blank confusion for what felt like an eternity before Eliza gave voice to what we were both thinking.

"What? You mean today, right now? Just like that?"

"Yes. Miriam is our resident AI for this project. She keeps the lab space ready to go at a moment's notice. In cases like your father's we find it's best to get started right away, unless the patient objects."

Eliza turned and looked at me. "What do you think?"

"I haven't made any arrangements," I managed to stammer, still unsure about the sudden decision I was being thrust into.

"Roger has taken the liberty of personally seeing to all of your immediate obligations," Krysta said, adding a little blush to her smile. "We don't usually take such a hands-on approach to this but, for Roger, your case hit close to home."

I was floored by the continued revelations of what this man had done, not only for me but also for my children. Drawing in a deep breath, I silently resolved to thank him for the opportunity the next time I saw him. Then I exhaled and closed my eyes.

I focused only on the sound of my heartbeat thrumming in my ears and did my best to let go of any feeling of resistance or hesitation. When I opened my eyes again, Krysta and Eliza were still patiently waiting for my answer.

I nodded again.

"I think I'm ready."

~

I SNIFFED AND TOOK A SECOND TO STRETCH MY NECK. THE POD enclosure was a bit roomier than I'd expected, but my limbs were all secured in place, and tubes disappeared into the flesh of my arms and legs.

Through a thick sheet of protective glass, I could see an image of Krysta and Eliza. They were both sitting in a separate room, but the image was crisp and clear.

Even though they were staring back at me from a screen built seamlessly into the thick pane, I felt as if I could reach out and touch them. And yet, logically, I knew it was an illusion.

"What is real?" I whispered the words and allowed myself the pleasure of a mischievous grin.

Krysta spoke into a microphone somewhere in front of her. "Are you ready for the recording, Mr. Wade?"

I stopped smiling and nodded.

"Verbally, if you could. Please? I need to verify we have audio and confirm your consent."

"Yes," I said. "I'm ready."

"Great. We're just going to breeze through a little legal work and then we'll get on with it, okay?"

"Okay."

She smiled and picked up a clipboard.

"State your name for the record."

"Denton Ellis Wade."

"You're doing great, Dad," Eliza said, leaning toward Krysta's mic.

I smiled at her and winked. In truth, I was beyond nervous, and maybe a little scared. But I was doing my best to keep those feelings under control.

Eliza was right. I'd been given a new lease on life and this time I was determined to do things right.

No more surrender.

No more giving into fear.

No walking away.

Not this time.

"Denton Ellis Wade, do you agree to be bound by the non-disclosure agreements you have signed with Cyberternal Industries, Incorporated?"

"I do."

"Are you undergoing this procedure of your own free will, without coercion or promises of payment from Cyberternal Industries, Incorporated?"

"I am."

"Do you understand that this recording and any medical data obtained throughout the procedure or anytime thereafter will belong solely to Cyberternal Industries, Incorporated, and its affiliates, and will be used to advance technologies, which may or may not be used to generate revenue?"

"I do."

I watched Eliza turn to examine something outside the camera's field of vision and privately wished I could scratch my nose.

Krysta continued with her list of questions for the recording. "Do you understand that a complete neural map will be taken as part of the procedure? And that this map will be used post-procedure for comparison and research purposes?"

"Uh, I guess so?"

"Mr. Wade?" Krysta's tone was assertive.

"I do."

"Do you understand that this will be the first in a series of procedures, and that you will be required to complete the entire treatment plan prior to your release from this program?"

"Yes." I nodded.

"And do you agree to accept transportation and assistance for ongoing procedures, provided to you free of cost or obligation by Cyberternal Industries, Incorporated, through the duration of your treatment? Do you also acknowledge that said assistance is not to be considered as a form of payment for participation in this research?"

I laughed. "Yes. I do."

Krysta nodded at the clipboard and set it aside. "Do you have any questions for me at this time?"

"Will it hurt?" Eliza asked.

Krysta looked conflicted before nodding again. "I was going to cover that in a bit, but I suppose now is as good a time as any."

She looked up at the camera, speaking directly to me. "There is a chance that the nano-helpers won't be able to anesthetize certain areas, due to the strain it might put on the surrounding tissue. If that turns out to be the case, and if your charts are any indication, it probably will, we can do something for the pain once the procedure is over."

"What?" Eliza asked, incredulous. "What do you mean, 'once it's over?'"

"You won't remember the pain," Krysta said, still looking at me as she tried to reassure my daughter.

"You expect me to just sit by and watch my father being tortured in there? He might not remember, but I will."

"That's why family members are not permitted to view the actual procedure," Krysta said, turning to face her. "I'm sorry, Eliza."

"I will be okay," I interjected, cutting into the budding struggle for power my daughter wasn't equipped to win. "I'm tough. If you want me to have a chance at getting better, this is what needs to be done. I can handle it. I promise. Besides, I'll see you when it's finished. No memory, no pain. Deal?"

Eliza's reply came after a long, drawn out silence. "Deal."

The rest of the preliminaries went by in a blurred haze.

I was so wrapped up in my thoughts that I almost didn't realize the calibrations had finished and Krysta was about to usher Eliza from the room.

"Hang in there, Daddy," Eliza said, wiping a tear from her eye.

I startled back into the present and blinked at the screen inside the glass shell. "Eliza, hold up."

She cast her gaze away from the camera for a minute before looking back. Suddenly, words escaped me. "I... uh... I love you. If something happens, will you tell your brother and sister that—"

"No," she cut in, shaking her head. "I love you, too, Dad. But no, I won't tell them anything. You can tell them yourself when you're done."

With that she turned and walked out the door, leaving Krysta to offer me a consoling smile before ducking out to escort her to a waiting room down the hall.

"Real smooth," I whispered to myself. "Real freaking smooth."

Nearly five minutes passed before Krysta returned.

"She'll be okay," she said. "You've got a really tough daughter, Mr. Wade. You did well."

"I think I blew it there at the end," I said. "Maybe I shouldn't have said anything about things possibly going wrong."

"Not at all. I think what you did is a very important part of the process. And trust me, she heard you. She isn't ready to handle the thought of losing you just yet. If you want my guess, I'd say she'll likely apologize for the outburst as soon as you walk into the waiting room."

"You think so?" I asked.

"Well, this isn't exactly my first rodeo, but people have surprised me from time to time." She turned back to her clipboard. "It looks like we're all set, if you're ready to begin?"

That was the cue. The therapy session was over.

"Let's do it," I said. Then I closed my eyes and tried to relax.

The pod rotated backwards until my head and feet felt level. Cold air flooded the small chamber and Krysta cleared her throat.

"There's a chance you may lose consciousness. If that happens, you might not remember this conversation, but just in case you do, try not to freak out. Some people wake up in new surroundings and, well... Let's just say we've had a few who didn't handle it quite as well as they might have."

"Try not to freak out," I said, my voice strained and a little uneven. "Check."

Honestly, I wasn't sure what else to say.

According to Krysta, there was a good chance I was about to feel a whole lot of pain. From what I gathered, it could be overwhelming and I might pass out. Of course, they would give me meds that would make it so I didn't remember said pain, but I could wake up somewhere unexpected with no memory of how I got there.

Awesome.

Bring it on.

"I'm uploading the nano-helpers now."

"Nano-helpers." I chuckled. "What a silly thing to call th—"

The burn of a million paper-cuts seared through my veins like lightning and my mouth filled with the coppery twang of tasted blood. This wasn't a test of will.

I wasn't fighting for a cause like the hero in some movie. I had no intention of holding out until the last possible second to yell a single word of import.

All I wanted to do was to scream in agony, but no sound could escape my lips. The impulse was there, but I somehow lacked the ability.

Wave after wave of fire coursed upward as the tiny machines infiltrated their war zone and stormed toward the enemy gates. Every last nerve in my body was a live wire. Every muscle twitched and cramped of its own accord.

And then the world went dark.

4

I n the darkness, there was no world. There was nothing. And yet, somehow, there was no nothing, because nothing was something.

In the darkness, there was only the absence of anything.

I had no thoughts, no reasoning. I experienced no time, and yet time passed. I had only my awareness to keep me company, but even that was silent. I was an aura of uncertainty surrounded by the vast unknown, and unable to reach out or question my own existence.

I was something and I was nothing all at once, until everything changed.

When I opened my eyes, I was no longer in the pod. In fact, if I was sure of anything, it was that I wasn't on sub-floor 126 at all.

Krysta's words echoed in my mind.

"Try not to freak out," I mumbled, stumbling over the sound of my own voice. "Check."

Somehow, it seemed as if eons had passed since I'd last heard my own inflection.

A slight seaward breeze tugged at my hair and clothes. The sun was shining and large, billowing clouds rolled across the sky like lazy giants.

There was no cityscape or smog, only the shifting forms of shapes begging to be named by an imagination starved by the void.

I turned and surveyed my surroundings. I was standing on the white marble steps of a ruin atop a small island, and I wasn't alone.

Roger was sitting nearby. When I turned to look at him, he stood.

"There you are," he said. His tone was casual, and it looked like he was wearing some kind of bathrobe. It drew a stark contrast to the near-permanent business casual attire I was used to seeing him in.

I looked down at myself and saw the same drab linens. "What is this?" I asked.

Roger chuckled. "A toga? No? Maybe. I'm not sure, actually."

"Where's Eliza?"

He stopped laughing and his smile faded as he looked out toward the sea.

"Roger. Where is my daughter?"

"Damnit, Denton," Roger said. "How can I answer that question? I know you must be confused. You have to believe me when I tell you that it wasn't supposed to be like this."

I looked at my toga again before following his gaze to the endless blue water. After breathing in a huge gulp of salty air, I thought about the lizard that had slithered against Eliza's leg in the lobby. "Am I dead?" I asked.

Roger remained silent, still watching the waves dance on the rocks below.

"Is any of this real?"

He turned to face me and shrugged. "What is real? Are you real? Am I real? Ultimately, that's for you to decide."

I pinched my arm. "I feel real."

Roger nodded.

"Is this EndWorld?" I asked at last, giving my suspicions life.

"Almost," he said, still refusing to look me in the eye. "This is the tutorial program that gates access to EndWorld."

"What did you do? What did you do, Roger? What in the hell have you done?" I tried to get ahold of myself, but the questions burst from my mouth before I could stop them. "What happened to Catch-22?"

"The Digital Consent Law of 2022?" Roger asked, looking up from the rocks below. He let out a long sigh. "I know this is going to be hard for you to accept, but you gave your consent. You're here of your own free will."

"You're trying to tell me that I wanted this? No way," I spat. "This isn't what I signed up for. I agreed to treatment. That was it. Now I wake up and I'm here."

"This wasn't me," he said, lifting his hands in a defensive gesture. "It was your decision to come here. You have to trust me, Denton. I know it's confusing, but you wanted this. Please, if you'll allow me to explain—"

"Go on then," I shouted. "Explain it to me. Tell me how I got here."

I don't know what I expected him to say. If I was here, it meant there was no going back. Still, the anger I felt was overwhelming. I needed something, anything to hold on to.

Why had he robbed me of my last few months with my children? How could he do something like that? Even through my anger, I could see how that didn't make much sense. Why go through all the hassle to get rid of me? It wasn't like I was going to get better. All he had to do was sit back and wait. My clock would have run out sooner than later.

Had I died in the pod? Was that it? That was something I could understand. It was a risk. I knew it when I gave my authorization for the procedure. But I'd never agreed to be brought over to EndWorld.

"We've had this conversation five times now," Roger said, sitting back on the step. "Each time it's gotten more difficult."

"What are you talking about?"

He plucked a blade of grass and began nibbling at it, spitting little bits here and there. I could remember doing the same as a kid and the humanizing effect helped calm my nerves.

"What do you mean, Roger?" I asked. "We've never had this conversation before."

"You didn't die," he said, then quickly added, "Well, I mean, you did. Last week, actually. But last week, as it happened for the rest of us, never happened for you. Your last memory was in the pod. That was a little over three months ago."

Three months?

He shrugged. "Krista told me you were in agony when the nano-helpers completed their baseline scan. They'd already begun the procedure, and it isn't normally a concern, but the pain is probably the last thing you remember. I'm sorry about that."

"I thought the scan was just for comparison," I said, narrowing my eyes at him.

"It was. It is. A baseline neural scan isn't enough to port someone to this side on its own," he explained. "We had to merge the data from that scan with the rest of the data from your EndWorld transition. Even then, this was a risky operation. As you can probably tell, the last four attempts didn't turn out as well as we'd hoped."

I let out a huff and sat down on the step beside him. "You're telling me that I chose this? I don't see how that makes any sense."

He laughed, but there was no joviality in it. "No, I suppose it wouldn't make much sense at all. Would it? Your disdain for EndWorld was no secret. It wasn't until near the end that you began seeing things differently."

"What if I don't want to be here?" I asked. "What if the choice you say I made was wrong?"

Roger cleared his throat and stood, pacing toward the edge of the cliff before answering. "You can jump now and it will be over, the program will acknowledge your choice and your data will be scrubbed from the system," he said. "Or you can finish the tutorial, get a taste of what you might be missing out on, and tell your guide you don't want to enter the world beyond. Then jump."

I stood up and took my place next to him at the edge of the cliff. Closing my eyes, I drew a deep breath and felt the tug of the wind on my robe and skin.

"But—" Roger started.

I opened my eyes.

"Part of the tutorial includes an opportunity to say goodbye. To Eliza and Sophie and Jacob. Helen too."

I let out the breath I'd been holding and glanced over at him. "You serious?"

"This last week has been hard on them. On all of us, really."

"I can say goodbye? That's possible?"

Roger nodded. "You don't even have to tell them what you intend to do. Just say goodbye. Give them a measure of peace before you leave."

I thought for a minute, allowing the breeze to take my mind wherever it might go. "They think I'm staying?"

I waited for a response, but none came. Roger's gaze remained fixed on the horizon and I could see his exhaustion plainly across his features. The slumped shoulders, the bags under his eyes, how had I missed it before?

"Do they know how much trouble you've run into?" I asked.

He shook his head. "We knew there was a risk. No matter how hard the machines worked or how close we got, it wasn't enough. We were too late. The cancer was aggressive, but we thought we had it under control. At least enough to complete the transfer. There just wasn't enough data."

"And you've been working to get it right ever since?"

He nodded again. "I think I was beginning to get used to failure. This was our last shot. I know you weren't ready for this, not at the stage you were in when the first scan was taken."

He turned to face me, abandoning the picturesque view.

"If you aren't ready for this, Denton, I'll respect your wishes. I won't bring you back. This is it. I just want you to know that I'm not here to trick you. I'm not trying to push this on you in any way. We all just want you to find happiness, however you choose to pursue it."

Then he held out his hand and gave me a gentle smile.

I looked down at his empty palm and then offered my own, shaking his hand in a gentleman's agreement.

Complete the EndWorld Everlasting tutorial for an opportunity to see my family one last time?

Those were terms I could live with.

5

After saying our temporary goodbyes, Roger exited the program. In his absence, I was alone, surrounded by the miraculous splendor of the digital landscape. Birds cried out their lonesome songs as they drifted on the thermals.

The white marble ruins reminded me of the life I'd left behind. The last page in my book had been turned, and I'd missed out on the final chapter.

The idea that I had died months after stepping into that pod was still hard to accept. It was almost as hard to believe as the notion that some other version of me had chosen this path.

But what reason would Roger have for lying?

And why go to the pain and expense of getting me here when things hadn't gone according to plan?

I had far more questions than answers.

"Hello, Traveler," a soft, feminine voice said, startling me out of my wandering thoughts.

I turned around to find a beautiful woman draped in thin, wispy white fabric that fluttered in the gentle breeze. Her hair was raven-black against her pale skin and her green eyes sparkled in the sunlight.

"Hello," I said, confused. "Are you the tutorial?"

She laughed and put a hand to her mouth in an effort to hide her growing smile. "This," she gestured to the surrounding space, "is your tutorial. *I* am Ayva."

"Oh," I said, feeling the heat of embarrassment burn my cheeks. "I'm sorry. To be honest, I'm still not sure how any of this works. I hope I didn't offend you."

"No offense taken, Traveler." She reached out her hand and smiled openly. "Do I have your permission to access your personal information?"

"Is that a requirement to finish the tutorial?" I asked, unsure of the implications such an agreement might pose.

"It is," she answered. Her tone was the epitome of politeness and her smile seemed to vaporize my concerns like ether.

With no alternate course of action standing between me and my family, I sighed and nodded. If I wanted to finish this, my only option was to play along.

"If you'll take my hand," she said, "I will access your information and we can continue with the tutorial."

I placed my hand in hers in the best gentleman's handshake I could muster. Firm enough to show I was still in control of my faculties, but gentle enough for a woman's finer sensibilities.

As far as I could tell, Ayva could be anything from a well-scripted computer program to a fully fledged AI, and I had a feeling all of this could be part of a larger test, somehow.

Ayva closed her eyes and her lashes fluttered as she processed whatever data I'd given her access to. When she finished, she blinked and then looked right into the core of me.

She smiled again, but this smile was different. It felt even more genuine, if such a thing was possible. It was as if she could see everything I was, everything I had ever hoped to be.

It felt like she saw something inside of me that I couldn't see on my own. That she accepted the wonderfully flawed and broken man who stood before her on this strange island of make-believe.

I didn't know how to process this. I felt both naked and surprisingly unashamed. Looking down, I was comforted by the knowledge that I was, indeed, still wearing my toga.

"Thank you, Denton Wade," she said, placing her other hand on top of mine. "I'm sure this is a very new and unusual experience for you."

"You can say that again," I said, cautiously withdrawing my hand. Then I cocked my head and asked, "What all does this tutorial entail?"

She didn't respond. Instead, she turned to appraise our surroundings.

I continued my quest for information, trying to gauge what stood between where I was and the goodbye I was looking forward to. "You're not going to have me jumping through hoops of fire or grappling with a minotaur or an ogre or something, are you?"

Ayva merely laughed.

The sound of it was like music.

"Can you give me a hint?"

"You'll see," was the only reply she left me with. Then she turned and walked up the marble steps of the ruin like mist flowing over water.

When she reached the half-way point, she turned and beckoned for me to follow before once again resuming her ascent.

I followed, climbing one step after another, until I reached the top. The view was even more amazing from this vantage point. Ayva stood in front of an ivy-covered rail and stared off at the endless horizon. When I joined her, she nodded, but didn't stray from her vigil.

"Look at this world, Denton. Can you see any of its imperfections?"

I glanced around, turning full circle as I surveyed the view from the peak. The world was more than just beautiful. It felt... *real.*

"It's perfectly imperfect," I responded. "From the cracks in the marble to the patterns in the leaves, nothing is repeated and not a single pixel is out of place."

"But there are imperfections. This is not EndWorld," Ayva said, her voice full of wistful abandon. "This world is different. It is unique; imperfectly perfect, as one might be inclined to put it."

There was that enchanting smile again.

I didn't understand. "What do you mean?" I asked, dumbfounded by the strange twist of conversation.

It was then that Ayva turned to me, fixing her green eyes on mine. "This place wouldn't exist without you, Denton."

"Me?" I asked, incredulous. "It's a tutorial program. Maybe this instance wouldn't exist, but I imagine there are at least a thousand other people standing where I am right now."

One of Ayva's eyebrows darted upward, and she glanced back toward the sea. "This place is unlike any I've ever visited," she said. "No one in all of creation has set foot upon this threshold but us. Each tutorial is different, yet they are all the same: gateways to EndWorld. Yours is not the same."

"Is there something wrong with my tutorial?" I asked.

When she didn't respond, the worst possible conclusions filled my mind, and I scrambled to make sense of the situation. Was the code here as doomed as Roger's previous attempts at bringing me over?

A sinking feeling threatened to consume me from the inside and I stared down at the crashing waves so far below. I could barely make out their distant roar as the sound flitted on the wind, each fragment but a faint glimmer of what it should have been.

I didn't want to give voice to my worst fear, but I had to know. "Are you trying to tell me I can't say goodbye to my family?"

"There is nothing preventing you from seeing your family once you have finished your tasks here, Denton. I only meant to say that your tutorial is the first I've ever encountered with another way out," Ayva explained. "It is both beautiful and terrifying."

It was then that I understood what she was trying to say. It was what Roger had told me about before he left. I had a choice. She was talking about the ocean. It was another path, one that didn't lead to EndWorld, but to oblivion. The great beyond.

"You are still trying to decide which fate you might embrace?"

"I have to finish the tutorial," I said, trying my best to avoid the question.

"And what will you do then?" she pressed.

"I will see my children and show them I'm okay. I'll tell them I love them. After that? I can't say I know for sure just yet."

It was a little white lie. For some reason, I wanted to tell her. I wanted to confess my deeply rooted distrust of a supposed eternal man-made construct, but I was beginning to feel like Ayva had skin in the game. What would it mean for her if I rejected EndWorld?

"I see," she said, and it seemed she understood. Her gaze at the horizon softened, and she turned to face me again, this time with a melancholy smile. "Are you ready to begin your first quest?"

"Let's do it," I answered, trying to sound more confident than I felt. "Bring on the fire."

"Please wait while I conjure flaming hoops, Denton Wade," Ayva replied, closing her eyes in a manner that suggested the task required deep concentration.

"Wait, hold up. You mean I really have to jump through hoops of fire?" I asked, shocked.

Ayva opened her eyes and laughed. The unexpected humor caught me off guard and I stared at her in disbelief. It took a few seconds to realize my mouth was hanging open, and I quickly shut it before shaking my head.

"Was that a joke?" I asked.

"Turn around," Ayva replied, still smiling.

When I turned, I was relieved to see five half-pillars jutting from the ground behind me. They were directly in front of the stairs we'd just climbed. Whatever this was, it seemed better than the flaming circles of varying sizes I'd half-expected.

New Quest Alert! You've been offered a quest:
Choose Your Weapon.
Before you begin your journey in EndWorld Everlasting, you must choose a weapon.

Hint: The weapon you choose will influence certain things, such as starter skills and home location upon entering this new world. Choose wisely. This quest will be complete when you choose from the available weapons within the EndWorld Everlasting tutorial.
Reward: *Weapon of choice.*

The text popped up in a dialogue box on the right side of my field of vision. At the bottom, there were two options: *Accept* and *Decline*. I focused on the option to accept the quest and the box flared, then disintegrated.

Out of nowhere, a different type of weapon appeared on each of the marble pedestals. A brutish battle axe floated in the air above the first. The second had a pair of crossed, curved daggers, both a little longer than my forearm. The third, a wooden staff with a circular jewel of some sort affixed at the head. The fourth, a simple bow and quiver. The fifth, a plain-looking one-handed sword.

I glanced back at Ayva, surprised to see her looking on with genuine interest.

My eyes were drawn to the staff at first. I'd always loved playing casters in traditional role-playing games, but mages typically started out slow, growing in power as they gained knowledge. It was a class I loved to play, but would choosing that path slow my progress in the tutorial?

It was a question worth considering.

"Conflict wages within you, Denton," Ayva observed.

I stepped closer to the row of weapons. It seemed entirely inconceivable that a realm as expansive as EndWorld could be limited to five classes. What if the weapons represented archetypes? The hulking barbarian, the master of stealth and trickery, ranged casters (both support and damage), ranged physical attackers, and one-handed weapon specialists, which must include the tank classes.

I tried to remember every game I'd ever played that featured advanced skill trees. If hybrid classes existed in EndWorld, the path of the sword might also include variants of the classic Battle Mage archetypes. That could prove interesting. It was a play style I'd flirted with once or twice before.

Reaching out, I gripped the hilt and tested the weight of the weapon in my hand. I pulled cold steel from its sheath. The blade was dull and the pommel plain. Standard starter weapon fare. Without thinking, I swished the sword in a crisscross pattern in front of me.

"This will do," I said.

> ***Item Obtained!*** *You've acquired:*
> **Squire's Training Sword.**
> *[One-Hand Sword]*
> *2-5 Physical damage.*
> *Quality: Average.*
> *Rarity: Common.*
> *Durability: 2/10.*
> ***Quest Complete!*** *You've completed:*
> ***Choose Your Weapon.***
> *Congratulations! You have obtained your first weapon.*

Upon dismissing the text, the ground began trembling beneath my feet. It was a slow rumble at first, as if the island itself was growling its disapproval of my choice. Then the tremors quickened.

I stole a look behind me, but Ayva was nowhere to be seen.

When I returned my attention to the pillars, the four remaining weapons disintegrated and then vanished, floating away in tiny wisps of dust on the wind. I watched in awe as the worn marble pedestals sunk back into the ground without leaving a trace.

The tremors turned to violent quakes, and I rocked back on my heels, trying my best not to stumble backwards. Fighting to keep my balance, I crouched low to the ground and grit my teeth.

Tiny pebbles near my hands and feet danced as they bounced back and forth before rolling toward the spot where the weapons once stood. There they coalesced, clumping together like stubborn lumps of starch in an otherwise perfect Thanksgiving gravy.

The tip of the sword I now held in my hand thudded against the bare, packed earth. It was then that I realized what was coming next. This was no simple earthquake. No. It had to be a test. A trial to gauge my mettle and teach me about the combat system in the process.

Ayva wasn't here, so that meant no outside help would be given. I was on my own.

The growing mound of rock and debris clenched itself into a fist the size of a basketball before spreading its fingers wide. From somewhere deep within the ground I could hear a muffled roar. Then the fingers dug into the soil as the creature pulled itself upward.

Another earthen hand breached into the atmosphere, followed by the crown of a massive head.

6

The large, earthen golem towered above me. Bulging muscles of stone shook as it bellowed a mighty war cry. I wiped the resulting dust and grime from my face and concentrated on the creature.

*You **Inspect** the Rock Golem.*
Level 2. Hit Points: 65.

New Skill! You've learned the skill: INSPECT: RANK 1.

*You can now **Inspect** objects and creatures.*
***Inspect** is a Basic Skill.*
Huh? Bet you never saw that one coming.

The monster had sixty-five hit points and was double my level, but I still had my sword and I'd already gained a crucial skill. Besides, this was a tutorial, right? How hard could it be?

The golem leaned back and clenched both fists behind its head before driving them into the ground between us with blinding speed. The strike was too far to land a direct hit, but the resulting shock wave drove me backward while the rippling earth flung me into the air.

I landed in a crumpled heap.

A quick look at my health bar indicated the strike had cost me ten hit points. I was now down to forty HP and my sword was several feet away, where it stood tip-first in a mound of grass.

This was no joke.

What use was a sword against a seemingly impervious rock monster like this? Still, it was my only hope. I jumped to my feet and barely had enough time to roll toward the grassy hillock before another massive swipe rent the air where I had been crouching just moments before.

With my sword safely within my grip, I took a quick inventory of my options. The beast was strong and dealt powerful blows. I doubted I could parry any of the moves it had used thus far and besides, my sword only had two durability left. Even if I could withstand the incredible force behind the attacks, I wasn't sure how much damage the worn metal could take.

I would have to do better at dodging.

One thing I had going in my favor was that while the golem's attacks were fast, it telegraphed its movements as it prepared each strike. As if to illustrate this observation, the golem drew its left arm back, readying another swipe.

This time I rolled forward, narrowly dodging the incoming blow as I closed the distance between us. Now standing at its feet, I doubled my grip on the hilt of my blade and slashed it against the monster's hardened skin.

Tiny clumps of rock fell and scattered across the ground and the golem cried out in pain. Then it lurched forward and the force of its knee struck my chest. I found myself airborne once more as I flew across the makeshift arena and crashed into an ivy-covered pillar.

Fifteen more hit points drained from my health bar and my vision pulsed as I struggled to catch my breath. One thing was certain, tutorial or not, the pain I felt was very real.

*You **Inspect** the Rock Golem.*
Level 2. Hit Points: 61.

I only managed to inflict four HP at the cost of fifteen. I glanced up at my health bar. 25 HP left. Exchanging blow for blow with the golem was a losing strategy. The thing hit like a Mack truck. I had to learn to anticipate and dodge the close-range strikes and counterattack at each opportunity.

I picked up my sword and limped back toward the fight. Once again, the golem bellowed its war cry, assaulting me with a torrent of wind and grime.

Wind. Of course. A rock golem was essentially a creation of the elements. My sword only dealt physical damage, which put me at a significant disadvantage. But, just as I'd learned to inspect the creature as a matter of intuition, there had to be other skills and abilities I could acquire in a similar fashion.

I held my left hand aloft and shielded my eyes against the blast, concentrating on the rush of air. Then I focused on my sword and willed the tempest into the cold steel.

*You cast **Wind Blade** on your **Squire's Training Sword.***
New Spell Acquired!
*You've learned the spell: **WIND BLADE: RANK 1.***

*You can now cast **Wind Blade** on your weapon.*
***Wind Blade** increases attack speed and adds wind damage to attacks.*
Only one weapon-enhancing effect may be active at a time.

A hefty weight tugged at my spirit as the spell took effect, but my sword felt lighter in my hand. Underneath my red health bar was a new one that represented my remaining magic points. The blue status bar drained as I watched it until it stopped at the halfway point. It read 10/20 MP.

The golem roared and slammed both fists against the ground, snapping me from my revelry of having just learned magic. This time

I anticipated the attack and rolled to the side, evading the cone-shaped reverberation of earth.

A massive right-handed swipe followed. Again, I ducked and rolled toward its feet. Twin orbs of wispy-green air encircled my blade as I slashed against the golem's trunk-like legs. Hewn rock fell in clumps and I circled behind the beast, dodging the retaliatory strikes I'd learned to avoid.

The golem's health bar sank below half until 30 HP remained. It turned as I pressed my assault, shaving another 5 hit points and equalizing our health pools. And then it laughed.

The effect was paralyzing as I watched the lumbering behemoth lower its arms and shake with mirth. Had I passed some unannounced test of strength? Unsure of how to respond, I looked around, once again searching for Ayva. There was still no sign of her.

It was the two of us, the rock golem and I, squared off in the small space at the top of the lonely island. Its gravely laughter continued, and I felt a smile tug at the corners of my mouth. Then my own laughter followed.

I lowered my weapon and breathed a sigh of relief, relishing my first moment of triumph in this strange world between worlds. The blade of my new sword had a few impressive chips and dings. After inspecting it, I wasn't surprised to see the durability had dropped to 1/10. The golem had been a tough and wholly unexpected foe. Honestly, I was surprised I fared as well as I had.

The golem was still laughing. Long, low rumbles shook its frame as it looked down at me, both hands clutched to its massive belly. My smile and the sense of accomplishment I'd felt only moments before soured.

That's when it struck me. Full on, foot to chest.

The wind gushed from my lungs as I was flung backward, sliding in the dirt like a rag doll. When I finally came to a stop, my vision pulsed again, this time with flashes of red.

Each breath was a labor as I tried to fight the growing sense of panic.

***Warning:** Critical Health. 5/50 HP remaining.*

This wasn't going well. I suddenly had a new appreciation for how cunning the creatures in this game could be.

The golem advanced as I searched for my sword. It was nowhere to be found. I had even less hope of defeating the hulking monster without a weapon.

Thud. Thud. Thud.

Step after slow, thunderous step, the golem made its approach. I looked up in an attempt to gauge how much time I had left before I had to act or be crushed underfoot. There. Half the distance between us was my sword. The glowing orbs of the wind buff had worn off, and it was once again just a dull chunk of crudely forged steel.

There was no time to think, no chance to hesitate. I only had one option left, and the window was closing.

I ran toward the beast, sliding like a runner stealing home base to retrieve my sword. Once I had the hilt firm within my grasp, I closed my eyes and tried to recall how I'd used the spell.

Thud. Thud. Thud. Thud.

The golem was almost upon me. It reared back and bellowed, signaling the double-handed attack that was sure to come. Dust and debris pelted my face, and I concentrated on the raw power, focusing it toward my dented blade.

*You cast **Wind Blade** on your **Squire's Training Sword.***

Again, the twin orbs encircled the steel. Again, I felt the internal drain as my MP bar dwindled. This was my chance. The golem raised both fists above its head and prepared to strike. Seizing my few remaining seconds, I hacked and slashed at the leg that had sustained the most damage from my previous attacks, allowing the wind to fuel my strikes.

You hit the Rock Golem for 4 HP + 2 Wind damage.
You hit the Rock Golem for 3 HP + 2 Wind damage.

You hit the Rock Golem for 5 HP + 2 Wind damage.

The last blow broke through the golem's knee and I darted to the left as it toppled to the right. Spinning with my momentum, I flanked the beast as it fell. Then I let loose my own war cry and jumped, plunging my blade deep into its armored back.

Critical Strike! *You hit the Rock Golem for 12 HP + 4 Wind damage.*

You have defeated the Rock Golem.
You have gained 350 Experience Points.
*You have found an **Elemental Shard**.*
*You have received 30 **Silver Coins**.*

*ALERT! Your **Squire's Training Sword** has shattered.*

The jagged remnants of my blade jutted out of the lifeless hunk of stone and I looked at my shaking hands, staring in disbelief at the broken hilt. My whole body trembled as I fought to contain the overflowing deluge of adrenaline coursing through my veins.

"WELL DONE, DENTON WADE." AYVA'S GENTLE, FEMININE VOICE SENT an involuntary shiver down my spine.

I turned to face her and noted the unveiled look of admiration in her eyes. "Was that fight supposed to be that hard?" I asked, still breathing heavy from pain and exertion.

Ayva reached out and placed her hand on my shoulder. In an instant, I felt a surge of renewal travel through me. A quick look to my status bars confirmed I was once again at full health and mana.

"You learned magic," she observed.

"I guess I did." I shrugged. "Though, I'm not sure how much good it will do me without a proper weapon." I punctuated the last bit by holding the hilt of my sword aloft, preparing to toss it.

"Keep it for now," Ayva said. "You may need it."

New Quest Alert! You've been offered a quest:
Fix Your Weapon.
Your weapon has been broken. See a weapon specialist or blacksmith to get it repaired.
Hint: *Broken weapons are next to worthless. Taking good care of your weapons and equipment is essential for success in EndWorld Everlasting. This quest will be complete when you have repaired your weapon.*
Reward: *100 Experience Points, 50 Silver, 1x* **Item Repair Voucher.**

I accepted the quest and chuckled. Another errand.

Of course.

I looked around the makeshift arena before finally spotting my query and retrieved the trampled scabbard. Without a proper blade to secure the sword within the sheath, I'd have to carry both separately.

"You could place them in your inventory," Ayva suggested, as if reading my mind.

"How do I do that?" I asked.

"You need only think of the word 'Inventory'," she explained. "Focus on it, and the interface should engage."

Inventory.

It felt odd to be staring into what amounted to an unfathomable abyss. There was no discernible User Interface (UI). My mind rejected it at first, preferring instead to recall the many in-game incarnations of inventory UI's I'd encountered over the years.

There was no physical bag, nothing to put my hand into. It wasn't a box on a screen. It both existed and didn't. It was, and it was not, and yet I could feel it, like some strange sense of intuition.

I wondered about the elemental shard I'd received upon killing the golem and was immediately rewarded with a mental image of what my inventory contained.

Elemental Shard x1.

30 Silver.

This was weird.

"How do I—"

Ayva grinned. "Imagine placing the items into your inventory and they will go there. To retrieve an item, simply imagine it in your hand with the inventory system open. It may be awkward at first, but it will become second nature in time."

I shrugged. "Sounds simple enough."

I focused on the broken hilt of my sword and the dented scabbard and then imagined placing them inside the void. They disappeared. The absence of their weight in my hands felt strange. Then I had an idea. I looked at the broken blade still embedded in the golem's rocky corpse and imagined placing it in my inventory as well.

Ayva's giggle brought a flash of heat and embarrassment to my cheeks as I realized she could tell what I'd just attempted to do.

"That won't work, silly," she said. "I'm afraid you'll have to find other materials if you want to repair your sword."

"Well, it was worth a shot," I said.

I pulled the elemental shard from my inventory, holding it up to the light of the sun. It was a slim crystal, measuring about four inches in length, and appeared to be infused with an earth-like energy that swirled and danced within its depths.

Ayva continued her instruction. "By default, EndWorld Everlasting utilizes the auto-loot feature. If you would rather, you can change your settings to manually loot. Most travelers prefer the default setting."

I nodded and, hoping to avoid further embarrassment, placed the shard back in my inventory.

Then I busied myself with scanning the parts of the island that were visible from where we stood. "There doesn't appear to be any active settlements in this place. Where am I supposed to find a blacksmith or a weapon specialist mentioned in the quest? Do I need to search for a wizened old hermit or something?"

"That quest cannot be completed here, Denton," Ayva explained.

"Not here? Are you saying the tutorial extends to areas beyond this place?"

"No. That quest can only be completed in EndWorld, I'm afraid."

Ayva's response took an eternal minute to sink in.

"How does that work?" I asked, doing my best to keep the sour look from my face. "I can't finish the tutorial unless I finish the quest, but to finish the quest I have to exit the tutorial?"

"Not exactly," she said. "You have already completed the requirement for the tutorial by accepting the quest. Whether you choose to complete the task or not is up to you. Quests are not binding, you see. You don't have to do something in EndWorld just because someone asked you to; and that includes quests within the tutorial."

A wave of relief washed over me and I let out an exaggerated sigh. "You had me worried, there," I said with a forced chuckle. "What else do I need to do before I can see my family?"

"Yes, of course, Denton." Ayva flashed a knowing smile. "You must be anxious to see them. You are almost there. But, before we can move forward, it is time for you to choose your skin."

"Choose my what?"

7

"Choose my skin?" I asked. "You mean, like, my in-game appearance?"

Ayva swirled her finger in my direction and my now-filthy toga disappeared, leaving me standing in front of her in nothing but a pair of loose-knit linen shorts.

"Ummm?" This was the only thing I could bring myself to verbalize.

When I looked up, I could see a strange mirror-like surface in front of me. The image I saw reflected how I'd grown used to seeing myself in the months leading up to my visit to the Cyberternal Industries home office. Being reminded of the sickness that had assaulted my body, and the treatments that only seemed to make me feel even worse, made me wonder about my current existence.

"This is how I remember myself," I said, "before I climbed into the pod. But I don't feel like that man. I feel alive. I feel..." I glanced at the pile of rocks that had been a formidable foe only moments before. "I feel strong; capable, you know?"

Ayva nodded. "It appears you are a very capable Traveler, Denton. While each trial is unique to the person, not many Travelers could have slayed a beast such as that one. Your body may have been weak, but your spirit remains strong."

"You're saying I don't have to look like this?" I asked. "Can I be something like a half-dragon, an elf, or a troll? What kind of limitations are we talking about?"

"There are no clearly defined fantasy races in EndWorld," Ayva said. "At least none that are available to Travelers as selectable skins. Each Traveler is limited only by the confines of their own mind."

"Limited by the confines of my own mind, huh?" I asked, instinctively toying with the idea of testing my limits.

"The human psyche is much more delicate than most people think," she said. "Try to push the boundaries if you'd like, but most Travelers I've encountered usually choose the best version of themselves their mind can accept."

"What do you mean?" I asked.

"A very old man could be younger, and yet not too young. His mind must be capable of accepting the change. In kind, a fat man could be skinny, but only as skinny as his mind would allow."

"That sounds a little bizarre," I said. "I would have guessed that EndWorld was full of strange, new possibilities."

"EndWorld is a place of endless possibilities, Denton," Ayva replied. "However, this restriction is a matter of the id, the inner ego, and what is referred to as the super-ego. All of these together form the basis of what your mind will accept as truth. As such, it is the very nature of one's view of self: their identity. To push that boundary too far is to risk a rejection of the self and jeopardize the acceptance of a new reality."

I looked into the reflective surface while Ayva's words began to sink in. Most modern games offered players a way to escape themselves, transforming who and what they were for countless hours at a time. But there was always real life to return to, if only for food and sleep. The confines of one's humanity served as an anchor, grounding the player with what was real: hunger, thirst, fatigue. So much could be faked inside those fictional worlds, but the body and mind still required care.

I guess it was starting to make sense. If the tutorial was unique for each player, each trial suited for a person's strengths and weaknesses, then it was understandable that an individual's sense of identity was a fundamental part of the experience.

"So, how does this work?" I asked. "I don't see any UI controls. Is there another secret word I need to think of to access a hidden menu or something?"

Ayva moved to stand beside me, but her reflection wasn't present in the makeshift mirror.

"Concentrate on your appearance," she said. "Test the boundaries of your mind, if you will. The system will not allow you to go beyond the threshold of your capabilities."

I thought of my father. I don't know why his face was the first to pop into my mind. Perhaps it was because I imagined I might have aged as he did. That was before my first round of nuclear medication, before my hopes of being a grandfather myself one day had been dismantled before my very eyes.

My reflection did not change.

I felt Ayva's hand upon my shoulder and when I turned to look at her, I found myself drowning within the depths of her beautiful, green eyes.

"Your spirit is strong, Denton. Perhaps too strong for something such as this. It knows that old age is no longer a path that is open for you. Growing old might be possible for other men, but that isn't your path." She smiled, but it felt like so much more than just a simple gesture.

My heart warmed, and I redoubled my focus on the reflection. I thought of the moment when my suspicions were confirmed, when the doctor told me I was out of options. Slowly, the image began to change.

"Our hopes and our fears are often the strongest connections we have with our sense of identity," Ayva said, her voice sounding distant and full of sadness. "Even among my kind."

The man staring back at me was how I'd imagined myself in the days leading up to the end. Sunken, shadowy eyes stared out of tight-skinned sockets and an expressionless look of malaise permeated the stillness in the air.

"Is this who you would choose to become?" she asked.

I shook my head, unable to take my eyes from my reflection as the phantom before me mirrored my movements.

"Try again."

This time I closed my eyes and thought of my children. I walked through the precious memories of their births. I could remember looking into Helen's eyes with unfathomable pride each time she delivered one of our beautiful babies into the world. I could almost see my shaking hands as I severed the umbilical cord that tethered them to the utopia they'd been forced to leave behind.

"Oh, that's much better," Ayva exclaimed.

When I opened my eyes, I saw a man I almost didn't recognize. My reflection was a little taller, a little more muscular, and more handsome than I'd ever considered myself to be.

"This is how your children must see you," she added.

"But this is never how I've seen myself," I protested. The man staring back at me was full of confidence and could easily be described as twice the man I'd ever hoped to be.

"Your bond with your children is strong, Denton. You are willing to believe what they believe. Therefore, your mind is capable of seeing the man that they have seen."

I thought about changing it, of toning down my appearance until it more closely represented the man I'd been before the sickness had taken hold. But then I stopped and concentrated on the reflection, hoping I hadn't caused it to change. This wasn't about me and it never had been.

"I choose this," I said, nodding my approval. "If this is who my children see when they look at me, then those are shoes I'd like to try to fill."

"I am pleased with your choice," Ayva said, waving away the reflective pane.

"What now?" I asked.

"Would you like a chance to choose a new set of armor?"

I looked down at my thin linen shorts and remembered my missing toga. "Yes, please," I said. "I think that sounds better than running around in my skivvies. What do I have to do this time, another rock monster?"

Ayva laughed. "There are no monsters to fight this time."

"Oh?" I asked. "Going to take it easy on me?"

"That depends," she answered. "Some Travelers enjoy this next part, others not so much. How do you feel about crafting?"

"Wait. You're saying that I get to make my first set of armor?"

"Does this please you?" she asked.

I nodded. "Actually, yes. That sounds like it could be fun."

With another wave of her hand, Ayva brought up a new interface in front of me. Each panel presented a reflection of my new skin, and each wore a different set of starter gear.

"You have already selected your weapon," she said, "and while you can still change your specialization within EndWorld, there are certain benefits to staying true to your established choice."

"Okay," I said.

"Each set of gear represented here comes with the standard armor class strengths and weaknesses. Heavy armor will reduce your movement and attack speed, but will also increase your defense. Light armor increases your agility, but does not offer the same defensive bonuses."

I considered this carefully as I rotated through the carousel. If I had any aspirations of being a true Battle Mage, I would want to combine the best of both cloth and leather armors. Metal pieces would be too unwieldy if I went up against another foe like the golem.

Then again, who was I kidding? Had I changed my mind about EndWorld? I was doing this for the kids. For Helen. After our conversation when I first arrived on this island, maybe even a little for Roger. But, if I was going to act the part, I might as well get into it a little.

None of the options seemed to have any real flair or flourishes, pretty standard for starter gear. I stopped at a panel that displayed a stylish-looking cloth doublet and rugged black leather pants with reinforced knee joints. Given the natural fighting style I'd adopted when squaring off against the golem, it seemed like a good fit. I turned to Ayva and nodded.

"I think this will do," I said.

"Very well." Ayva dismissed the carousel with the flick of her wrist. "Is this where you'd like to start your work?"

I looked around and shrugged. "Does the location make any difference?"

She raised an eyebrow and smiled. "I don't suppose so, but perhaps you might choose a particular site for inspiration and aesthetics? Having something pleasing to look at while you work couldn't hurt."

I couldn't agree more. "How about over there?" I asked, pointing toward the edge of the cliff where a few crumbling pillars stood sentinel over the endless ocean.

"You would look out over the abyss?" Ayva asked.

I couldn't be sure, but it felt as if she was a little hurt by my response. Then I understood. The ocean was the other exit, the one that didn't lead to EndWorld. That wasn't what I'd meant at all.

"No," I answered. "I'd rather face this way, so I can look out over the island. If that's okay."

Ayva's frown dissipated and she closed her eyes. Then a large workshop filled the area in front of the pillars.

"There we are," she said.

I walked up to the workspace and ran my hand along the surface of the worktable. I could feel each ripple of the woods' grain beneath my skin and the air was filled with the scent of tanned leather.

"This is really impressive," I observed. Then I concentrated on the items I wanted to craft and a translucent interface came into view. "Oh," I said. "That's handy."

"Indeed," Ayva replied. "It seems you are ready to begin your task. I shall return when you have finished."

I didn't look up. "Could you stay?" I asked.

"I cannot provide assistance," she stated.

"No, that's not it." I looked into her eyes and offered a hesitant smile. "I think I could use the company, that's all."

Ayva's brow furrowed as she processed my request. After a drawn out pause, she gave me a gentle smile of her own. "Of course, Denton. I will stay."

8

yva stood nearby, watching as I worked through the complex series of instructions. Crafting in the tutorial was difficult, but I could tell this was only an introduction.

I'd been provided with all the leather, cloth, and metal accessories needed to complete each piece, and I assumed this wouldn't be the case once players reached EndWorld.

After all, someone had to turn the hides into leather and whole cloth didn't just grow on trees. Likewise, the rivets, buttons, and various clasps would likely be made by aspiring blacksmiths, bone workers, and glass blowers to fuel the economy and level their crafts.

For a long while, we sat in silence. Then, at last, I finished the final stitches on the drab brown shirt I'd managed to sew together.

"How does it look?" I asked as I pulled it over my head.

It wasn't a masterpiece; I knew that much, but it wasn't half bad, either.

"Quite fitting," Ayva said with a nod.

Her reply didn't give away much, and I decided to keep the silence broken while I selected the next garment to to work on.

"You were going to leave earlier," I said, swiping through the options in the crafting interface.

"Yes."

Another hard stop.

"Where do you go?" I asked.

"Nowhere," Ayva replied.

How could that be possible? Not ready to start in on the leather pieces just yet, I selected the doublet that would go over the shirt I'd just made and began organizing the required materials.

"Nowhere? What does that mean, exactly?" I asked.

"I am still here," she said. "I go nowhere, I simply observe without being observed."

"Why?"

Ayva leaned back and I watched as the wind played with a wayward strand of her dark, silky hair.

"I usually find it's best to allow Travelers to interact with their environments without outside influence," she said at last.

"Oh," I replied, surprisingly let down by her answer.

"This upsets you?" she asked, her look of concern growing as she leaned in.

"No," I said, searching for the right words. "It's just that I was enjoying your company, I didn't mean to intrude. You don't have to stay."

The quiet stillness settled back into the space between us before she spoke again. Her words were soft and filled with care.

"I enjoy your company as well, Denton. I will stay, if you would like."

I nodded and returned my focus to the task at hand. I wasn't sure why, but Ayva's presence was comforting. This wasn't about gaining any sort of favor or competitive edge. Was it attraction? I mean, she was gorgeous and there was something of an aura about her, sure, but that wasn't it either.

I completed line after line of fine stitch work and mulled it over in my mind. Using the thimble on my finger, I pushed and pulled, fighting the needle through the thick layers of cloth.

The hard, dexterous labor truly gave me a keen sense of appreciation for the marvels of technology that had shaped the world I'd left behind.

But there was something else that began to form as I labored to piece and stitch together my armor: a deep sense of accomplishment. It was hard work, and yet here I was; creating something with my own two hands.

Ayva looked on in silence as I moved from the doublet to the pants, donning each piece as I finished it before moving to the next.

Then I stopped. I stared at the pattern for my boots for what seemed like ages before I picked up a thick leather sole and turned it over in my hands. It was a simple design, but I felt somewhat intimidated by the notion of it. A boot. Surely, a moccasin would have been easier.

I let out a sigh and decided to eat the toad, throwing myself at the task with the utmost of determination. I picked up the leather punch tool, which looked more like a tiny iron spike with a rough wooden handle, and then I grabbed the wooden mallet.

The first few holes felt awkward, but they seemed to match the spacing requirements specified in the pattern, so I kept going. By ten, I'd found my rhythm, and it wasn't long before I'd completed the entire perimeter around the first sole. In an effort to preserve my momentum, I moved on to the second and repeated the process.

"Huh," I said aloud. "That actually doesn't look too shabby."

"Not as hard as you thought?" Ayva asked.

I shook my head. "It wasn't bad," I admitted. "I've never made boots before, but I can't imagine many people do these days. I mean, I'm not done yet, so who knows what might happen before I finish, but I feel good."

Ayva laughed. "Good," she said, giving me an encouraging smile. "I believe in you."

Fastening the sides of the boots to the soles was another story. The foul-smelling glue burned my nose, and the vapors made my head swim.

"Ugh, this stuff is disgusting," I observed aloud, but Ayva merely looked on, unperturbed by the caustic aroma.

Once the glue had set, it was time to thread a tough length of sinew through the newly attached sides and the holes I'd punched into the hard leather soles. This proved to be a difficult and messy task.

After coaxing the needle through the thick, sticky material just a few times, I found my hands cramping from the strain. The thimble was dented and covered with the now tar-like glue.

Much like in real life, using the right tool for the job appeared to be a big contributing factor towards achieving success. So, too, was the ability to improvise with what you had on hand. Looking around the workbench, I located a pair of pliers I'd used earlier and tossed the crumpled thimble to the side.

"Very clever, Denton," Ayva said, nodding her approval.

I wasn't sure whether she was referring to my astute and observable troubleshooting skills or the very personal train of thought that led me there. What limits did someone like Ayva have within the tutorial? Was this a result of taking her hand, giving her access to my 'personal data?'

As if answering my question, she raised an eyebrow and smiled.

9

With the workshop gone, the man staring back at me in the freshly conjured reflective surface looked confident and strong. The armor I'd fashioned wasn't perfect, but it looked good. What more could you ask from a set of starter gear? I glanced at Ayva and she nodded her approval.

"Not bad at all, Denton Wade."

"Not bad at all," I agreed. Then I turned to her and smiled. "What's next?"

"Would you like to see your family before you go?" she asked. She raised her eyebrow in a manner that suggested she already knew the impact her question would have.

Tears dripped down my cheeks as I nodded. The sudden reminder of where I was and why I was here stung deep and my heart ached within my chest.

For a brief moment, I'd allowed myself to get lost within the tutorial. Making my own armor had been difficult, but it had also taken my mind off the anguish I'd grown so accustomed to. It had shown me that there was still something else besides just pain and grief and loss.

"Yes," I said once I'd rediscovered my ability to speak. "Can I see them now?"

"Very soon," Ayva replied. "First, how would you like to appear?"

"Appear?" I half-imagined bursting into some sort of virtual waiting room in a cloud of smoke, but the mental image didn't fit into what I'd seen of the EndWorld experience so far.

"Would you like to use your chosen skin and armor, or would you prefer your original appearance and attire from the life you left behind?"

I considered this for the briefest of moments. There was only one answer that made sense. I had to be the man they'd always known me to be and prove that the sickness did not define the man I'd become.

"I think I'd like them to see me like this," I said.

"As you wish." Ayva nodded. "Sadly, there is a limit to how long visitors can interact with the system, the time you have is not limitless."

"I understand," I said.

I didn't like it, but it did make sense. This was the gate to EndWorld, after all. If the founder of Cyberternal really had created the cyberworld for his son, there had to be a legitimate reason to let go. Otherwise, what purpose would there be for a world beyond the gate?

"I can open up access to your tutorial, if you'd like. Or, if you aren't comfortable sharing this echo of your soul, we can move to a more neutral ground."

"This would be great," I said, indicating the flat area where we stood.

To be honest, I couldn't imagine a more perfect place. Behind us, the sun was beginning to set and the horizon was painted in the most brilliant hues.

Ayva clapped her hands together and the mirror-like window dissipated before the workshop once again faded into view. Behind me, I heard the now-familiar sound of living stone and spun around to see the golem's corpse tremble as it started to reform.

"Wait a minute," I said, carefully backing away from the shifting pile of rocks. "What's all this?"

Brushing itself off, the golem stood tall and proud, with the jagged remains of my sword still jutting from its back.

"Can I at least have the blade of my sword back?" I asked.

The golem grunted and then gave a rumbling chuckle. It shook its head.

I guess not.

"Wouldn't you like to show your family everything you've managed to accomplish?" Ayva asked.

Still a little perturbed about the blade, I nodded. Seeing the golem I'd managed to defeat might actually be pretty cool. Or, how did Eliza put it? Chill?

"Yeah, I suppose that would be chill," I said, doing my best to sound aloof.

Ayva only smiled in response.

Within the short span of just a few minutes, I was staring into a blue portal. It reminded me of the classic video games of my youth. By now, I suppose I realized that wasn't much of a coincidence. The shifting vertical pool of liquid electricity rippled as a small hand emerged.

I dropped to my knees, breathless as I waited. Finally, Jacob stepped through and looked around. He blinked several times, and it looked as if he was trying to make sense of the landscape he was seeing. Then his eyes focused on me and his face brightened.

"Dad," he exclaimed, rushing towards me.

Behind him, the portal began to shift and Sophie stepped through, followed soon after by Eliza.

I held my children and openly wept as I hugged them close. When I leaned back to take another good look, I could see I wasn't the only one shaken by the encounter. All three had wet cheeks and red-rimmed eyes, and Helen and Roger now watched, hand-in-hand, in front of the open portal.

"How do you feel, Dad?" Sophie asked, her pretty blue eyes gleaming in the orange-violet hues of the sunset.

"I feel good," I said. "Really good, actually."

Sophie was our middle child. Just a few years younger than Eliza, she would have turned fifteen in the months since I'd entered the pod for my first treatment at Cyberternal.

"Happy birthday, baby girl," I added, giving her blonde hair a gentle tussle.

She looked at me and then to Eliza, confusion plain on her gentle features.

Roger stepped forward and knelt down. The kids turned, and he did his best to explain.

"Your dad doesn't remember anything that might have happened during the last three months. We tried as best as we could, but the cancer spread much faster than we'd anticipated. Despite how hard they tried, the AI's couldn't save those memories."

"You don't remember the zoo?" Jacob asked, looking sad.

I shook my head and placed a hand on his shoulder. "I'm sorry, sport. I wish I did."

"Me too," he said with a huge grin. "That would have been fun."

"We didn't go to the zoo," Eliza explained, fixing her little brother with a sisterly glare. "You were too sick."

"I was testing you." Jacob laughed. "You pass."

"Pass the gas," I said, giving him a gentle pinch. It was the kind of response I knew he'd get a kick out of and he immediately started dancing around making crude noises.

"Fart! Farty, fart-fart," he exclaimed.

Helen looked on disapprovingly while Sophie and Eliza rolled their eyes.

"You don't remember the pain, then?" Sophie cut in.

The only pain I could remember was inflicted within the pod when the nano-helpers did their thing. Somehow, I suspected this wasn't what she was referring to.

"The last memory I have is going to Cyberternal Industries with Eliza," I explained, looking to my oldest daughter. "When we first met Krysta."

Eliza's expression darkened for a moment, but then she forced a smile. "And then you were here?" she asked.

"And then I was here." I nodded, gesturing to the space around us."

Ayva stepped forward. "Your father has done some very impressive things here in the EndWorld tutorial," she said.

Eliza looked skeptical.

I concentrated on my inventory and retrieved the broken hilt of my sword. "I got this," I said, showing them the shattered steel.

Sophie and Eliza leaned in to take a closer look, but Jacob did not appear to be impressed.

"It looks broken," he said.

"Yeah," I admitted. "It wasn't when I got it, but that guy over there," I pointed to the golem, "had some powerful moves and pretty tough skin."

Jacob gasped and ran toward the golem. "Whoa," he exclaimed. "This guy is so cool."

"You had to fight a rock monster?" Sophie asked. "That's intense."

"And I won, too." I laughed. "Can you believe it?"

Eliza smiled approvingly. "That's pretty chill, pops."

There was something different about the way she was acting and it hurt my heart to wonder why.

There was no telling what might have happened in the months since I'd last seen her. It was possible that she'd chosen to distance herself from me near the end. If that was the case, I couldn't blame her for avoiding the pain. She still had her whole life in front of her. If taking a step back was what she needed, I could understand.

Jacob was climbing on the golem now, and I felt the familiar need to caution him against harm. "Be careful, buddy," I said. "He still has a piece of metal sticking out of his back from where my sword shattered."

"Whoa," he exclaimed again, vying for a better foothold to see the wound on the golem's back. "That's so wicked."

Ayva waved her hand, and the blade vanished. "Then she turned to Jacob and asked, "Would you like to give it a try?"

I frowned, but then she winked and conjured a simple wooden sword and offered it to my boy.

The rock golem smiled and moved side-to-side, gently tapping his earthen hands on Jacob's forearms as the two began to spar.

The rest of us sat down to talk and it wasn't long before Roger looked at his watch.

"Time's almost up," he said, eliciting groans all around.

Even Helen seemed disappointed by the news. She'd hardly spoken a word the whole time they'd been here, but I could tell there were still things yet unspoken between us.

She stood and wiped the tears from her eyes, then walked over and wrapped her arms around me.

"I love you," she whispered before nodding to the kids and walking back through the portal.

Roger approached next, gripping my hand in his right while placing his left on my shoulder. "You did well here, Denton," he said. "I mean it. That was impressive."

I glanced back at the golem still goofing around with Jacob and smiled. "It doesn't look so tough now, does it?"

Roger only laughed before leaning in. "I know there's a lot between us that you don't remember, but just know... I'm going to miss you, man. Whatever you decide, I support you."

Then he, too, vanished through the portal, leaving me alone with Ayva and my three children.

Sophie was next to say goodbye. Burying her face in my chest, she began to sob. Her whole body trembled as she clung to me, not wanting to say the words that would end our time together. Even though I couldn't articulate it at the time, I understood.

"I'm so proud of you," I said, leaning her back so I could get one final look at her.

She wiped at the tears in her eyes and tucked a strand of hair behind her ear. "Thanks, Dad. I'm going to miss you so much."

"I know," I replied. "But I'll always be with you."

"Yeah," she said, giving me her best attempt at a smile. "I know."

After giving me one final squeeze, she turned and walked towards the portal. My heart broke anew as I watched her disappear through the electric blue void.

Jacob came next, barreling into my legs like a little freight train.

"Ooph," I exclaimed, struggling to maintain my balance.

"Hey, Dad?" he asked, giving me an appraising look.

"Yeah, bud?"

"I love you," he said, then launched himself at me once more, this time embracing me in his signature bear hug.

I wiped the tears from my eyes and then bent down, wrapping him in a hug of my own. "I know, son. I love you, too. You grow up and be strong. Be stronger than I was, okay?"

"No sweat, old man."

I laughed, and I was surprised at just how good it felt.

"I'm proud of you, Dad," he added before darting off through the portal.

My heart sank. There was so much I felt like I needed to tell him, so little advice I'd been able to pass on about how to be a man.

I let out a sigh. Jacob was a lot like I was as a child. He was strong and resilient. I had to trust him to choose his own path.

Ayva bowed her head toward my eldest daughter and backed away, leaving me to stand alone with Eliza.

I could tell then, and there was no escaping it. My daughter had matured a lot in the time I'd missed. A knowing sorrow filled her gaze and there was a depth of wisdom about her that wasn't there before.

It made me wonder if she didn't know exactly what I was thinking.

"Eliza—"

"Dad," she cut in, "before you decide..."

"Decide?" I asked, trying to feign ignorance to what she might be referring to.

"Three months ago," she said. "I know what that means. I know how you felt about EndWorld back then. It seems like a lifetime ago to the rest of us, but for you? That's the last thing you remember, isn't it?"

I nodded.

"So, there has to be a failsafe, right? A way for you to bug out of the system?"

Again, I nodded.

Despite how unkind the truth was, I just couldn't bring myself to lie to her.

"This is going to be hard for you to understand right now," she said, stepping closer. Her eyes glistened with determination and she stood a little taller.

"What is it?"

"Roger got me an internship with the company."

"Oh?" I asked, genuinely surprised. "With Cyberternal?"

She nodded. "You were proud when you found out, and it made me happy. Really happy. You were so excited. Then you took a turn for the worse. It was hard watching you suffer, but I knew I'd be there for you. Watching over you in a way."

"Hey, now," I said, doing my best to reassure her while trying to ignore the grisly details of my death. "I am excited for you, Eliza,"

Working for Cyberternal Industries... it was a good gig, a career even. To get in this young, she had an incredible future in front of her. How could a father be anything but excited and proud?

"I don't doubt you are," she went on. "You've always wanted what was best for me, no matter what. But I'll never forget what you said."

I waited for her to continue. When she didn't, I couldn't help but ask.

"What did I say?"

She gave me a quivering smile and fresh tears dripped from her eyes. "You told me I'd be your guardian angel. And I believed it. There was nothing else I wanted more."

"Eliza..."

"And now what?" she asked. "Will you just fade away into nothing?"

"Come on, that's not fair."

"Nothing is fair," she shot back, suddenly raising her voice. "Life isn't fair. Death isn't fair. I already lost you once, Daddy. I can't bear the thought of losing you forever."

I wanted to protest. I wanted to argue. But neither of those things felt right. So, I held my tongue and wrapped my arms around her as silent tears fell down our cheeks.

"I love you." She breathed out a long, unsteady breath and began backing away toward the portal.

My words caught in my throat, and I tried to find my strength.

"I love—" I started, but she was already gone.

10

The portal closed before I could act on my initial impulse of diving in after Eliza. Defeated, I slunk to the ground and buried my head in my hands. It wouldn't have made a difference. That door wasn't for me. I didn't have a body left to go back to.

Ayva leaned down and wrapped her arms around me, infusing me with her quiet, calming spirit. My sobs subsided, and I lifted my eyes to stare at the spot where the portal had been only seconds before. They were gone, and there was nothing I could do to bring them back.

"Bittersweet, is it not?" Ayva asked.

She was right. It was bittersweet, through and through. I had the opportunity to say goodbye, and yet I had to watch my entire world crumble before my eyes. It was too much, and yet it wasn't enough. I would endure that pain for the rest of eternity if it meant I could spend one more minute with them.

But that time had come and gone. There would be no more, not in this world or even the next.

The words Eliza left me with lingered, searing into my mind like a red-hot iron. Somehow, she'd seen right through me. I couldn't believe just how much my little girl had grown up in the short time I'd missed out on.

Ayva took my hands and helped me stand. Then she led me to a collapsed pillar near the edge of the cliff where we could sit. I don't know why, perhaps I just needed a distraction, but I looked for the golem. He was nowhere to be found.

"I dismissed him," she said. "His presence was no longer required."

What about me? I wondered. Was this it? The tutorial was over and my presence here was no longer required. I had two options, the void or the world beyond. But what of the promises this other me had made?

EndWorld Everlasting. It wasn't heaven, and it wasn't hell. Maybe it was a combination of the two. Or maybe it was something else entirely. I couldn't make up my mind, but there was one thing I knew for sure. My little Eliza, now all grown up, had shaped her life around being a part of the world where she'd thought I was going. And now? Nothing was certain, for either of us.

The deepest part of me suddenly wished I was the other man I'd become, the one who had known for sure that this virtual world was the one he wanted. At the beginning of the tutorial, I could only imagine what might have changed my mind. Now, after speaking with Eliza, I was pretty sure I knew.

Ayva placed her hand on my knee and looked into my eyes. There was kindness in her gaze and understanding. She didn't need to speak the words, I already knew what she might say.

I let out a sigh and glanced at the last fading rays of sunshine as the violet-hued clouds won the battle for control of the horizon. In my mind, it seemed like an apt metaphor. My time in the tutorial was coming to an end. I didn't have long before it would be time to decide.

We sat in silence and I reveled in the soft tug of the near-evening breeze. It brought with it all the intoxicating aromas of the island, jasmine and wild roses, magnolias and gardenias. How had I not noticed it before?

My day had been chock-full of adventure and accomplishment. I once again retrieved the remains of my sword from my inventory, testing the weight of it in my hand. Even without the blade, there was a steadying, familiar feel to it. Next, I summoned the elemental shard I'd received upon defeating the golem.

I was instantly reminded of the trip we'd taken with the kids just before I found out about the first tumor. Topaz Mountain in the deserts of Utah. The elemental shard looked like a giant crystal of topaz, bleached by an unrelenting sun and filled with the living energy of earth. Although I could hear nothing, the shard seemed to be singing to me. The inaudible sound echoed inside my head. It was nothing short of beautiful.

"A special gift from the elements," Ayva explained, staring at the gem that filled my palm. "It's very rare to see its like within the tutorial."

"What does it do?" I asked.

She shrugged in response. "It's a calling. The shards mean different things for different people, and they do different things based on the path the Traveler chooses. I can't say I know much more than that."

"I see," I said, losing myself once more within the shardsong.

I closed my eyes and placed the objects inside my inventory again. The music faded and I let out a long breath. Then I stood.

"Wait," Ayva said, grabbing hold of my hand. A sudden surge of energy pulsed through my skin and she instantly let go.

I looked down at her, confused by her sudden reaction and the influx of power infused in her touch.

"I would give you something, if you'll allow it," she said, her voice soft and quiet, her words almost swallowed by the wind.

After an awkward pause, she held out her palm much as she'd done when I first began the tutorial. I reached out and took her hand in mine.

Once again, the spark of power surged through my fingers and up my arm, this time taking hold deep in my chest.

New Hidden Trait! You've acquired a new trait: **SECOND CHANCE.**

Hidden Traits are special, always-active abilities.
*You aren't sure what **Second Chance** does, but it sounds like something*
worth having. This Hidden Trait is extremely rare.

"A gift for you, from me," she whispered. "Also quite rare."

I looked back towards the ledge. "What happens if I jump?" I asked. I hated the pain the question seemed to inflict, but a part of me couldn't let it go.

Ayva shook her head. "This I do not know, Denton Wade. Possibly, you will cease to exist. Perhaps you will only exist outside of this construct. I know little of that path or the secrets it keeps. I know only my own fear when I look into the depths of the waves. I see only oblivion."

My mind traveled back to the void before the tutorial, the time without time, the place without place. Being without being. A shudder rippled down my spine and I shook the thoughts from my head.

"And if I choose EndWorld?" I asked.

"If you choose EndWorld Everlasting, you will awaken alone in a new place, surrounded by the many faces of those who would join you. You will make friends and possibly some enemies. There will be many paths and the lines between right and wrong may blur. You will discover who you are, yet I cannot guarantee you will like the person you find you have become. That will depend on the choices you have made."

"That's all?" I asked with a nervous chuckle.

"You and I will probably never see each other again," she added with a surprising note of sadness. "Still, a part of me will always be with you. An echo, much like the song of the shard you now possess."

Unsure of how to respond, I asked the only other question I could think of. "And what will happen to this place, this island? Can't I stay here instead?"

"You cannot. This place will cease to exist. The resources will be gathered back into the larger system to be used for new tutorials for other Travelers who come this way."

I nodded. It made me a little sad to think the island and its ruins would be erased, but that was the way of things. It was a reality I didn't enjoy, but was beginning to accept.

Life was nothing more than a series of transitions and forks in the road. It was finally time to choose my path.

Gathering my courage and bringing myself to look into Ayva's eyes, I struggled for the right words.

As if sensing my turmoil and trepidation, she offered me another smile. This one was sad and tears began to well in the pools of her eyes.

"I'll do it," I said at last, though I was still wrestling with the internal conflict of my soul.

"You will travel to EndWorld?" Ayva asked, looking hopeful. "This is what you have decided?"

"I think so," I said.

"You must be sure, Denton."

I took a deep breath and then nodded. "Yes, I'm sure. My daughter needs me and," I looked around one last time, "and this was fun."

Ayva's green eyes sparkled and her grin was infectious. "Then there is only one last thing for you to do."

"Oh?"

She waved and a door appeared before me.

"Pass through the door," she said, "and you will find your new life in EndWorld Everlasting."

"I guess this is goodbye, then?" I asked.

"Yes," she answered. "I suppose it is. Goodbye, Denton. I am very glad to have met you."

"The feeling's mutual," I said.

Then I opened the door and stepped inside.

A sick sense of falling engulfed my being, drawing me further into the unknown as I traversed the space between two worlds. Deeper and deeper I went until I could no longer tell if I was falling down or flying upward. Then a sudden rush of speed sent me tumbling head over heels and, all at once, everything stopped.

I opened my eyes, blinking back my growing sense of disbelief. The night was black and so many impossibly bright stars peeked out from behind the gaps in the golden-tinged clouds that had swallowed the moon.

I was lying in what felt to be the soft loam of an undisturbed wilderness. The air was infused with the woodsy scent of pine and firs and the forest was filled with a strange and foreign night song. Insects thrummed and chirped their peaceful cadence as I sat up, struggling to regain my bearings. Other sounds greeted me, but I was disheveled and couldn't concentrate long enough to place them.

My mind was still reeling from my experience in the tutorial. A very loud part of me couldn't believe the choice I'd made.

What was I thinking? What had I done? I thought of Eliza and her parting words. There was so much I didn't know about this place, but she promised to be my guardian angel. What did that even mean? An intern wouldn't have any power to directly influence the game, not with all the safeguards Cyberternal Industries must have in place. I could only guess the sentiment was that she'd be watching over me in spirit, working for the company to ensure the systems remained operational.

That made much more sense.

I closed my eyes and shook my head, performing a mental reset of sorts. None of those thoughts would help me now. I had much more pressing concerns at the moment.

An owl hooted nearby, and I thought I could hear the faint baying of wolves from somewhere far away.

So, this was EndWorld.

I swallowed hard and pushed myself to my feet, taking the chance to better survey the immediate area. Trees. Besides the stars and the clouds, that's all I could make out at first. The rest was enshrouded in the thick cloak of night. I knew it would only take my eyes a few moments to adjust to the darkness, but I couldn't shake a feeling of urgency to understand my surroundings.

Without the requisite light to see where I was, I performed a quick self-assessment. I wasn't missing any limbs and everything seemed to be working as expected. That was a plus. On the downside, I hadn't the foggiest clue where I was. Still, I wasn't without options.

Map. I concentrated on the word, willing it into being.

Item not found.

Well, at least that was something. Even if I didn't have a map at the moment, it appeared to be an item I could obtain. I looked around again, hoping to find a chest or something on the ground nearby.

No such luck.

Drawing my gaze upward, I surveyed the horizon between the trees, pivoting in place as I turned. That's when I saw it: the distant, flickering glow of a campfire halfway up the next ridge.

My spirits brightened. A campfire in a place like this could only mean one thing. People.

It was too dark to make out the whole lay of the land but, depending on the roughness of the terrain between here and there, I estimated it would take about thirty to forty-five minutes. Unless I ran into trouble along the way, that is.

Wait.

I thought about my plan for a moment.

No. An encounter on a night like this might be a blessing, but it could just as easily be a curse.

I'd read too many fantasy novels as a kid to get sucked into blind hope when it came to campfires. As far as I knew, that camp could be filled with hulking ogres or flesh-eating trolls. Truth be told, there was a whole lot I didn't know about this strange, new world.

Friend or foe, there was no way to tell who I'd run into from where I stood right now.

What else could I do? Stay here until morning, alone and essentially unarmed? Or, I could stumble around aimlessly until I spotted some other kind of shelter. Then what?

I shuddered at the thought of crawling into a dark cave without some kind of torch or light to see if it harbored any other occupants.

Looking back at the branches I'd found myself lying under when I came to, I focused my vision. The trunk of the pine was tall and thin, and a soft bed of old, brown needles littered the ground, promising a fairly passable bed. I suppose staying put was an option, but I'd be exposed if I fell asleep. None of the branches promised enough support for an overnight vigil.

Considering the lack of other, more sensible options, I decided to round the travel time up to a solid hour and started to stretch. I could always make the call once I'd managed to get close enough to observe what kind of camp I'd happened to discover. If it didn't look good, I'd turn around and find somewhere safe to hole up for the rest of the night. What harm would that do?

Off in the distance, a chorus of howls echoed in the darkness. The sound was carried by the wind as it creaked and moaned through the upper boughs of the trees. I couldn't be certain, but the wolves sounded more distinct than they had just moments before. Perhaps I was beginning to shake the mental fog after all.

More howls burst forth from somewhere behind me. If anything, it sounded like the pack was getting closer.

I didn't know much about wolves, but the one thing I did know was that they had an incredible sense of smell. I pulled my broken sword from my inventory, clutching the hand-and-a-half hilt like I would a baseball bat. It was no use. The shattered blade wasn't even long enough to be considered a decent knife, let alone a long dagger. I stowed it again and scanned the forest floor.

Nothing.

If I headed for the camp now, the wind would be at my back, which meant my scent would carry forward. My mind raced. If the wolves pressed closer as I traveled, it could be simple chance or a scripted encounter. Either way, they wouldn't be hunting me through any fault of my own.

On the other hand, my scent would precede me on my trek toward the camp. Could ogres and trolls smell humans? I wasn't familiar enough with the lore to know.

Another round of howls pierced the night. The longer I stayed put, the fewer options I had at my disposal.

It was time to move.

My mind took me back to my childhood, to hunting trips with my father. It felt like a lifetime ago, but it reminded me to keep an even pace. The wolves couldn't smell me, and they wouldn't unless the wind changed. There was no reason to draw their attention by running through the woods, creating a commotion. That would only stoke their burning desire for the hunt.

The terrain sloped downward as I went and the going was easy. With the wind at my back, it seemed like I was making good time. The wolves were still somewhere behind me, but not nearly as close as they'd been before. Still, I scanned the ground as I went, looking for a branch that might be suitable as a club. I probably wouldn't have much luck as long as I was surrounded by pines, but it didn't hurt to keep my eyes open.

The moon had freed itself from the clutches of the clouds while I walked and it was much easier to see forest around me in the pale light.

A twig snapped somewhere to my left. I froze. It was more instinct than anything else. My breath grew shallow and restrained as I focused on the sound. Nothing else followed but the soft serenade of the forest.

I took a few more steps and then stopped to listen once again. Nothing.

Just like the major cities in the world I'd left behind, forests were also full of activity. It was a fact often overlooked due to the sense of serenity they often evoked. This forest was likely no different, but I decided it would be better not to let my guard down. Just in case.

The wind shifted then and the gradual decline of the slope steepened. I had to keep pressing forward. Beneath my feet, the loam gave way to the odd rock and then boulders as I made my careful descent. I could only hope the wolves wouldn't catch onto my smell before I hit rougher terrain. If left to their own devices, they'd likely stick to the game trails, and I'd be safe. Worst case, I might have to make a run for it and hope for the best.

Knowing the wind was against me now, I quickened my pace. As long as the moon remained unhidden, I wasn't too worried about stumbling in the dark. I could see well enough. It was the wolves that concerned me most. With no weapon to fend them off with, I'd be in pretty bad shape if they caught up to me now.

The trees were beginning to thin as the pines gave way to more leafy varieties. I wasn't an arborist by any means, but if I was going to come across a downed limb to use as a club or staff, this was where I expected to find it.

The eager cries of the beasts rang through the forest behind me as the pack picked up my scent. I was running out of time. Looking down in a panic I stumbled forward, crashing down on the rocks and debris. The fall shaved a few hit points from my health bar, but I scrambled back to my feet.

Up ahead, I could see a large branch. I made my way to it, and then lifted it up for a better view. The thickness was right and the wood was dead, but the branches would have to go. I snapped them off at the base as I went. Then, satisfied with my work, I tested the weight of it in my hand. Yes. This would do nicely.

Item Obtained! You've acquired:
*A **Makeshift Club**.*
[Club]
1-3 Physical damage.
Quality: Poor.
Rarity: Very Common.
Durability: 8/8.

Well, at least my new weapon was better than nothing, which was precisely what I'd had only moments before. There was only one thing left to do. I concentrated on the power of wind, visualizing the golem's breath as it had torn at my skin during our battle in the tutorial.

*You cast **Wind Blade** on your **Makeshift Club**.*

The now familiar twin orbs of green spiraled around the club's wooden shaft, infusing it with the power of wind and illuminating the area with a dull glow just as the moon was swallowed by the cover of clouds once more.

Another round of howls, this time much closer than the last, spurred me into action. Holding the club aloft to see by its light, I ran through the trees, doing my best to avoid any outcropping of rocks or broken limbs. The trunks were growing thicker with the decrease in altitude and branches slapped at my skin despite my efforts dodge the worst.

Sensing a growing darkness in front of me, I skidded to a halt just feet away from a steep ledge. I peered over the side to see the ground resume about twenty feet below. Resting my hand on the trunk of a nearby tree, I paused to catch my breath. I could climb down with the help of the exposed roots, or I could try to go around. Since wolves couldn't climb, the path straight down seemed the logical choice.

A strange whirring sound approached fast from behind me and, before I could turn to look, a curved dagger sank deep into the bark near my hand. I let out an involuntary yelp and stared in disbelief before making a hasty jump into the open air.

After a gut-lurching free fall, I landed with a resounding thud that shook my bones. Five more hit points vanished from my HP bar as I struggled back to my feet. Wolves were one thing, but I suspected they didn't throw daggers. Something or someone else was on my trail. It was time to move.

Running headlong into the thick brush, I tried to face the onslaught of branches against my face with all the poise and dignity I could muster. Which wasn't much. My heart raced within my chest, but I was encouraged by the slight incline my path was taking. This meant I was starting the climb of the next ridge and, while I couldn't see it from where I was now, the camp would be somewhere dead ahead.

With any luck, I'd find other Travelers, friendly folks like myself, and an end to my flight. If it really was ogres or trolls, I might be able to draw my pursuer in and then escape in the resulting commotion. It was a stretch, but staying put wasn't an option.

Upwards I climbed, grabbing hold of anything that seemed sturdy enough to bear my weight. I'd never been hunted before and I found the experience slightly invigorating, if not entirely frightening.

Within minutes I could see the distant, flickering firelight through random gaps in the trees. It wasn't a direct view of the camp, but I could tell from the dancing reflections that I was getting close. I stopped and looked behind me, listening for any sign of my pursuer. Only the sound of my own thudding heart greeted me in the darkness before the frustrated whines of the wolves and the snapping of branches somewhere nearby reignited my desire to flee.

Winded as I was, I fought the urge to stop and rest. Dirt and grit tore at the skin of my hands as I pushed myself to go on. Then, just as the slope started to level out, I glimpsed the shifting shadows of people up ahead, cast by the dancing firelight. People. Not ogres or trolls, but possibly just as dangerous.

"Hold on, quiet. Did you hear that?" One of them asked. His voice wasn't too gruff and carried an edge of alarm.

It wasn't a sure sign I hadn't alighted upon a merry band of thieves or roguish bandits, but it was better than the cold, hard tone of a fearless killer.

"No," a woman answered. "Guilly over here's too busy licking his chops for me to hear a damn thing."

"Sorry," the man she'd referred to said sullenly. "I'm starving."

My stomach rumbled as I tried to catch my breath. Now that I thought about it, I was famished. But at the moment, finding something to eat was the least of my worries, what with a dagger-throwing maniac and a pack of wolves hot on my trail.

Quiet as I could manage, I crept forward, inching my way closer to the camp.

*You use **Sneak**. Your **Sneak** skill is now level 1.*
***New Skill!** You've learned the skill: SNEAK.*

You can now reduce your chance of detection by people and creatures.
Raising your skill will make you harder to detect.
***Sneak** is an Advanced Skill and may reduce your trustworthiness with*
Travelers and Townsfolk if you are caught.
Aren't you a clever, sneaky bastard?

I raised an eyebrow at the unanticipated system message and found myself fighting to contain an unexpected chuckle. This whole experience was just chock-full of surprises.

Now, with a little more confident in my abilities, I slipped my club into my inventory and pressed forward again. I could always retrieve it if need be and it wouldn't help to have the swirling orbs giving away my position just yet.

"Maybe it was nothing," the original voice said and one of the shadows shifted closer to the fire. "Any more of that rabbit left?"

"Sorry," Guilly answered again, sounding just as sullen as before.

The man let out an exaggerated sigh and laughed. "No problem. Let's cook another. We can round up a few more tomorrow before completing the quest."

A quest. So, these people were likely the same as me, other players. Or Travelers, as Ayva had put it back in the tutorial. I'd have to stick with the going nomenclature if I wanted to fit in.

Crack!

A large branch crunched directly behind me and I felt the cold steel of a dagger's blade at my throat.

"Tell me you didn't just hear that," the man said, the panic creeping back into his voice.

"Yeah, I heard it," the woman answered.

"Me too," added Guilly and his large shadow grew as he stood and pulled a huge battle axe from its sheath on his back.

"Don't make a sound," a woman's voice hissed in my ear. I tried not to swallow as she pulled the blade tighter against my neck.

12

Guilly advanced a few paces, gripping his battle axe with his large hands spread wide upon the handle.

"Who's out there?" he shouted.

"Shhh." My attacker pressed herself closer, reaffirming her threat of violence by tilting the dagger's blade upward. The action lifted my chin and exposed more of my vulnerable neck.

"What do you think, Sven? Should we check it out?" the woman standing by the fire pressed.

Sven leaned back on his heels, scanning the darkness for trouble. "I don't know, Ruby. Could be nothing, could be something, hard to say for sure. Throw another log or two on the fire and be careful the rabbits don't burn or we'll spend half the day tomorrow chasing tails to bag our mark."

Ruby added more wood to the pit, keeping her eyes fixed in our direction. I wanted to call out, but I wasn't sure how death worked in EndWorld and something told me I shouldn't be in a rush to find out.

"Easy now," the rogue whispered in my ear. Then she shoved her knee into the back of my leg, easing me down into a silent crouch.

My mind raced with useless thoughts as I fought for a single good idea. Every scenario I came up with ended with my blood spilling on the forest floor. At least for the moment, that was an outcome I preferred to avoid.

"What do you want from me?" I whispered.

"Shhh."

The reply was quiet but harsh, and yet I hadn't felt the bite of her blade dig any deeper. Was this a good sign? I was hopeful, but things hadn't exactly gone my way since arriving in this strange place.

"Sven?" Guilly asked.

After a moment, Sven answered. "It's probably nothing, just the woods playing tricks. Keep your weapons ready, though. You never know when we might need them."

"Maybe it's sprites or brownies, forest folk and the like," Ruby offered, then her voice turned cold. "Or spirits."

"Leave us be, spirits," Guilly's shout echoed around us. "We don't have any quarrel with you."

"C'mon," Sven said, turning back to the fire. "Mind the rabbits before they turn to ash."

We remained where we were as the scene played out before us. The three of them poked at coals and turned the rabbits on their spits while the delicious aroma wafted in our direction. My stomach rumbled, and the blade flinched, inflicting a burning pain and shaving off a single hit point.

"Sorry," she breathed. "Try not to do that." Her grip loosened a bit, and she pulled the dagger away slightly, giving me a little more room to breathe.

What was this? Remorse? Blood trickled down my neck and I did my best to swallow softly.

"What do you think for tomorrow?" Sven asked. "Wake at first light, finish the quota on our rabbits, and finish our objective before we head back to Fort Morrow for the turn-in? Maybe see if there aren't a few upgrades we can afford?"

"Or more pie," Guilly offered.

"Is that all you can think about? Food?" Ruby insisted.

"I get hungry," he answered. "And that pie was good. Besides, it added three whole stamina points for the effect's duration. Six hours. That's better than any piece of gear I've seen at this level."

So, they were definitely Travelers. The woman behind me seemed to agree as she let out a sigh of relief.

"Let's sit and listen a while longer," she whispered. "They might be like us, but that doesn't mean they're good."

This floored me. To be honest, I didn't know what to think, but I found myself giving a slight nod of agreement. The crazy knife ninja had a point. Just as she'd managed to get the drop on me, these three could just as easily be of ill-repute.

And what if she'd somehow managed to save me from a far worse fate? I was beginning to see how that might be a possibility.

"Okay, now," Sven shouted in our direction. "The rabbit's almost done, so if you're finished skulking around in the dark, you might as well join us."

"Sven?" Ruby asked in a hoarse whisper.

The rogue's grip tightened on her dagger, but this time she kept the blade tilted away from my skin. Still, she made no effort to move from our hiding spot.

"Been tracking them since we heard the noise," Sven explained, his voice loud enough that the words were obviously for our benefit as well. "Come on out," he added. "I promise we won't bite."

With a groan of displeasure, my assailant withdrew her blade and stood before offering her hand. I took it and she helped me up.

"Play it cool," she whispered. "They could be up to something."

Something about her voice sounded familiar, but I couldn't for the life of me understand why. For all the hilarity of the situation, I got the impression that somehow this shadowy stranger had a genuine concern for my wellbeing.

How odd was that? To say I was confused by the plethora of mixed signals would be a broad understatement at the very least.

When I didn't move, she gave me a gentle prod. "Go on, I've got your back."

With no other apparent options, and still reeling from the strange turn of events, I put my hands in the air and placed one foot in front of the other.

Sven made no attempt to retrieve his bow, though I could see it plainly as it leaned against a mossy stump within arm's reach.

"Two of them," Guilly mumbled, his words barely audible over the crackling fire and the sound of our footsteps. "Your tracking skill is getting better."

"Level 3 already," Sven said, confirming the observation.

"No sudden movements now," Ruby warned. She drew her staff and a soft white glow emanated from the stone mounted at the top.

"She's a healer," the rogue whispered. "You can tell by the color inside the stone."

"That's right," Ruby said. "And I've got good hearing, too. The big fella here is a hungry axe-wielding maniac and Sven is deadly accurate with a bow. We're not some defenseless children gone camping in the woods, so best not try anything funny."

"I'm not a maniac," Guilly objected. "I am hungry, though."

"Just what do you call that berserker thing you do, then?"

"I call it **Berserker**," he answered with a shrug, clearly dumbfounded by her lack of understanding of his skill.

"Whatever." Ruby brushed off his indignation. Then she looked back in our direction. "Into the firelight with you. Let's take a look."

As we stepped into the camp, I chanced a look at the strange woman now standing beside me. Her clothes were pitch black, and she wore the hood of her cloak low over her eyes. I couldn't see her face, but the feeling of familiarity persisted.

"Some night, eh? What brings you to our humble abode?" Sven asked with what appeared to be a genuine smile.

"I just got here," I explained. "I spawned on the next ridge over. Then I saw your fire. Spawned? Is that the right term?"

Sven laughed. "It's good enough."

"Anyway, there were wolves. I didn't want to get caught in the dark."

"Yeah, we could hear them. They sounded close not long ago."

"They were dire wolves," the woman next to me interjected,

correcting our assumptions. "Just pups, a few level 3's but level 4's mostly."

"Level 4?" Guilly asked. "Here?"

She nodded.

Sven whistled, shaking his head. "That's no joke."

I thought of the golem and felt a chill of fear creep into my chest. Multiple mobs at or around level 4? It occurred to me then just how close I'd been to being torn to shreds.

Everything shifted as I began seeing the situation differently. Whoever this woman was, she very well might have saved my life on the hill back there. Though, the manner in which she did it left much to be suspected. I wasn't sure what to believe.

"My name is Denton," I said, hoping to break what was left of the ice between us and the party we'd managed to crash. I already knew their names from the conversation we'd observed from the shadows, but now that I could see them clearly in the firelight, I gave them each an appraising once-over.

"I'm Sven, Archer with Ranger specialization," Sven said, offered his hand in the way of a greeting.

I shook it, noting his tall, wiry frame and his dirty blond hair that draped at shoulder-length. Though he was skinny, his handshake was firm and the muscles in his arms had clear definition.

His choice of weapon made immediate sense.

"Guilly, Hungry Axeman Extraordinaire."

I wasn't sure whether he was joking or not until his lips spread wide in a goofy smile. The man was huge and if his attacks were half as ferocious as his appetite seemed to be, heaven help anyone who found themselves in his way. I shook his hand and chuckled. "Good to meet you."

"Greetings, Denton. The name's Ruby. I'm the group healer, as your friend already noted, but don't think that doesn't mean I have a few tricks up my sleeve."

"Ruby," I said, nodding my hello.

Her cloak was white and long and her staff had bits of ivy that spiraled up toward the gem.

She noticed my gaze and smiled. "We got lucky with an item drop. I didn't expect to replace my starter weapon so soon, but it's been quite nice."

"I bet," I mumbled in agreement, thinking of my own lackluster situation.

Sven chuckled and retrieved one of the spits before casting a roaming glance at my empty belt. He raised an eyebrow. "Did you lose your weapon on the way here?" he asked.

"Uh, not exactly," I explained, pulling the club from my inventory.

"A stick?" Ruby asked with incredulity. "You finished the tutorial, and all you got was a crummy stick? How does that work? That wasn't even an option in mine."

"My sword broke."

Sven nodded. "That's not too uncommon, actually. I'm guessing you got a quest to repair your weapon before you left, right?"

Now it was my turn to nod.

"Yeah, I figured. We've got a buddy in town, in Fort Morrow," he said. "He's a pretty good smith, and he should be able to help you out. But he doesn't do freebie work. You might have to shell out some coin or run a few quests to make it square."

"Of course," I said, excited at the prospect of fixing my blade and completing the quest. "Your friend can give quests? Does that mean they're an NPC, then?"

Guilly laughed as he picked up the rabbit on the other spit and offered it to my cloaked companion. "Jörgen, a Non-Player Character?" he asked. "Nah. He's a Traveler, like us."

"Oh, that's good to know," I said.

"He's pretty cool about it. It's not too big of a deal if you forget, like some people I know," Ruby added.

"Hey—" Guilly started, but Ruby ignored his interruption.

"Jörgen has been in EndWorld a while now. He's from one of the previous spawn cycles. Came to Fort Morrow in the caravans from another territory just a few days before we started showing up."

Hmmm. That was interesting. So, fellow Travelers could give quests?

It made sense in a way.

Players always inevitably asked for one thing or another in every single multi-player game I'd ever encountered. This usually resulted in an off-market trading system. There just wasn't a good way to formalize such a thing in most games. The companies who tried usually ended up with clunky, half-baked solutions people circumvented anyway.

Besides, if people wanted a system like that, they could just use an auction house. Right? I mean, why deal with a clunky trade mechanic simply because the game wanted a cut of the rewards?

But having the ability to offer quests...

Maybe this place was different.

I was definitely interested in seeing how the system worked in EndWorld.

All eyes rested on the hooded rogue.

"Raven," she said, taking a limb from the roasted animal and passing the rest on.

That was it. No explanation, no banter, just an awkward silence that blanketed the group, perforated only by the sounds of the fire and the nocturnal song of the surrounding forest.

Finally, Guilly broke the tension. "Well, now that introductions are all settled," he said, rubbing his hands together, "let's eat."

Within minutes we were sitting around the fire, eating roasted rabbit and conversing like old friends. It was hard to believe I'd been running through the trees and underbrush as if my life depended on it only a short while before. This was a nice change, and even Raven seemed to have relaxed a little.

There was so much I didn't know about EndWorld: the lore, the bestiary, the economy, and who knew what else. Any opportunity to learn about my new life was welcome, so I listened intently as the group shared some of their exploits with us.

"And that's how Ruby and I ran into Guilly," Sven said after recounting his tale. "We've been together ever since."

Guilly shrugged. "You have to understand, Denton. They really are good pies. Try one when you get to Fort Morrow. Trust me. So good. Three whole points to stamina."

Everyone but Raven laughed at this, though she didn't seem entirely displeased with the conversation. Or the company, for that matter. The longer I sat near her, stealing occasional glances in her direction, the more I felt the connection between us that I'd suspected earlier.

There was something about her, something that evoked strong feelings within me, both foreign and familiar. No matter how hard I tried to quell them, I just couldn't manage to shake it.

"Stamina, that increases your health pool, right?" I asked.

Guilly nodded.

"How long have you been here?" I prompted. "In EndWorld, I mean."

"We arrived toward the beginning of the spawn cycle," Ruby said. "Twelve days for me."

"Ten," added Sven.

"Thirteen," Guilly said, looking slightly embarrassed. "I wasn't into questing or grinding when I first got here. It wasn't until I grouped with Ruby and Sven that I started trying to level."

"And now look at you." Sven laughed. "Almost caught up already."

"What level are you now?" I asked, suddenly feeling like a total noob.

"I'm actually surprised you haven't checked," Sven said. He gave me a meaningful look and then nodded toward Raven. "She did, even before you two reached the fire. But I guess that makes sense if you just arrived."

Raven flinched slightly, and I felt my cheeks grow hot with embarrassment, though obviously for a different reason. She'd been caught in the act of scoping out the party, while I hadn't even thought to check. I was definitely a noob.

"Do you mind if I inspect you now?" I asked.

"Knock yourself out." Sven chuckled.

*You **Inspect** Sven Tillerson.*
Level 4. Archer class. Specialization: Ranger.
*You **Inspect** Ruby Michaels.*
Level 4. Mage class. Specialization: Healer.
*You **Inspect** Guilly Ortega.*
Level 3. Warrior class. Specialization: Berserker.

I turned to Raven and asked, "May I?"

She only shrugged in response.

*You **Inspect** Raven Cross.*
Level 3. Rogue Class. Specialization: Shadowdancer.

A Shadowdancer? I wasn't sure what that was, but I imagined all these specializations had to be low-level incarnations of more advanced classes. No doubt more would open up as each Traveler progressed down their chosen paths.

Perhaps one day, this Shadowdancer would hang up her daggers, trading them in for a pair of ninja katanas or claw-like fist weapons. My mind spun with all the possibilities.

"Satisfied?" Raven asked, though it was clear she wasn't looking for an answer.

"Yeah, thanks," I said, returning my attention back to the other three. "Do people usually camp out in the wilderness like this?"

"We've actually got rooms down at one of the inns at the fort. Paid through the whole week, believe it or not," Sven replied, tossing Guilly a wide grin.

"Oh, come on. You're not going to start that again, are you?" He protested.

"What?" I asked. "This sounds juicy."

"Oh, brother. I'll never hear the end of it, will I?"

"Your best bet when you hit the town is to collect quests, as many in the same area as you can find," Sven explained. "That's what we did. Got a whole list of them, too. Kill so many wild boars, collect a number of sprigs of pigeonweed, and the like."

"And five rabbits apiece," Guilly grumbled.

"We'd just about finished up our quests for the day," Ruby went on, "when this old lug convinced us we could bag the remaining rabbits on our way back in no time flat. Maybe a few more to sell, if we were lucky. Just stop a while and cook two, he said."

"And as you can see, night crept up and here we are," Sven finished. "Could have bagged the ones we needed on the way to town, no problem. Might even be snuggled in those soft beds we paid for, but no. We'll have to get them in the morning, on top of replacing the ones we've eaten tonight."

"Bet you're glad we stayed out now, though," Guilly countered. "If we hadn't we probably wouldn't have run into these two."

"Not before heading to the arena anyway," Ruby added.

"The arena?" I asked. "Player versus Player?"

"Sure, if that's your thing," Guilly said, pausing to pick a piece of meat from his teeth. "Though, we were thinking of pitting ourselves against the trials instead."

"Feats of strength and coordination," Sven explained. "Put a good team together and you can bring in some decent coin and loads of experience to boot."

Ruby nodded. "It's also a good way to increase your reputation with the crowds. Better reputation means discounts at shops, new opportunities, you name it. The arena isn't the only way to go, and it isn't for everyone, but that's what we've decided to do."

"And the arena, it's at Fort Morrow, is it?" I asked. "I think I'd like to see that."

"No," Sven said. "Not Morrow. The arena is actually at the capital, Castle Harrund. The castle is at the center of the region. Folks usually head there around level 5, but Fort Morrow is the closest settlement to where we're at now. It's a good first stop."

Just then, a thunderous howl shook the air around us, piercing the night with terrifying ferocity.

Raven glanced up and cocked her head to the side. "Mother dire wolf is calling her wayward pups home. There will be hell to pay for straying so far from the den, but at least we won't have to worry about them tonight."

There was something in her voice that made my blood run cold. All at once the warmth of the fire wasn't enough to keep a shiver from running down my spine. From the looks of it, I wasn't the only one impacted by the dreadful sound.

"An alpha, this close to Fort Morrow?" Ruby whispered.

Raven would say no more.

13

I awoke to the cold bite of morning. Opening my eyes, I watched the sun fight for purchase in the eastern sky as tiny wisps of smoke danced off the ash-covered embers. The smoldering heap was all that remained of the night's fire.

Propping my head in one of my hands, I played through the events that had led me to this point and looked around the camp. The rest of my new companions were all showing the first signs of wakefulness, save one.

Raven stood watch nearby, her back leaned against the sturdy trunk of a large tree. Even in the growing daylight, she was surrounded in shadow and mystery. The hood of her black cloak still draped low, covering much of her face. Though I couldn't see her eyes from where I sat, I could tell she was watching me.

"Good morning," I called to her.

"Morning," she responded coolly.

Guilly stretched and yawned. "Morning already?" he asked. "Oh, man. I could really go for some breakfast."

"You remember that next time you want to stop and cook up some of our quest items, would you?" Ruby chided.

"Geez, someone's grumpy," he teased.

"Maybe I wouldn't be so grumpy if someone didn't threaten to wake the dead with their blasted snoring all night," she said, tossing his good-mannered ribbing right back.

Sven stretched and got to his feet. "All right, that's enough, you two. Let's get squared away and head out. If we're lucky, we can bag the rest of these rabbits and turn in the lot of them in time for a late lunch."

Then Ruby turned to me. "We'd invite you along with us, but there's no telling how long we'll be. Besides, at level 1, joining our group wouldn't be very good for experience points. Not for us and certainly not for you. No, you'd be better off doing a few in-town quests when you can get them and hunting lower level mobs."

I nodded. "I understand."

"Any plans yet?" Sven asked.

"I was thinking I might try to make my way to Fort Morrow to see Jörgen," I said. "Hopefully, I can get working on having my sword fixed." I shrugged. "Who knows, maybe I'll see you all in town before you head off to the arena?"

"Sure thing," he said. "We're staying at the Bearded Goat."

"You're joking, right?" I asked. "Is that really the name of an Inn?"

"Best one in town as far as I'm concerned," Guilly answered. "They have mead and ale and all sorts of spirits. And the stew, you've got to taste it. Fresh baked br—"

Ruby silenced any further recital of the menu with a stern look.

"What about you?" Sven asked Raven. "If you don't have plans, you're welcome to head out with us. I mean, if you'd like. We could use another level 3."

Ruby cast a sideways glance at Sven, but before either of them could back out of the offer, Raven shook her head.

"Thanks, but I think I'll head into town with Denton," she said softly. "Just to make sure he gets there in one piece."

Sven nodded, obviously pleased with her response. "That works, too," he said. He looked a little relieved as he gathered up his bow. "Everyone ready to move out?"

Within just a few short minutes, I found myself watching the three of them weave through the trees. And then they were gone.

I turned to Raven and asked the one question that had been burning in my mind since our encounter. The one thing I couldn't ask in front of the others. "Why did you attack me?"

I couldn't see her face beneath the hood, but I could have sworn she rolled her eyes.

"Well?" I prompted. "Was it the wolves?"

She nodded. "Dire wolves, much like normal wolves but bigger and meaner. Not exactly something you want to mess with, especially not at level 1.

"But then what about back there?" I asked, pointing to the spot where she'd held her knife to my neck.

"EndWorld isn't always a nice place," she answered, stiffening a little. "What I did was for your own good. I don't regret it and I won't apologize."

"I'm not asking you to," I was quick to respond. "It's just, I don't know. All of this is new to me. I'm trying to understand. That's all."

"I guess I can't argue with that," she said, lowering her gaze once more. "I admit, you have a right to be upset."

Though it wasn't an apology, I figured it was the closest I was going to get. Somehow, I was okay with that. What if Sven, Guilly, and Ruby hadn't been good folks, was there a limit to how cruel people could be within this virtual world?

I considered Raven again, this time seeing her in a new light. What had she been through since arriving in EndWorld?

Seeing no further point in sticking around the small camp, I pulled my makeshift club from my inventory and kicked dirt over the lingering coals. "Shall we head toward Fort Morrow?"

Raven stood and adjusted her cloak. Then she invited me to her party. Just as when I'd been offered quests, the dialogue box opened, and I concentrated on accepting the invite.

Party Invite Accepted.
You are now in a party with Raven Cross.

Note: Party members have access to view your health and magic points, as well as other vital stats.

Warning: Your party may be disbanded automatically if the members of your group travel to different areas.

I started off in the direction taken by the others.

"This way," she said, heading off on another course.

"We're going to Fort Morrow, aren't we?" I asked, confused.

"Yes. And Fort Morrow is this way."

Unsure of what to do, I watched as she headed off through the woods. Not wanting to get lost by myself, I decided to follow.

We walked along in silence, making our way up rolling slopes, weaving through the trees as we went.

Neither of us spoke a word, and the gentle quiet was enough to remind me just how different this place was from the life I'd left behind. The air smelled fresh and clean and time seemed to pass a little more slowly here. Every minute promised something new.

I had so many questions, there were so many things I wanted to know, but I resisted the urge to break the peace. Raven didn't talk much, and yet she'd cared enough to act in what she felt was my best interest.

Then her haunting words came back to me. *'EndWorld isn't always a nice place.'* That's what she said, wasn't it? What if there was more to that statement than I'd first realized?

What if Raven was exactly the type of person I should be afraid of here?

If I was going to survive in this place, I was going to have to start asking questions and I needed to know more about the people I chose to be around.

I stopped walking. After several steps, she stopped and waited, then turned. "What's wrong?" she asked. "Why did you stop?"

"What's wrong? This is," I said, pointing at her and then to me and back again. "The more I think about it, the more I realize I don't have the slightest clue who you are. And here I am following you through the forest, too nervous to ask you anything because I don't want to come off as a total noob. But that's exactly what I am, isn't it?"

"What is it you want to know?" she asked.

"That's just it, I don't know," I stammered. "I don't know enough to know what I should be asking. You're a level 3 Rogue Shadow-dancer, whatever that is, and you could be leading me to a horrible and untimely death. All I know for certain is that those guys went one way and we're going another, though we're supposed to be headed to the same place. It just doesn't make sense."

"Just a little further and I think you'll understand." The cold disregard in her voice had melted, and she sounded pleasant. As if the two of us were old friends taking a stroll through the woods.

Again, I was struck by a sense of familiarity, this time it resonated within her new, kinder tone.

I was torn. Should I follow her a bit longer, or head off in the direction I thought the others had taken? Truth be told, I thought I knew where they might be, but a part of me wondered if I really did. I was sure I wouldn't be the first to get lost in these woods and I certainly wouldn't be the last.

"How much further," I asked.

"Only about fifty yards. It's just on the other side of this hill."

If she wanted to kill me, she could do it here. Why would she need me to walk another fifty yards? Then again, maybe there was a fate worse than death in EndWorld? In the end, it was the feeling that I knew this woman from somewhere, somehow, that won out.

With a sigh, I clenched my fingers tight around the club in my hand and resumed walking. Fifty yards and not a single step more. That's all I would give her before turning back towards camp so I could try to follow the trail the others had left behind. It might be dangerous, but at least I'd know what I was getting into.

If things turned out bad here, I'd have to fight. There wasn't a doubt in my mind that I'd lose, but at least I'd go down swinging.

As we crested the hill, my mind struggled to comprehend the sight that greeted us. The rising slope gave way to lower terrain and in the distance, rising above the leafy tops of countless trees, was Fort Morrow. It was only then that I started to understand.

"This is what you wanted to show me?" I asked. "It's beautiful."

Raven nodded, then confirmed my guess. "This is Fort Morrow," she said. "It's the central hub of the kingdom's southern territories. With the exception of the dire wolves, you'll mostly find mobs ranging anywhere from levels 1 to 3 on this side of the fort."

I assumed EndWorld Everlasting was like many of the other games I'd played throughout the years, which meant mobs weren't large groups of irate players, but a term used for loot-dropping creatures or humanoids. Such creatures would likely be a source for experience points, as long as they were close enough to your current level.

"And the other side?"

"Level 2 through 5." Then she pointed northward, beyond the borders of the fort. "Kingsroad is up that way, follow it and you'll end up at Castle Harrund."

"That's where the arena is?" I asked.

"Yes. Also, High Town and Low Town are quest hubs for higher levels, both are located within Harrund's outer walls. There you can find skilled smiths, advanced trade crafters, and vendors who sell rarer items than you'd likely encounter at Fort Morrow and the surrounding townships."

As I scanned the horizon, I was awed by just how massive the area appeared to be. And this was just one starting location. Guilly said Jörgen was from a Traveler from another starter area and he'd arrived by caravan just a few days before the first of us started showing up. I was just beginning to realize the scope of what that must mean.

"How big is this world?" I asked.

"It's big," Raven answered. "About ten times bigger than Earth, if not more."

Then my eyes were drawn to a darker part of the sky. The horizon was filled with the jagged tops of gnarled pines.

"What's that over there?" I asked.

"A swamp," she answered. "It's nasty place, just beyond Fort Morrow to the Northeast. Before that, the road splits south of

Morrow, Kingsroad West going away from Morrow will take you all the way to Elswood Village. To the East is the Dark Forest. Both are townships of Harrund's kingdom. The ice-capped peaks in the North-west are called the Frostwind Mountains. That's really all I know."

"I see," I said, trying my best to remember it all. "How do you keep track of all that? Do you have a map? I tried to activate the command, but it was a no-go."

Raven nodded. "You can pick one up at the Cartography shop at Fort Morrow. It goes in your inventory and populates as you visit new areas. But as long as you can remember about where things are by the time you get one, it should fill in everything we just discussed."

"That's useful. What about combat?" As long as she was feeling inclined to talk, I figured I might as well try. "Any tips you can give me?"

"You fought in the tutorial?" she asked.

"I did."

"Did you win?"

I nodded. No one seemed inclined to talk much about their tuto-rial experiences, so I decided to keep the details to myself for now.

"At level 1, that's all you really need to know," she said. "Best not to overthink it. But one thing I can tell you for sure is that you should lose the stick when we get to town. The durability won't last and your damage will suffer. You can finish your starter quest by repairing your weapon, or you can buy a new one."

With that she reached into her cloak and pulled out two square objects, each wrapped in a linen cloth that had been soaked in wax. Then she offered one to me.

"You're probably hungry. This should help."

When I unwrapped the stiff cloth, I found what looked to be some kind of nature bar. Chunks of flattened oats were mixed with honey, nuts, and dried fruit.

"Thanks," I said, taking an experimental bite. It was good.

"No problem."

Combat-wise, I hadn't managed to learn anything I didn't already know, but learning more about the area was invaluable. We sat a while in silence, crunching on the snack she'd provided while looking out on the land below. That's when I decided to thank her for all her help by sticking my foot in my mouth.

"You know," I said, shifting to look at her. "Ever since last night, I've had the strangest feeling. This is going to sound weird, but it feels like I know you from somewhere."

Raven seemed to shrink a little under my gaze, lowering her head so her hood shielded even more of her features.

"Sorry, it's nothing," I quickly added. "This place must be doing weird things with my head. That's all."

We skirted several packs of lesser wolves and other forest animals on our journey, walking for another hour in silence. My boots were starting to come apart at the sole and the sun was burning hot in the sky when she stopped.

Scanning the forest for more creatures and losing myself in my thoughts, I hadn't noticed. My attention was elsewhere and I nearly bowled her over but managed to step to the side just in time.

Raven cocked her head and looked at me from beneath the cover of her hood before speaking. "I'll leave you here," she said. "I have a few things I need to do before I head in to town. Up ahead is Kingsroad, it'll take you to the southern gate. If you hit a fork, you went the wrong way."

I stared at her for a moment before the words seemed to click. "Oh," I said. "Uh, thank you for... well, for everything."

She turned to leave, then stopped short.

"The others are staying at the Bearded Goat. I've got a room at Harold's Tavern on the other side of town. It isn't as fancy but Harold probably has another vacancy, if you're interested." She didn't look at me this time, but I thought I could hear a smile in her voice.

"Thanks," I said. "I'll have to check it out."

With that, she nodded and walked off into the woods, leaving me to finish my journey to Fort Morrow alone.

Kingsroad was filled with people headed to or from the fort. Many of them looked as if they were newbies like me, complete with starter gear in various states of disrepair and disarray. I looked down at my boots, which were now in pretty bad condition. It was becoming clear that I probably didn't have much of a future as a cobbler.

"Which way to the fort?" I asked a passerby.

The man pointed over his shoulder and kept walking. Then a teenage boy who was headed in the direction the man pointed stopped and looked at me.

"You're going to Fort Morrow?" he asked.

The kid was about the same age as my Sophie, around sixteen. He was lanky, with reddish-brown hair and a goofy grin. He was wearing a baggy brown robe with short sleeves and carried a fairly straight staff adorned with a glowing blue gem.

*You **Inspect** Zachary Smith.*
Level 3. Mage class. Specialization: Frost.

"Yeah," I said, giving him a smile. "That's exactly where I'm headed. My name is Denton."

"I'm Zack," he replied. "Nice to meet you." Then he stuck out his hand.

I returned the gesture. "Likewise," I said.

He beckoned me over to join him. "Seems like we're headed in the same direction. Morrow's my next stop."

14

We'd been walking along Kingsroad a while before Zack turned to me and asked, "So, how long have you been in this world?"

"Just got here. Last night, in fact," I replied. "You?"

"Eight days for me."

I looked back in the direction he left behind. Though still passable, the dirt road was marred with the deep ruts of wagon wheels, likely left by heavy caravans traveling during the last rain.

Off in the distance, a dark shadow seemed to hang over the woods. This was one of the areas Raven told me about.

"You spawned back that way?" I asked. "That's the Dark Forest, right? Elwood Village?"

"Sure is," Zack said, giving me a thumbs up and a cheesy grin. "People there are pretty friendly, too."

"Oh yeah?" I asked, surprised at his description of such a gloomy-looking place. "What brings you to Fort Morrow, then? Anything special?"

He paused long enough to kick a rock down the dirt road before answering. "Just going to take a look around. I'm actually on my way to Castle Harrund. Got a date with a shopkeeper or two, I'm going to try to find me an arcane spell."

Another surprise. When I inspected him a minute ago, the system told me he was specialized in Frost magic. Why would a Frost Mage be looking for arcane spells? It was an interesting question and one that might help me better understand how magic worked, which would probably be important if I wanted to become a competent Battle Mage.

"An arcane spell?" I asked. "Aren't you specialized in Ice-based magic?"

Zack looked at me in surprise before answering. "Well, that wasn't exactly my choice. My staff sort of chose for me. I just want to try a few different things to see what fits."

Given his answer, it was apparent that specializations weren't set in stone.

I thought about this for a moment. Ruby had chosen the staff as well but, for whatever reason, her choice had caused her to spawn as a healer.

"That makes sense," I said after a while. "There's still a lot I don't know about how all of this works. I thought about taking the staff myself, but I went with the sword instead. I figured I'd try to become a Battle Mage if things worked out. To be honest, I'm not even sure if that's a possibility."

Zack shrugged. "I don't know about any of that. I've always liked playing as a mage." Then he gave me another quick look-over, eyeing my belt for the tell-tale sign of a swordsman, but I wasn't wearing my blade or the empty scabbard. "You chose the sword, huh?"

I nodded.

"I haven't seen a single sword since the tutorial. As far as I'd heard, most warrior classes start out in the Frostwind Mountains. Why are you hiding yours? I'd like to take a look, if you don't mind."

"There isn't much to see," I admitted, pulling the broken hilt from my inventory and offering it to him. "It shattered when I dealt the final blow in my trial."

He took the hilt in his hand and stared at it while we walked.

"Geez, what did you do to the end of it? Do you still have the blade? My staff broke, too. But I collected the pieces and got it repaired in the first town. Maybe you could do that?"

I let out a breath I hadn't realized I'd been holding and took back the shattered weapon. "I sort of lost it."

He blinked and shook his head in disbelief. "How did you manage to lose a large piece of metal? Kind of an important part of a sword, don't you think?"

I looked at the thinning group of merchants and Travelers around us and slowed my pace. I wasn't sure why people didn't talk much about their tutorial experiences, but I didn't want to put myself at risk.

Once we were safely out of earshot, I leaned in and whispered, "I lost it in the tutorial when I stabbed a golem. The blade broke off in its back and I couldn't retrieve it. I'm just hoping a smith in town can come up with a way to fix it."

"I'm not sure you can fix a sword without a blade, can you?" he asked. "You might have to buy another one. I bet a lot of the vendors sell swords, though. This is a second-tier town, so you shouldn't have a problem finding one. Then again, I'm not much of a crafter myself. Just take a look at these robes." He laughed.

"Yeah, something tells me you might be right," I said. "I've heard of a merchant smith in town, Jörgen, he's a Traveler like us. I figured I'd talk to him and see what he has to say about it."

"That sounds reasonable." He shrugged and offered a smile.

We walked the rest of the way in silence and, as we neared Fort Morrow's southern gate, the dirt road transitioned into a cobbled street and the line of people began to thicken.

Just visible on the horizon, the gray stone walls of the fort towered over the treetops. The banners atop the parapets waved in a breeze I couldn't feel, and the first murmur of sounds one might expect from a medieval cityscape reached my ears.

My heart thudded within my chest as my excitement grew, and I was surprised by my sudden eagerness. I cast a glance toward Zack to gauge his reaction.

He was stepping on tip-toes in an effort to look over the heads of those in front of us, bobbing this way and that to get a better glimpse of the scene obscured by those before us.

Having kids of my own, I couldn't help a slight chuckle. It was clear he was in a hurry to get in and take a look around before continuing his journey toward the castle.

"You've got a long road ahead of you?" I asked.

A distracted nod was his only reply.

"Why don't you go on ahead," I suggested, clapping a friendly hand on his shoulder. "I'm going to take my time and try to get a feel for the place since this is my starting area."

He looked at me for a moment before nodding again.

"Safe travels, eh?" I said. "And good luck finding the spell you're looking for."

Returning my smile, he offered his hand again. "Take it easy, future Battle Mage," he said as we shook our goodbyes. "Mind if I add you as a friend? Maybe you can show me that new sword when you get it fixed?"

Of course, I thought. Why hadn't I put that together before? Without phones or email, having a system to keep in contact with people in this world would be an important part of the experience.

"Sure thing," I replied, doing my best to hide my surprise. "I don't know how to add you, though."

It struck me then that I hadn't gotten a single offer from any of the other people I'd met since finding myself in EndWorld. I suppose it was possible none of them knew how to send an invite, but the prospect didn't seem likely.

"I'll send the request," Zack said, squinting his eyes as if he were focusing on a faraway object. "You can pull up the interface by focusing on the menu and navigating to the Social tab."

Within a few seconds, I was prompted with the friend request, which I immediately accepted.

"See you around?" he asked.

"See you around," I answered with a chuckle. "Thanks for the company, and for the tip."

Then, with a roguishly goofy grin, he was off, ducking and weaving through the crowd like a kid on his way to his next class between bells.

The encounter left my heart aching. Zack reminded me so much of my own children, and yet he was here in EndWorld. Which meant that, like me, he was dead. It was a hard reality to swallow.

Even thinking about the truth of it threatened to take me down a dark path. I couldn't imagine losing one of my kids and my heart went out to his parents. All things considered, I might have died, but they were still alive. Helen and Roger would take care of them. They would keep my children safe.

I resolved to try my best to look after Zack if I ran into him again. Maybe he didn't need a father figure here in this game world but, despite his humor and quick wit, he looked like a kid who could use a friend. Someone who could see him for who he really was, who believed in him, and would be there for him if the enchantment of this place ever wore off.

THE SIGHTS AND SOUNDS OF THE CITY UNFOLDED AROUND ME AS I passed through the open gate. Thick wooden doors sat ajar on their massive hinges and guards clad in fairly ornate leather armor stood by, keeping a watchful eye on the crowd. Shops and traveling merchants lined the streets, where countless voices joined the throng.

"Advanced weapons, blades and spears," a man called out. "Twenty silver, fifty silver, up to one gold. Step right up, we won't be undersold."

"Staves, trinkets, and baubles. Get your magic items here." A woman from somewhere a little further in joined the chorus.

Then a rather large man leaning against his cart smiled and winked at a pretty woman in front of me before starting on his pitch. "Tasty treats. Delectable delights. Food to enjoy now and some for the road. Step right up, folks, Fat Anthony has what your stomach needs."

*You **Inspect** Fat Anthony.*
Level 16. Trader.
*Your **Inspect** skill is insufficient to reveal further details.*

The afternoon sun was getting long in the tooth and the smells from Fat Anthony's cart reminded me that it had been hours since I last ate. A loud grumbling sound emanated from my belly and I found myself wondering about the pies Guilly talked so much about. I hadn't even thought to ask where he'd gotten them, or even what kind of pies they were. As if reading my mind, Anthony nodded at me and started his pitch again.

Up ahead, the crowd started thinning as the cobbled street opened to a grand courtyard. That was the place I wanted to be, where I could stop and sit and collect my thoughts. I needed to get away from all the bodies and the noise. All of a sudden, it seemed like I couldn't get there fast enough. A familiar sense of panic and hyper-vigilance crept in as people pushed and shoved, elbowed and shouldered, each trying to get wherever they were going without much concern for those around them.

I lowered my head and focused on the barely attached soles of my boots, drowning out the noise of the street one inhale and exhale at a time. Before I knew it, I was in the courtyard. Sitting down on a stone bench, I struggled to rouse myself from the trance. I'd felt disconnected from the rest of the world for a long time and the anxiety was hard to shake, but this wasn't how my children would want me to live. If I was going to be a part of this place, if I was going to be happy in EndWorld, I had to work on becoming more like the man my kids knew me to be.

From the safety of my seat, I watched the people as they passed by. I even inspected a few, but stopped when a particularly gruff looking man gave me a dirty look. The others hadn't seemed to notice, but he must have had the same skill as Sven. Not wanting to risk offending anyone else, I decided to cool it for now. Besides, there were other things for me to worry about. I was hungry, I only had thirty silver to my name, my boots were all but busted, and I had a sword in desperate need of repair. On top of all that, I still hadn't decided where I was going to stay for the night.

One thing was certain, I'd need to get started on tackling some quests if I wanted to improve my financial standing. Otherwise, I might find myself sleeping in the woods again tonight. As a level 1 noob without a proper weapon and any advanced skills, that didn't sound particularly appealing. My best bet was to stick to delivery-type quests for now, saving low-level combat until I had a decent weapon as Raven suggested. With that decided, I only needed to figure out where I could find quests to accept.

Spotting a guard nearby, I got to my feet and walked over to where he stood. Then, disregarding my inclination to avoid inspecting everyone I encountered, I decided to chance it.

*You **Inspect** Tommy Lewis.*
Level 18. Town Guard.
*Your **Inspect** skill is insufficient to reveal further details.*

Nothing there seemed too out of the ordinary and I resolved to focus on leveling up my **Inspect** skill further once I secured a better weapon and headed outside the city walls.

But why did the system message indicate my skill was too low for these last two? It hadn't done that before. Perhaps it was our level difference?

"Excuse me, sir?" I asked.

The man looked at me with what appeared to be a mixture of annoyance and distrust. It was as good a sign as any that I'd also need to work on increasing my reputation.

"I'm looking for a blacksmith by the name of Jörgen. Would you happen to know where I can find his shop? And, by chance, is there a place where a new Traveler can pick up quests from the local townsfolk?"

"Well, aren't you just full of questions on this fine afternoon?" the guard grumbled. "Tell you what. You go fetch me a loaf of bread and some cheese from Fat Anthony back down the way and I'll give you those answers you're looking for."

New Quest Alert! You've been offered a quest:
The Hungry Guard.
You've asked Guard Tommy Lewis for information. Before he'll give you the answers you seek, you must bring him something good to eat.
This quest will be complete when you deliver a loaf of bread and some cheese from Fat Anthony's cart to Guard Tommy Lewis.
Reward: *100 Experience Points, Information, 5 Silver, Improved familiarity with Guard Tommy Lewis.*

I sighed and looked down the cobbled street. Somewhere back there was Fat Anthony's cart and the food items I needed. With one final glance at the guard, I nodded and accepted his quest.

"Now get lost," he said. "And don't come back until you've brought me something to eat."

I sighed and stepped past merchants and idle shoppers as I retraced my steps to where Fat Anthony was hawking his goods. Since I was fighting against the natural flow of foot traffic, the trek was a little more difficult this time, but I was a man on a mission.

I had no intention of letting a simple pick-up and delivery quest get in my way. The guard might have been rude and condescending, but he had information I wanted and the other rewards certainly wouldn't hurt.

"Ah, yes," Fat Anthony said after finishing another recital of his pitch. "I see your nose led you back and, truth be told, something told me I might see you again. You've made an excellent choice, friend. Feel free to browse, but be forewarned. There are no free samples."

"I am hungry," I admitted, "but for now I just need to pick up a loaf of bread and some cheese for one of the guards."

"Is that so?" Fat Anthony asked. "Do you happen to recall which guard sent you?"

"It was... Tommy Lewis?" I replied.

The large man smiled and wiped his chubby fingers on his apron. "Of course."

He reached into his cart and retrieved a covered basket. "That will be thirty silver. Are you sure I can't get you something else?"

"Thirty silver?" I asked, baulking at the dent the purchase would put in my wallet.

At this rate, completing the quest would drain all my current funds. The five silver reward the guard had offered was a complete joke. If I accepted Anthony's price for the bread and cheese, my coin would go down to a measly five silver from thirty. And that was after receiving the award. It wasn't exactly a step in the right direction.

Not by a long shot.

I started to wonder if I should just walk away. There had to be other means of obtaining the information I was looking for.

Noticing my reluctance, Fat Anthony rubbed his chin in thought. "Say, you're new here, aren't you?"

I nodded.

"Alright," he said. "Well, I suppose I could give you a discount since you're just starting out. How about twenty silver? That's a whole ten silver off my normal price, and I'll even throw in a sweet roll for your trouble. It's always nice to see folks helping out the guards."

This deal was only slightly better. Finishing the quest would cost me twenty silver, leaving me with only ten. With Tommy's reward of five silver, I would be left with just fifteen of the thirty silver I had on hand. The more I thought about it, the more it seemed like this quest wasn't a good deal at all.

Then again, I wasn't sure if there were consequences for abandoning a quest once you'd accepted it. I really should have been a little more inquisitive about the requirements.

"Okay," I answered after a long pause. "I'll take it."

"Very good," Fat Anthony said with a wide grin, rubbing his hands together like a greedy cartoon villain. "Focus on your currency and imagine yourself retrieving the desired amount from your inventory."

My time with Ayva in the tutorial seemed like ages ago, but it was remarkable how strange it felt to have an NPC like Fat Anthony instruct me on the user interface instead.

I found myself wondering if all Non-Player Characters would know I was so new as I imagined placing the twenty silver in my hand.

While Fat Anthony's tip had been helpful, it kind of ruined the whole immersion aspect I'd come to enjoy so far. There was probably a way to turn it off, and I resolved to look into it later.

Retrieved 20 silver coins.

When I handed the coins to Fat Anthony, he quickly stashed them into a pocket and passed me the goods.

"A deal's a deal. Here's the package for Tommy," he said with a smirk. "And don't forget your roll. Please, do come again."

With the quest items in hand, I turned and made my way back to the square. Behind me, I could hear Fat Anthony laughing. What was up with these NPCs? I was beginning to wonder if maybe Fort Morrow wasn't my kind of town.

I bit into the sweet roll as I walked. Before I could even chew, I gagged, spitting it right back out again. Fat Anthony's laughter turned into a wheezing fit of hilarity. The thing was beyond horrid. It tasted like a frosted heap of clay and dung. I could only imagine he'd been watching, waiting for the punchline of the joke I hadn't realized he'd played.

There was no point in going back and confronting the man. What could I do, yell at him and create an even bigger spectacle of myself? Threaten to beat him with my stick? No. I wasn't going to give him the pleasure. It was obvious I had been the brunt of a prank. The best response would be to leave it at that and learn from the experience. At any rate, I was beginning to see Raven's point. Blind trust in this place could be dangerous.

Now furious, I headed straight for the guard. There was nothing I wanted more than to deliver his stupid bread and cheese and be done with the business altogether. The sooner I could find Jörgen and get started on some real quests, the better.

Something inside me yearned for the protection of a real weapon. It wasn't that I wanted to inflict harm, though the thought of kicking Fat Anthony in the balls did seem rather appealing at the moment. No. For some reason, lacking a proper weapon in this place made me feel incomplete, as if without it I was at the whims and mercy of those I might encounter. And, as I'd just experienced, that wasn't a good feeling.

Tommy Lewis was eying me with interest as I approached. He adjusted his scabbard on his belt and I could tell he was trying his best to hide a smile. So that was it, then. Both of them were in on the joke. It made sense, but that didn't stop me from being disappointed. Had I somehow managed to bump into the two worst NPCs in town, or were they all like this?

"Here's your bread and cheese," I said, handing him the package.

"Thanks, noob," Tommy replied. He took the bundle and dropped five silver pieces in my open palm. I watched as my total increased back up to fifteen.

"Jörgen's shop is on the other side of the fountain," he added. "It's the one with the anvil on the sign. You can get quests by talking to townsfolk or other Travelers. And, since we're a little more familiar now, here's a bit of free advice. Try to be a more careful who you accept quests from in the future."

Quest Complete! *You've completed:*
The Hungry Guard.
You've received: 100 Experience Points, Information, 5 Silver, and Improved Familiarity with Tommy Lewis.

It took everything I had not to punch the guy in the face and I was still fuming by the time I reached Jörgen's shop. When I opened the door, a bell on a curled strip of metal rang out, announcing my arrival. A man with long, blond hair pulled back in a ponytail looked up from a ledger. He was wearing a thick blacksmith's apron and smudges of soot darkened his cheeks. The cross-hilt of a large, two-handed sword sheathed on his back peeked over his shoulder.

"Are you Jörgen Olsen, by chance?" I asked.

He squinted at me and smiled. "That's me," he said, his words sounding almost foreign with his thick accent. "Welcome to my shop. Feel free to take a look around, if you'd like."

I let out a breath, doing my best to let go of the anger I had toward the other townsfolk. I might not have been able to stand up to a fat merchant or a fort guard, but at least I could try to channel it into something more productive. Something like forging new, more advantageous relationships.

"My name is Denton Wade," I said, taking a chance on this encounter going better than the last. "I ran into a few Travelers last night, you might know them. Sven, Guilly, and Ruby. Sound familiar?"

Jörgen nodded, bristling a little at the mention of their names. "They're good people. Didn't stop by last night after questing like they planned. Has something happened?"

"Everything is fine." I explained, noting his concern. "They should be on their way back to town as we speak."

He seemed to relax a little, so I retrieved the broken hilt from my inventory and set it on the counter. "They told me you might be just the man I need to see about something like this."

Jörgen stared at it long and hard, bending in close to get a good look before he picked it up and tested the weight of it in his hand. He looked at me, then back at my shattered weapon, giving a long, low whistle.

"That's some break," he said at last, setting it on the counter once more.

This was it, the moment of truth. Knowing I only had ten silver to my name, I steeled myself for disappointment and asked, "How much would it cost to repair my sword?"

15

Jörgen didn't reply right away, and the silence felt heavy in the air between us. After what seemed like an eternity, he looked into my eyes and sighed, picking up the remains of my sword again to examine the spot where the blade had shattered.

"When I was a boy, I read a book about a great warrior," he said. "He was just a mouse, but he was a mouse who dared to stand up to wild cats. They captured him and broke his sword, the last memento he had to remember his father by. Then they threw him in a dungeon and forced him to wear the hilt around his neck as a mark of shame."

"That's a little depressing," I admitted.

"It was very sad, but that was not the end," Jörgen said with a grin. "This little, ferocious mouse escaped and went on a quest to a great, faraway mountain. He faced perils and met many new friends. The road was tough, but he made it. Once there, a mighty blacksmith forged his father's broken sword anew, crafting the blade from the heart of a fallen star."

"Now that sounds more like a story I'd enjoy," I said, unable to resist a smile.

I could almost envision the upcoming quest. *Retrieve the heart of a fallen star, collect rare and dangerous reagents, all to obtain the most epic sword ever.* Were things really starting to turn around?

"Yes." He nodded. "But it was just a book. I cannot attach a blade to this hilt with my current skill, not even one made from the heart of a star. As far as I know, it is a myth. A legend; nothing more than make-believe. The metal would always be weak and no such joint could ever withstand the heat of battle."

All my soaring hopes crumbled as reality came crashing in. It seemed that even in this fantasy world there were limits.

Seeing my look of despondent agony, he reached across the counter and clapped me on the shoulder. "Do not despair, little mouse. All is not lost."

"You're not going to suggest I wear this thing around my neck like an amulet, are you?" I asked with incredulity.

He laughed long and hard. "It would not make such a good amulet, I think," he said. "But even for me, it is plain to see this hilt does have magical properties."

After noticing my look of skepticism, he added, "Maybe not plain for you, but as a skilled smith, I have learned a few things. Yes?"

I nodded, slowly, furrowing my brow as I tried to work out what he might be trying to tell me. I couldn't come up with a single thing. Magical properties in a sword I couldn't use? What good was that? After the day I'd had, I was eager for even the slightest semblance of good news, but my mind was too tired to put the pieces together.

"What does that mean?" I asked.

"This hilt is a relic."

My eyebrows shot up like startled crows. "A relic?" I echoed. "That's a good thing, right?"

"Indeed," Jörgen replied. "Relics are very rare, usually imbued with the power of great events or a focusing of the will when the wielder calls upon a strength that exists outside themselves. And then, a cataclysm occurs, creating something new out of the old."

"Something new out of something old," I said, weighing the words aloud. "How can relics be rare then? Sven told me it's quite common for Travelers to break their weapons in the tutorial."

"Yes, this is true." Jörgen nodded. "It isn't that the sword broke. No, that would be too simple. Yet, only in breaking did this weapon gain its potential."

"That seems ironic," I said, "being as it can't be fixed. So much for being special. What good is it if I can't actually wield it? I need a weapon if I'm going to be able to level and make my way here."

He stroked his chin, apparently thinking through the implications. "I don't know. But..."

"But?" I asked, prompting him to complete his train of thought. I don't know why, but I was also clinging to the idea of some new hope.

"I would like to hold on to it for now, to study it more. If you don't mind. I promise I will return it to you. On my honor, as both a shopkeeper and a smith, this I swear to you."

Allowing Jörgen to borrow the hunk of metal seemed like the natural choice. There was always the chance that he'd steal the broken weapon but, even if he did, what difference would it make to me? It wasn't like it was doing me any good as it was now. And what would I sell a chunk of a tutorial weapon for anyway?

Besides, there was also the chance I could use this strange turn of events to my advantage.

"Well," I started, "I'm kind of without a suitable weapon. Is there any chance you could cut me a deal on something a little more durable than this? A sword, perhaps?"

I pulled out my makeshift club and set it on the counter.

Jörgen looked at my improvised stick of doom and chuckled. "You made this?"

"It was the best I could do under the circumstances," I replied. "I was being pursued by a pack of wolves, or dire wolf pups, as I was later informed."

"No, no. It's quite good, especially considering the circumstance," he said, waving off my explanation. "I could sell this."

"Really?" I asked. "Who would buy something like that?"

"You'd be surprised. It might not be much now, but to the right crafter it would be quite a suitable base. Many fine weapons start out looking like this," he explained. "Tell you what, I'll give you two options. I can give you five silver for it now, no questions asked. Or I can take it on consignment and you get ten silver when it sells."

I frowned, but nodded all the same. "Consignment, I guess," I said. I'd already figured that if push came to shove, I might find myself sleeping under the stars again tonight and it was beginning to look like that might be the way of things for the foreseeable future.

"What's wrong?" he asked. "You don't like this deal?"

"No, it's not that," I answered. "Every little bit helps, I suppose. It's just that after buying that stupid guard his lunch for a worthless quest, I'm down to fifteen silver and I don't even know where I'm staying tonight. I could take the five up front, but it probably wouldn't make much of a difference, anyway."

After listening to my explanation with increasing intensity, Jörgen slammed his fist against the counter and his face turned a bright shade of red. Then, with surprising speed, he flipped up the walk-between, storming from behind the counter and heading straight outside. The bell rang as the door slammed shut and I found myself standing alone and dumbfounded in the now empty shop.

A few minutes later he returned, practically dragging the guard, Tommy Lewis, behind him.

"Is this the scoundrel who gave you the quest?" he growled, shaking the man by his collar.

Tommy shook his head slightly, silently pleading with me to hold my tongue.

There was no quest prompt and no pop-ups offering me one choice over the other. Still, two things were becoming very clear. First, this wasn't the first time Tommy had pulled his stunt, and second, this modest blacksmith was apparently in a position to do something about it.

I was starting to realize that Jörgen was no ordinary Traveler. The man had to have some serious clout with city officials if he could put the smack down on their fellow NPCs with impunity.

"That's him," I said, much to Tommy's discomfort. "He sent me to Fat Anthony for bread and cheese, but the reward for the quest wasn't worth the trouble. Maybe it was my fault for being so naïve."

"How much did you spend?"

"Twenty silver," I answered.

"And you were given a 'sweet roll'?" Jörgen asked, giving Tommy's collar a fierce jerk upward.

I nodded. All at once, the heat of embarrassment burned my cheeks. It felt horrible having my weakness paraded in front of me like this, even if Jörgen's heart was in the right place.

The sweet roll wasn't just a prank. It was a painful reminder that this wasn't the sort of life I would have chosen for myself. I was so far out of my element, but I was trying to be strong. I was trying to remember why I'd decided to come to this place.

Living in EndWorld and becoming the best version of myself I could be was for my children. It was silly, and I knew that. I mean, there was no way for them to know how I was getting along in this strange land, but somehow it mattered.

I had to believe that.

Jörgen gave the trembling man another shake. "Tell him the cost of the bread and cheese you sent him to buy," he demanded.

"Three silver," Tommy said through clenched teeth.

My head began to spin as I realized the whole extent of the trick. I hadn't just been insulted, the whole thing had been a scam. Talk about an insult to the injury.

"Pay it back," Jörgen said. "Every last coin."

"Now wait just a second," Tommy protested. His eyes seemed to lose focus for a moment. It was as if he was looking at something far away.

Perhaps a quest prompt.

Then, with another fierce jerk and a raised eyebrow from the tall, muscular blacksmith, Tommy changed his tune. "Fine." With an effort, he slammed fifteen silver coins on the counter.

"All of it," Jörgen whispered, nodding toward the counter.

"That is all of it, I already gave him five silver as a reward. Five plus fifteen is twenty. We're even."

Jörgen looked to me for confirmation and I nodded. It was true, but the imposing blacksmith was not satisfied.

"A reward is a reward," he said. "Payment for services rendered. You owe this man a total of twenty-five silver, not twenty. Twenty-five silver, and not a copper less. Do you understand?"

Tommy grumbled and rolled his eyes but complied all the same, placing another 5 silver on the pile.

"Now get out of my shop. If I hear of you pulling your tricks again, I'll be sure to have a little chat with the captain of the guard. Perhaps he's a lot less lenient regarding matters such as this, yes?"

I was still staring at the door well after the chime of the bell had faded. I took a deep breath and turned.

Jörgen gestured toward the pile of coins.

"You'll run into all types here in EndWorld. As unfortunate as it may be, this isn't the first time those two have taken advantage of newbies," he said as I was placing the currency back into my inventory.

"To be honest, I was starting to wonder if the whole thing wasn't a scripted encounter," I admitted. "I have to say, I wasn't exactly expecting to be taken advantage of by a couple of NPCs on my first day."

He laughed then, bracing a callused hand against the worn wood of the counter. "Those two ruffians aren't NPCs," he said. "They're just a couple of miscreants who've managed to worm their way up in level and favor. But mark my words, things have a way of coming back around in this place."

"Travelers?" I breathed, not knowing what to make of this new information. "But how can that be? The data I got back when I inspected them was different than the other Travelers I've encountered so far."

"Ah, yes. I see now," he said. "It's a common trick. The Inspect skill is only so useful and it can cause a fair amount of confusion. With enough skill in deception, anyone can manipulate what others see. Some choose to try to level the skill enough to overcome this, but good old intuition suits me well enough."

I caught myself frowning at this, unable to determine which path would suit me best.

"Nothing to worry about, little mouse," Jörgen said, clapping me on the shoulder with affection. "You have many adventures ahead of you in this place, this much even a simple blacksmith can see. There will be plenty of time for you to decide which road to take."

Despite his self-deprecating words, I had no doubt that the man standing before me was anything but a simple blacksmith.

"But first," he went on, smiling. "Something tells me this adventure of yours begins with a tale of two swords."

New Quest Alert! You've been offered a quest:
A Tale of Two Swords.
Jörgen Olsen has offered you a unique quest.
Allow Jörgen Olsen to hold on to your broken sword. In exchange, you will receive a replacement blade. Return to Jörgen's shop when you are stronger to learn more about the nature of your relic.
The completion requirements for this quest are unknown.
Reward: 5,000 Experience Points, 3 Gold, additional information about the nature of your broken sword.

16

My eyes went wide as I read through the quest. Five thousand experience points? Something told me it would be some time before I'd be strong enough to meet the requirements, but there was no way I could turn down such a generous offer. When the shock subsided, I looked at Jörgen and nodded, accepting his offer.

He rubbed his hands together with eager excitement and hopped back behind the counter before retrieving a fancy-looking one-handed sword. He pulled it from its sheath and tested the weight of it in his hand before he stared down the blade itself, squinting one eye to gauge the truth of the metal and the sharpness of the steel. Finally satisfied, he gently offered it to me.

I took the sword in my hands, taking care to mind the razor-sharp cutting edges. It was beautiful and seemed to glow slightly with a faint light of its own.

Item Obtained! *You've acquired:*
Truthseeker.
[Bastard Sword]
10-15 Physical damage.

Strength +1, Dexterity +1.
Quality: Excellent.
Rarity: Rare.
Durability: 15/15.
Craftsman's Mark: Jörgen Olsen.

I stared at the stats in utter disbelief. This didn't make sense. The sword he was offering me was far beyond the quality of the starter blade I'd used to defeat the golem.

As if sensing my trepidation, he explained. "It is a good weapon, much better than you might encounter for a few levels. But you must understand, despite how generous it may seem, the deal is not so one-sided. Offering fair trade is very important for my reputation, you see."

When I didn't respond, he continued. "If I can learn more about your relic, I'll likely gain a significant amount of skill and experience. My standing as a shopkeeper will grow. And I might even get more opportunities to handle other relics in the future. So you see, it's not such a bad trade for me at all."

What he was saying made sense. If relics were as rare and powerful as it seemed, a merchant could probably do very well by immersing themselves in such a market. Besides, if Jörgen wanted to steal my relic, he could have simply offered me a paltry sum of coin at the start and been done with it.

"Thank you," I said, sliding the cold steel back into the safety of its sheath. Then I set about securing the ornate scabbard to my belt.

Somehow, Truthseeker felt right and comfortable as it hung at my side. I was eager to get out into the woods to test its blade but, even from within the shop, I could tell the hour was growing late. Going out into the world at large at this hour would be reckless, even with this new, powerful weapon in my hand.

Jörgen retrieved four packages from beneath the counter and grinned. It was clear that he was going to enjoy what happened next.

New Quest Alert! You've been offered a quest:

> *Welcome to Fort Morrow.*
> *Deliver packages to:*
> *Beatrice Potts, Map Vendor at Cartography & More.*
> *Kenneth Johnson, Trade Goods Supplier in the Central Market.*
> *Marianna Sweet, Innkeeper at The Bearded Goat.*
> *Harold Strong, Innkeeper at Harold's Tavern.*
> ***Reward:*** *500 Experience Points, 10 Silver, Increased reputation with*
> *Beatrice Potts, Kenneth Johnson, Marianna Sweet, and Harold Strong.*
> ***Additional Reward:*** *Variable.*

"You don't have to deliver them all tonight," he reassured me. "Do what you can and then drop the rest off before you head out of town, but don't wait too long. I've got a reputation to keep."

I accepted the quest and placed the parcels in my inventory. I wasn't sure how many of the deliveries I could complete before the last hours of light faded, but I could certainly get started. And what's more, two of the locations would take me to places where I could inquire about a room for the night.

Things really were starting to look up.

"Thank you," I said, shaking Jörgen's muscled hand with gusto. "I won't let you down."

"My pleasure," he said with a smile, nodding toward the door. "You better get a move on if you want to catch a few of them before nightfall. I'll be closing shop soon, so you can stop by in the morning to collect your delivery fee."

WHEN I STEPPED OUT OF JÖRGEN'S SHOP, I WAS GREETED WITH A surprisingly cool breeze. It seemed that even with a few hours of light left, the heat of the day was beginning to wane.

I looked around, shielding my eyes against the brightness. Even more bodies filled the square than before as people milled about the shops making last-minute purchases before the night stole in.

Fort Morrow felt different, more welcoming somehow. I still felt out of place, but I no longer sensed a growing hostility as I had before. What's more, I held my head high and walked amongst the crowd without anxiety. Was it Truthseeker hanging at my side, or was it something else?

I was still pondering the origin of my new-found confidence when I spotted a storefront with a large compass painted on its wooded sign.

Given the emblem, it seemed reasonable to assume that this was the cartography shop. Easy enough. With any luck, I'd find Beatrice Potts inside. Then I could deliver the first of Jörgen's four packages and be on my way.

The door creaked as I twisted the knob and pulled it open. Inside, dusty scrolls were scattered in heaps and piles across every bench and table. I resisted the urge to cough and instead lifted a fist to my nose, doing my best to avoid breathing in the tiny airborne material that floated in the fresh stream of sunlight.

It looked like the shop was empty at first, but then the slightest movement caught my eye. The dancing flicker of candlelight illuminated the far wall, and then I saw her.

The proprietor of the shop, a studious-looking woman, sat in the corner, peering through a magnifying glass at an unfurled square of parchment.

The woman didn't look up, but greeted me all the same. "Shut the door behind you. I'm in the middle of a very delicate task and I could do without the breeze interfering with my work."

I closed the door as quickly and quietly as I could before gingerly making my way through the towering maze of scrolls.

It was clear to see that Beatrice was trying to concentrate, what with the annoyed glances she shot my way each time I inadvertently bumped into part of the mess.

Redoubling my efforts, I twisted and turned through the maze, drawing ever closer to her workspace. By the time I made it to where she sat, I'd had three near-misses yet somehow managed to avoid knocking over a single scroll.

__Hidden Quest Complete!__ You've completed:
__Avoiding Beatrice's Ire.__
You have successfully avoided raising Beatrice's ire.
__Reward:__ 200 Experience Points.
+100 Favor with Beatrice Potts.

The surprise notification flashed in my log. A hidden quest? I read through the text with great interest, pausing for a moment on the last line. While the experience points were nice, it was the increased reputation that caught my eye.

Favor was apparently different from the familiarity gain I'd received from the wayward Traveler, Tommy Lewis. Was this what Ruby had meant when she'd told me about the benefits of raising reputation?

In a way, I supposed familiarity was just that, familiarity. It could be either good or bad depending on how someone felt about you.

Favor had a little more obvious connotation.

Beatrice was still concentrating on her work at hand. She bit her lip and wet the tip of a quill in a nearby inkwell.

Thinking better of breaking the silence, I decided to look on instead. With the slightest movements, the feathered pen in her hand inflicted tiny black lines on what appeared to be a very detailed map.

She set the pen and the magnifying glass aside and donned a strange pair of binocular glasses one might expect to see as part of a steampunk spectacle. Once satisfied, she went back to filling in what looked like the coast of an otherwise unmarked sea.

Long minutes passed with only the sound of her quill scratching on the parchment and the creaks and groans of her chair to fill the silence.

My stomach growled, reminding me that I should eat soon, and Beatrice looked up as if shaken from a trance.

__Hidden Quest Complete!__ You've completed:
__Gaining Beatrice's Sympathy.__
Beatrice Potts looks upon you with sympathy.

Reward: *300 Experience Points, +100 Favor with Beatrice Potts.*

"You sound hungry," she said, taking off the strange glasses and setting her pen to the side once more.

"It's been a long day," I admitted. "I still need to make my way to the two inns and make arrangements for the night."

"Well, I suppose that will do for now," she said, giving me her full attention. "I'm sorry to have kept you waiting."

"It's quite alright," I said, waving off her apology. "I enjoyed watching you work. It isn't every day you get to see a master cartographer in action."

To be honest, I'd been hoping to trigger another gain in favor and was a little disappointed that hadn't done the trick. Still, every word of what I'd said had been true.

Beatrice smiled and intertwined her fingers in her lap. After a few seconds of awkward silence, I realized she was waiting for an explanation for my unexpected visit.

"Right," I said, fumbling in my inventory for the package I'd been asked to deliver. After two failed attempts to retrieve the right one, I presented her with the correct parcel.

"Oh, yes. Very good," she said. "And sooner than expected, I must say. Jörgen always takes such good care of his clients."

She set the package aside and took a closer look at me. "You're new here," she observed. "Have you just arrived?"

"Last night." I nodded.

Then, in the silence that followed, I realized another reason Jörgen might have sent me on this particular errand.

Clearing my throat, I posed the now obvious question. "Say, you wouldn't happen to know how a new Traveler like me might find himself in possession of a map, would you?"

I added in an exaggerated wink for effect.

"As a matter of fact," Beatrice said, leaning forward and beckoning me closer. "I might know just the place."

Ten minutes later I was back out in the square, the proud owner of a fully integrated map and compass. Beatrice had even been so kind as to explain a few of the more advanced functions.

By messing with my menu interface, I could toggle a mini-map on and off and even shift it around within my field of vision. This would be handy. And, just as Raven had said, everything I remembered from her introduction to the area was visible within my expanded map interface.

Checking the markers on my mini-map, it was clear that the nearest objective was nearby. I examined the marker before allowing the mini-map to fade from my field of vision. It was Kenneth Johnson, the Trade Goods Supplier in the Central Market.

I had just enough time to swing by his stand before choosing one of the inns. So, determined to avoid being left out in the dark, I made my way across the cobbled square and down an adjacent street.

Kenneth Johnson was a mousy-looking man with gray hair and spectacles. He wore a thick leather apron and greeted the regulars who milled about his stall with uncanny enthusiasm.

"Mary, such a pleasure to see you this evening. Did you have any trouble vanquishing those rats? Grissak, I didn't expect to see you back so soon. What's this? You've leveled up already? Where does the time go?"

I couldn't help looking at the burly man. He was clearly a Traveler, wearing a set of rusty, dented plate armor and sporting a gruesome battle axe. Upon hearing his name, he perked up and stepped forward.

"Do you have any more of those sharpening stones, Kenneth?" Grissak asked with a smile that seemed to be just as broad as his massive shoulders.

I decided to wait for the crowd to thin before approaching the stall, taking advantage of the passing time to find the correct package so I wouldn't look like a bumbling idiot as I had in Beatrice's shop.

There were still several people hovering around the stall when Kenneth waved me over with a smile. "I won't pretend I don't see you lurking around over there. Come on, come on, time's a wasting," he said.

I returned his smile and stepped forward. His eyes settled on the package before drifting toward the scabbard at my waist.

"Is that Truthseeker I see hanging from your belt?" he asked in awe and a few of his patrons turned their appraising gazes in my direction.

Not knowing how I should react to the unexpected attention, I nodded sheepishly and offered the merchant his parcel.

At this, Kenneth took the box and laughed. "It's a remarkable sword for someone of your level." he quipped. Then he added, "I hope you'll forgive me for saying so, but it's a terrible fit. I've seen some fine matches since he arrived, but I'm afraid Jörgen's made a grave mistake this time around."

"What do you mean?" I asked, utterly confused by the man's strange antics.

What was it to him which sword the blacksmith had given me? Was he somehow implying that I wasn't worthy of wielding a weapon such as this? I couldn't detect any malice or sarcasm in the man's voice, so I was at a complete loss.

As if sensing the cause of my discomfort, Kenneth explained. "Truthseeker is a fine weapon. Yes, it's true. And from what I can tell you'd make a fine swordsman. I sense something else, too. Magic? Yes. But rarely are things so simple. A blade must match its wielder if the two are to fight as one, you see."

"What are you suggesting," I asked.

"Why, sell it to me, of course," the merchant exclaimed to the raucous laughter of those gathered nearby.

When I didn't reply, he continued. "Ask anyone around, I'd offer you a fair price. How's five gold sound?"

New Quest Alert! You've been offered a quest:
An Enticing Offer.
Kenneth Johnson would like to buy Truthseeker, which he insists is an imperfect match for you.
To complete this quest, accept Kenneth's offer.
Reward: 5 Gold, Increased Favor with Kenneth Johnson.

Someone in the crowd whistled their approval.

"With five gold, you'd be able to buy any sword you wanted in all of Fort Morrow. Mark my words," a woman standing next to me added.

"Fort Morrow? Forget about it, he'd be able to buy any sword in all of Harrund," another person in the crowd contested.

I considered this for a moment. It seemed like a good offer, but it felt... wrong. Jörgen had given me this sword, and I didn't feel ready to part with it. "That seems like a lot of gold," I said at last. "But I think I'll hold on to it for now."

Then I dismissed the quest.

"Let's not be so hasty," Kenneth insisted. "Tell you what, how about I sweeten the deal? I'll give you six shiny gold pieces and three of my best healing elixirs."

New Quest Alert! You've been offered a quest:
An Even More Enticing Offer.
Kenneth Johnson would like to buy Truthseeker, which he insists is an imperfect match for you.
To complete this quest, accept Kenneth's offer.
Reward: 6 Gold, 3 Healing Elixirs, Increased Favor with Kenneth Johnson.

I was about to turn down the second quest when Kenneth leaned in closer and placed a gentle hand on my shoulder.

"No need to decide now, friend. Sleep on it and come back tomorrow morning. Give me your answer then. Just be sure not to spiritbind it or else I won't be able to offer you nearly as much."

I wasn't sure what he meant about spiritbinding, but I nodded and made my farewells before heading toward the closest inn.

When I stopped in front of my destination, which turned out to be none other than The Bearded Goat, I could smell the delectable aromas coming from the kitchen within.

The day had been long and my mind was weary from all the unexpected twists and turns I'd encountered along the way. With any luck, I'd be able to deliver the package, grab something to eat, and rent a room for the night without encountering any trouble.

Pushing the swinging, saloon-like doors open, I entered the dimly lit establishment.

So, this was the place where the others had been staying.

I looked around in hopes of finding someone who could point me in the right direction. Serving girls holding wooden trays stacked to the brim with dishes and drink wove their way through the standing crowd to eager diners sitting at tables.

Most of the patrons who hadn't yet found a seat stood with glass or tankard in hand, conversing with others who found themselves in a similar predicament.

And the food.

Freshly baked loaves of bread were pulled, golden brown, from a wood-fired oven. I looked on as some of the seated patrons helped themselves to skewers of roasted meats, while those seated at the table nearest to me dined on what appeared to be the very same stew Guilly had gone on about.

It was all I could do to keep myself from drooling.

After asking a passing waitress for help, I spotted Marianna Sweet. She was a gorgeous woman with curly brown hair and stood behind a long counter in the back.

I watched her dual wield mugs full of frothy beverages in her strong hands and listened to her exchange jibes with the regulars. Filling orders suddenly seemed like an art form, each laugh and smile and joke a carefully choreographed move in a delicate dance.

Finally catching her eye, I lifted the parcel I'd received from Jörgen and nodded in her direction.

"Pardon me fellas," she said, tossing a damp serving towel across her shoulder and strutting out from behind the bar. "It seems my package has arrived."

Something in her voice left me wondering if she was talking about the parcel itself or if she was referring to me.

Truth be told, it made me uncomfortable. My nerves settled,

however; when she took the parcel from my hands and gave me a little wink.

"I've been waiting for this," she said as she began opening the wooden crate in front of me. "You didn't take a peek, did you?"

Not wanting to compete with the noise around us, I just shook my head.

"No? Well, I wouldn't have blamed you if you did. After all, who can resist taking a look at Jörgen's goods?"

Again, I wasn't certain if I was reading too much into what she was saying or if she was doing it on purpose.

She pulled a brand-new cast-iron skillet from the package and set the crate to the side. Then her eyes, too, strayed toward my belt.

"Oh, my," she exclaimed, clapping her free hand on my chest and holding the skillet aloft with the other. "Talk about taking a peek at the goods. Who would be tempted to sneak a glimpse at an old thing like this when they're sporting that kind of steel?"

"I, uh—"

She walked her fingers up my chest and placed one on my lips. Then she squinted her eyes, still looking at my sheathed sword. "And, would you look at that, it isn't even spiritbound."

17

arianna Sweet didn't insist on buying my sword like Kenneth had, nor did she offer any sort of compensation for the delivery as Beatrice did. That said, she couldn't resist a few more teases with her over-the-top innuendos before breaking the tough news.

Had I missed an opportunity to win her over with hidden quests and increased reputation? Perhaps, but I wasn't much in the mood for flirting.

Either way, I'd missed the boat. The inn was already at full capacity for the night. Even considering the three rooms vacated upon the departure of Sven, Guilly, and Ruby, it seemed as if the Bearded Goat was the place to be.

With no other options left, I set my sights on the last stop for Jörgen's quest.

Of course, Harold's Tavern was on the other side of the fort and the mere thought of the trek made my feet ache. I was hungry and growing ever wearier from the day's travels, but there was nothing else for it. After taking a deep breath, I started walking.

The scene that greeted me outside the packed inn wasn't what I'd expected. Stepping back out into the cool night air, I was immediately taken aback by the bustle of activity as Travelers, I assumed, gathered together in groups to discuss their latest adventures and discoveries.

My curiosity was piqued, and I noticed my steps slow, but I redoubled my resolve and pushed myself toward Harold's. Something told me that in a place like this, information was key.

In bypassing this opportunity, it was possible I was missing out on a piece of information that might help me avoid mistakes like accepting bad quests from people looking to make some easy coin off noobs like me. Or worse, what if I walked right past someone sharing details on hidden quests and cool rewards?

The night was young, but the day had been a long one. Besides, there was always tomorrow. As for now, I decided to finish my quest, while securing lodging and some kind of nourishment. With any luck, I might find a source for information at the tavern over the course of a hot meal.

There was also a fairly good chance I might run into Raven. To be honest, I wasn't sure what to think about the sullen and secretive woman. No matter how hard I tried, I couldn't shake the feeling that we'd met before but, after the way she reacted when I brought it up, it was obviously a topic she wasn't interested in discussing further. If even for my ultimate benefit, her actions in the forest confused me.

How was one supposed to react when a hidden stranger pressed the cold steel of her blade against one's throat to prevent them from exposing themselves to another group of strangers?

Yet, like Jörgen, she'd been protective and helpful, even if it was in her own, unconventional way. I felt a strange sort of kinship with her, just as I had with Zack, the young man I met on the Kingsroad outside the fort's southern gates.

The last few remaining stitches on my boots and a prayer were the only things keeping my soles between my feet and the cobblestones. I'd only been here for a short time, but I'd already experienced so much. But that wasn't all. I'd managed to make a few friends and felt all the richer for it. Inwardly, I marveled at what a strange place EndWorld had turned out to be.

Even now, I could feel the weight of Truthseeker on my belt. It was an impressive sword, one I hoped I might prove myself worthy of.

And there it was. With one random thought, my mind touched on the very notion I'd somehow managed to avoid since my arrival.

Things had happened so fast, I hadn't given much thought to the consequences of my actions. What was my worth? To know that, I had to know who, or what, I was.

One thing I knew for certain, and it was a truth that stung very deep, I was dead. In death, I shared the same fate as every other soul trapped in this place. But what was EndWorld? Did it exist? Did we? I had so many questions and none of the strength it took to give them voice. I suppose my greatest fear was that I was no longer myself, but a programmed simulation of the man I used to be: an artificial intelligence with a forced identity, doomed to dance to the long-silent fiddle of a dead man until the day the lights went out for good.

Glancing up at the marker on the mini map, I took note of my progress and let out a long sigh. What use was this chain of thought, anyway? It didn't seem to be doing me a lick of good. No matter what, whoever or whatever I was, I was here. Certainly, that was all that really mattered for the time being.

The real question was how I could better integrate myself into this new way of life. After all, I wasn't here for me, but for my kids. I imagined the way to make them proud would be to try to fit in and do well for myself here, but how?

I wasn't like Jörgen or that guard, Tommy. Both men seemed to be embracing their new lives in EndWorld, even if the paths they chose were different from one another. The blacksmith was chaotic good to the guard's lawful evil. I couldn't help but smile at my overly simplistic generalizations, throwbacks from old school gaming that was well before my time, but they seemed to fit. I mean, Tommy hadn't exactly broken the law when he'd offered me his quest. He merely exploited the rules of the system and took advantage of my noobish ignorance.

No. I wasn't like them, nor like any of the people now gathered about in the street, it seemed. But, just like all of them, EndWorld was my new home. This was my new life.

Something told me the sooner I learned to embrace it, the better off I'd be.

If only it were that easy.

The torches along the cobbled streets were stretching further apart, allowing the night's shadows to flicker as they danced to a song I couldn't hear. Harold's Tavern was drawing closer and the small groups of people began to thin.

By the time I reached my destination, I could see why the Bearded Goat had been so packed. This part of the fort seemed run down and almost forgotten.

Shady figures glanced up from their secretive dealings as I neared the entrance and their gazes lingered until I stepped inside.

Taking in my new surroundings, I immediately scanned the tavern hall for Raven, hoping to find some kind of anchor in the crazy underworld I'd managed to stumble into.

No such luck, though upon closer inspection the denizens of the place weren't as intimidating as I first expected.

Sure, there were a few obvious rogues in the mix, kitted out in their leather attire with gleaming daggers worn proudly for all to see, but the rest of the crowd looked surprisingly normal.

A large, hairy man wearing nothing but what appeared to be a pair of rusty iron underwear and some kind of leather suspenders gripped me by the shoulder and grinned.

"Welcome to Harold's, noob," he exclaimed, shaking my hand with unrestrained gusto.

*You **Inspect** Elyograg Nightly.*
Level 4. Brawler class. Specialization: Hand-to-Hand.

"Aye," Elyograg exclaimed, raising my hand in the air like I'd just won a championship bout. Several people in the nearest booths began exchanging coins.

"The name's Ely. Dinner's on me tonight, buddy," he said with a chuckle, giving me a huge, toothy smile. Then he winked as one of the rogues tossed him a small sack.

"I don't get it," I said, looking from one person to the next and back at the half-naked brawler. "What just happened?"

"You inspected me," Ely explained as he ushered me in toward the bar like an old friend. "It's a little game we like to play. We take turns greeting the new folks and place wagers on whether we can get them to inspect us. I won."

"Yeah," I said, unable to resist a chuckle. "I noticed."

Ely grabbed a couple of the bar stools and then held up a meaty palm, hailing a gruff-looking man behind the counter. "Hey, Harold, we've got another noob. Swing over here when you get a chance, would you?"

Harold glanced up and set the glass he was drying lip-down before picking up another. "These dishes ain't going to dry themselves, keep your panties on," he grumbled, eyeing Ely's sparse attire.

The big man's jaw dropped and several patrons within earshot snickered. Then, before Ely could recover from his shock, Harold gave me a sly wink and grabbed another glass.

"They aren't panties," Ely stammered. "It's a subligar and you know it. And besides, those glasses would dry themselves if you left them long enough."

"Forget the glasses, man. Harold's nailed it. You're wearing a damn iron diaper, that's what it is," one of the rogues chided.

Ely's cheeks flushed pink, and he looked like he was about to burst with rage when he suddenly let out a hearty guffaw.

"Ha," he laughed. "I guess I'll just have to take this old subligar off then, right? But I have to warn you, I don't have another pair of trousers in my inventory." With that, he turned from the bar and gripped the sides of his bottoms.

"Noooooo," a chorus of voices shouted back and for a moment even Harold looked dismayed.

"You sure?" Ely asked, laughing again. "I hear there's a wicked moon out tonight." Then he turned back toward the counter before giving his iron britches a tug downward.

"Aww, man, I'm trying to eat here," the rogue whined.

Harold frowned. "Cut that out, you daft lump of hog tripe. I don't need no naked men running around in my establishment."

"Okay, okay," Ely said, hiking up his drawers. "Now how about a round of drinks for me and my new friend here?" He turned to me. "I didn't catch your name."

"Denton."

"A round for me and my new friend, Denton," Ely said, correcting himself.

He turned to me again and asked, "You hungry?"

I nodded.

"And two specials," he hollered over the counter.

Harold shook his head and was about to turn away when I caught his attention.

"Hold up, Harold. I have something for you, actually."

"Eh?" Harold squinted his eyes and ambled over. "You say you've got something for me? What is it? Well, don't just sit there, let's take a look."

"It's from Jörgen," I said as I handed him the final parcel for my quest.

"Is that so?" Harold's eyes lit up as he took the package.

"What's all this about?" Ely asked, raising an eyebrow.

"A quest," I explained. "Standard delivery type from Jörgen. He's a blacksmith here in town."

Ely laughed and shook his head. "I get that, but how did you get him to give you one? Man, I'm telling you, that guy doesn't hand out quests to just anyone. I know half a dozen people who would love to be in your shoes right now."

Then he glanced down at my belt and his eyes went wide. "What is that?" he whispered after glancing around nervously.

I followed his gaze toward my sword and rested my hand on the pommel. "It's my new sword."

At this, Ely put his arm around my shoulder and pulled me closer in a half bear hug. "Put it in your inventory," he said, his voice low enough that I had trouble understanding what he was saying at first. "Do it now."

"But—" I looked around the tavern, taking in the other customers, who all seemed to have their weapons clearly visible.

Ely squeezed me tighter and grumbled. "Trust me, Denton. I'm trying to save you a whole lot of heartache. Put it in your inventory, nice and easy. Don't make a show of it. Just act natural. I promise, I'll explain later."

Whatever it was, I wasn't looking for trouble, so I did as he said and tucked Truthseeker into my inventory. Once I had, his grip loosened, and he gave me a smile.

"Sorry," he said. "When the place clears out a bit, I'll tell you why and I'm sure it'll all make sense."

I nodded my understanding just as Harold returned with our drinks.

"These are on the house," he said, "As long as you don't mind doing me a favor in return?"

"Sure. What is it?" I asked.

"Stop by Jörgen's tomorrow morning and give him this. He'll know what it's about. And I hope I can trust you'll make sure the seal isn't tampered with along the way?"

*You've received **A Handwritten Letter**.*

"Not a problem," I said. "I'll deliver it first thing."

"Great." Harold smiled. "I'll be out with your supper just as soon as it's done cooking. Let me know if you need another round."

Ely raised his glass in salute before taking a huge swig. "Oh, yeah," he said after gulping it down and letting out a long sigh of contentment. "I'll tell you what, Denton. No matter what anyone tries to tell you, Harold here sure knows how to make a good brew."

Harold waved him off with a smile and wandered back toward the kitchen.

"He seems like a decent guy," I said, gesturing toward the old man. "I have to admit, I wasn't sure what to expect when I got to this part of town."

"Yeah, he's pretty great." Ely nodded. "Most people prefer the Goat, but this place can't be beat. Don't let the area fool you. It doesn't matter where you are. There are always people looking to take advantage of the unsuspecting. It might look like a stand up place to the uninitiated, but there's just as many shady characters at the Bearded Goat as anywhere else, if not more."

"Really?" I asked, a little taken aback by the assertion. "It didn't look so bad. Besides, the whole place was packed to the brim."

"Absolutely." Ely took another hearty swig. "A place like that is the perfect spot to run a con." Then he turned to me. "Look, I'm not saying I'd vouch for everyone here. Not in a heartbeat. But when you walk through the door to a place like this, most people know to watch themselves. A place like the Goat? It lulls you in, convinces you that everything in the world is just right. Next thing you know..."

Ely didn't finish his thought, but I got the feeling I knew where it was headed. It didn't take a master sleuth to put it together.

He'd been swindled at the Bearded Goat, that much was clear.

I wondered if that wasn't the real reason he was sporting the rusted iron subligaria and leather suspenders. It made sense. Still, there was something I didn't understand.

How had he managed to obtain the brawler class and hand-to-hand specialization? Were the tutorials different depending on the person? I decided to ask.

"When I inspected you, I saw something that didn't make much sense," I started.

"Oh, yeah? What's that?"

Harold approached with two large bowls and a plate of artisan rolls. He slid a bowl in front of each of us and set the bread between. Gesturing toward Ely's near-empty glass, he asked, "Refill?"

I looked down at the steaming meat and vegetables and my stomach rumbled in anticipation as Harold filled Ely's glass. The aroma of the stew wafted up in tendrils, flooding my mouth with drool I was barely able to contain. Then, with a shaking hand, I wielded the wooden spoon. Fearing it might be too hot, I blew on the loaded spoonful before taking my first, tentative bite.

"Good, huh?" Ely asked, clearly pleased with my reaction.

The stew seemed to melt in my mouth, sending waves of euphoria through my body. Never before had I felt what I was experiencing in that moment. All I could manage was a small nod between successive spoonfuls. In the upper right corner of my vision, a small icon sprang to life, the buff duration increasing with each bite.

*You are **Well Fed**.*
*While active, **Harold's Stew** provides:*
*+1 to **Intellect**, +3 to **Stamina**, and +1 to **Strength**.*
*Current Duration: **30 Minutes**.*
*Max Duration: **12 Hours**.*

"You should try your drink," Ely suggested, nodding toward my glass. "It's honeyed dandelion wine. I promise, you've never tasted anything like it."

"If the dandelion isn't to your liking," Harold cut in with obvious anticipation, "I've got a keg or two of my best strawberry cordial down in the cellar."

"I've never tried the cordial," Ely admitted. "It's a bit outside my price range."

I took a sip of the dandelion wine and my eyes went wide. The cool liquid was sweet and complimented the heartiness of the stew with perfection. "Oh, wow. That is good."

"Ha," Harold exclaimed. "So, you do have good taste after all. When I saw your glass still full, I was started to worry there mightn't be any hope for you." He looked at Ely and back at me. "Ah, to hell with it. While I'm in a good mood, I'll bring you each a swig of my cordial. On the house. But don't you go blabbing about it or I'll have half the town beating down my door for free drinks. That's the last thing I need."

"Deal," Ely and I both chimed in unison.

Harold nodded and then vanished through a door that lead down into the basement. I took full advantage of his absence to stuff my face with stew, watching in awe as my buff timer increased.

I wasn't sure if I was imagining it or if it was some sort of confirmation bias after seeing the stat increase on the buff, but I did feel stronger and smarter. One thing was indisputable, a glance at my health bar confirmed my stats had increased by 30 hit points as a result of the additional stamina.

"What were you going to ask a minute ago," Ely queried, reaching for one of the artisan rolls and tearing it in two.

18

E ly shrugged. "Hand-to-hand? There isn't much to tell, really. I chose daggers at first but, after an unfortunate chain of events, I found myself near penniless."

"What happened?"

"I made a couple pretty big noob mistakes," he said, clearing his throat. "Ended up without any weapons or even a scrap of armor to my name."

"That's pretty harsh," I conceded, thinking back to the rudimentary club I picked up in the woods shortly after my arrival in EndWorld. "So you improvised?"

"Damn right, I did." He beamed, pulling a pair of fist weapons from his inventory and placing them on the counter for me to see. "I got knocked down pretty hard, but I wasn't ready to give up just yet. It was slow going, I'm not going to lie. I just used my hands at first, but then I had an idea. If the system was smart enough to recognize my switch to hand-to-hand combat, it made sense that it would recognize some kind of fist weapon. There was only one way to find out for sure, so that's when I made these."

The fist weapons looked a lot like brass knuckles, but they were made from carved wood and had inset bone pieces that protruded menacingly at the knuckles.

"How did you carve the wood without a knife?" I asked.

"How did people carve wood back in the Stone Age? I found a few sharp looking rocks and got to work," he said, clapping me on the shoulder before stowing his weapons back in his inventory.

Just then, Harold returned from the basement carrying a large wooden carafe. He stopped at the far end of the counter long enough to retrieve three fresh glasses and walked toward us.

"Gentlemen," he said, setting the glasses on the counter in front of our plates. "Have I got a treat for you."

With steady, reverent hands, Harold poured the fizzy pink liquid into our cups.

"Oh, man," Ely breathed. "That smells heavenly."

"Just wait until you have a taste," Harold quipped. "You ain't seen nothing yet."

I picked up my glass and examined the contents. It looked a lot like strawberry soda. Bubbles jumped and danced across the surface, tickling my nose as they burst, releasing even more of the intoxicating aroma. Harold watched with eager anticipation as we brought our glasses to our lips to take a sip.

"Sweet ambrosia," Ely exclaimed, thudding his fist hard on the countertop. "Harold, you dog. You've ruined me. Dandelion wine? Pleh. I don't know if I could ever go back to the stuff after tasting the likes of this."

Harold laughed and looked at me, waiting for my reaction.

"That good, huh?" I asked.

When Ely nodded, I took a small sip, holding the sweet, bubbly liquid on my tongue while I tried to process the beautifully complex flavors caressing my senses. It was almost too much. The cordial tasted like the sweetest strawberries I could imagine, but there was so much more to it than that. There was chamomile and vanilla and a hint of some kind of warm spice I couldn't quite identify.

"I think he likes it," I heard Ely say with a deep chuckle.

"That has to be the best drink I've had in my entire life," I admitted, still somewhat dumbfounded by the sensory overload.

"Ha," Harold laughed. "Give it a few more sips and it'll get even better," he said with a wink, filling up his cup while Ely and I exchanged surprised glances.

"Even better than this?" we both asked in unison.

"Only one way to find out," Harold answered before strolling away with glass in hand, leaving the carafe for us to finish.

He was right, of course. The strawberry cordial did get better with each sip. It was so good, in fact, that we'd finished our first glasses before realizing our meal was starting to get cold.

All at once, I had a much better appreciation for Guilly's apparent food fixation. Despite all my misgivings about EndWorld, this was something I could understand. It felt good to experience something new, to live in the moment, and to enjoy the friendly company of strangers.

It wasn't until after I'd finished my meal and downed another glass and a half of cordial before I realized I hadn't remembered to inquire about the possibility of renting a room.

"Harold," I called, flagging the barkeep over. "I know it's late, but is there any chance you've got a spare room I could rent?"

"A spare room?" Harold asked. "I sure do. It'll run you ten silver a night."

"Could I pay you for two nights now and bump my reservation out a bit once I make more coin?"

"Nah," Harold waved his hand. "Don't worry about it. We'll settle up in the morning. After that, you can stay for as many nights as you've got the coin for."

"Thanks," I said with a grin.

"Don't mention it. And listen, if you start running low on funds, you just let me know. Given the opportunity, I might be able to point you in the right direction before you end up sleeping in the streets."

Ely blushed a little and busied himself by trying to get the last few drops of cordial out of his glass and onto his tongue.

"Sounds good," I said.

Despite his gruff demeanor, Harold was a good man with a big heart, that much was clear. I didn't need to look any further than the guy sitting on the barstool beside me to see the impact of the tavern owner's generosity firsthand.

"Harold?" I asked, finally deciding to voice the question that had been eating at me since I'd walked through the door.

"Yeah?"

"There's a woman staying here, a Shadowdancer with black hair and two daggers. She goes by the name of Raven. Any chance you've seen her?"

"This Shadowdancer, she's a friend of yours?" Harold inquired with the faintest glimmer of suspicion in his eyes.

"We met in the mountains when I first arrived," I answered with a nod, taking care to leave out the part about spawning in EndWorld with a pack of dire wolf pups hot on my trail.

Harold rubbed at the stubble on his chin for a moment. "Is that so?" he asked after a long pause.

"We were walking toward Fort Morrow when she had to split to finish up some errands," I went on. "That's when she told me about your tavern. Of course, Jörgen asked me to deliver your parcel when I visited his shop, so it seemed like this was the natural place to end up."

"It is," Harold quipped, "for some."

"I guess I was expecting to run into her here," I continued, looking around the near-empty tavern lounge. "But I haven't seen her all night."

"Well, that makes two of us," Harold returned. "I guess there's no harm in saying that much, but I don't usually comment on the comings and goings of my guests. It ain't good for business, if you catch my drift."

With that, he turned and disappeared into the kitchen.

"Huh." I said, looking to Ely. "To be honest, I really didn't expect such a cold reaction to what seemed like a simple question."

He shrugged and took a moment to finish off the rest of his stew before responding.

"You might appreciate it a little more if someone comes in here looking for you when you don't want to be found."

My mind immediately went to the guard I'd ran into earlier and the sour look on his face when Jörgen had demanded he return the silver I'd paid to complete his quest.

"I guess you're right," I admitted. "I can see how a little anonymity might be worth a lot in a place like this."

"Hmm," Ely grunted and gave me a knowing smile. "You've already run into a bit of trouble, haven't you?"

"Yeah, I suppose you could say that," I said.

"Happens to the best of us." He laughed and slapped me on the back.

Considering the hints I was able to pick up regarding his situation, I didn't have much doubt he knew all about the sort of trouble I'd managed to get myself into.

"You know," he added after a moment. "I think I might be familiar with the woman you were asking about. Raven, was it?"

I nodded.

"She hide in her hood a lot, not very social?"

I perked up at his description. "That's pretty much exactly how I'd describe her."

"Yeah. Thought so. I mean, I can't do much but confirm what you already seem to know. She's been staying here for a few days. Haven't seen her since yesterday morning, though."

"Makes sense," I said. "We were in the mountains last night."

Ely raised an eyebrow. "Oh?"

I quickly waved off any idea of funny business and explained. "I met her just before stumbling into the camp of three other, uh, people like us."

"Travelers?"

Again, I nodded.

"How did that turn out?" he asked.

"Well enough, I suppose." I picked up my glass of dandelion wine and contemplated the tiny bits of sediment swirling at the bottom.

What else could I say?

The strange, sullen woman had held a dagger to my throat to protect me from a possible bad run in with three other strangers? And now I was looking for her? Yeah, something told me no matter how I tried to phrase it, the story just wouldn't come out right.

"You took a risk," Ely said, then eyed the surrounding area. "Which reminds me, that sword of yours—"

"My sword?"

"It isn't bound."

"Spiritbound?" I asked, recalling the way both Kenneth and Marianna had reacted to my weapon.

Ely nodded. "If it were a rusty training blade or a dented falchion, no one would care. Your sword, though. It's worth a lot. That much anyone could tell just by taking one look at it. I mean, I'm no expert in long blades, but you don't really need to be, do you?"

"You weren't the first to notice," I said, admitting a certain naivety in the way all this worked. "Truth is, I don't know much about the process of binding items, or the benefits or drawbacks of doing so. One of the merchants offered me a good price for it, but he indicated it would be a lot less if it was bound. Honestly, I'm at a loss. None of this was covered in the tutorial."

"You can say that again," he quipped. "If I had a silver piece for everything I've encountered so far that wasn't in the tutorial... Well, let's just say I wouldn't be wearing this iron diaper."

We both laughed at his joke. It was funny in a dark, cynical way that seemed to fit the mood perfectly. We were two schmucks trying to find their way in a world that was just a little bit bigger than we were used to, and one of us had the metal underwear to prove it.

"A non-bound item can be stolen without any real consequence," Ely went on. "As long as the thief isn't caught. But a bound item is something else entirely. Let's say you formed a spirit bond with your sword and I took it. Could I use it? Yes. Nothing would stop me from swinging it around like a buffoon, but the stats wouldn't be anywhere close to what they are now."

"That's why the merchant wouldn't pay much for a bound weapon? It's virtually useless?" I asked.

"Not exactly," he explained. "A bound weapon can be unbound. It isn't easy, near impossible for someone in our level range as I understand it. A specialist can do it for a fee, but it probably wouldn't be very economical. Not even for a sword like yours. If the merchant could undo the binding, it might not be an issue for them. Would it be worth it? I suppose it would depend on the item."

"That complicates things, doesn't it?" I asked, scratching my chin. "How could you tell my sword wasn't bound? And, for that matter, how would I go about binding it? I mean, I've already equipped it. Isn't that enough?"

"Not in EndWorld," Ely explained. "As far as knowing whether or not your weapon was bound, it's a lot like how you inspected me when you first entered the tavern. You can inspect items just like you can inspect people. One thing's for certain, a fancy sword like that is sure to be checked out by anyone with enough sense to look. Only, you can't tell when someone inspects your gear. It's either a given or it's just not possible at our levels."

"I see," I said, slowly absorbing the information over a sip of my dandelion wine. The drink was good, but Ely had been dead on. I, too, had been spoiled by the dreamy taste of the strawberry cordial.

"It'll never be the same." He sighed, nodding toward my glass.

"Tell me about it."

"Binding an item is fairly straightforward," he continued. "All you have to do is focus on it, really concentrate, and then feel for it with your heart and mind. It sounds weird, but that's the best way I can explain it."

"That doesn't sound too complicated," I said. "Is that all, just feel for it? How will I know if it's working?"

"When you've found it, the item will sort of sing to you, but no one else will hear it. Try not to freak out. Just imagine it as the item reaching out to bind with your spirit. That's pretty much what's happening."

I took another hefty swig of my wine and pulled Truthseeker from my inventory. "Here goes nothing," I said, closing my eyes.

Nothing happened.

I looked at Ely, who greeted me with a smile.

"Done already?" he asked, though it was clear he knew the binding didn't take.

"Not yet," I said. "Just concentrate on the sword, huh?"

"Yep. Block everything else out of your mind. Don't sweat it if it takes a while. Just remember, it's your first time. It'll get easier once you've figured it out."

"Hmm," I grunted before closing my eyes again.

Long seconds passed while I focused on Ely's instructions. Blocking out the ambient noise in the tavern, I reached out for the object with my mind, silently whispering its name as I searched.

A cold shiver ran down my spine as I sensed a foreign presence.

The sword.

It didn't sing.

The space inside my mind was dark, illuminated only by a pale light somewhere off in the distance. I don't know how but I knew it was Truthseeker, and yet the blade seemed to regard me with cold indifference.

I drew nearer to the sword with each soundless step until it was finally inside my reach. Extending a hand within the void, I couldn't feel the touch of its grip against my palm. Instead, I grasped nothing but wisps of light and shadow.

You do not seek the truth, the blade's words chided with a steely grumble. *You run from it. Why should one such as I bind myself to one such as you?*

What was I supposed to say? Did the sword actually want me to plead my case before it would pledge itself in service to my cause? And what cause was that? I was still new to this world, weaponless.

My training sword had broken and Jörgen had entrusted me with his blade. What more was there to say?

According to Ely, the weapon was supposed to sing. All I had to do was reach out? Yeah, right. This wasn't what I'd expected. Not even close.

When I didn't offer an immediate response, the weapon began to shine with an intense brightness. Everything was consumed by its scathing white light.

Insolent soul. Do you think yourself above my inquiry, or are you too ignorant to answer?

"What would you have me say?" I asked aloud, shielding my eyes from the glare. "I'm a man without a sword. It seems you're a sword without a man."

That is no reason to submit, the blade scoffed.

"You're probably right," I admitted. "I'm still very new to this place and there's a lot I don't know. But I want to believe there was a reason Jörgen offered you to me."

There was a long pause, so I continued. "A merchant offered me six gold for you today. He said we weren't a good match, wants me to sleep on it. Someone told me that was enough gold to buy any sword around here I wanted, but I chose this. I chose you. If you don't find me worthy, well, I won't try to convince you otherwise."

This seemed to have an effect. The light dimmed and Truthseeker began to hum with a low frequency that reverberated through my being.

Perhaps one such as you can learn to seek truth.

Then the expanse was gone, and I was just a guy sitting at a tavern bar in a strange, new town once again.

Ely grinned from ear to ear. "I was starting to have my doubts, but it looks like you did it."

"Did I?" I asked before looking down at the sheathed blade.

Something was different. The sword and scabbard in my hands felt lighter and electric, as if filled with some new-found energy. I could no longer hear its voice, and yet I knew it was there. It felt as if the blade had chosen to submit. I wasn't sure why. Perhaps it was because I'd told it the truth. Maybe it was something else. One thing was certain, whatever its reasons for choosing me, I'd found my new sword.

The gentle weight of the linens and the soft crackling of a fire within the hearth were as a siren song, keeping me trapped within the comfort of my bed well after sunrise. For a long while I could do nothing but lay there, imagining the world hadn't changed. Things were normal again and life was full of smaller, more realistic possibilities.

There was no such thing as magic or talking swords. There were no forts or castles. The only quests involved cooking pancakes and bacon when the kids came to visit. Eliza, Sophie, and Jacob would barge through the door any minute now, all eager to start the day. When they did, I would roar and hug them tight before they could pull me out of the covers and toward the kitchen.

I smiled, taking in a deep breath of the morning air then stretched with my eyes still closed. It was a horrible, simple thing, but it was enough to shatter what was left of the half-dream.

I stretched, and I felt no pain. There was none of the weakness or nausea that came hand-in-hand with the medication I was forced to take. This wasn't a dream. Everything about EndWorld was real. It was a fresh start. It was... a world without my children.

My heart broke anew.

A simple stretch was all it took to remind me of everything I'd been forced to leave behind. The kids. Helen. The pain and fatigue had been worth every moment I'd been able to spend with them. A voice from the darkest part of me reasoned that they had Roger now. They could be happy without me. That might be true, but it did nothing for the family-sized hole in my heart.

Rising from the bed, I begrudgingly surveyed my surroundings. The room was small but quaint and aside from the fireplace, there wasn't much to look at. A wooden dresser faced the footboard and a small, glass-pane window bathed the walls in sunlight.

It didn't matter where I wished I could be, not anymore. There was nothing I could do to go back. This was my new reality and the sooner I got used to it the better.

Sounds from the street trickled in as vendors shouted to hawk their wares over the clomping of horse hooves on cobblestones. Commerce, it seemed, was just as robust near Harold's Tavern during more respectable hours as in the town center the day before.

Harold looked up from behind the bar and nodded a greeting as I descended the stairs. With Truthseeker bound to me, I wore it proudly at my side.

"Looks like someone's fit for a day full of questing," he said, drying a glass and fetching another from the rack. "I might have a lead or two, if you're interested."

"Of course." I smiled, slapping thirty silver on the counter. "Ten silver a night for three nights, wasn't it? This should cover last night through tomorrow."

The expense also left me with a paltry five silver to my name.

Harold looked at the coins and frowned. "I respect a man who's eager to settle his debts as much as anyone, but are you sure paying for three nights in one go should be your first priority?"

"What do you mean?" I asked.

He glanced down at my boots. "It looks like you'll be needing new gear soon. Those clodhoppers seem fit to fall to pieces if the wind blows hard enough. It takes more than just a fancy sword to keep a body in fighting shape, mark my words."

"Fair enough," I replied. "I think I'd still like to pay for the three night, if you don't mind. I can always use the need for new boots and a good meal as motivation."

"Suit yourself," Harold said, tucking the coins into his apron. "Breakfast is on the house, you'll be on your own for the rest. We have our standard fare, but sometimes I get the urge to cook up something special. You'll usually know when that happens because I update the Specials board over there. Seems to draw a crowd whenever I do."

He pointed to a black slate mounted to the wall on the far end of the bar. The board was blank.

"No specials today?"

Harold shook his head. "Don't have the ingredients I need." Then he grunted. "Huh. Maybe that's something else you could help with, eh? Tell you what. If you can bring me thirty pieces of quality hare meat before sundown, I'll cover your dinner. Sound fair?"

Repeatable Quest Alert! You've been offered a quest:
Something Special.
Deliver 30 pieces of quality hare meat to Harold at Harold's Tavern.

*Hint: Harold doesn't want scraps. Only **High-Quality Hare Meat** will do. Deliver all 30 pieces before sundown. This quest is repeatable, check with Harold to see what ingredients he needs before completion.*
Reward: Harold will cook something special. Dinner is on the house. In addition, you will receive 4,000 Experience Points and improved standing with Harold.
Bonus Reward: Unknown.

"That does sound like a fair deal," I agreed, accepting Harold's quest for hare meat. Then he added another to my list.

New Quest Alert! You've been offered a quest:
Creatures in the Cellar.
Widow Wilson is in need of a hero. Creatures have infested her cellar.

Hint: Can't find Widow Wilson? A marker for her house has been added to your map.
This quest will be complete once you've eradicated the infestation in Widow Wilson's cellar.
Reward: 1,500 Experience Points, 50 Silver, and Improved Favor with Widow Wilson.
***Bonus Reward:** Unknown.*

"Now, if you were to ask me," Harold said. "I'd suggest swinging by the Widow's house on your way back from outside the keep. Hunting for certain cellar-dwellers during the heat of the day can take a lot longer than if you catch them towards early evening. Just don't take too long if you want to deliver the hare meat in time."

He gave me a sly wink and went back to drying the glasses on the bar. "Have a seat and I'll bring you out some grub. I'm sure you must be getting eager to start your day."

Something almost motherly in Harold's tone suggested the days around here started early, which was a key piece of information that I might want to keep in mind in the future. For my own good, of course.

"Thanks," I said, taking note of just how empty the tavern was.

The food, which included some sort of egg scramble with strange vegetables, a few pieces of bacon, and two slices of toast, was oddly delicious. Each bite replenished my well-fed buff by thirty minutes until it was capped at the full duration limit.

*You are **Well Fed.***
*While active, **Harold's Country Breakfast** provides:*
*+1 to **Strength**, +3 to **Stamina**, and +1 to **Dexterity**.*
You also receive a bonus to Experience gain.
*Current Duration: **12 Hours.***
*Max Duration: **12 Hours.***

Twelve hours for a food buff with a bonus to experience gain? Now I finally understood how breakfast could be the most important meal of the day. The silent quip was worth a chuckle, and I waved to Harold as I left the tavern.

Outside, the rest of the fort was full of busy, bustling life. Travelers and townsfolk alike ebbed and flowed around the carts and merchant stalls.

Feeling the sudden urge to browse the eclectic collection of goods and hardware, I buckled down and pushed myself toward Jörgen's shop. After all, I'd finished the quest to deliver his packages the night before and I still needed to drop off Harold's letter. Two for the price of one. While I could have stopped by later, my promise to take care of the tavernkeep's delivery first thing made it an easy choice to start the busy day.

It wasn't long before I found my pace within the crowd, losing myself in my thoughts as I made my way back toward Jörgen's shop.

The fort was picturesque, almost castle-like with all its turrets and towers, but even a noob like me could tell it had been built with military precision. Every structure had a purpose. I could easily imagine how the fort guard might defend such a place, scouting threats from high towers, sniping with longbows from the outer walls.

"Traveler," a familiar male voice called, stirring me from my thoughts.

I looked up and scanned the throng, leaving my fantasy of calculated warfare somewhere on the far border of memory. There was no way of knowing whether I had been the target of the shout, but something about the voice tickled recognition.

"Traveler, a moment. Please?" the voice insisted with an accompanying grip fixed on my arm for good measure.

I spun around, placing my hand on the pommel of my sword out of instinct.

"Whoa, there," Kenneth stammered and stepped backward, waving his palms in a gesture that suggested he meant no harm. "I only wanted to inquire as to whether you had a chance to consider my offer."

Then the merchant looked down at my side and frowned. "Oh," he grumbled. "I see you've attempted to bind the blade."

*Quest objectives failed. You can no longer meet the objectives for your
pending quest:*
An Even More Enticing Offer.
This quest has been removed.

"And what's it to you?" another voice cut in from behind me.

When I turned to look, I saw Ely standing firm with his chest
puffed out and his balled fists planted on his hips.

"Well, certainly," Kenneth stammered, "I intended no disrespect,
Ely."

"You two know each other?" I asked, trying my best to come to
grips with the situation.

"That we do," Kenneth answered.

"Yeah," Ely said. "We've done business before, if you could call it
that. More like highway robbery."

"Now, now," Kenneth chided. "A deal is a deal, is it not? You
agreed to the bargain of your own free will. And besides, I believe we
both found ourselves in less than ideal circumstances as a consequence of the trade."

"Whatever," Ely spat, dismissing the merchant's retort. "Denton
bound his sword. How does that concern you?"

"I could ask you the same, except you've gotten the details all
wrong. Denton didn't bind his sword. Not fully, anyway. Truthseeker
isn't like an ordinary blade. It's different. It's special. And it isn't suited
for someone like him."

"Someone like me? What's that supposed to mean?" I asked,
finally inserting myself into the conversation.

"Bah," Kenneth said. "I meant no insult by it. The two of you, well,
you're not well matched, it's plain to see."

"And that's for you to decide?" Ely growled. "What's it to you
which blade Denton decides to wield?"

"No, it's not for me to decide at all. It is the blade that chooses. I
have no influence over the sword. Ask Denton yourself. I'd wager the
blade didn't sing. It didn't, did it?"

Ely looked at me with a quizzical expression.

I sighed. "No. You're right, Truthseeker didn't sing," I answered. "I guess you could say it was more like a hum."

"You see?" Kenneth smiled. "It's plain as day. The blade isn't right for him. It was only a partial bond at best."

"And I suppose what you'll say next is that you'd be more than happy to relieve him of the burden?" Ely glared.

"Well, not exactly happy." The merchant wrung his hands and glanced back at the sword. "A partial binding isn't always as difficult to remove as a successful one, though sometimes it can prove much worse. It really depends. I'd be taking a chance."

He seemed to think it over before nodding his head. "Three gold, as is. That's my final offer."

New Quest Alert! You've been offered a quest:
Kenneth's Final Offer.
Kenneth Johnson would still like to buy Truthseeker.
To complete this quest, accept Kenneth's offer.
Reward: *3 Gold.*

I couldn't help but sigh as I read the text. Was he right? Three gold was still a lot of money and I still needed to upgrade my gear. The sorry state of my boots sprang to mind.

"Wait a second," Ely said, looking first at me and then to Kenneth. "Did you just offer him a quest?"

"I'd be much obliged if you'd keep your big nose out of our dealings," Kenneth shot back, the flash of anger on his face melting back to a pleasant smile.

"You were reading quest text just then, weren't you?" Ely asked.

I nodded.

"I knew it. Don't do it, Denton. I don't know what Ken's up to, but—"

"Kenneth."

"Whatever," Ely snapped. "You don't offer a man a quest for a simple merchant transaction. What are you up to, you thieving rat?"

"Thieving rat?" Kenneth stammered, his cheeks burning red. "My transactions are nothing but fair. I would never resort to petty thievery. How dare you?"

"How dare I? I'll show you how—"

With the conflict on the edge of coming to blows, I made my choice. "Gentlemen," I said, then once more. Firmly.

Ely and Kenneth both turned to face me.

"You've come to a decision, then?" Kenneth asked, looking hopeful.

"I have," I confirmed. "I'll be holding onto Truthseeker. It was a gift from a friend and that isn't something I'm willing to turn my back on. Now, if you'll excuse me, I have a quest to turn in."

I rejected Kenneth's final quest and set my path back down the busy street toward Jörgen's. It wasn't long before I heard Ely's heavy footsteps as he jogged to catch up.

"Hey, man. Hold on a second," he huffed. "You're not upset with me, are you? I was just trying to help."

"No," I answered, still keeping pace and weaving through the crowd toward Jörgen's shop. "I'm not upset. Frustrated, yes. Very."

Ely grabbed my arm and pulled me to a stop but let go when he saw the look in my eye.

"Sorry," he mumbled, stepping backward. "Look, man. I got your back. The last thing I want is for you to end up like me. No weapon, no armor, and doing whatever it takes just to survive. It sucks."

"I appreciate that, I really do," I said. "I get that you were just trying to help, but if I'd chosen to sell, it would have been my decision to make. Not yours."

"I know, man," Ely replied, glancing away. "Look, what else was I supposed to do? If there's one thing I know, it's that if Kenneth offered you a quest for the sword, it wasn't going to turn out well. And, trust me, I say that from personal experience." After a small pause he added, "Your sword is special, Denton. I'm really glad you kept it."

My hand felt a sudden draw toward the hilt of the blade and I rested my palm there comfortably. "Yeah," I said at last. "I think you're right."

"And I don't care what that skunky merchant says," he said with a chuckle. "It clearly suits you."

We walked the rest of the way toward our destination without incident or delay. When we entered the shop, Jörgen looked up from his familiar spot behind the counter.

"Ah, Denton. Welcome back. Looks like you've made another friend. Better company than the last, I hope?"

"I'm Ely," Ely said, approaching the counter and shaking Jörgen's hand.

"Well met and welcome," Jörgen replied. "What can I do for you gentlemen this morning?"

Ely snickered. "Gentlemen. That's a good one."

"Actually," I answered, handing Jörgen Harold's letter. "I've completed your delivery quest and I even have something to give you from Harold."

Jörgen's eye dulled for a moment as he seemed to consult his user interface. "Well, would you look at that? Someone doesn't waste any time, does he? I knew I was right about you, Denton. Good job."

I handed him Harold's letter and a dialogue box popped up.

Quest complete! You've completed a quest:
Welcome to Fort Morrow.
You receive 500 Experience Points and 10 silver.
Additional Reward: -500 Favor with Kenneth Johnson.
5 silver.

"Tell me, though," he went on. "What's all this with Kenneth Johnson? I've only known the guy a short while, but he never struck me as a rash merchant."

Too many thoughts and explanations ran through my head as I took in the quest completion message. 15 silver was a nice reward, but the unexpected hit to my reputation with Kenneth stung a little. I was beginning to understand how interconnected things were in this place. Decisions had real impact, though the results weren't always immediately obvious.

In truth, I didn't know how to respond to the question and Ely seemed content to hold his tongue for once. He was right. This was my business to sort through. So, I did the only thing that made sense. I unstrapped the belt around my waist and placed Truthseeker on the counter, scabbard and all.

Jörgen's face paled, and I watched as the natural joy drained from his eyes before he returned my gaze. Then he frowned.

"You should have sold it while you had the chance."

A long, cold silence followed before he continued. "Denton, I'm not sure what protection this blade can offer in its current state. A partial binding. I don't understand how this could have happened. Truth be told, I'd have a hard time believing it if it wasn't staring me in the face. Even so..."

"It's a rare thing, then? This partial binding?" Ely asked.

"I've heard of it, but I've never seen it with my own eyes. Honesty, I thought I was better than this."

"What do you mean?" I asked. "How is this your fault?"

"I don't know that it is." Jörgen shrugged. "I figured if I matched the blade to the wielder, all the pieces would fall into place. It was a nice theory, but now I'm not so sure. If I had to do it over again, I'd have made the same choice. I'm at a complete loss."

Ely shifted his weight from one foot to the other, capturing Jörgen's attention.

"Yes, it's a good question." Jörgen chuckled.

Ely looked at his feet, suddenly awkward.

"What?" I asked. "What's a good question?"

"If I'm not mistaken," Jörgen answered, "your friend here was just wondering what made you so special. Out of all these people, why did I think you were worthy of Truthseeker."

"Well," Ely started. "I mean, those weren't my exact thoughts, but it's pretty close." He shrugged. "Sorry, Denton."

I stared at the sword on the counter for a while before responding.

"No. There's no need to apologize," I said. "It's an honest question. You're right. I wondered the same, myself. I walked in here after being swindled in the street with not much more to my name than the busted hilt of my training sword, fifteen silver, and stick I picked up in the woods. I was greener than green and had just made about the dumbest mistake I could have made.

"When you put the pieces together, it doesn't make much sense. Kenneth was right. How could a sword like that be right for a person like me?"

Ely and I both looked to Jörgen for a response.

20

The unnamed path outside the eastern gate was quieter than Kingsroad had been to the south. Unlike my previous, more conversational jaunt with the young Frost Mage, Zack, this stretch was eerily quiet. The woods consumed the plodding sound of our footsteps and any hint of birdsong. A handful of Travelers made their way along the packed-earth trail around us, but no one spoke.

Ely and I walked side-by-side, hiking toward a spot in a nearby meadow he claimed would be great for grinding. I still wasn't sure how all the mechanics worked.

The range and proximity of mobs, he said, was enough that we could both gain experience points without impacting the leveling rate of the other.

We wove through the trees and my mind wandered. The spot sounded like a good place to start, and we'd already stopped by the home point on our way out of town.

Binding to the stone wasn't like claiming weapons or equipment. The experience of attuning myself was strange and, as Ely warned, much different from when I'd attempted to bind Truthseeker.

There was no singing, and I wasn't whisked away to some imaginary encounter. Instead, a sublime feeling of peace washed over me as I'd touched my palm to the glowing obelisk.

Fort Morrow was now my home.

The surrounding trees began to thin, bringing my attention back to the present. Up ahead, the path cut into a sprawling meadow filled with tall grass and dappled with aromatic wildflowers. Travelers were locked in combat, facing off against an assortment of creatures.

The sight of it stopped me cold. What I saw reminded me of my first experience with a Massively Multiplayer Online Roleplaying Game.

MMORPG's had been old hat for ages by the time I got to play, but the view in front of me scratched that same itch.

Suddenly, I couldn't wait to grind experience points on mobs and collect loot. Even my quest for high quality hare meat didn't seem quite as daunting.

Ely chuckled as he strapped on his fist weapons. "You feel it too, eh? All the eagerness and nostalgia wrapped into one?"

I nodded, and he pointed to a corner of the nearest field. "That area over there would be a great place to start out. There's a pretty decent group of starter mobs, which should be good experience for the first few levels."

"Thanks," I said. "Where will you be?"

"Just over there," he answered, pointing to a copse much further away. "I'll be fighting bandits that spawn around the trees for a while. I need to collect a few more bandanas for a quest. We should be far enough to avoid experience points loss, that way we don't need to drop party."

"Sounds good," I agreed.

We parted ways then, and as I walked toward the starter field, I felt another surge of emotions.

Flashes of my first moments in EndWorld came crashing back. It felt like I'd been a part of this world for ages, but it had really only been two days. Two days without fighting a single mob.

I unsheathed Truthseeker and recalled my encounter with the golem in the tutorial, instinctively willing the power of wind into my blade. Twin orbs of green swirled around the gleaming steel and I scanned the area for potential prey. Oversized bees and plant creatures seemed to flit about the field without a care in the world. Perfect starter mobs.

That's when I saw it.

A large rabbit with long ears hopped out of a tuft of grass, brown coat gleaming in the late morning sun. It stared at me with its beady, black eyes before turning to nibble on a nearby flower.

With any luck, I'd be able to finish Harold's quest in no time.

I strengthened my resolve, thinking of Raven and how she moved through the woods like a shadow. Then I took a step, followed by another, silently approaching my target and gaining confidence with each successive stride.

Now within striking distance, I steeled my heart and steadied my blade. The rabbit turned, and I stared into its eyes once more.

This creature wasn't like the golem. It didn't appear to be aggressive. Now it was I who was the hunter, and the thought was slightly jarring. But, if I really hoped to survive in this world, it was something I was going to have to get used to.

I raised my blade.

You hit the Meadows Rabbit for 5 HP + 2 Wind damage.

Seven damage from my first strike. Not bad.

As I prepared a second attack, I couldn't help but wonder how high the damage might have been if I'd managed to fully bind Truthseeker.

You've been hit! The Meadows Rabbit hits you for 20 HP.
You've been hit! The Meadows Rabbit hits you for 18 HP.
Warning: *Critical Health. 12/50 HP remaining.*
You've been hit! The Meadows Rabbit hits you for 20 HP.
You have died.
You have lost Experience Points.

~

Pain engulfed every fiber of my being and everything faded to black as I slumped into the soft embrace of the meadow grass. The whole encounter was over so fast that my mind was reeling. I fought through the sensory overload and struggled to grasp even a hint of comprehension.

What just happened? I felt as if I'd been ripped to shreds. While I was still trying to process, a message popped up and illuminated the darkness.

Return to home point?
Yes. | No.

I reviewed the logs. Then I reviewed them again.

Never in my life had I expected to be beat down by a rabbit but, according to the text, that's precisely what had happened.

"Oh, man," I heard an unfamiliar voice exclaim. "Take a look at this noob. I think he just got killed by that rabbit over there, but wow, look at his sword. Guess he overestimated himself."

"You know anyone who can rez?" a female asked.

Rez. I was familiar with the term from my experience playing other games. Apparently, the designers of EndWorld had incorporated at least one form of a resurrection spell or a skill that would bring the dead back to life. By the countdown timer on my status bar, it looked like I had one hour to find assistance before I was forced back to my home point. Or, by selecting 'Yes' at the prompt, I could return now.

I decided to wait to see how things played out.

"Around here? No way. The only reason I can think of for someone with that skill to be in the Meadows is if they were power-leveling a friend."

"Or they could be gathering," the female offered. "There's plenty of resources around here. You never know."

"I guess."

"We could shout?" she offered. "It's worth a shot."

"Sure. I guess it is worth a shot," the guy answered. I could almost hear the shrug in his tone. "But I wouldn't hold your breath, buddy," he added, chuckling at his own joke.

One didn't have to be a genius to figure out the last bit was purely for my benefit, and at my expense.

"Can anyone around here rez?" the woman shouted.

It was no use, no one in the Meadows answered their plea. Then, after a few minutes, they both offered their condolences and went on their way.

Who could blame them? Neither of them had the skill required to help and, like me, I imagined they had a whole list of quests to finish before the light waned.

I looked at the countdown timer. It had been fifteen minutes since my ill-fated encounter and I was burning daylight. If I wanted to make any sort of progress today, I'd need to make a decision soon.

A rabbit. A silly, stupid rabbit. That was all it took to steal the wind from my sails. It was hard to believe someone like Jörgen could have such a high opinion of my capabilities.

That was it. I decided I was done waiting around. There were quests to finish and I would have plenty of time to brood while making the trek back.

I focused my will on the menu and released.

A sudden, dizzying whirl of motion pulled at me, whisking me away from the Meadows and back toward the home point. The next thing I knew, I was standing in the town square wrestling with an overwhelming flood of vertigo.

"You never get used to it, do you?" a gruff voice asked.

I turned and saw a large, older man with a battle axe grinning at me. He was bear like in size, with wispy grey hairs that seemed to cover any body part not hidden by his leather garb.

"First time," I managed to say, fighting back another wave of nausea as I placed Truthseeker in its scabbard.

"Oh, brother," the man said. "You get used to the sick feeling, a bit, but the loss of experience points is where it really hits you. I don't imagine it gets any better. Especially as you gain some levels. Best to find out now, I reckon. Maybe you'll learn not to be as foolhardy as this old ruffian."

"Thanks," I said, offering my hand. "The name's Denton."

"Well met, Denton. You can call me Pops."

I raised an eyebrow and the man burst into a hearty laugh.

"Yeah," he said. "I know. It's just, ever since the missus and I had grandkids, Pops sort of became my new moniker. Going by anything else would just seem, I don't know, strange?"

"Fair enough." I laughed. "Pops it is."

"There's another thing you should know about dying," he said.

"What?" I asked. "Pain and loss of experience points isn't enough?"

"Afraid not," Pops said. "I'm guessing you ate breakfast this morning? If you didn't, you might want to start looking into it."

"I did."

"Yeah, you're going to love this." He pointed upward with a thick index finger. "Take a look at your food buff duration."

A groan escaped my lips when I saw it. The duration for my status increase had dropped to a measly five hours.

"You've got to be kidding me," I said, shaking my head.

"Hardship helps us appreciate the little things, I suppose. Where you headed?" Pops asked.

It took me a moment to gather my thoughts as I tried to refocus after the strange experience of dying. "I guess I need to walk back to the Meadows," I said at last. "I was supposed to be grinding on starter mobs. That is, until I got killed by a rabbit."

"I suppose they'll do that. Won't they?" Pops nodded. "Those hairy little fiends are some vicious beasties, what with their fast attack speed and high overall damage. Best to avoid them until you're sure you're strong enough."

"Don't have to tell me twice," I said with a shrug.

"Funny thing, though," he went on, "there are a lot of quests that involve killing the buggers. But mark my words, no matter where you go or how strong you get, there's always a rabbit somewhere that'd be more than happy to tuck you in for a nice little dirt nap."

"No joke?" I asked.

"I wish it was. Welcome to EndWorld, eh? Anyway, I'm headed back to the Frostwind Mountains. Those cave trolls better watch out." Pops grinned and brandished his battle axe. "I'll be ready for them this time. You take care of yourself, you hear?"

"You too," I said, shaking Pops' hulking paw again before making my way toward the eastern road.

As I exited the gate, I thought about Pops with his battle axe and Ely with his improvised fist weapons. Both seemed tempered by their experiences. Made wiser by their mistakes.

I could only hope time would have the same effect on me.

Once I'd stepped back into the uneasy quiet of the forest, I felt a strange pull to an area that must have been due North of the meadow. A small path broke off through the underbrush, and I couldn't quite recall if I'd seen it there before.

Stopping dead in my tracks, I peered through the branches and leaves.

There was no sign of fresh footprints, and no real indication anyone had been down that way in the recent past. And yet the feeling that I needed to venture off into the shadowy unknown coursed through my veins, causing my heart to race.

I couldn't quite explain it. Even Truthseeker lent its weight in its scabbard, pulling me ever so slightly northward.

A murder of crows took flight from a nearby tree, cawing their displeasure at my presence. The sudden, ominous interruption sent a shiver down my spine.

I stood there for a while, transfixed by that feeling I couldn't quite explain. Then I thought back on my pitiful encounter with the rabbit.

I thought about Jörgen and what he'd said before we left his shop. Why he'd entrusted me, of all people, with Truthseeker.

It wasn't that I was *The Chosen One* or some epic hero in the making. In fact, it had more to do with my broken blade than anything else.

Was my shattered hilt a possible relic?

How could that be?

Jörgen only speculated that I might be capable of great things. Then again, who wouldn't be capable of great things if they had access to one of the finest weapons in the region?

I chuckled.

Apparently, this guy.

I pulled up my menu and looked over the map.

The meadow was ahead of me, straight down the path Ely and I had taken before. This other path...

A darkened area on the map, yet undiscovered in my travels. If I had to guess, it looked to be some kind of swamp.

I swallowed hard and shook my head.

No way.

The last thing I needed was to get sucked into some mire or find myself charmed by ghost lights or swamp spirits.

Instead, I pulled up my active quests, looking for the one Ayva had given me in the tutorial.

New Quest Alert! You've been offered a quest:
Fix Your Weapon.
Your weapon has been broken. See a weapon specialist or blacksmith to get it repaired.
Hint: Broken weapons are next to worthless. Taking good care of your weapons and equipment is essential for success in EndWorld Everlasting. This quest will be complete when you have repaired your weapon.
Reward:** 100 Experience Points, 50 Silver, 1x **Item Repair Voucher.

Fifty silver. It was enough to cover five more nights at Harold's Tavern.

I looked down at Truthseeker. It wasn't the blade I was supposed to fix when I'd gotten the quest. I'd given that one to Jörgen.

Fat chance.

Something told me it would be a long time before I could finish that particular quest. And what then? Would the reward be worth the effort by the time I could actually finish it?

I mentally scrolled through the quest list until my eyes settled on the task Jörgen had given me.

A Tale of Two Swords.
Jörgen Olsen has offered you a unique quest.
Allow Jörgen Olsen to hold on to your broken sword. In exchange, you will receive a replacement blade. Return to the blacksmith's shop when you are stronger to learn more about the nature of your relic.
The completion requirements for this quest are unknown.
Reward: *5,000 Experience Points, 3 Gold, additional information about the nature of your broken sword.*

Setting my path back toward the meadow, I started walking again. Whatever it was that was drawing me toward the swamp would have to wait.

I had to admit, I'd been so enamored by receiving Jörgen's prized blade, Truthseeker, that I'd almost forgotten about the Two Swords quest.

And I still wasn't sure what it would take to become strong enough to satisfy the objectives. One thing was certain, though. I hadn't met the requirements with my failed attempt to bind the blade.

Dying to a rabbit didn't help matters, either.

Aside from dying being an incredibly painful experience, and one I wasn't keen on repeating any time soon, Pops was right. I'd lost about ten percent of my Experience Points.

The hit set me back even further from leveling up.

Yeah. So much for getting stronger.

Finding myself in the Meadows once more, I unsheathed my sword and set my sights on an over-sized flying insect. The thing was as large as a medium-sized dog, but had all the markings of a standard starter mob.

It was time to take ahold of my fate.

I was ready to fight.

No, it was more than that. I didn't just want to fight. I wanted to win, and I was determined to avoid making the same stupid mistakes.

*You **Inspect** the Meadow Wasp.*
Level 1. Hit Points: 35.

Satisfied with the level and difficulty of my prey, I renewed Wind Blade and inched closer.

21

Wasp after wasp fell to my blade. Each kill netted only 100 Experience Points. After ten, my muscles ached. After twenty, the sickly warm entrails covered my armor.

Soon after that, the repetitive monotony of leveling stole my kill count. It felt as if I'd bested hundreds of the winged devils, and still, my Experience bar only inched forward.

An hour passed and then another as I lost myself in combat. And all the while, I daydreamed of vanquishing prey of epic proportions while I rested to recover my hit points and mana between spawns. Bees were fine for now, but my pride begged for something bigger.

Dragons and wyverns, thundering ogres, and large beasts of epic proportions filled my mind.

One day.

For now, my biggest foe had been a rabbit. It was a challenge I was eager to attempt again, but my quest wasn't that easy. I couldn't kill just one. I needed thirty pieces of high-quality hare meat if I wanted a free meal at Harold's.

It sounded like such a silly little thing. And yet, a free meal could mean a new pair of boots.

I looked down at my sorry excuse for shoes, a remnant of my crafting session within the tutorial. A new pair of boots might increase my stamina or dexterity and would surely improve armor and reduce damage taken. All the simple, little things added up. They made a difference.

It was settled. I'd kill as many of these stupid wasps as it took. I would level up until I could fight the rabbits.

Then I would fight. And I would win.

My stomach grumbled. The food buff I received at breakfast was ticking down at an alarming rate. It was another bitter reminder of what my foolishness had cost.

Not this time.

I was going to be better.

I had to be.

*You **Inspect** the Angry Meadow Bee.*
Level 2. Hit Points: 55.

I blinked in disbelief and checked again. Sure enough, I'd somehow managed to find a tougher version of the same mob. At least, they looked similar enough. Wasps and bees were quite different back in the real world. What was I getting myself into?

Scanning the meadow, I tried to determine what made this mob different from the rest. It was slightly larger than the wasps and pathed closer to the tree line. Could it be unique?

Another bee flitted nearby. I inspected it to be sure.

*You **Inspect** the Angry Meadow Bee.*
Level 2. Hit Points: 57.

Nope, not unique. The bees had all the appearances of being a slightly harder version of the wasps, perhaps with better experience rewards and a chance at loot? It was worth a shot.

I decided to wait until the two mobs had pathed far enough apart to avoid any chance of linking. The last thing I needed was to have a swarm of level 2 mobs tearing into me at the same time.

It wasn't long before the first bee pathed away from the second, giving me the perfect opportunity to engage. I spent the last of my MP, recasting the wind enhancement on my blade, and prepared to strike. With the bee's back to me, my swing rang true and deep.

Critical Strike! You hit the Angry Meadow Bee for 16 HP + 4 Wind damage.
New Skill! You've learned the skill: SNEAK ATTACK.
You can now do more damage to unsuspecting objects and creatures.
Sneak Attack is an Advanced Skill.
Strike from the shadows to pierce their hearts.

The bee glowed red as it turned and focused its attention on the source of the attack. I parried and ducked each successive blow, expending my stamina at an alarming rate.

With whatever berserker buff the bee had activated, it was becoming apparent that I might have bitten off more than I could chew.

For the second time today.

No. I refused to allow myself to be beaten like this. I didn't want to die again. Besides, I was too tired to make another walk of shame from the home point.

My eyes darted around the blur of movement in front of me, desperately searching for something, anything I could use to regain an advantage.

You've been hit! The Angry Meadows Bee hits you for 10 HP.

Pain surged through my arm as the bee's stinger slashed at my flesh, drawing blood. Without thinking, I whipped my sword around, grazing its body as it prepared for another strike.

Glancing Blow! You hit the Angry Meadow Bee for 3 HP + 2 Wind damage.

Glancing Blow! You hit the Angry Meadow Bee for 4 HP + 2 Wind damage.

You've been hit! The Angry Meadow Bee hits you for 12 HP.

Again, I swiped at it, barely connecting as I fought through the pain.

Glancing Blow! You hit the Angry Meadow Bee for 3 HP + 2 Wind damage.

Panic surged within my chest. The bee's hit points were below half now, but with each successive strike my odds of success dwindled. One unlucky critical hit could tilt the scales to a point beyond recovery.

I needed to do something different if I wanted to win.

Parrying another attack, I chanced a second look at my surroundings. Not five paces away was a large, upended tree trunk. Roots hung in the air like outstretched arms awaiting unsuspecting prey.

It might work.

Ducking another stinger thrust, I rolled toward the rotting wooden obstacle and then darted the rest of the way.

The bee followed, growing redder in its mad pursuit. I could only guess this meant it redoubled the berserker buff when I'd broken away. If so, it was likely its attacks would come faster and the hits would be harder.

Great.

I waited for the bee to strike as I inched toward the stump, preparing to make my move. Then, just as it slashed, I spun around a dangling clump of roots.

The bee shook with fury, filling the air with the loud hum of its transparent wings.

This was it. I thrust my sword between a gap in the roots, burying the blade deep into its abdomen. Then I repeated the attack again and again.

You hit the Angry Meadow Bee for 5 HP + 2 Wind damage.

You hit the Angry Meadow Bee for 4 HP + 2 Wind damage.
You hit the Angry Meadow Bee for 5 HP + 2 Wind damage.

With only 5 HP remaining, the bee began to twitch. Then it aimed its stinger between the roots and toward my chest.

Wasps and bees *were* different. While a wasp could attack endlessly until unprovoked, a bee would literally give its life for the hive. My eyes grew wide as I realized what was about to ensue.

A fresh wave of adrenaline kicked in and everything moved in slow motion as I threw myself to the ground.

*The Angry Meadow Bee uses **A Stinger for the Queen.***
The Angry Meadow Bee misses.
The Angry Meadow Bee dies.

You have defeated the Angry Meadow Bee.
You have gained 300 Experience Points.
*You have found an **Intact Bee Stinger.***
*You have found a **High-Quality Honeycomb.***

Congratulations! You are now Level 2.

22

A rush of euphoria surged through my veins, filling my HP and MP bars to full. A quick examination of my status bar revealed that I'd gained ten additional points to each. My wounds were healed, and my stamina had been renewed.

The pain in my limbs vanished in an instant and Truthseeker felt lighter in my hand. After all the fighting and the growing fatigue, I suddenly felt like I could do it all again and run for miles. Life was good. I was stronger. Even the gentle meadow breeze smelled sweeter.

I could do this.

Looking around to gauge which bee I should kite to the stump next, a blinking scroll near my status bar caught my attention. I squinted my eyes to focus on the icon and read the resulting text.

Congratulations, Traveler of EndWorld,
on reaching Level 2!
With each level, you will gain access to new skills and abilities.
New paths will open before you
and the realm of possibility will grow.
What you do and how you choose to live
in EndWorld Everlasting

is a choice only you can make,
but it is our sincerest hope
that you will always strive to be
the very best version of you.

New skills and abilities? That was certainly something I could get behind. As for the other stuff, my mind went back to Fat Anthony and Tommy Lewis. Were they just doing what the system message said, being the best versions of themselves, however bad that may be?

Whatever.

Thinking too much and dwelling wasn't going to get me on the path I needed to travel.

I set my mind back to the task at hand and targeted another bee. Starting with another sneak attack, I landed a critical hit before making a mad dash to the safety of the hanging roots.

Another bee down. This one didn't net quite as much experience points. Only 200. Even so, it was still a huge improvement over the wasps.

I received one to two pieces of honeycomb with every kill, but only one in about five were of higher quality. Each time a bee used and missed its final attack, an intact stinger would drop. It was a rare, but welcome occurrence.

The honey dropped often enough that I couldn't be sure how much it might be worth. Still, I decided to hold on to everything I got. Just in case.

The stingers, though. I considered the implications. Poisons? Alchemical ingredients? Something like that could be useful. With any luck, they'd fetch a decent price at one of the vendors in town.

My food buff wore off after I killed my twenty-third bee. Without the bonus to experience gain, the twenty-fourth only netted me 100 experience points. With the drop in stats each fight seemed increasingly more difficult.

The experience points slowed to a trickle as I spent longer recovering between mobs. Since I'd hit level 2, it was probably still better experience points per hour than fighting wasps, sure; but the loss I felt from the fifty percent reduction was palpable.

I sat hard on the grass and put my head between my knees. Without a spell or ability to heal myself, I was stuck meditating to restore my health and mana whenever my bars dipped too low. It was a perfect time to think and reflect on what I'd learned.

Truthseeker felt like an extension of my being, even if it wasn't fully bound to me. The more I attacked and parried, blocked and thrust, the more natural it felt. I knew I was gaining skill, but I couldn't help the overwhelming sense of amazement with how fast it seemed like I was progressing.

The only thing missing was a new spell.

Learning Wind Blade might as well have been a fluke or a boon from the tutorial. Even after doing it once already, I had absolutely no clue how I was supposed to discover something new on my own.

Was it even possible outside of the tutorial? I found myself wondering if perhaps there was a different set of rules now that I'd entered EndWorld.

I tried to picture flames shooting from my palm or harnessing and whipping tendrils of arcane energy toward my foes.

It was a pleasant thought, but no such luck.

Too bad.

My somewhat limited gaming experience seemed to point in one sure direction. I'd need to find a trainer or a source for scrolls if I wanted to increase my arsenal of magic tricks.

It occurred to me then just how foolish I'd been on the Kingsroad before making it to Fort Morrow. There I was, walking side-by-side with a Frost Mage. Why hadn't I thought to ask about learning magic? Zack very well could have had the exact answers I was now looking for.

I shook my head.

There was no use beating myself up about it. Besides, asking too many questions went against the noob rule. Sometimes it was best to learn by doing. Asking for too much information or for too much help could close doors quicker than if you'd just sat back and observed.

Strengthening my resolve, I decided to do just that. I would observe and I would do and I would learn by doing. In time I was sure I'd learn more about how things worked in EndWorld.

For now, I had to be content with killing bees.

Even if the experience was slow.

ELY LOOKED LIKE DEATH. DIRT AND GRIME COVERED HIS TORSO AND legs and a fresh cut on his cheek was encrusted with blood. He wore a massive loop of red bandanas from a makeshift loop on his waist, an obvious challenge to any bandits who might want to try their luck against his armed punches.

I imagined I looked just as gruesome to the casual passerby.

We walked together in silence for a while, neither of us possessing the energy it took to sustain a conversation. We were tired, exhausted from a full day of grinding.

Up ahead, the sun was just beginning to tease a magnificent sunset. The long day in the Meadows had come to an end, but it was still some hours before darkness blanketed the world. Plenty of time, Ely had said when he'd approached my camp, to turn in quests and finish our own business before we met up at Harold's.

I'd agreed. Even with the roots of the upended tree to hold my prey, my muscles were sore and weary from the countless battles. Every time I glanced toward my progress bar, my weariness was renewed. I was quite a ways off from level 3 despite my efforts.

As if to punctuate just how far I had to go, a Meadows Rabbit poked its head from a nearby stump and wiggled its nose in our direction.

Cheeky little bastar—

"Dumb rabbits," Ely spat.

"One day," I said to the creature, shaking my fist in its direction. "One day."

Ely raised an eyebrow.

"It's a long story," I offered. "One rife with struggle and revenge."

"Oh, man." He chuckled. "You didn't try to fight one of those, did you?"

I suppose my expression said everything.

Ely laughed. Then he slapped me on the shoulder hard enough that it almost bowled me over.

"Don't worry," he said after mostly regaining his composure. "You're not the first one to die to a rabbit and you won't be the last. Those things are vicious."

"You got that right." I smiled in an effort to regain what was left of my dignity.

"You didn't check it first?" he asked.

I shook my head. "It was a noob mistake. I know. I guess you could say I learned my lesson, though. I examined every last wasp and bee I fought before I even thought of engaging."

"It gets to be second nature," he said, and I felt him retreat a little. His gaze grew long and his lips tightened. It was as if he was replaying parts of his history in EndWorld within his mind.

Then he perked up, and looked down at the blade tucked safely inside its scabbard at my waist.

"How did your sword hold up?"

"Really well," I answered. "Honestly, if this is what it's like to wield Truthseeker when it's only partially bound, I can't imagine how powerful it would have been had the binding been complete."

"Maybe it's stubborn," he offered. "You know, like, maybe it wants you to prove yourself before it will give you its full strength."

"You think so?" I asked, hardly able to contain my excitement.

Ely shrugged. "I wouldn't hold your breath or anything, but I've seen stranger things."

I had to admit, the idea of a weapon that grew in strength as the wielder advanced wasn't exactly revolutionary. It was a pleasant thought and it had been done countless times before in books and legends and all the nameless games that had faded into oblivion.

But the real question was, did such a thing fit with the way EndWorld worked?

Only time would tell.

I glanced toward the skyline. The sun was dipping below the walls of the fort and people lined up at the gate before us as they shuffled their way forward.

"You have much to do before you head to the tavern?" Ely asked.

The question pulled me back from my thoughts of Truthseeker and what potential it might hold.

"A few things. I've got to go see a widow about a cellar and I might stop by the merchant stalls if there's enough time."

"Oh? What are you looking to buy?"

I pointed at the remnants of my boots. "It'd be great if I could replace these," I said, "but I'd probably settle for selling some of the loot I picked up today."

"Hmm," Ely grunted. "Probably not a good idea. I'd hold off on selling just yet."

After staring at him for a moment in confusion, he explained. "Look at all these people," he said. "They're all coming in from the fields, all packed to the gills with loot to sell. It drives prices way down. Best bet would be to wait until the morning or take a look at the auction house."

"There's an auction house here?" There was no hiding the surprise in my voice.

"Of course." Ely laughed. "The auction house connects all the nearby kingdoms. It's a way for Travelers to help regulate their own economy. As long as we have the AH, we aren't at the mercy of the NPC-governed market."

"Eh aetch?" I asked.

"Yeah," he said. "A. H. It's short for Auction House."

"Oh," I said, feeling my cheeks burn. "I guess I should have known that."

"No worries, man," Ely said, tossing me a wide grin. "It's a lot to take in all at once. Can't blame a guy for getting a little mixed up. It's natural to have to find your rhythm, I imagine, but you're doing great. Keep your chin up. You'll catch on before you know it."

An auction house. Here. In EndWorld? I considered the implications for a moment. This was good news.

"Thanks," I said. "I really appreciate all the help you've been giving me. I feel like such a noob and I'm trying my best not to be a burden."

"Nah." He dismissed my words with a quick wave of his hand. "We all start out as noobs, Denton. Besides, all things considered, I'd say you're learning really fast. I mean, this is what? Your second full day here? Give yourself some credit."

"Anyway," he continued as we rounded a corner just inside the fort. "This is my stop. I've got to turn in these bandanas to the captain of the guard and then I'll be a couple more hours running errands. See you at Harold's?"

I nodded and tossed him a mock salute before heading toward the marker on my mini-map for Widow Wilson's estate.

According to the advice Harold had given me, this was the perfect hour for an encounter with rats.

The wrinkled, old widow weighed the sight of me as she might appraise a mangy beast of burden. Awkward moments passed, and she took in every last detail as she contemplated my worth.

"And what might your name be?" she finally asked.

"Denton," I answered, then quickly added, "Denton Wade."

"Well, Denton Wade, I suppose you'll have to do," she said with a huff, giving me a brisk nod before beckoning me inside. Then, to herself, she added, "Honestly, I don't know why I even bother if this is the best they can do."

"Excuse me?" I asked, unsure of how to handle her unexpected contempt.

"Never you mind. I grow tired of having to explain myself to the lot of you. Travelers. Always showing up, leaving half the work, and expecting full pay at that."

"I'm not sure I—"

"Why, just the other day one of you hooligans tried to make off with my silver," she cut in. "I'll have you know he didn't get off easy. Three weeks service in the fort guard if I recall, so be sure to watch your sticky fingers. You can rest assured that I will."

"Look," I said, preparing to abandon the quest entirely. "I don't know what sort of people you usually deal with, but I don't want any trouble. I'm just here to kill the rats in your cellar."

"Rats? In my cellar, you say?" Her eyes gleamed with newfound interest. "I'm guessing it was Harold who sent you? Is that it?"

I nodded.

"Well, then. That's something else altogether, isn't it? Indeed. Why didn't you say so?"

Without waiting for so much as a reply, Widow Wilson grabbed me by the arm with more strength than her tiny frame suggested and ushered me inside.

Once past the threshold, she led further into an adjacent room and then into a very large kitchen. The place was well decorated and felt warm despite her initial harsh demeanor.

I was still trying to process it all when she came to a stop near a large, wooden countertop.

Looking around, I saw a space that felt loved and well-cared for. Scraps of freshly cut vegetables lined the counter and a large knife sat gleaming in the candlelight. Nearby, a crackling fire danced within the hearth and a large cast-iron pot hung above the flames.

I couldn't help but take in the delicious aroma of the bubbling stew. "Harold ought to be careful," I said absentmindedly.

"Eh?" Widow Wilson asked. "Why's that?" Her brow furrowed in confusion. "What's that old bum got to do with my kitchen?"

"Oh." I turned to face her, suddenly a bit embarrassed over my comment. "I'm sorry, that must have been my stomach talking."

"I see." The widow looked toward the pot.

I couldn't tell if it was just the glow of the firelight or if a flush of pink had blossomed on her cheeks. Either way, the hard lines of her face seemed to melt a little, growing softer.

"Go on," she said without looking back from the flame.

"Harold makes some excellent food, don't get me wrong but, whatever you're cooking smells amazing."

The widow seemed to consider this for a moment.

After a brief pause I realized how I must have sounded, like a street urchin begging for scraps. And after she'd already mistaken me for some hooligan who might make off with her possessions the moment she turned her back.

In an attempt at damage control, I added, "I'm not trying to suggest anything. It just smells good, that's all. I haven't eaten since breakfast, so maybe that has a little something to do with it. But no bother, I do have dinner plans. I promise. I'll be eating at Harold's once I'm through with my quest here."

> *Hidden Quest Complete! You've completed:*
> ***A Widow Most Flattered.***
> *You have successfully flattered Widow Wilson.*
> *This is no easy task.*
> ***Reward:** 500 Experience Points.*
> *+20 Favor with Widow Wilson.*

"No offense taken at all," she said, turning to smile at me. "The old man will never admit it, but I can cook him under the table any day. With one hand tied behind my back if I want to be fancy."

She laughed.

"Tell you what," she added. "Do a good job for me down there, complete my quest, and perhaps I'll have a piping hot bowl waiting for you."

For a moment, I couldn't help but picture my own grandmother standing before me, waiting with a bowl of my favorite soup. My breath caught, and I tried my best to blink away the sudden burst of emotion I felt welling within my chest.

Despite the widow's initial sternness, it was beginning to look like my luck had taken a turn for the better. I might not have been able to secure the high quality hare meat for Harold, but this quest had opened up a surprising opportunity.

As if to punctuate my sudden eagerness to complete the task, my stomach let out a very loud grumble. "That sounds like a good deal to me," I agreed.

The widow laughed and then, with a slight gesture of her hand, she pointed at a recessed door that seemed to be enshrouded by some sort of elusive shadow.

I furrowed my brow and took a tentative step toward the darkened threshold.

"Not so fast," she said, gently grabbing me by the arm. "It's black as sin down there. Do you have any spells or abilities that might permit seeing where there is no light?"

Shrugging, I shook my head. "No such luck."

With a kind smile, she turned and retrieved a lit candle from the dining room table.

Despite everything I'd seen in the world so far, the candle, nestled in the center of a silver saucer, drew me out of my sense of immersion. It was beautiful, and the attention to detail was nothing short of staggering.

Brilliant, white wax had dripped from the flame in perfectly shaped rivulets, frozen in time by the cool evening air. Not a single bead had reached the immaculately polished metal.

Widow Wilson offered me the flame and then pulled the cellar door open. It creaked on its hinges, revealing a few wooden stairs that trailed off into the darkness, the rest were shrouded in the shadows of the unknown.

"Fifteen of the beasts should do the trick," she said with a wide grin. "Bring me whatever stolen goods you find. I'll warn you though. The little filchers will take anything they can get into, so watch your pockets."

"Will do."

"And Denton Wade?" the widow asked.

"Yes, ma'am?"

"Please be careful with the candle. The candelabrum was a wedding gift from my sister many years back."

"Candela—?"

"The silver platter that collects the wax," she explained. "It's special to me. Understand?"

I nodded and, resting one hand on the rickety banister, held the light aloft with the other.

The old stairs creaked as I descended into the depths and shadows danced behind every wooden surface. With only the flickering light of the borrowed candle to guide my path, I took each step in careful stride.

A quick glance toward my status bar revealed the quest's updated objectives.

Defeat creatures infesting Widow Wilson's cellar: 0/15
Retrieve stolen items: 0/10
Return all stolen items to Widow Wilson: 0/1

As I stepped off the final stair a new message flashed into my field of vision.

You have entered a low-level dungeon:
The Widow's Cellar.

Now that was interesting.

24

A dungeon. I gulped, hesitating at the bottom of the stairs before taking another step. Nothing leading up to the moment I passed through the recessed cellar doorway had hinted that I might find myself inside a dungeon so soon.

But what did it mean? I couldn't help but wonder what was so different between a place like this and an open area like the Meadows. Was it nothing more than an instanced quest zone, a place where I could finish the widow's challenging quest without outside interference? Or was it a traditional dungeon with harder mobs and a chance to receive better experience and loot?

Recalling my encounter with the Meadows Rabbit, I swallowed hard. One thing I knew all too well was that the NPCs of EndWorld had no problem handing out quests that were well above one's current capabilities.

Pops had warned me about encounters with rabbits when I'd come to at the home point. No one had warned me about rats. Then again, no one had cautioned me about the potentially deadly final attack of the bees either.

One thing was certain, this place appeared to be much larger than the size Widow Wilson's house suggested.

It looked like a cellar, though.

Wooden beams jutted from the dirt to support the weight of the buildings above. The earthen floor was lined with a maze of nailed crates and boxes of various root vegetables.

Stealing my nerves, I pressed onward into the darkness.

"Rodents of unusual size? I don't believe they ex—"

A sudden sound of scurrying cut off my half-hearted attempt at lightening the mood.

"It calls us rodentses," a harsh whisper echoed from behind a large wooden barrel.

"It has candle," another added in hushed tones with greedy interest. "We kills it. We take candle. This good, good."

My eyes widened, and I tightened my grip on the hilt of Truthseeker, preparing to free the sword from its sheath.

"Hello?" I called out, hoping to learn more about my potential adversaries. "I can hear you. I'm here on a quest. Have you seen any rats?"

Another sound of scampering was my only answer. Then a wooden box clattered to the ground beside me.

"Again. It calls us rodentses. Stupid human. Death beckons it."

One of the creatures growled and let out a low hushing sound. "Shhh."

Another crate fell and a massive oaken keg rolled behind me, blocking my path to the stairs.

I pulled my sword free and whipped it in the direction of the commotion. The hard wooden pillar of the last stair-rail pressed against my back as I prepared to square off.

These were not rats.

Instead, a seemingly intelligent foe lurked within the shifting shadows.

I was outnumbered.

My candle flickered in the damp cellar air. It fluttered and nearly died in the mildewy draft.

There was nowhere to run.

The scuffling grew louder as the creatures inched closer.

My hands trembled.

Then the candle went out.

I closed my eyes against the darkness and thrust every last ounce of my will into the cold steel of my sword. Energy drained from me in a torrent, pouring through the heart of the blade and then surging into the surrounding air.

New Spell Acquired! You've learned the spell: TEMPEST.
*You can now cast **Tempest**.*

Tempest infuses your body and weapon with the power of a violent storm, adding moderate wind damage to attacks and increasing both attack speed and dodge.
Only one weapon-enhancing effect may be active at a time.

My magic bar dropped to 5 MP but my mind, body, and spirit felt unbelievably light. A strength unlike any I'd ever known surged through my veins. The darkness receded as wisps of green swirled around me, illuminating the repulsive faces of two rat-like humanoids staring in stunned awe.

With each passing second, the opportunity to maintain my advantage was dwindling. I stowed the flameless candle and redoubled my grip on the hilt of my sword. Then I yelled a savage battle cry, throwing myself headlong into the nearest foe.

Barreling my shoulder into the chest of the first creature, I spun and sliced at the second. Truthseeker connected.

Critical strike! You hit the Cellar Kobold for 18 HP + 12 Wind damage.
Critical strike! You hit the Kobold Foreman for 20 HP + 12 Wind damage.
Dodged! The Cellar Kobold misses its attack.
You hit the Cellar Kobold for 9 HP + 6 Wind damage.

Without skipping a beat, I dodged and thrust, parried and cut. Dealing with the first long enough to engage the second, each of my strikes rang true without trading a single blow.

Both creatures were sustaining heavy damage, but I knew the onslaught couldn't last.

I had no idea how long Tempest would remain active and I couldn't bring myself to look at my status bar. The seconds were ticking down, but I didn't want to know. Not now. Not with my life and the threat of excruciating pain hanging in the balance.

You've been hit! The Cellar Kobold hits you for 10 HP.
You've been hit! The Kobold Foreman hits you for 15 HP.

Pain blurred my vision, and I felt the burning sting of a deep wound in my side. And yet, not all was lost. Ribbons of green light filled the air, indicating my buff was still active.

With one last burst of effort, I slashed and hacked. Truthseeker seemed to glide through the air of its own accord until the beasts slumped over in defeat.

At last. The fight was won.

You have defeated the Cellar Kobold.
You have gained 200 Experience Points.
You have defeated the Kobold Foreman.
You have gained 250 Experience Points.
*You have found a **Rusty Copper Dagger**.*
*You have found a **Flint and Tinder set**.*
*You have received **5 silver**.*
*You have retrieved **3 stolen items**.*

I glanced at my status bar. 35/60 HP. 5/30 MP. The green icon for Tempest blinked rapidly and then vanished. With the battle behind me, the weight of the world came crashing down on my shoulders. I gave in to the wave of exhaustion and fell to my knees.

Two out of fifteen Kobolds.

Thirteen Kobolds remained.

Seven more stolen items.

More rustling sounds came from afar, deep in the cellar's depths.

I closed my eyes and cleared my mind. What I needed now was health and mana. Given another encounter without access to Tempest, I was as good as dead.

The sounds of shuffling in the darkness grew louder as another Kobold approached. It kicked at the ground and rifled through boxes, sniffing and snorting as it neared.

Each passing second brought a renewed internal struggle. The urge to stand and prepare to face the looming threat was all-consuming, but my mana was still far from full. Every precious second brought me closer to the minimum amount I needed to cast Tempest.

And still, the Kobold wandered closer.

The stench was overwhelming. Mold and decay filled my nostrils and my breath caught in my throat.

The creature stopped.

It sniffed and then startled. "What has it done?" it spat. "Kobold blood is spilt. Kill it good, good. Kill it dead. Death takes it."

"Human in dark place?" another Kobold voice a little further away asked. "It kills brothers?"

"Kills brothers dead, cold."

"Death beckons it," the second hissed.

"Yes, yes. Death beckons it," the first agreed.

The Kobolds advanced just as the last tick of my mana recovered. There wasn't a moment to lose. Once again I poured everything I had into Truthseeker and felt the torrential reverberation of magic swirl around me.

"Be wary, brother. It has trickses," one of the Kobolds warned.

The patter of their footsteps quickened, and both dashed toward me. The glint of their crude weapons were clearly visible in the pale green glow.

This encounter, I knew, would be different. The Kobolds had initiative, and with it came a hefty advantage. I wouldn't be able to land any surprise attacks to start the fight. I'd have to make up the damage elsewhere.

Truthseeker hummed in my hands. Tiny vibrations ran down the hand-and-a-half hilt and up my arms. As strange as it seemed, the blade appeared to be trying to communicate with me. Images flashed in my vision.

Smooth strikes and artful parries replaced the frenetic hacking and slashing of the previous battle. Listening to the quiet voice of the blade, I danced around the Kobolds. I avoided blows and dealt my own.

Each round of parries and thrusts increased the growing rage of my opponents. Their carelessness widened my window for attack and each strike further drained their dwindling health.

You've been hit! The Cellar Kobold hits you for 9 HP.
You've been hit! The Cellar Kobold hits you for 12 HP.

The blows landed, but I fought through the pain, intent on maintaining my momentum.

You've been hit! The Cellar Kobold hits you for 11 HP.
You've taken a critical hit! The Cellar Kobold hits you for 18 HP.
Warning: *Critical Health. 10/60 HP remaining.*

Stars burst behind my eyes as one of the Kobolds landed a heavy strike to the side of my head. The coppery taste of blood filled my mouth. I didn't have to look at my status bars to know the gravity of the situation. One more round of damage and I was done for.

They renewed their advance, pressing me back against the stairs as I attempted to dodge or deflect their blows. It was a losing battle. Every inch I gave was one inch closer to death.

With my back to the wall once more, I strained to turn the tide of battle. Parry, counterstrike. Dodge, slash, thrust. The precious few seconds I had of the Tempest buff were wearing thin. Though I didn't want to admit it, I knew this tactic was unsustainable without the buff's increase to dodge.

Something had to change. Fast.

An image of the golem from the tutorial flashed in my mind, another message from Truthseeker. How could the sword know about the time before I entered EndWorld? There was no time to ponder the question further. Seeing an opportunity, I deflected a downward strike from the nearest Kobold and rolled forward.

I was now standing behind my foes. Rallying the last reserves of my strength, I focused it into one massive, spinning slash attack. A shockwave burst from Truthseeker as I spun, knocking my attackers forward.

The blow connected, and both Kobolds fell to the ground in a heap. Exhausted, I gasped for breath. The air was like cement and the cellar seemed to spin around me. My vision pulsed red.

You have defeated the Cellar Kobold.
You have gained 200 Experience Points.
You have defeated the Cellar Kobold.
You have gained 200 Experience Points.
You have found a **Crude Shield.**
You have found a **Scroll of Earth.**
You have received **3 silver.**
You have retrieved **2 stolen items.**

I couldn't go on. I didn't have any fight left. What I needed was to rest so I could recover my mana without interruption.

Behind me, I heard a deep, raspy voice ask, "What is commotion? Where brothers? Find outsider. Kill."

Was this the dungeon boss? There was no way to be certain, but there was one thing I did know.

I wasn't ready to find out.

MY HANDS TREMBLED AS I FRANTICALLY PULLED THE FLINT AND TINDER from my inventory. Behind me I could hear the sound of Kobolds rummaging in the dark on their quest to find the interloper in the domain they'd claimed as their own. I needed time to recover.

I needed a distraction.

Sparks blinded me in the blackness. Again I struck the flint. Again and again. Finally, the small bundle of tinder took the glowing red ember.

I blew gently on the tiny spark, giving life to a small flame. Then, pulling the candle from my inventory, I lit the wick.

Taking the scroll I'd gotten from the last fight from my inventory, I focused my concentration on the strange-looking words. How much was the spell worth on the market? Hesitation wasn't an option. I didn't have the luxury of time.

The scroll crumbled between my fingers.

New Spell Acquired! You've learned the spell: **EARTHBLAST: RANK 1.**
You can now cast Earthblast at your foes.

Earthblast deals elemental earth damage. Critical strike chance is increased with each successive use.
Hint: Elemental damage is affected by your foe's resistances and weaknesses.

"There, there," a raspy voice called out in excitement. "It has fire. It has light in dark place. We kills it. We takes fire. Come, come."

While the Kobolds rushed both around and over crates in their pursuit, I set the candle on the ground and inched backward. I could barely make out the shapes of barrels and boxes in the dim light, but I pressed deeper into the shadows.

I thought about Widow Wilson and the care she must have taken to keep the silver from tarnishing and my heart broke.

After she'd warmed up to me, there was little I could do to keep myself from comparing her to my own late grandmother. The creatures would take her candle, but I would live. And, with any luck, I'd get it back before the quest was finished.

The Kobolds were upon the flame within seconds and I watched from behind two crates as three stepped into view.

"It leaves candle," one said. "It leaves candle for Kobolds?"

"It not know Death comes?" asked the furthest from me.

"Without candle, Death beckons," answered the third. "Death beckons it. Death take it. We take candle."

"Boss is much happy with candle. Boss reward us good, good," the first replied, shaking with what appeared to be mirth.

Even with my newly acquired spell, I knew I couldn't fight all three and win. Not in my current condition. I had no mana and only 10 HP.

Let them take the widow's candle to their boss. Let them collect their reward. I needed time to rest, to recover.

Breathing a silent vow, I promised myself that I would do whatever it took to retrieve the lost item. I'd fight every last one of them if I had to.

Tick by tick, my HP and MP bars slowly filled. The red pulse of my vision waned and my hands steadied. Each breath became less labored than the last. The pain lifted and my heart slowed in my chest.

Glancing at the quest requirements revealed that I'd managed to secure 5/10 of the stolen goods. If the first two fights were any indication, retrieving the rest shouldn't be much of a problem. Just as long as I could maintain better control of the encounters.

I let out a quiet sigh and leaned against a nearby crate. I'd only killed four out of the fifteen Kobolds I needed for the quest. Each encounter had taken a tremendous toll. There had to be a better way.

I needed to find a method to isolate and engage individual Kobolds if I didn't want to spend ages recovering between fights.

Tempest made me feel almost invincible. Unfortunately, as the most recent encounter had demonstrated, almost invincible wasn't good enough.

Even if I managed to avoid every attack, the mana drain from casting that one spell alone prevented me from engaging another group until I'd fully recovered.

I'd be here until morning at this rate.

My mind wandered back to my old gaming days, how did we do things back then? I smiled as I recalled spending hours looking for a group, traveling to parts unknown, setting up camp, and then sending one unlucky player to play fetch with mobs over and over again.

If done right, the rewards were worth the wait.

I would have to be both puller and tank. The problem was, I wasn't in a party and had no way to heal myself if things got dicey. I had to find a safe way to lure the Kobolds to my location. Once I figured that part out, I could fight unimpeded without attracting the attention of the rest of the mobs in the cellar.

Was it really possible? There had to be a way, I was almost sure of it. As a matter of fact, the concept wasn't much different from how I'd fought the angry bees in the Meadows earlier that day.

Too bad I didn't have more candles.

What did I have? I looked at my inventory.

18 Silver Coins
1 Elemental Shard
96 Honeycomb
32 High Quality Honeycomb
13 Intact Bee Stingers
112 Insect Wings
1 Flint and Tinder
1 Crude Shield
5 Stolen Goods

I considered the shield for a moment, even going as far as strapping it to my left arm.

The weight of it pulled me off-balance.

That wasn't going to work.

It was too bulky for my purposes. A smaller buckler might do to preserve maneuverability, but this one was much better suited for a full-on tank build. I took it off and stowed it away.

Even if the shield had been a good fit, it still didn't solve my biggest problem. I couldn't see.

There was no electricity in EndWorld. Not in the traditional sense, anyway. I couldn't just flip on a light switch and call it good.

Tempest provided enough light for close combat and I imagined Wind Blade might as well, but neither of those helped with the bigger problem. I wanted to pull the Kobolds one-by-one to a spot where I could fight without drawing the attention of the others. But how could I do that if I couldn't even see the buggers?

It was a serious predicament, and I was really starting to regret my hasty decision to part with the candle when I did. Surely, I could have used it as a lure instead? What was I thinking?

I was just about to curse my stupidity out loud when I was overtaken by a sudden idea. A lure. Yes, that was it. I needed to lure the Kobolds away from the boss. While it was true, I no longer had the candle, I did have something else.

In fact, I had a lot of it.

Honeycomb.

Back on Earth most honey was synthetic these days. The thought sparked a memory I'd long forgotten. The time I took my girls to an apiary and watched them lick the stickiness from their fingers as they chewed on the waxy comb.

"Everyone loves honey," the beekeeper had said. "It'll be a shame when all the natural stuff is gone."

He was right. The synthetic stuff tasted similar, but it was nothing like eating the real thing, unprocessed and right from the wax. The feeling was hard to explain, especially to someone who never had the chance to experience it like I had.

I pulled a honeycomb from my inventory and licked the sticky sweetness from my fingers.

Everyone loves honey.

Probably even Kobolds.

25

I fumbled on my hands and knees, crawling through the darkness toward the flickering light of the candle.

The Kobolds had gathered on the other side of the cellar, their shadows loomed larger than life around me. There were so many. I couldn't make out what they were saying, only the occasional comment made sense.

They were waiting for the boss to grant them an audience. It was the perfect time to get close.

Inch by inch I went, for what felt like miles. My path wound around boxes and crates, beside loose vegetables and gnarled roots, and over the odd sack of grain. It smelled like damp, cold earth and sweat.

Was the smell coming from me or the cellar? Or both? Honestly, I didn't know where one odor ended and the other began.

It had been a long day.

I took a tentative sniff. The resulting dry heave confirmed I was wearing most of the foul scent.

When I finally made my way within clear sight of the ragtag gathering of rat-like creatures, I was taken aback by the sheer size of their leader. He stood tall in the middle of the throng. The gargantuan beast was at least a head-and-a-half taller than the rest of his Kobold kin.

A glowing crystal was affixed to what appeared to be a leather belt around the boss's forehead. It bathed the area with a pale blue light that contrasted well with the dancing warmth of the candle.

This larger Kobold had muscles that bulged beneath his ragged cloth armor and leather duds. A menacing, rusty pickaxe hung from a makeshift loop on his tattered belt and he rested a hand on it as he surveyed his gathering of minions.

There were ten of the little ones. Add the boss, and there were eleven Kobolds in total. Just enough to complete the widow's quest.

Great.

I looked at the boss again and a cold shudder ran down my spine. The question running through my mind had become an unfortunate staple of my existence. Ever since the moment I'd entered the Cyberternal Industries headquarters, it hadn't been far from my thoughts.

What had I managed to get myself into?

It seemed like a lifetime ago, back there in the lobby with my daughter. It was another life. And that was another version of me. This was my new reality.

I'd managed to make a few friends so far on my journey but, for the moment, I was alone. This was a challenge I had to face on my own.

Gritting my teeth, I found my resolve and returned my attention to the task at hand. One of the Kobolds held my borrowed candle aloft while the others looked on in revered silence.

The boss nodded his approval before taking the tribute. "Is good," he said. "Chieftain keeps it safe, keeps death away from Kobolds. You earn reward, young one." Then he opened a hand, revealing what appeared to be a small number of dried corn kernels.

The Kobold Foreman knelt and bowed low, touching his head to the boss's foot before graciously taking the gift. Though the light was dim, it was clear that the significance of the offering was much more than it appeared at face-value. After all, I'd just spent the last few minutes crawling over more loose corn kernels and bits of grain than I dared count.

Surely, any of these minions could have taken all they wanted without fear of reproach. The bundles of stolen goods I'd managed to loot seemed to support the hypothesis.

"You bestow great honor. Kobold not fail great chieftain."

The boss grunted his approval and stowed the widow's precious candelabra in his inventory. Meanwhile, the Foreman distributed the reward to the waiting hands of his fellows and their eyes glistened in the pale blue light as they accepted their payment.

Despite the agony I felt over losing the candle, the display was touching, in a way. There was something awe-inspiring about watching the camaraderie and respect. On some level I suppose I understood these creatures. They didn't seem so different from the rest of us. Maybe they didn't belong in this cellar, but so what? They appeared to be intelligent beings, perhaps they could be reasoned with.

The boss looked upon his followers and smiled. "Soon Death comes. Death takes all humans. Takes Travelers. Death have them for good, but not Kobolds. Kobolds take candles. Kobolds remain when Death moves from this place."

"Death takes them. Kobolds remain," the group chanted, holding their weapons high. "Kobolds take candles. Then only Kobolds remain."

My stomach lurched. Whatever understanding or sympathy I'd had for these creatures crumbled under the cold weight of their words.

Something bad was coming to Fort Morrow, something only candles could stop. Whatever it was, they were content to let it take us all.

And here I was. One man with a quest. Clear a cellar. Which, as it turned out, also happened to be a low-level dungeon. A storyline. An unknown enemy lurking in the darkness. Death and candles.

All the pieces were coming together, even if I didn't quite understand how it all fit.

There was more to this quest than I'd first assumed. This was something bigger.

And yet, the knowledge that this quest was important still didn't solve the problem at hand.

Forget the boss. No matter how lucky I got, there was no way I could take a group that size. Two had been almost too much and left me vulnerable for minutes at a time as I rested to recover my health and mana.

No.

I had to do this right.

One at a time.

To do that, I needed a distraction. A tribute. Something the rotten scavengers would take to their leader.

An idea popped into my head and I couldn't help but smile.

What if I laced the honeycombs I'd found that morning with the toxins from the stingers?

I pulled a handful of the honeycombs from my inventory and placed them in a neat pile, then retrieved the 13 **Intact Bee Stingers**.

Tiny drips of venom oozed from the hollow cores, and a slight scent reminiscent of bananas filled the air.

I took one stinger in hand and examined it in the low light. A small sack pulsated where the organ had detached from the bee.

Perfect.

***Warning!** You lack the appropriate level of alchemy skill for this action. If you proceed, your ingredients will be destroyed, but you may gain valuable experience.*
Would you like to continue?
Yes. | No.

Well, so much for that idea.

Crafting would have to wait, though I now had a finer appreciation for how valuable it could be.

I put the stingers back in my inventory and placed the first few honeycombs at my feet.

Taking a few steps backward, I stacked another small mound and another, staggering each pile far enough to be visible from the next. Retracing my steps, I placed the rest of the bait, all the while using the crates as a natural funnel.

Within minutes, the bait had all been placed and the trap was set.

It was now or never.

I closed my eyes and took a deep breath. Then I picked up a turnip and tossed it at a crate nearest the first pile.

A loud thud echoed through the cellar and the light shifted as the boss snapped his head toward the sound. With a guttural command, he ordered his minions to investigate.

It was too late to turn back now.

The Kobolds advanced, stopping in groups of two or three to gather the delicious, sticky bait. They chattered in excitement as they fumbled over one another to collect their discovered treasure. As one group stopped, the others advanced, seizing upon pile after pile, and thinning their own ranks as they drew near.

At last, I was faced with a lone Kobold sitting hunched over the final pile of honeycombs.

Casting Wind Blade on my sword, I readied my attack and launched forward in a dizzying blur of motion.

A critical hit. Followed by another before the creature could even react. Within seconds my foe lay vanquished upon the cellar floor.

There was no time to review the loot or experience points rewards that scrolled down my log. I had to make every second count.

Rounding the corner, I attacked the next Kobold.

Another critical strike.

Then the sole of my boot caught on a root and I tripped. This time I couldn't avoid taking a few scrappy hits before the fight ended.

Second Kobold down.

A chunk of life drained from my health bar. I'd lost twelve hit points. No good. I had to be faster, less clumsy. I cursed my poorly crafted boots.

There was obvious wisdom in Harold's words and in that moment, I couldn't help but reflect on how right he was. It wasn't just about how fancy your sword was. The condition of the rest of your gear was just as important, if not more so.

There were still eight normal Kobolds left between the boss and where I now stood. I hesitated, realizing with frustrated indignation that making the best of each moment would be crucial to my success.

It was time to move.

I sucked in a breath and rolled forward, catching the next Kobold by surprise. Two critical strikes and I just managed to parry the creature's retaliating strike before I finished him off.

Honey dripped from the Kobold's chin, betraying the unrestrained greed that had gotten it killed.

26

The large Kobold stared off in the distance, waiting for the minions that would never return. My chest heaved as I sucked in each breath. I did my best to stay quiet but, despite my ragged breathing and an accidental bump into a nearby crate, the boss didn't seem to notice.

Fourteen Kobolds lay in crumpled piles in periodic intervals, all of them dead on the cellar floor. One more kill. One more package of stolen goods.

I was beyond ready to be finished with this quest and the sooner I could put the whole dungeon behind me the better.

My health and mana ticked upward. I'd gotten dangerously low with the last few encounters, but the breakneck pace was the only way to maintain my element of surprise. I felt like a rogue. A very bad, magic-wielding rogue with a hand-and-a-half bastard sword instead of lithe daggers and I had very little skill in the way of stealth.

Another tick. Within a few minutes I'd be ready to engage. I did my best to psych myself up for the challenge. There was no denying this Kobold was a monster. His muscles flexed and his eyes glinted with a budding rage. His minions still hadn't returned, and he was growing impatient.

With a sudden bellow, the beast clenched his fists and shouted into the darkness beyond the glowing sphere of light emanating from his forehead. "You no take candle from Kobolds. You no take candle. Death take you." His words were as cold as ice and there was no fear in the threat.

My spirits sank. There would be no surprise attack against the boss. I silently wished I'd discovered some sort of healing spell to augment my fighting abilities. With the right amount of mana management, I'd be able to better sustain the amount of time I could remain engaged in battle and reduce my recovery afterwards. I made a mental note to look into it when I got out of this place.

I imagined myself waking up in my room at Harold's and rubbing the stiffness from my limbs before grabbing breakfast. My stomach grumbled. It had been so long since I'd last eaten. In my fantasy, the morning air was cool, and I left the tavern to peruse the shops that lined the streets of Fort Morrow.

Minutes trickled by and I continued to imagine myself navigating the next day while I waited for my health and mana to return to full. Still, the boss looked on, listening for any sign of the threat that had decimated his entourage. My breath had returned to normal, but my heart still thudded loudly within my chest.

Forcing my thoughts back to the present, I contemplated the best possible strategy for attack. He was still alert and getting more irritated with each passing moment. Facing him head-on seemed to be my only option and, unlike the bees in the Meadows, I wouldn't be able to get him caught up in the terrain while I placed strategic blows. If the smaller Kobolds were any indication, his strength and reach were far too great for such cheap tricks.

Too bad.

Stepping from the shadows, I held Truthseeker in a defensive stance and ventured into the blue glow of the Kobold gathering place. The boss didn't notice me at first. I contemplated rushing headlong into battle. With any luck, I'd land the first strike before he managed to free his rusty pickaxe from his belt.

It was a good plan. As good as any, really. Tightening my grip, I prepared to run. And then, in an instant, none of it mattered.

The boss jerked his head in my direction and let out a screech-like howl.

*The Kobold Boss uses **Staggering Shout.***

A sickening wave of nausea washed over me, drowning any thoughts of a preemptive attack. The dazzling blue light of the gem affixed to the creature's forehead grew brighter and pierced my every thought. The cellar spun and my balance wavered.

Truthseeker grew heavy in my hands. Then the tip of the blade swung forward, cutting into the packed earth. Without an ounce of warning and despite my best efforts to stay upright, I found myself careening toward the ground.

*You have been inflicted with **Staggering Daze.***
You have been inflicted with Heavy.
You are now Confused.
You have been Slowed.

The Kobold Boss charged toward me. Yelling and swinging his pickaxe, he covered the distance within a few quick bounds.

Before I had a chance to recover, the beast brought his weapon down hard, embedding the rusty spike in my left shoulder.

I cried out in pain.

***Critical Strike!** The Kobold Boss hits you for 40 HP.*

Preparing a second blow he raised his axe again, lifting me up slightly as he freed the weapon from my flesh. The rusty tip now glistening a purple-hued crimson in the blue light of the glowing crystal.

On nothing but pure impulse, I unleashed a torrent of stone from the palm of my outstretched hand. The boss stumbled backward as shards of rock ricocheted off his head.

*You cast **Earthblast.***
***Critical Strike!** The Kobold Boss takes 25 HP Earth damage.*

Within a matter of seconds my life bar had dropped to below half and, while I'd managed to land a good hit with Earthblast, it had cost me dearly.

The unexpected force from casting the spell felt invigorating against the agony in my shoulder. But the incantation shaved 10 points off my MP pool, leaving me with 20.

This meant two things.

First, at the cost of 10 MP, I could cast Earthblast two more times before I ran out of mana.

Second, and far more serious, at a cost of 25 MP, I no longer had access to Tempest.

*You **Inspect** the Kobold Boss.*
Level 4. Hit Points: 70/95.

Things weren't looking good. I rolled the numbers around in my head. For every one point of damage I took, I'd need to deal twice as much damage to the boss. And then five more points on top of that. Furthermore, the rodent-like humanoid was twice my level.

I gulped audibly and then, upon locking eyes with the boss, scrambled for my blade.

Whatever I did, I had to take better control of my impulses. While the surprise critical strike was nice, the movement speed increase from Tempest alone would have greatly improved my chances of success.

Angered by my resilience, the Kobold shouted once more. This time I was ready. Ignoring the piercing shriek, I noted the resist in my log.

Not today, rat-man. Not today.

I felt a smile tug at my lips. It was an involuntary response to an impossible situation, but it felt good.

Maybe things weren't as impossible as they seemed.

I grit my teeth and swore a silent oath. One of us was going to take a dirt nap tonight, and it wasn't going to be me.

I still had options. I could cast Earthblast twice and hope for the best. Or I could cast Wind Blade once. Since unlocking Rank 2, the spell now cost 15 MP per use.

There was no logical reason to use Rank 1 to save MP. Not this time. This wasn't a fight of attrition. I needed to pull out some serious damage over a short duration. Otherwise, the boss would wear me down and the cost of each mistake I made would become exponentially deadlier.

The boss shuffled his feet and swapped the dripping pickaxe back and forth between his massive hands while he considered me. Then he shifted, preparing a second charge.

The moment called for decisive action.

I needed to make a choice.

What would it be? Wind Blade or Earthblast?

The boss charged.

Stomp. Stomp.

Stomp.

I raised Truthseeker to meet his downward strike and spun sluggishly to the opposite side as the pickaxe slid down the angle of my blade. With a clumsy pivot, I found myself staring at the Kobold's unprotected backside.

The tip of my sword sank deep into the creature's flank.

Critical Strike! *You hit the Kobold Boss for 15 HP.*

I reached forward with my left hand, sending another blow toward the back of my enemy's head.

*You cast **Earthblast**.*
The Kobold Boss takes 17 HP Earth damage.

The force from the blast jerked my injured shoulder, and I stumbled backwards several paces before falling hard on my rear, wincing in pain.

Truthseeker felt heavy and unwieldy in my shaking palm and my vision began to fade between dark pulses that threatened to absorb the pale blue light.

Forcing thoughts of sleep from my mind, I focused on what little strategy I could come up with.

One Earthblast left.

That's all I had the MP for, but I wasn't sure I could withstand the pain of casting with my left hand another time. And I certainly couldn't swing my sword with that arm, either. I would have to change tactics somehow.

The Kobold Boss turned. Red rage glowed in his eyes and his stone, fueled by his mounting anger, grew painfully bright.

I let my head slump downward, and I closed my eyes while the boss drew near. Sleep beckoned. If I let him finish me, I'd end up at the home point.

I could return and face him again.

No.

I pressed the tip of my blade into the cold earth as I forced myself to stand. Leveling my gaze at the beast, I let out a battle cry so fierce it stole the confidence from the Kobold's curl-lipped sneer.

"Yeeaaaaargh!" The sound tore out of my throat like a creature released from a long-forgotten cage.

The Kobold halted in its tracks and stared at me, dumbfounded by my sudden change in disposition.

I had no more tricks. With only 10 MP to spend, there was no hope of learning a new spell or ability that might help turn the tide. All I had was what little strength I could muster and my own ingenuity.

Latching on to the anger surging in my chest, I shouted my challenge.

"I will not be defeated by you. Not today. Death will not take me, Death will take Kobolds. And I will take candle."

The boss howled, furious with indignation.

I had killed his minions and threatened to take his most prized possession, the one thing that would keep Death at bay.

He lowered his head and began to charge.

Again, I closed my eyes. I listened to the sound of his footsteps as he advanced. And then, when the moment was right, I loosened my grip on Truthseeker and lifted my right arm.

*You cast **Earthblast**.*
***Critical Strike!** The Kobold Boss takes 25 HP Earth damage.*

Once the spell left my palm, I swung my left hand hard against the pommel of my sword and scooped up the falling hilt with my right. Swinging the blade with all my might, I spun away from the beast and then towards it in a full, circular arc.

Pain lanced through my shoulder, but the weight of the steel propelled my swing, building centrifugal force into the attack.

The blow connected.

***Critical Strike!** You hit the Kobold Boss for 17 HP.*

The boss flew backward and landed with a sickening thud several feet away.

I blinked through my disbelief and nearly dropped my sword. My shoulder felt like it was on fire but the fight wasn't over.

Not yet.

Rising to his feet, the Kobold stooped to retrieve his weapon from the packed dirt. Then he turned his gaze back upon me, unleashing a glare that caused my breath to catch within my chest.

At once he started to chant and guttural words I couldn't understand assaulted my senses. My limbs grew heavy. Then the ground beneath my feet began to boil as previously unseen roots broke the surface and twisted around my feet and legs.

The Kobold Boss took one step closer. Then another. And yet another.

Each movement seemed like an incredible burden, but he did not stop his approach and the intensity of his chanting only seemed to grow.

Holding Truthseeker aloft, I kept the tip pointed toward the creature's chest. I still had 20 HP left, and I knew his hit points were dangerously low.

*You **Inspect** the Kobold Boss.*
Level 4. Hit Points: 1/95.

A status message flashed in my log. I ignored it. Nothing but a single hit point stood between me and the end of this tiresome quest.

Whatever the message said, it could wait.

Still chanting, the Kobold Boss raised his pickaxe high above his head and prepared to strike.

I grinned. Within just a few more steps, the beast would be within striking range and the fight would be over.

Then something strange happened.

***Absorb!** The Leech Root drains you for 5 HP.*
The Kobold Boss gains 5 HP from the Leech Root.

My eyes went wide in disbelief and the boss used my moment of distraction to strike.

Out of instinct, I tried to roll to the right to avoid the blow but my feet were firmly stuck in place by the entangling roots. It took everything I had to whip Truthseeker upward in time to catch the brunt of the attack.

Bouncing off my blade, the pickaxe tore at the flesh of my left leg.

***Glancing Blow!** The Kobold Boss hits you for 10 HP.*

The roots tightened around my legs, further immobilizing me where I stood. The tables had turned in one agonizing moment.

I was quickly running out of options, even as the boss continued pressing his offensive advantage. He swung wide, and I reacted, whipping Truthseeker to meet the blow.

A loud clang reverberated down the blade and through my hand before echoing off the far cellar wall.

The Kobold Boss stepped closer, closing in on the little space I had to defend and narrowing my parry window.

Again, he swung his pickaxe. Slower this time and exaggerating the telegraphed movements of his strike.

I was tired and my thoughts swam through my brain like slow-moving mud. Still, I wasn't stupid. If left unblocked, the strike would ring true and, even as slow as it was, with only 5 HP remaining, it could finish me off. But I knew he was up to something.

As soon as our weapons met, the Kobold Boss spun around in an imitation of my previous attack. And with another screech, the roots binding me in place tightened even more.

The rusty head of the pickaxe whirled through the air as I brought my blade up to meet the attack.

My vision filled with sparkles of dancing fire and I felt the hilt of Truthseeker being torn from my grasp. My single-handed grip had proven too weak, and the blade seemed to cry out as it was flung into the darkness outside the makeshift arena.

The roots pulsed and I could sense the life beginning to drain from my flesh.

It was over. I had lost.

The glowing blue light of the boss's gemstone seemed to dim, waning in brightness as it was overtaken by my encroaching desire to sleep.

I— No... No!

If I was going to die again, it wasn't going to be like this. Not without spending every last ounce of fight I could muster. I wasn't done yet.

Opening my eyes, I grit my teeth before punching the Kobold Boss square on the nose.

You hit the Kobold Boss for 6 HP.
You have defeated the Kobold Boss.
You have gained 2,500 Experience Points.

New Skill! *You've unlocked:* ***HAND-TO-HAND.***

Hand-to-hand _is a Combat Skill._
Wise Warrior once say:
A man without a weapon is a man without fist or foot.

The pale blue light faded, and the gem went dull as the Leech Roots released their grip on my legs, retracting back into the earth. Without their grip to prop me up, I slumped to the ground.

Meanwhile, a list of loot drops scrolled through my log.

I was too tired to look. For now, I was content with the Quest Complete indicator beneath my mini-map.

One item I desperately hoped the boss would have dropped was Widow Wilson's candle. I imagined it in my inventory and it appeared in my hand. After inspecting the candelabrum for damage, I sighed with relief and relit the wick.

With the candle and its silver saucer safe in hand, I knew what I needed was to rest and regain some of my health. But first, I had to find my sword.

After fumbling in the barely lit darkness for several minutes, I finally felt Truthseeker's hilt safe within my hand. Once I pulled it into the light, I let out a sharp gasp of dismay.

There was a large chip missing from the blade where the boss's spinning attack had struck.

I sighed to myself and slid the sword back into its sheath. There was nothing I could do about it now. Best to leave it until the morning when I could show Jörgen and get his opinion.

With any luck, he'd be able to make the necessary repairs without too much trouble. As for now, I was eager to return to the house and turn in the widow's quest.

My stomach grumbled. Perhaps I might even receive a bowl of my long-awaited reward.

I turned and walked back toward the prone form of the boss, pausing briefly to pay my respects to the clever warrior before heading toward the creaky, wooden stairs.

27

Widow Wilson turned to face me as I stepped through the darkened threshold and into the light of the kitchen. Without saying a word, I gently blew out the flickering flame and placed the borrowed candle on the counter.

"Oh my, if you don't look a little worse for wear. All finished, I take it?" she asked.

I glanced at my quest log to be sure, then nodded. "Ten stolen items and fifteen Kobolds, including one boss. I think that just about does it."

Retrieving the packages of stolen goods from my inventory, I placed them on the countertop next to the candle.

"You didn't run into too much trouble, I hope?" Widow Wilson asked.

An exhausted chuckle escaped from somewhere deep in my chest while I looked at the ceiling and shook my head.

"I guess I managed," I said. "But I have to say, those weren't exactly rats down there, were they?"

The widow laughed and smiled knowingly. "I wasn't the one who said they were rats. An infestation of creatures, perhaps."

"But—" I started to protest.

"You must be hungry," she cut in, interrupting me. "I believe I promised you a bite to eat, didn't I? Come and sit. I'll ladle you up a bowl of my soup. I think you'll like it."

With that, she turned and walked toward the large cast-iron pot hanging above the fire and began to fill a wooden bowl. Tendrils of steam filled the air and my mouth began to water.

"Careful, now. It's hot," she said as she offered me the meal.

After a moment spent looking on while I ate, the widow spoke up. "Care for some bread? A drink, perhaps?"

"Both would be amazing," I answered around a mouthful of soup. Then, after swallowing, I added, "Sorry, I guess I was so hungry that I seem to have forgotten my manners. Yes, please."

"Entertain an old woman's curiosity and answer me this, was it Harold?" she asked after handing me a goblet and a small loaf of bread. "Was he the one who told you there were rats in my cellar?"

Again, there was something knowing in the tone of her voice. Like she was trying to make a gentle point.

I thought back to my conversation with the barkeep earlier that morning and shrugged. Honestly, it felt like such a long time ago, but deep down I knew there was truth to her words.

"No," I answered at last, admitting my wayward assumption. "Now that I think about it, I don't suppose he did mention rats specifically. I guess I just sort of filled in the blanks."

There was a funny glimmer in the widow's eye then and she smiled. It was a kind smile, and I was once again struck with the image of a doting grandmother, this time imparting her wisdom on her young charge.

"Often in this world," she said, "you'll find things aren't always as they first appear."

After a brief pause, she continued. "We're all guilty of it. Filling in the blanks, that is. Just as I might have mistaken your intentions upon your arrival on my doorstep, I suppose you could say. Perhaps we'd all be a bit better off if we pursued the truth first, before jumping to conclusions."

"A lesson well-learned," I agreed, dipping a chunk of the bread into the broth. "Those Kobolds were a nasty bunch. They fought much harder than the rats I expected to encounter, that's for sure."

"And yet, you appear to be much stronger than you were before you ventured into the dark. Two new spells, I see. That's quite impressive for one so new."

I stopped chewing.

"Oh, no need to fuss. I am well-versed in the arcane and elemental arts, myself," she explained. "Used to be quite skilled in my day, if you can believe it."

"Is it normal then?" I asked. "Learning spells in combat, I mean."

I was referring to Wind Blade and Tempest, of course. Obtaining a scroll as a random drop from a mob or finding it in a treasure chest didn't seem too far-fetched. At least that was something I could understand. But if there was a way to better control when and how I learned new spells, I was ready for a lesson.

"So eager," the widow said approvingly. "To answer your question indirectly, it is common for some. Less common for others. Would you like some advice on the matter?"

"Yes, please." I nodded my head vigorously.

"My advice is simple enough, though it might not be the answer you were hoping for."

"Go on," I said. "I'm listening."

"One would be wise to prepare for the worst without relying on inspired intervention. Use the tools you have and use them well. There may be a time when you desperately wish to learn something new, when all the while you had the perfect answer already at your disposal."

After a moment of steady silence, she added, "Like items and potions, spells and abilities are merely tools one uses. If the world and the problems you encounter are a lock, you must come to realize that you are already the key."

"Oh," I said.

I was pretty sure I understood the first part, but what was all this about locks and keys?

"Use what you have wisely and you will go far," she explained. "Of course, new tricks are always welcome, but seldom are they the only answer.

Nodding my head, I decided to chalk it up as a reiteration of her previous point.

I couldn't rely on learning new tricks in the heat of battle. It just wasn't sustainable. Simple enough.

As if sensing she might have lost me, the widow pointed to my bowl and grinned. "You better eat before your soup gets cold."

My stomach agreed, so I happily obliged.

After I'd finished my bread and emptied the bowl, the widow handed me a package.

"Take this to Harold," she said. "He'll know what it's about. I suspect you might have been hoping for a reward. Don't worry. Harold will take care of it."

I raised an eyebrow, but she didn't offer another word of explanation.

Sensing our interaction was done for the night, I cleared my dishes and started to see myself out.

Then I stopped and turned to face the wizened old woman. "Widow Wils—"

"Bah," she spat. "Enough with formalities. You can call me Margaret, if you'd like."

I nodded and smiled. "Thank you, Margaret, for giving me a chance and for the best bowl of soup I've ever had the privilege to enjoy. It was truly amazing and I hope we meet again."

Hidden Quest Complete! You've completed:
A Widow Less Bitter.
You have received Margaret Wilson's approval.
Reward: 1,500 Experience Points.
+50 Favor with Margaret Wilson.

A rosy hue blossomed on her cheeks and she politely cleared her throat. "I trust we will, young man. I trust we will."

I chuckled. "Have a good evening, Margaret."

"You as well, fabled Rat Slayer. Now make haste to Harold's before the cold of night takes you."

And with that, I stepped out onto the cobbled street and made my way toward Harold's Tavern.

I thought about my day and allowed my mind to wander as I walked. With each stride I relived the failures and the triumphs and considered my accomplishments.

Every muscle in my body seemed to be crying out in pain and exhaustion, and yet there was a new spring in my step. I had single-handedly defeated my first dungeon.

Soon I would be at Harold's and something told me Ely would be sitting at the bar, waiting and wondering what had taken me so long. I took in a deep breath of the night air and immediately felt a smile pull at the edges of my mouth.

As luck would have it, I just so happened to have an amazing story I couldn't wait to tell.

28

By the time I neared Harold's Tavern, I could tell something was off. What greeted me wasn't the abandoned night-time byways I'd traversed the night before, but a scene much like the one outside the Bearded Goat.

Crowds lingered on the normally empty street outside Harold's establishment and an excited energy permeated the charged evening air.

It was strange. Surreal even. In fact, now that I considered it, the feeling went back to the very moment I stepped foot outside Margaret Wilson's house.

I'd been so caught up in my elation over my narrow victory against the Kobolds that I hadn't noticed it at first but, once recognized, there was no denying it.

Something in Fort Morrow was very, very different.

It wasn't the walls or the parapets. Not the banners or the empty market stalls. I couldn't quite put my finger on it. Yet with the gathering crowds in this part of town, at this hour, I knew I wasn't the only one who felt it.

As I approached Harold's Tavern, I couldn't help but stop to listen.

A bevy of sound assaulted my senses, interrupting the thoughts swirling in my head.

Harold's was much more active tonight than it was when I arrived the night before. Raucous laughter filtered out the doorway as another would-be patron stepped through the threshold about twenty paces ahead of me. Seconds later, I heard a much louder version of the cheers and groans that resulted when I'd first inspected Ely.

Coins were still exchanging hands when I entered. A number of eager eyes jerked up, ready to take the next bet, but the few regulars sitting nearest the entrance waved them off. I wasn't just another noob mark.

The dismissive look on their faces echoed the feeling I got whenever I thought of Harold and his hole-in-the-wall tavern. For better or worse, these were my people. I belonged here.

Scanning the crowd, I felt the growing sense of unease in the pit of my stomach. Booths and tables were packed tonight and patrons lined the walls with cups in hand. The scene before me bore a much closer resemblance to the Bearded Goat than my expectations of Harold's.

A slight wave of panic washed over me and I even considered slipping off to my rented room, bypassing the crowd altogether. I could always deliver Margaret's package to Harold in the morning.

Then I spotted Ely's bulky frame seated at the bar. He turned and smiled, waving me over with apparent excitement.

Letting out a held breath, I nodded and began weaving my way through the standing bodies. When I finally made it to the bar, I realized he wasn't alone.

"I believe you two know each other?" Ely asked, raising a glass of dandelion wine.

Smoldering eyes blinked at me from the shadowy depths of a familiar hooded cloak. Then a pair of pale, feminine hands retracted the covering.

I took a step backward and my mouth dropped open in disbelief. "Ayva?"

"Raven," she corrected, giving me a sideways look that suggested this wasn't the time to discuss her resemblance to the woman who guided me through the tutorial.

"Right," I said, allowing my mind time to process before I continued. "Sorry. It's been a long day."

29

Raven stared into my eyes, searching without a hint of locating whatever it was she hoped to find. The awkward silence that settled between us felt louder than the clamor inside the packed tavern.

Ely lowered his glass and scanned the room. "Some night, huh?"

Breaking free of Raven's stare, I matched his wandering gaze.

"There," he said, pointing a finger to a nearby booth. "Looks like they're leaving. Let's grab their spot before someone else does."

Scooping up his plate, Ely pressed into the crowd with a grim look that dared anyone to spill his drink.

Eager for a chance to sit and rest, I followed close behind. Ely continued and, as if by magic, a path melted before us as we made our way to the table undisturbed.

I recalled my first encounter with the muscled and scantily clad pugilist. I couldn't help but smile. Given my own response at the time, the reaction of the newcomers gathered in small groups wasn't much of a surprise.

Behind me, Raven and another mysterious woman took our flank, weaving through bodies as the impromptu gatherings reconvened, continuing their paused conversations.

"Denton," Ely said, once we'd all reached the now-vacant table, "you already know Raven. This," he pointed to the other woman, "is Attia. She's not only the best healer I've come across in EndWorld, she's also smokin' hot."

Attia shook her head and, though I couldn't see it, I could almost feel the eye-roll.

Like Raven, Attia wore a cloak; though hers was sewn from an exquisite fabric of dazzling white. Her face was hidden within the shadow provided by the hood, but dark hands reached up to pull it back, revealing beautiful, deep brown eyes and a shy smile.

"Pleased to meet you," I said, offering my hand.

She shook it.

"I'm pleased to meet you, too, Denton."

A surge of renewing energy rushed through me as our skin touched. I watched in awe as my minor wounds and abrasions healed before my eyes.

"Whoa," I breathed.

Attia's smile widened to reveal a row of straight, white teeth. "That better?"

"Much. Thank you," I replied, still taken aback by the unexpected healing ability she'd used, and seemingly without an ounce of effort.

"Attia is studying to become a white mage," Ely explained. "Besides being stunningly gorgeous, she's already mastered several branches of the healing arts."

"I wouldn't say I've mastered anything," Attia said in protest, taking a seat beside Ely in the booth. "I'm only level 4, remember?"

"Okay, maybe mastered wasn't the right word, but you're an amazing healer. There's no arguing that fact."

Attia blushed and turned away, using the opportunity to hail a nearby waitress. Meanwhile, Raven took her seat beside me on the bench and leaned close.

"I'm sorry I didn't show up last night," she whispered. "Things got... well, complicated."

"I understand," I said, noting the regret in her eyes. "There's really no need to explain."

"Actually, there is," she said, leaning even closer. "But not now. Not here. Even in a place like Harold's, you never know who might be listening."

Then she turned and flashed a smile at the waitress. "We'll take two bottles of Harold's Strawberry Cordial. You can put it on my tab."

"Yes, of course, Ms. Raven," the waitress said with a polite smile. "Do you need anything else?"

Raven glanced around the table. After we all shook our heads, she answered. "That will be all for now. Thank you, Leah."

When the girl had gone, Ely put his hands up in protest. "I don't have much coin, Raven. I'll pitch in what I can, but it won't be a lot."

She laughed. "I don't want your coin, you big lug. And don't start getting all precious about hand-outs now. The way I hear it, the two of you had no problem sampling a glass of the cordial last night when Harold offered it."

Ely's mouth dropped open, but no words escaped his maw.

"Besides," she continued, "I owe Denton for leaving him in the woods and not meeting him here like I'd arranged."

"You left him in the woods?" Ely asked, then turned to me. "I don't remember you telling me she up and left you out there."

"I seem to have made it just fine," I said with a shrug.

"Okay, then. That explains Denton, but what about me? Do I just get to bask in his radiance?" he asked with a mischievous grin. "Not that I'm complaining."

Raven made a show of being in deep thought before answering. "Well, I just so happen to have a quest chain that might be a bit too much for me to handle on my own. I don't know the specifics yet, but there's a chance I could use some of those muscles of yours. You wouldn't begrudge a girl a flagrant attempt at bribery, would you?"

Ely grinned wide and thrust a fist into his open palm. "Your level 5 quest line? By all means, bribe away. Just tell me what needs punching."

Raven nodded. "You've got yourself a deal."

The change in Raven's demeanor now that the shadows of her hood no longer enshrouded her face left me speechless. Confusing emotions struggled for purchase as I wrestled with nailing down exactly how I felt about the change.

The whispers and secrets I could understand, but this? Her pleasant behavior coupled with the uncanny resemblance to Ayva left my mind reeling as I struggled to make sense of it all. Too many conflicting emotions left me feeling confused and unsure.

Where was this woman two nights ago when we met in the woods? Where was her overwhelming generosity when I needed it the most?

None of this made sense, and yet here we were. The four of us, all strangers just a few nights ago, now thrust together in a strange combination of ones and zeros on some server cluster somewhere.

EndWorld Everlasting. What is real?

The deep sense of irony I felt when I thought of those words now left me shaking my head.

"What?" Ely asked, confused. "I'm not above selling my body for some of Harold's cordial. I know you know what I'm talking about. You tasted it last night. So worth it."

"No." I laughed. "Sorry, my mind was somewhere else. Besides, now I know your weakness. Just you wait until I get a tough quest. Heaven knows I could have used your help tonight."

"Yeah, what was up with that? You came in looking like you got ran over by a bus. There's dried blood on your armor, too. Did a wagon break loose in the market and roll over you after we parted ways?"

"That's actually not too far from how I felt," I said. "Thanks again, Attia."

"My pleasure," she said. "Acts of random healing is actually a part of a quest I'm on right now. So, really, it was you who helped me."

"Well? If it wasn't a wagon, what kind of trouble did you run into?" Ely pressed.

"Kobolds," I answered. "Quite a few of them, actually."

"Kobolds?" the three asked in unison. "Here?"

Just then, a loud groan of disappointment sounded from somewhere near the entrance, interrupting our conversation. It only took me a few seconds to realize who had cost many of the newer gamblers their ante.

I couldn't believe my eyes.

Cupping my hands as I stood, I called the older man over. When Ely looked at me questioningly, I explained.

"Everyone, this is Pops."

30

Pops nodded to the members of our group and pulled up a chair before sitting at the end of the table.

"Hello, everyone," he said.

"I'm Ely," Ely said, leaning forward and offering his hand.

"Nice to meet you, Ely."

"I'm Attia."

"Attia. What a pretty name. Very pleased to meet you."

"Raven. Nice to meet you, Pops. You know Denton, then?"

Pops nodded as he shook her hand. "Yes, we met this afternoon. And it's very nice to meet you, Raven."

"This afternoon?" Ely asked. "Out in the Meadows?"

"No, no." Pops laughed. "At the home point. Here in town."

Hoping to head off any further discussion that might lead to an embarrassing recall of my encounter with the Meadows Rabbit, I decided to change topics.

"I didn't expect to see you back so soon. Weren't you headed to the Frostwind Mountains?"

"That was the plan," Pops said with a shrug.

"Was it…"

"The cave trolls?" Pops finished my thought. "No. Not this time.

Just a few fellow travelers trying to get a leg up in the world by whatever means necessary, I guess."

"PvP?" Raven cast a sideways look in my direction that seemed to suggest more than I was picking up on.

"You mean player verses player?" I asked.

"Yes," Attia said with a frown.

"But shouldn't it be called TvT? You know, Traveler verses Traveler, to fit in with EndWorld's terminology?"

Attia's frown turned into a sad smile.

"PvP is an old idea from an old life, and some ideas never really die," Pops explained. "Here in EndWorld Everlasting it means something else altogether."

"And it usually isn't as simple as an argument between Travelers," Raven added.

Pops nodded and continued. "If you ask me, most of the people who gank and kill other people outside the arena haven't really considered the very real implications or consequences of their actions. They're truly acting as if they're just a part of some elaborate game. It's all about that endorphin rush."

Ely slammed his fist on the table. His jaw was tight and his eyes narrowed. "I'm getting so tired of people like that," he said, his voice low. "Don't make excuses for them, Pops. They come to a place like this where almost anything is possible and treat it like they would any old game. But people get hurt here. For real. It isn't just a game. You can't just log in and log out whenever you want to. This is our lives now. Consequences matter."

Seeing the fire growing in his eyes, I imagined him reliving the moments that led up to his current situation. Harold had been kind enough to give him a helping hand, but it was clear the road hadn't been an easy one to travel.

It was impossible to guess the full details of what happened to my new friend, but there were a few things I'd managed to put together. Whatever it was, it hadn't been pleasant. And somehow that NPC merchant, Kenneth Johnson, had played a part in it.

Attia put a gentle hand on Ely's bicep and I watched with interest as his shoulders relaxed.

"You're a healer?" Pops asked, giving Attia and appraising look. "I haven't run into many people with the ability to soothe like that. Quite the impressive talent you have there, young lady."

"Thank you. I see you have a talent for observing aggro and threat levels. You must be a tank class then?" Attia asked, giving Pops a look of her own. "I wouldn't have expected that given your—"

"Lack of armor?" Pops laughed, running a hand over his hairy forearm.

"Right." A flush of color darkened her cheeks as she looked away.

"Wait up, hold on a second," Ely cut in. "How can you be a tank? I mean, no offense, but you're all flesh and leather. Where's your tin-can suit and shield?"

Pops was still laughing when Leah brought out the bottles of cordial and began setting out fluted glasses. She cast a furtive look toward Raven before she set a final glass in front of the old man.

"Thank you, Leah," Raven said, flashing a kind smile.

"Will there be anything else?"

"Actually," I said, "I know it's pretty busy right now, but could you let Harold know I finished one of the quests he gave me this morning? I've got something for him when he can catch a break."

Leah nodded. "It might be awhile. Like you said, it's a busy night."

"That's fine."

After she retreated back into the crowd, I found myself facing four sets of raised eyebrows.

"What was that all about?" Raven asked. "Harold gave you a quest?"

I shrugged off her question. "So, Pops, how does that work, exactly? I saw the battle axe and I guess I assumed you were some kind of warrior or berserker class. You probably get that a lot, huh?"

"Well, yeah. The great axe and leather doesn't help matters. That's for sure," Pops answered, though Raven didn't take her eyes off me. "I suppose I could make use of something with a bit higher defense rating, but I just couldn't justify the spend at this level. The runes actually make up a lot of the difference."

With that he pulled his axe from his back and showed us the charred markings of symbols burnt into the wooden handle. I wasn't sure if my eyes were playing tricks on me, but I swore I saw coals smoldering deep within the ebon-black runes.

"That's really quite impressive," Attia breathed. "I honestly haven't seen anything like it until now."

"We each have our own paths," Pops said, tossing us all a wink.

"But that's not it, right?" Ely asked, probing further. "It can't just be the runes on your axe. That's why you're a tank? That doesn't make much sense. I mean, what's stopping me from scratching some symbols into these and calling it a day?" He punctuated the remark by tossing his crude fist weapons on the table.

"Ely," Attia protested. "Should we all just start throwing our weapons on the table now? Be nice."

"No, no," Pops said, smiling. "He's right. If it were just the runes, anyone could be a tank if they bought the right weapon or visited a rune shop or, like he said, scratched some markings into what they've already got. That wouldn't make for a very balanced system, now would it?"

"I don't suppose it would," I answered.

"Activating the runes requires a certain skillset, I guess you could say," Pops explained. "There are different specialties, of course. Tanking just happens to be the one I chose to pursue."

"So you're a...?" Ely pressed.

"I'm a Runewarrior, defender class," Pops said, slinging his axe back into its place on his back. "I'm sure there will be fancier titles as I become more proficient, or so I'm told, but that's what it is for now."

"A defender class with a great axe," I mused.

"My level 5 quest is to find a greatsword that's been forged in the heat of battle," Pops explained. "I thought I had a good shot at it with those cave trolls, but I guess the other folks had different plans."

Raven smiled and picked up the nearest bottle. "Best not to dwell on it. There will be other chances. Now, who's ready for some of Harold's cordial?"

"Count me in," Ely said, putting away his weapons. "I might not get how this whole rune thing works, but cordial is definitely something I can understand."

"Excellent. I'll begin pouring just as soon as Denton starts telling us about that quest of his. Was it the Kobolds, then?"

All eyes were on me once again.

I sighed.

"It's not really a big deal," I said. "Besides, Harold actually gave me two quests. One was to collect high-quality rabbit meat, which I failed to do."

"And the other was the Kobolds?" Raven pushed.

"Well, yeah." I shrugged. "I actually thought I was supposed to kill rats, so the Kobolds were a bit of a surprise. I guess I managed, though."

"Hmmm," Raven hummed. "That's interesting."

Attia tilted her head in thought, then asked, "What do you make of it?"

"Sounds like a main story quest," Raven said. "But level 2 is a little low for something like that. Still, Kobolds? That's not your everyday run-of-the-mill mob for someone just starting out."

"I was level 1," I corrected.

"Level 1?"

"Harold gave me the quests this morning before I had a chance to grind experience points out in the Meadows," I went on. "That's how I met Pops. I tried to fight a rabbit on the first go. It didn't end well."

"Alright, that settles it," Ely said, licking his lips. "A deal's a deal, as they say. So, how about we start pouring some of that cordial?"

Raven nodded and uncorked the first bottle. "A deal is a deal."

Though she began to pour, I got the feeling I hadn't heard the end of the matter. And yet, all I wanted was to sit and relax and listen to someone else's stories for a change. The day had been long and arduous and my own tales were growing heavy.

The sweet bouquet of the bubbling strawberry cordial filled the air. The aroma was intoxicating, and I knew Harold hadn't lied when he warned us the drink would only get better with each sip. My mouth watered in anticipation, but my heart felt heavy as I realized even this felt out of place.

If the Kobolds were right, then Death was coming to Fort Morrow, and I'd somehow managed to get myself knee deep in the thick of it. Even though I wanted to believe the worst was behind me, something told me there would be plenty to worry about in the days ahead.

"Why are you so interested in Harold's quest?" Ely asked as he picked up his glass. "It's not that uncommon for the old boy to toss out a quest or two. I know I've gotten my fair share."

Raven shrugged and kept pouring. "Did you get your quests straight away, or did they come once you found yourself in a situation where you needed some help?"

Ely's cheeks flushed the color of the cool, pink liquid. "I guess you could say I was in a bit of a bind."

"That's just it." Raven's eyebrows shot up. "Harold helps Travelers in need. That's sort of his shtick, see?"

"Yeah?"

"So, the question is, why does Denton need help?"

"Why does anyone need his help?" I asked, suddenly pensive. I wasn't sure if it was the first sip of the cordial or just a desire to be a part of the conversation that obviously concerned me, but the thought suddenly felt as if it would tear itself out of me if I didn't give it voice.

"What do you mean?" Attia asked.

"Why does Harold help anyone?" I said, doubling down on my point. "I mean, really. It doesn't take a rocket scientist to see that I'm out of my league, does it? You know, considering I never wanted to be here in the first place."

All eyes were on me again.

"Let's just spill out the facts, shall we?" I went on, emboldened by the silence. "I broke my sword in the tutorial and all I get for my trouble is a stupid Earthen Shard. But that's not all. Before I can turn my back on all of this, I get the world's biggest guilt trip from my oldest child. The next thing I know, I'm falling head-long into accepting this crazy adventure. And what happens next? Rainbows and butterflies? Of course not. I get chased through the woods by rabid wolves, assaulted at knife-point in the dead of night, and taken advantage of by the first person I meet in town. And when I finally catch a break by receiving an amazing sword, I can't even manage to bind it correctly, and then—"

I didn't have the strength to give voice to what happened next, but the silence that followed was too heavy to bear.

"And then Harold gives me a quest. So, naturally, into the dungeon I go, but what do I find? Rats? Easy experience and loot galore? No. No, of course not. I find Kobolds. Two at a time and a boss that nearly kills me, all the while going on about Death and how it comes for us all. And it takes everything I've got just to survive, but you know what? I do it. I win. But my new sword is chipped and I still feel afraid and alone and so far out of my element that it's hard to breathe. I don't know. You tell me, does that sound like a handout to you?"

No one blinked. No one said a word.

Even the people in the surrounding booths and tables stopped talking.

An awkward silence was all that remained.

"I'm sorry," Raven said, lowering her eyes. "I guess I never really thought about any of this from your perspective. I didn't mean to belittle the trials you've gone through. I can honestly see how it must have been really hard for you."

The sudden gentleness of her words struck me harder than a swift rebuke. Who was this woman? She wasn't as soothing as Ayva had been, but she wasn't as hard or as harsh as the woman I thought I'd met in the woods.

"No, I'm sorry," I whispered, picking up my glass with a trembling hand. "I guess I'm still trying to process everything. I... I love my daughter. I love all my kids. I mean it. They always saw the best in me and I guess on some level I'm still trying to come to terms with that. And with all of this."

Attia reached out her hand but, before I could stop myself, I pulled away. I suppose something inside of me knew that no amount of soothing could take away the pain. I might find temporary relief in her touch, but it couldn't last. This was something I had to handle on my own.

Harold cleared his throat.

"What's all this?" he asked. "Never before have I seen such long faces with a bottle of my finest open on the table."

"It's my fault," I said, feeling sheepish. "It must be something in the air tonight."

Harold looked at me, considering my words. "Yes. That's not far from the truth. Is it? A strange night, indeed. Nothing for it, though. Business is good. Life goes on and all that."

When I didn't respond, he continued. "Miss Leah tells me you have news for me, is that right? Something from Widow Wilson, I presume?"

I handed him the package.

Harold looked at it for a long while before opening a small note and shifting a hand into his apron. After a bit of fumbling, he retrieved a pair of dented spectacles and began to read.

Breaths were held while his eyes traced each line of text and it seemed as if he might never speak, leaving the rest of my companions to exchange curious glances across the table. But, at last, he looked up with a stern expression.

"Hmph," he grunted. "Seems I was right about you, Denton."

Not knowing what to say in response, I remained silent and hoped the man might provide a better hint at his meaning.

A slow smile warmed his face. "Margaret is a good friend of mine. We go way back, you see. I suppose you could say we're like family," he went on. "What you did for her tonight, that was no simple thing. And it won't be soon forgotten. I can assure you of that."

Taken aback, I did my best to handle the compliment with some sense of poise and dignity.

"Thank you," I managed to mumble. The words felt like concrete in my mouth.

Harold looked at each of my companions in turn and then smiled. "Quite the group of Travelers you've managed to stumble into, if you can excuse an old man's bold observations. Would you mind if I include them on the next part of your quest? One can never really know for sure in this crazy world of ours, but something tells me you may find yourself glad for the help."

Before I could answer, I felt an over-eager kick from under the table. Looking up, there was no mistaking the source. Ely's eyes were as wide as saucers and a stupid smile played about his lips.

I took a sip of my cordial to chase away the sudden dryness in my mouth and nodded.

"Very well," Harold said with a light chuckle. "If you wouldn't begrudge a fellow a bit of time to manage his business, I'll give Denton his reward and get the particulars in order once this crowd has thinned. Fair?"

"Fair," we all agreed.

Several pairs of watchful eyes cast furtive glances toward our table long after Harold had slipped back into the crowd and emerged once again behind the bar.

"Well," Attia said, keeping her voice low. "We seem to have found ourselves a bit of unwanted attention."

"At least most of it seems benign," Pops grunted.

"How—" I began to ask.

Ely chuckled. "Open your Party interface. The old man must have grouped us up, that's why Pops can sense external aggro levels. Am I right?"

Pops let out a silent chuckle of his own and smiled.

"Well, so much for keeping things low-key," Raven said. "Then again, something tells me we're about to have bigger concerns than a little attention in Harold's tavern."

This made me think of her earlier promise to explain her disappearance. I couldn't help but hear the words echoing in my mind.

'... you never know who might be listening.'

I took another sip and swallowed hard.

Attia's brow furrowed. "What do you mean?"

"I think Denton was right," Raven said. Then added, without waiting for a response, "Something feels different. All these people must feel it to. Did you see the sky above the swamp?"

"There was a black cloud," Attia said. "Like black smoke, but not like smoke. Not exactly."

"Almost like a shadow." Pops nodded.

"Whatever it is," Raven said, "I think it explains why so many would flock to the city. The question is, what does this shadow mean for Fort Morrow?"

"And, more importantly, what does it mean for us," Ely added.

31

It was nearly two hours later when Harold finally stepped out from behind the counter and made his way back to our booth. The two bottles of strawberry cordial Raven bought were long gone, and we were nursing a third that Attia, Ely, and Pops had pooled their spare coins to procure.

I'd offered to pitch in, but apparently the prospect of a group quest was more than enough to cover my share.

"Still pretty busy out here," Harold said to no one in particular as he neared the table. He stopped to wipe his hands on his apron before continuing. "I don't reckon it'll be dying down anytime soon. There's more gossip to be had than I know what to do with, that's for sure."

Smiles faded and flushed cheeks sobered at the prospect of waiting even deeper into the night.

"Never you mind, though," he went on. "I won't keep you any longer. If you'll follow me down to the cellar, we might just find ourselves a bit of privacy. What do you say? I'm sure Leah can handle things while we're gone."

The question hung on the air until I realized the others were waiting for me to answer.

"Sure," I said with a shrug and without an ounce of ceremony.

The cordial had put a fine finish on an extremely long and arduous day. My eyelids drooped. Each blink seemed to last just a little longer than the one before it. Stifling a yawn, I slid out of the booth behind Raven and followed as Harold made his way toward the cellar door behind the bar.

Every Traveler who knew anything about the establishment, and many of the newcomers who didn't, watched in silence. Only a few raucous voices carried the weight of the still-full tavern. A pair of dice tumbled and rolled across a wooden tabletop. When the clatter stopped, a winner's cheer punctuated our descent into the most sacred area of Harold's domain.

In the hour of our waiting, I'd learned a little about Harold's Tavern and the famous strawberry cordial I'd become acquainted with. As it turned out, Harold and his ambrosia-like beverage were famous well outside the walls of Fort Morrow. What's more, rumor had it there wasn't a single proprietor of inn, tavern, or bar who wouldn't part with a handsome sum of gold to find a copy of his recipe in their possession.

And the cellar was where the magic happened.

It wasn't at all like the dark dungeon that lurked below Margaret's kitchen. Instead, flames danced at regular intervals, held aloft like beacons in beautifully ornate wall sconces. Oaken kegs were stacked in perfectly aligned racks that ran perpendicular to the far wall like long aisles of books in a library.

I knew very little of the tavern business, but I suspected the contents of one rack alone could be worth tens of thousands of gold. Even more if the kegs were filled with Harold's special strawberry concoction.

Out of the corner of my eye, I caught a glimpse of Ely licking his lips and rubbing his massive paws together. I smiled, to which he merely shrugged and returned my grin with a sheepish one of his own.

Finally, upon reaching a large table adorned with scrolls and brewing implements, Harold stopped and turned.

"There," he said, eyeing us all with an expression of inquisitive expectation. "Well, let's have it."

"Uhhh," I started, unsure of what else the older man was looking for.

"Bah," he said, waving me off. "You've already given me the package from Margaret. No, someone else has something for me, don't you? I can feel it in my bones. Which one of you is it? Don't make me guess."

"I'm sorry, Harold," Raven answered. "I didn't want to steal Denton's spotlight."

"Don't worry about Denton," he replied with a devious grin. "There's no harm in waiting a little longer. We'll get him straightened out before you know it. First things first."

She laughed and stepped forward, holding something small in the palm of her hand.

"A side quest?" he asked as he retrieved the object and began inspecting it. "Discovered this while you were tracking the pups, did you?"

Raven nodded.

"Not the best of omens, is it?" he asked aloud, though the question didn't appear to be meant for anyone in particular.

"What is it?" Attia asked, stepping closer.

"Corpse bloom," Harold answered with a measure of fearful reverence. "It's very rare and hasn't been seen in these parts for years. Some say it's the first sign of dark days ahead."

He handed it back to Raven and nodded. "All the same, it's quite the find and might prove to be very useful if what I suspect is true. I'll need you to deliver the flower to a friend of mine tomorrow. He's an alchemist here in Fort Morrow."

"Thank you," she said, stowing the black blossom in her inventory. Then, after she read and accepted her new quest, Harold grinned.

"Knowledge is a very precious commodity," he said, "and it should always be duly rewarded whenever possible."

Without warning, the faintest glow seemed to emanate from

Raven's skin and she looked down at her hands in awe. "Ding," she exclaimed.

The others cheered while I looked on, dumbfounded.

"I don't understand," I mumbled. "What's a ding?"

"She leveled up," Attia explained.

"Sorry," Raven said with an awkward shrug. "It's kind of a thing. Sort of a throwback to old school online gaming, or so I've heard."

Harold smiled. "I must admit, from what I gather, much of your old world is strange to me," he said, "but this tradition is one I've come to enjoy."

Then he nodded in my direction. "Prepare yourself, Denton."

I took a step back, unsure of what exactly he was suggesting I prepare myself for, when I felt the same sensation I'd encountered in the Meadows that morning. A wave of renewing energy washed over me and I closed my eyes, basking in the sheer, quiet bliss of the moment.

When the feeling subsided, I opened my eyes to see the others staring at me expectantly.

A quick look at my log confirmed my suspicions.

Quest Complete! You've completed:
Creatures in the Cellar.
You've received: 1,500 Experience Points, 50 Silver, and 100 Improved Favor with Widow Wilson.
Bonus Reward: *A length of Silver Chain.*
Congratulations, Traveler of EndWorld,
on reaching Level 3!

While the system message didn't include any words of wisdom this time around, I did notice the visible increase to my health and mana pools. 20 HP and 15 MP? Excellent.

"Uh, ding?" I said at last, feeling a goofy smile taking root at the corners of my mouth.

"Congo rats," Ely exclaimed.

"Congratulations," everyone else said in unison with warm, genuine smiles all around.

It felt good to be surrounded by friendly faces. I had to admit, for the first time since I'd arrived in this strange place, I was starting to feel like I really belonged here. Quests and leveling up felt... normal. I barely recognized myself, but the feeling was good.

"Thank you," I said before looking to Harold. "So, I take it there's something else? Another quest you need us to embark on?"

"Oh, yeah." Ely laughed, striking fist to palm. "I'm ready to smash things up a bit. Let's do this thing."

Harold merely shook his head. Then, with a sigh, he added, "Not so fast. There are dark days ahead and heavy burdens to bear. I will give you the quest, but I'm afraid you will be unable to embark until after you've rested."

Ely shrugged. "Who needs rest?" he asked rhetorically.

I made a show of raising my hand.

"It matters not," Harold explained. "You are to meet with the Captain of the Guard tomorrow evening. He will direct you where to go from there. In the meantime, I suggest you sleep and get your affairs in order."

Then he looked at me and seemed to appraise the sorry state of my gear. "You have more coin and some items to sell at the markets, I hope?"

I hadn't bothered checking my inventory after each encounter with the Kobolds, but I knew I had at least a few things I could sell. I nodded.

"Good," he said. "I suggest you do just that. And get yourself some better equipment while you're at it. Perhaps Raven can spare some time in the morning to help you out."

"Of course," Raven said, glancing in my direction. "That would be perfect."

Something in her look suggested this was exactly the kind of opportunity she'd been hoping for. Had I not been as exhausted as I was, I might have wondered what she wanted to tell me so badly or perhaps what she wanted to know. But, as it was, I was beginning to feel I'd reached my limit of curious wanderings for one day.

"Then it's settled." Harold beamed. "And now, your quest."

New Quest Alert! You've been offered a quest:
An Errand for the Captain of the Guard.
The Captain of the Guard has requested a party of able-bodied Travelers to assist with a special errand.
Meet Captain Elsbaud tomorrow evening at the Northern Gatehouse when the moon rises.
Reward: None.

Pops grunted and Ely gave voice to our immediate concern, "No reward? You can't be serious, Harold. You mean to tell me we could show up and get assigned something like latrine duty and not get a single thing for it?"

"Ha," Harold chuckled. "Some might say that the adventures of life bring their own rewards, but worry not. Captain Elsbaud will tell you the details of his quest himself. I'm quite certain he'll also explain whatever reward he might be willing to part with upon successful completion of the task. And rest assured, it will not include latrine duty."

When no one replied, he spoke again. "I'm afraid that's all the information I'm allowed to divulge at this time. I suggest you take the opportunity to rest and prepare for what the morrow may bring."

Our deflated murmurs as we accepted the quest joined in a depressed chorus. "Thanks, Harold."

"And Denton?" he added.

"Yes?"

"You might find some benefit from stopping by Margaret's again tomorrow while you're out. If you do see her, please say hello to her for me. Would you?"

Raven raised an eyebrow, but Harold's errand didn't come with an additional quest prompt.

I answered her inquiring look with the slightest shake of my head before responding to Harold's request. "Of course. As long as you don't intend to have me fighting more Kobolds."

Harold laughed long and hard before answering. "No. I promise, no more Kobolds. At least not this time."

~

I AWOKE THE NEXT MORNING TO THE SOUND OF A FIRE CRACKLING IN THE hearth. Another day in EndWorld. Rolling over, I buried my head in the soft, feather-filled pillow.

My left shoulder ached where the Kobold Boss's attack had landed. My muscles were tightly bunched and filled with a dull, resounding pain despite Attia's healing touch and the invigorating rush that came with leveling up.

I groaned and rolled over, swinging my feet over the edge of the bed and flexing my toes on the cold, wooden floorboards. Yawning, I stretched and then took a moment to rotate and massage the stiffness from my shoulder.

I wanted to spend the rest of the day in bed, but I remembered Harold's advice from the morning before. I could sleep later. There was a long list of things to do before meeting the rest of the group later that evening. And, now that I thought about it, I suppose I was growing even more eager to hear what kind of explanation Raven had in store to account for her odd behavior and why she'd disappeared.

The sight of my boots sitting next to the door brought a sarcastic smile to my lips. They were in such a sorry state that there was no mistaking it. They had to be replaced, and I was certainly no cobbler.

With that thought in mind, I finished getting dressed and was about to open the door when I was startled by the sound of a gentle knock. Pulling the lock free, I opened the door.

Raven stood on the other side of the threshold looking somewhat surprised. "Oh," she said, taking a small step backward. "Harold said you were probably sleeping, but it looks like you're all ready to take on the day."

"Something like that." I laughed. "Though I'm not going to lie, it was a real struggle."

"Is your shoulder bothering you?" she asked.

"Oh," I said, noting that my hand had resumed rubbing the stiff muscles, seemingly of its own accord. "Yeah, I took a nasty hit from the pointy end of a pickaxe. It seems like everything external has healed, but I'm still feeling pretty sore."

Raven frowned. "Even after Attia healed you last night?"

I nodded. "Maybe it's psychological?"

She bit her lip and looked away. "Maybe."

After an awkward silence she added, "You want to head down and get some breakfast before we hit the market?"

To be honest, I was half expecting her to ask to come inside, and was fully prepared to listen to a long-winded explanation of what had happened back there on the mountain.

But breakfast also sounded really good.

"If we go now, we might beat some of the crowd," she said, smiling.

Thinking back, I recalled the vast number of bodies crammed into Harold's the night before and shuddered.

That settled it. The explanation could wait.

32

Raven stared at me from across her skillet-cooked breakfast and took a slow sip of her coffee. Then, setting her mug on the tabletop, she frowned.

"What's on your mind?" I asked.

"What you said last nigh. You know, about your experiences in EndWorld so far... I know I've played a big part in all of that, and I'm sorry," she said, shifting her attention to the potatoes on her plate.

"There's a lot you haven't told me," I said, picking up my own mug and sipping the delightfully hot beverage.

"I know."

"Like, why were you out there on the mountain in the first place? Why did you disappear? And why do you look exactly like... like someone else?"

"Not here," she said, her words suddenly quiet.

"Okay, not here," I said, acquiescing once again to the delay in her explanation. "But you have to give me something."

She shrugged. "I was out on the mountain because my main quest took me there. I was supposed to stop a particular threat, but I ran into you instead. To be honest, I didn't even realize you were a Traveler right away. It wasn't until we were close to the camp that I inspected you."

"Not knowing that I was a Traveler, does that really make it any better?" I asked, thinking about the edge of her knife pressing against my throat in the darkness.

"I don't know," she answered with a wry smile, nodding toward my injured shoulder. "Should we ask the Kobolds?"

"Fair enough," I said with a chuckle. Then I refocused my attention on my plate while my mind filled in the blanks with a number of things that went bump in the night.

Things could kill you in EndWorld. Sure, it wasn't a permanent death, but it was death all the same and far from pleasant.

I suppose I'd gotten off easy. For the most part, it was only my pride that had been injured. The pain you experienced was as real here as anything I'd ever felt. And, in the heat of the moment, I could imagine a person might do just about anything to avoid that level of agony.

At least she'd bothered to inspect me first.

After several forkfuls of silence between us, I looked up again. "Will you tell me today? I mean, I don't suppose you really have to tell me at all, but I am curious."

Raven nodded. "I'll tell you today. Probably."

"Probably?" I asked, suddenly feeling a little incredulous.

She only laughed. "I will. I promise."

When we finished our meal, we each settled our bill with Leah and headed out of the tavern and onto the foggy, cobbled street. The morning air was crisp and biting, colder than I expected for late summer or even the early days of fall.

Raven pulled her hood up over her head and rubbed the warmth back into her arms. "There's something unnatural about this cold," she observed. "I wonder..."

"What is it?" I asked, noting the concern in her voice.

"It's probably nothing." She shook her head and started walking toward the nearby shops. "You said you had items to sell, right?"

"Right," I said, hurrying to catch up.

She wove through the mingling window-shoppers and bargain hunters who were all perfectly content to mill about the byways, unperturbed by their innate ability to block foot traffic. I followed behind, though far less graceful in my pursuit.

When we reached a group of merchant stands at the edge of the square, she stopped and turned. "What sort of items do you have to unload?"

"I, well—" I pursed my lips and shrugged.

"You don't know?"

"A crude shield? Some bee stingers and several pots of honey. Maybe some other stuff, but I haven't really checked," I admitted, suddenly feeling a little sheepish for my decision to avoid the bother of keeping track of the loot from my dungeon run.

"Do you have any pieces of gear you could equip, or is this where we're starting from?" she asked, gesturing toward my now-shabby attire.

Again, I shrugged.

"You really don't know? How is that even possible?" Her words were stern, and yet it was clear she was smiling.

"I guess you could say I'm a little out of my element," I quipped. "I mean, come on. Who else dies to a rabbit the first time they draw their sword?"

"Actually, you'd be surprised," she said, chuckling from beneath her cowl.

"Well, okay. Maybe I'm not the only noob, but it's pretty clear I've got a lot to learn."

"We all do," she said. "Look, don't worry about what you have and haven't done or whether someone else seems to be fitting in better than you are. It isn't that simple. Life is complicated here, for every-one. Just take things one step at a time."

I nodded. "Fair enough, I suppose."

"It's the best any of us can do, really," she added before turning to face the shops. "I'm guessing you haven't messed with many of your system settings. You still have auto-sorting of your inventory enabled?"

"I didn't turn it off, if that's what you're asking. Stackable items still pop up in neat stacks. I'm guessing it's enabled?"

"Good. The advanced settings can be really useful, if you spend the time to tweak them, but for now the defaults will make our little errand a whole lot easier," she said. "Come on. Follow me."

Within a few short strides, I found myself standing in a dimly lit herb shop. The dusty aroma of dried herbs and flowers caressed my senses, leaving me feeling almost intoxicated by a myriad of pleasant scents.

Raven took one look at me from beneath her hood and shook her head. "Madam Comfrey's got quite the concoction brewed up this morning. Better let me do the talking."

"Uh huh," I said before I'd even managed to process her words. "That sounds great."

"Actually," she reconsidered, "maybe you'd better wait outside. Here, do this: think about your inventory and tell it to sort by item type. Then trade me your honeycomb, the bee stingers, and any other roots or items that show up in the alchemical ingredients list. I'll take care of this transaction."

"Okay."

The sorting was easy, but then I paused for a second, thinking about the logistics of handing her a massive pile of sticky honeycomb.

"Is there an easier way to do this?" I asked. "Can I trade items without pulling them out and physically handing them to you?"

"Yes," she answered. "Just visualize them in your inventory and then sort of will them to me. You should get a system message to confirm the transaction if you do it right."

Trade Pending.
Would you like to trade Raven Cross the following items:
1 Elemental Shard
48 Honeycomb
32 High Quality Honeycomb
13 Intact Bee Stingers

112 *Insect Wings*
Yes. | No.

"Yes," I said aloud.

"Oh, goodness. It sounds like I have a visitor. Please, do come in," Madam Comfrey cooed from somewhere deep inside the shop.

Raven grabbed my arm, yanking me to a stop before I realized I was moving. "Trade them," she hissed.

"I did," I whispered back, then read the error in my chat log. "Oh, wait. It didn't go through. I had a bound item."

"It's fine," she said, still keeping her grip firm and her tone low. "Just trade me the non-bound items."

A few seconds later, I'd manage to transfer everything but the elemental shard I'd received upon defeating the golem in the tutorial.

Raven nodded and shoved me outside the shop.

"I'll be there in a moment, Madam Comfrey," I heard her holler. "I was just browsing."

The door clanged shut, and I was once again surrounded by the growing crowd of morning shoppers.

"Hey, you. Give me ten silver," an unpleasant male voice commanded.

I looked at the miscreant and his companion and frowned. "Uh, no?"

"See, I told you," his buddy said. "It doesn't work like that. Maybe it has to be a chick, or maybe it only works for the herbalist."

I blinked. "You mean that smell in there?"

They both nodded and the first one spoke.

"Sorry about that," he said. "She robbed me blind in there with what she paid for my items. I was just trying to figure out how she did it."

"Sure," I chuckled. "And you were planning to give the coins right back if it had worked, right?"

The guy shrugged and flashed a twisted grin. "I probably would have kept them, to be honest. You know, all in the name of science."

"In the name of science," his friend mocked, thrusting a fist into the air.

"We could wait for that chick that went in with him," the guy suggested, rubbing his chin. "Maybe it works on the opposite sex?"

"Or," I said, placing my hand on the hilt of Truthseeker, "you could get lost."

"You can't use that here," the friend retorted, glancing at my ornate scabbard and the state of my shabby clothes.

"Oh, I assure you," I said, taking a step forward and projecting a confidence I didn't really feel. "This is the finest weapon Jörgen Olsen has ever forged. I can use it and it will be quite effective, despite the appearance of my armor. And, once I've informed the guards that you're trying to rip off innocent Travelers within the city walls, I'm sure they'd understand. In fact, I've got a meeting with Captain Elsbaud tonight. What did you say your names were, again?"

The two looked at one another in silence before backing off and vanishing into the growing crowd.

I was still grinning when Raven emerged from the herbalist's shop. It felt good to not only stand up for myself, but to have the opportunity to stand up for someone else for a change; even if she could most definitely take care of herself.

"Here," Raven said, handing me the bee stingers and 75 silver coins. "She drove a hard bargain for the rest of it, but her price was way too low for these. Probably best to put them on the auction house. They're too rare to sell at a steep discount, and besides, she'd just raise the price and use her herbs to entice a sale."

"How does she get away with it?" I asked, thinking of the encounter with her previous victims.

"Aside from the fact that a fair majority of the guards are guys?"

"Yeah, aside from that," I said, feeling a burst of heat on my cheeks.

"You'll find a lot of towns have their shady characters," she said without emotion. "Everyone serves their purpose in a way. Harold is a key part of both our stories, Ely's too, but the folks at the Bearded

Goat probably wonder why he runs such a shady-looking establishment."

"You're saying Madam Comfrey is someone's Harold?"

"Probably." She shrugged.

~

THE AUCTION HOUSE WAS PACKED. LONG LINES STREAMED FROM EACH OF the windows, where Travelers and native EndWorlders alike posted their goods and placed bids on every kind of item imaginable.

"Most low-level gear is best purchased directly from vendors or trade workers," Raven explained as we waited. "You can find the occasional good deal here but, as you can see, the wait can be substantial."

"Is it always this busy?" I asked.

"Not always. Once people start heading out the gates to quest and farm, it starts to calm down a little. That's usually when the crafters come to replenish their auctions and buy the more commonly farmed materials."

Despite the long lines, the pace was deceptively quick. One by one, the Travelers in front of us wove their way back from the window. Some wore smiles of triumph, while others were clearly disappointed with the outcome of their transactions.

Within about ten minutes, I found myself face-to-face with a cheery-eyed blonde who flashed me a disarming smile.

"Good morning," she said. "How can I be of assistance?"

"Good morning. I would like to sell these," I said, proffering the bee stingers.

She inspected them one by one before placing them gently on the counter. "Thirteen **Intact Bee Stingers**," she recited. "How would you like to post them?"

Raven stepped closer and withdrew her hood. "Can you tell us about the recent sales and current listings?"

The attendant looked to me for confirmation.

"Yes, please," I agreed, flashing a smile of my own.

"One moment," the attendant said.

She opened a very large ledger and began flipping through the pages. Then, upon finding the section she was looking for, she ran her finger along the lines of text.

"Ah, yes. Here we are," she exclaimed upon finding the information. "It appears this item is a very rare ingredient at the moment. There are only two intact specimens listed on the regional market. Several have sold in the last few days."

"How much?" Raven asked.

Again, the attendant looked to me for confirmation.

I nodded.

"The two available items are listed for 10 silver a piece. Historical sales suggest a median purchase price of around 12.5 silver per specimen of this quality."

"Buy them both," Raven said.

Shrugging, I returned my attention back to the attendant. "I guess I'm buying them."

"That will be 20 silver coins, please."

After handing the woman the fee, I waited while she opened a cabinet and retrieved the stingers. Once she placed them in my hands, Raven motioned for me to hand them back.

"Now list them in three groups of five. Minimum bid: 15 silver for each stinger, purchase price: 20 silver apiece. Auction duration: 48 hours."

This time the attendant smiled and offered her hands without waiting for a confirmation. "You understand there will be a five percent auction fee associated with this transaction, to be collected at the time of sale?"

"I do now," I agreed. It didn't take a math genius to realize just how good of an opportunity I'd somehow managed to stumble upon.

"And you agree to these terms?"

"Sure."

"Please say either yes or no, sir," the attendant prompted.

"Oh, sorry. Yes. I agree to the terms."

"Thank you. One moment, please."

I turned to Raven and smiled. "That was relatively painless."

"Excuse me, sir?" the attendant asked.

I looked back and raised an eyebrow. "Yes?"

"Your auction has ended."

When she slid a stack of coins across the counter, the meaning behind her words became clear.

2 gold, 85 silver.

I gulped and willed the coins into my inventory.

"Will there be anything else?"

Raven flashed me a mischievous grin and jerked her head toward a row of shops, replacing her hood as she turned.

"I think that will be all. Thanks for your help," I said, then turned to follow my guide through the crowd before I lost sight of her completely.

"You are very welcome, and thank you for your business," the woman called after us as we fought to break free of the growing lines.

Once we had reached an open section of the cobbled street, Raven stopped and turned to face me.

"So, there you have it. That's pretty much the auction house on the best of days."

"That was amazing," I said, still in awe of how quickly the stingers had sold.

"Just be careful," she warned. "Until you really start to understand how the market works here, it's probably best to limit yourself to the occasional dabble."

While I could understand the logic of what she was saying, my mind kept returning to the thought of farming the Meadows for more stingers. Sure, it would take a few hours, but I had a good system down.

I could almost count the coins pouring in with each drop.

"Tempting, isn't it?" she asked. "You're thinking about heading back out there and grinding out a few more drops?"

Sheepishly, I nodded.

"It probably wouldn't be all that bad of an idea." She shrugged. "Then again, maybe someone in line witnessed the transaction and is already on their way. Or maybe the person who bought those stingers got enough to maximize the skill gain of a particular craft. You could spend all day farming and flood the market. Next thing you know, they aren't worth a single silver."

"You think so?" I asked, suddenly feeling confused by the flurry of mixed signals.

"I don't know," she said. "But I do know we've got a group quest to prepare for and you need new gear. Let's see what tomorrow brings before we start daydreaming about striking it rich on low-level mobs. Fair?"

"Yeah." I sighed. "That's fair."

"Don't worry." Raven flashed me a disarming smile. "I'm sure there will be plenty of time to farm and make gold. You're practically surrounded by endless opportunities."

"I know, and I don't mean to come off as being ungrateful," I said. "I really appreciate what you did back there. I mean, I could have made out like the two chumps milling about the herb shop, angry and wondering how they got duped into selling their wares dirt cheap."

She nodded and leaned close. "So, what do you say we do something about those horrendous clod-hoppers you're kicking around in?"

33

The sun rose further in the sky and more anxious bodies filled the now-fogless streets. Far above, high, wispy clouds raced across the horizon, pulled by an invisible force while the air inside the fort walls remained eerily calm, cold, and oppressive.

"What's next?" I asked. "Armor?"

"A cobbler, to be more specific." Raven grinned from beneath her hood. "We can sort through the rest of your gear after that."

"A cobbler?" I chuckled, immediately thinking of a delicious, fruit-filled cake baked in a dutch oven. "But we just ate."

She was unimpressed with my joke.

"Why don't we just hit an armor shop and knock it out in one fell swoop?" I pressed. "Would a cobbler be that much cheaper?"

"Cheaper? No. Sure, you could buy your boots from any old armorer in town, if you were so inclined," she replied.

Frowning, I scratched at the stubble of beard on my cheek. "Why not, then?"

Raven started walking again. "You completed the tutorial, right? Light armor is one thing, but making a decent pair of boots takes specialized skill. Just look around. You think you're the only one flashing their piglets?"

She was right, of course. I looked down at my feet and felt a flush of embarrassment at seeing my exposed toenails, encrusted with dirt and grime as they were. It reminded me of the simple things I hadn't really taken the time to miss, like a hot shower or a nice, warm soak to soothe my aching muscles.

There it was. More bellyaching about the things I missed. I guess I'd been so focused on my own experience that I hadn't really taken much stock of the other Travelers around me.

Maybe it was easier to see my own struggle while assuming everyone else had it all together. This made me think of Zack and his mismatched sleeves.

Finally, I was beginning to see the bigger picture.

"When it comes to buying boots," she continued, "it's best to see an expert if you want them to last. Otherwise, you could end up with gear that looks like that," she said, pointing to the worn footwear of a Traveler standing in line at a stall as we passed.

I glanced at the boots and understood. It was more than just gear or loot. By actually looking at the people standing and walking along the street, I saw a much different story than the one I'd been telling myself.

Lopsided shirts and uneven pant legs were common. Most boots were just as bad or worse than my own. On occasion, I spotted the rare normal-looking piece of gear sticking out amidst a tutorial-made outfit ensemble. And now that I was paying attention, I realized those new pieces were a clear indicator of a person who was catching their stride: an upgrade.

But not all upgrades were created equal.

"You see? All these people and we're not so different," Raven observed. "The trick is in learning how things work here. It's confusing at first, but if you stop and listen, pay attention to the world around you, and watch what other people do, it isn't so hard."

I nodded my head in agreement and matched her stride. We walked the rest of the way to the cobbler's establishment in silence, and I found myself unable to keep my eyes off the other Travelers we passed.

The more I looked, the more I saw the confusing newness reflected in their eyes. And that overwhelmed gaze as they took in their surroundings was a direct translation of the way I'd felt when I first entered the fort.

Now that I thought of it, it wasn't just Zack's sleeves that had been mismatched. All of his gear had been equally out of sorts. He was just a kid, a Frost Mage traveling from here to there in search of arcane magic. And yet, he seemed to fit in. By all appearances he had been in his element, flitting through the menus like an old pro. I was starting to realize there was a lot more to all of this than I'd first considered.

Raven was right. I wasn't alone. Instead, I was surrounded by people who probably felt just as lost as I did.

THE COBBLER'S SHOP WAS AN OPEN-AIR STALL TUCKED BETWEEN TWO larger stores. As we drew near, I couldn't help but turn my nose. It reeked of burnt leather and the acrid stench of industrial glue so strongly that I could almost feel my nostril hairs curling in the fumes.

A tiny, old man standing doubled over a shoehorn looked up and grunted a hello without missing a beat. His tool worked back and forth in a blur of motion, scraping and sliding against the leather in perfect rhythm. Meanwhile, his shaggy canine companion glanced in our direction before letting out a depressed huff of indifference.

"Who do we have here, Rufus?" the man asked.

As if in response, the dog lifted one hairy eyebrow and tucked his nose under a paw.

"Ah, don't mind him," the man said, returning his attention to the boot he was working on. "He's still sore I wouldn't let him chew on that mangled piece of rawhide some greenhorn tried to sell me this morning."

Rufus snorted and let out another sigh before closing his eyes.

"The name's Jasper," the man added, "and if it's shoes or boots you're after, you've come to the right place. If it's advice or quests, I'm afraid I'm fresh out of both."

"Boots will be fine," Raven said, taking a step toward Rufus.

"Be careful," Jasper warned. "He isn't always the friendliest to strangers."

The dog yawned and stretched, then nuzzled his head against Raven's hand.

"Well, I'll be..." Jasper grunted. "It appears the old fleabag is just full of surprises this morning."

He took one look at Raven's pristine black leather boots and smiled before resting his eyes on my sorry excuses for footwear. The smile melted, and he glanced back at Rufus before meeting my gaze.

"Oh, my. Tell you what, son," he said. "Let's start this little transaction of ours off right, shall we? I'll buy those boots off you if you're keen to part with them. How does a silver a piece sound?"

I shrugged. The boots were all but done for anyway and I honestly couldn't see any reason not to sell them. After all, if his prices were too far off the mark, I could always find another shop and I wasn't above walking barefoot if I had to.

I glanced at Raven, hoping to gauge her reaction to Jasper's offer.

She shrugged and went back to petting Rufus.

"Deal," I said, bending down to unlace and remove the boots.

Once I'd handed them over, Jasper ripped off the soles with a few deft motions and a flick or two of his tool. Then he tossed the hard bottoms to the side and passed the gnarled leather to his dog.

Rufus began chewing in earnest.

It felt strange watching the fruit of my labors being torn to shreds by the mangy mutt, and yet it was oddly satisfying. I hated those boots.

"Well, then," Jasper said, standing and wiping his hands on his leather apron. "Would you like the coins now? Or shall I take it off the cost of your purchase?"

I wiggled my cold toes and leaned back on my heels. "Hold onto it for now. Let's see what you've got."

Jasper looked me over and I felt his eyes linger on Truthseeker for the briefest of moments.

"Some blade you've got there," he observed. "Jörgen's work?"

I nodded.

"Hasn't exactly been a perfect fit, has it?"

My heart thudded in my chest and I found myself fighting a strange mix of emotions. Some of the feelings were hard to identify, but two were quite clear.

On one hand, I was still ashamed that I had half-ruined an amazing weapon with my inability to fully bind the blade. And on the other, I felt the burning sting of embarrassment with the knowledge that even a humble cobbler could see my shortcomings.

"No," I said at last, thinking about the new chip in the steel as a result of my latest adventures. "I suppose it hasn't, though I'm sure it isn't due to any fault of Jörgen's, nor the blade's for that matter."

"Right you are," Jasper exclaimed. "A fine smith and a fine weapon, yes."

Although I knew it was true, his words stung, cutting deeper than the Kobold Boss's pickaxe strike.

"But make no mistake, you don't appear to be half-bad yourself," he added, giving me a nod. "A simple mismatch, I might say, and I don't think you'd find many who would disagree. Don't you worry. While I can't do anything about the blade, you won't find a more skilled cobbler in the whole region. I guess you could say that boots are my specialty. We won't be making the same mistake, mark my words."

"Consider them marked," I said, suddenly unable to resist a smile.

Raven stood and gave Rufus one last pat on the head and a scratch behind the ear. "I'll leave you two to your business, then."

"You're leaving?" I asked.

She stopped, but didn't turn around. "Only for a bit," she said, dipping her cloaked head low. "I have to check up on something, but it won't take long. I'll be back before you know it."

"Right." I chuckled. "Promises, promises. Now, where did I hear something like that before?"

"Ah, let the woman go," Jasper said, waving a dismissive hand in her direction. "It's probably for the best. Crafting the right pair of boots isn't always the easiest of tasks and it takes time."

"It's okay," I said. "I was just teasing."

"Oh, I see." The cobbler stroked his chin in thought, turning to Rufus as he did. "Teasing such a formidable-looking Shadowdancer? It seems this one likes to live on the cusp of danger. We'll have to keep that in mind while we craft his boots."

"See, Denton," Raven called back just before disappearing into the crowd, a humorous edge unmistakable in her voice. "I told you Jasper knew his stuff."

And then she was gone.

Minutes trickled by while Jasper worked in silence, first measuring every imaginable angle of one foot and then the other before setting about the task of customizing the soles of my new footwear.

"Just you wait, Denton my boy," he said at last, punctuating a renewed flurry of movement with his tool. "Once you've slipped your feet into a pair of my boots, you won't ever see footwear the same again."

"I'm going to hold you to it," I said, wiggling the warmth back into my exposed toes for the umpteenth time.

Long minutes trickled by and the steady rhythm of Jasper's handiwork became the backbone of the mid-morning chorus. Voices and clanging armor and the clamor of tools joined together to create a unique melody.

This, I realized, was the song of Fort Morrow.

Rufus twitched and kicked his feet, the scraps of my old boots discarded. A pathetic growl escaped his slumber before he went calm once more. Then the canine's chest heaved with a heavy sigh and Jasper let out a gentle chuckle.

"It's good to have friends," he said, nodding toward the dog. "Take ol' Rufus, here. He showed up one day when he was just a pup. I tried to shoo him off, if truth be told, but he stuck around. And I'm glad he did."

Unsure of what to say, I appraised the mutt in silence before I spoke.

"How long has it been?" I asked.

"Five? Six years now?"

I nodded.

"What about you?" he prompted. "What's the nature of the bond between you and that mysterious and good looking companion of yours? Friendship, or perhaps something more?"

"I don't quite know, to be honest," I said with a shrug, a little surprised by my own candid response. "About the friendship part, anyway. I guess we might be friends? It's kind of hard to say."

"I see," Jasper said. "Perhaps in time things will become clear. But, if you'll indulge an old man, may I offer a piece of advice?"

"Sure."

"If there's one thing I've learned in my long years, it's that friendship is a precious thing, and true friends are hard to come by. A true friend would do almost anything for you. That isn't something to take for granted."

He paused for the briefest of moments and the world seemed almost silent for the lack of rhythm from the pounding and scraping of his tools. "And that goes double for you, young lady."

Looking up with a snap, I watched Raven stroll into the cobbler's workspace. Nothing about her appearance had changed, but something felt different. She looked relieved.

Lowering her hood, she revealed a coy smile. Then she tossed the old man a wink and sat down beside me.

"Making progress, I see," she observed.

"Almost done, as a matter of fact. Just a few minor touches and we'll be ready to test the fit," Jasper replied.

"Did you find what you were looking for?" I asked, trying to keep my mind from dwelling on how much of the previous conversation she might have heard.

"I did," she answered.

Though her response was short, there was an unmistakable

thread of calm satisfaction in her voice. Whatever her errand, it was clear the results had worked out in her favor.

"There," Jasper announced. "Try these on for size." He handed me the pair of finished boots and leaned back, waiting for me to put them on.

> *You receive **Fencer's Boots of Focus.***
> [Feet] *Defense: 3*
> *Stamina +3, Intellect +3*
> *Strength +1, Dexterity +1.*
> *Requirement: Level 3.*
> *Quality: Excellent.*
> *Rarity: Rare.*
> *Armor Class: Medium.*
> *Durability: 10/10.*

To my surprise, it appeared as if my health and mana dropped significantly upon donning and binding the boots. I blinked in disbelief until I realized what had happened.

I hadn't taken damage or inadvertently cast a spell. The increase in stats had directly increased my resource pools without filling them.

"The buffs to Stamina and Intellect increase my health and mana?" I asked with a grin, expressing my appreciation for the cobbler's fine work.

Jasper nodded. "Three points each. I worked in a point to Strength and Dexterity as well. That should help even the odds a little when it comes to melee combat."

"Wow," I breathed, still having a hard time coming to grips with how much of a difference those stat points made.

Just by equipping the boots, I'd gained thirty points to both resource pools. And that was on top of whatever battle prowess the secondary stats lent to the mix.

"These are great," I added, noting Jasper's grin of approval. "You were right. I'll never look at a pair of boots the same way again. How much do I owe you?"

"35 silver, less two for those old scraps. That brings the total to 33 silver pieces."

After the briefest moment of consideration, I gladly forked over the coins. It was a steep price, enough to pay for three more nights at Harold's Tavern and a small meal, but there was no denying just how big of a difference this one piece of gear would make.

I thanked Jasper and said my goodbyes, shaking his hand and tossing a nod toward Rufus.

Of course, the dog wasn't at all concerned about our departure, having found a renewed interest in the scraps of my previous boots.

"One more thing," the old man called as we stepped back onto the cobbled street.

I stopped and turned.

"Sword or no sword, I think you're going to do great things, Denton. There's no doubt about that. But do me a favor, will you?"

"Absolutely," I answered in earnest.

"Don't go forgetting about ol' Jasper when you hit your stride. There will always be loot from treasure chests and dungeons and the like, but come back and see me from time to time and I'll fix you up right."

I smiled. "You've got yourself a deal."

Raven walked a short distance before she stopped. Then, without speaking so much as a word, she turned and considered me for a moment from the shadow of her hood.

"What is it?" I asked, unable to shake the uncomfortable weight of her gaze.

"You're going to do great things, Denton Wade," she said with a smirk.

"Oh, come off it," I quipped as I resumed course, but she didn't budge. "Are we going to get armor or not?"

"Actually..."

I stopped walking and turned to face her, waiting for what might come next and fighting to stand my ground amidst the shuffling bodies of the crowd.

Then she was gone.

34

Merchants lining the busy market-way continued hawking their wares, shouting pitches to the crowd that mingled ceaselessly around me. Bodies shoved and shifted. Then the space Raven once occupied was filled; her vacancy completely erased by a world that had moved on, unaware of her sudden absence.

A passerby bumped my shoulder while my mind struggled to comprehend what had just happened. The jostle sent me into a collision course with a woman who was weaving her way as she hurried to who knows where.

"Watch it," she exclaimed, leaving me to mumble my apology in her wake.

Then I felt the warmth of a body pressing close against my back and the gentle whisper of an exhale upon my neck.

The hairs on my nape stiffened and my breath caught within my chest.

"Boo," Raven whispered, sending a chill down my spine.

The word was almost too quiet to hear amidst the clamor of the throng, but the action reminded me of our first encounter on the mountainside. Only this time, I didn't have the edge of a dagger at my throat.

I turned and blinked away my disbelief.

"How did you—"

"I'm a Shadowdancer," she said coolly, as if that somehow explained everything. Then she smiled, revealing her amusement at my confused expression.

"Do you want those answers I promised you earlier?" she asked.

I nodded.

"Come with me," she said, taking my hand and leading me through the crowd and away from the area that housed Harold's Tavern.

After several minutes of dodging occupied shoppers and merchants alike, we finally stood in the shadow of an impressive bell tower. The rough-cut gray stone blocks were stacked with perfection. The structure was as formidable as any of the sleek walls that made up the fort's defenses.

Craning my neck to see, I noticed the tower stretched a good story and a half above the surrounding buildings. Far above, the massive, metallic bell glinted in the filtered sunlight as it started to heave first one way and then the other.

Twelve rich notes reverberated off the walls and buildings, singing the announcement of the hour to any who might care to listen.

"Here?" I asked once the bell's song faded, still looking upward.

"Not quite," Raven said. "You might want to make sure you breathe. Closing your eyes might help a little, too."

She gripped my hand tighter, and the world faded from view as I felt myself slip into the void that existed somewhere deep within the tower's shadow.

We emerged from the inky blackness once and then twice more, each time just long enough for Raven to use the tower's rough stone wall as a foothold. With quick, deft movements she propelled us upward before slipping back into the nothingness.

My stomach lurched as the sudden motion stopped and I struggled to brace myself. Beside me, Raven's chest heaved. She flopped down on the hard stone, laughing with what sounded like equal parts elation and exhaustion.

"I've never gone that far before." She gasped. "Certainly not with a passenger. Whew. My stamina is beyond depleted."

Chancing a quick look over the tower's edge, I felt my legs begin to falter. The ground spun with dizzying abandon as my mind tried to comprehend the impossible vertical distance we'd somehow managed to travel.

"You'd probably better sit before you end up falling," she warned. "Here, eat this. It should help with the jitters a bit."

"Thanks." I took the small piece of cured meat she held aloft and sat next to her, tearing off a chunk with my teeth.

"Don't mention it."

I chewed in silence, savoring the combination of smoke and spices and recounting memories from a different life. Like eating beef jerky with my dad on camping trips when I was just a boy.

Memory after memory played in my mind and, just as she'd said, my nerves began to calm.

For several long minutes we looked out across the fort in silence, watching with detached interest as unsuspecting people milled about the streets below.

I wanted to know so much, but I hesitated. Asking now didn't seem right, and yet the silence was beginning to wear at me.

"What I wouldn't give for a water balloon right about now," I said, finally giving in to my desire to break the quiet.

We both laughed.

It felt nice to enjoy a moment like this with someone. Laughing. Not overthinking every little thing.

With everything that had happened over the past few days, it was good just to get out of my head, if even just for a little while. No more reminders of what I'd left behind. Of what had been taken from me. A moment without the plague of regret.

"Who are you," she asked, looking me dead in the eye.

I shrugged, doing my best not to betray the shock I felt at her sudden question. "I'm me. Just a guy with a sword in a digital world."

"Just a guy with a sword, huh?" She didn't sound convinced.

I pointed to Truthseeker nestled in its scabbard.

"You know what I mean," she said, rolling her eyes.

After a brief pause, she changed tactics. "Look, I'll just cut to the chase. Some of the things you've said lead me to believe you aren't who you say you are. But you've somehow managed to gain Harold's trust."

"Uh. I guess so? I'm not sure what you want me to say."

"Denton, gaining Harold's trust... that's no small feat. And frankly, I'm confused. Did you work for Cyberternal, is that it? Did we know each other?"

"I never worked for Cyberternal Industries." I shook my head. "You'd think I'd be a lot better at all of this if I had. And as far as when we met, for all I know, it was in the woods with a pack of dire wolves hot on my heels."

She looked away and seemed to voice her thoughts aloud. "Or maybe you're just putting on a good show of being a total noob, trying to get close to me. But why?

"What would someone from the company want with me now? I've been trying to wrap my mind around it. I can't think of a single thing. I mean, if you're here, you're just as dead as I am. It's not like either of us are getting out of this place alive."

"I don't work for the company." I chuckled, but then sobered when I realized she was being completely serious. "I never did. I promise. My noobishness is, unfortunately, one-hundred percent legit."

"Are you sure?" She smiled. "I was going to say, you could probably stand to dial it down a bit. The act might be a little more convincing that way."

"Ouch," I said, grabbing my chest in mock desperation, as if her words had dealt a mortal blow to my heart.

"I don't know," I added. "All things considered, I don't think I'm doing all that bad. Especially considering the fact that I didn't really sign up for any of this."

Her smile faded. "What do you mean?"

"What? That I didn't sign up for this?"

"You had to sign up for it," she said, incredulous. "There's no getting around it. There are specific laws regarding consent when it comes to digitizing a mind. Some companies might have tried to skirt that line, but Cyberternal has always followed the law to the letter."

Now it was my turn to sigh. "It's a long story."

"Try me," she insisted.

"Oh, no. I don't think so."

"Come on, why not?"

"Are you kidding me?" I asked, still smiling. "You take me all the way up here, through shadow or smoke or whatever in between, on the top of this tower, promising me the answers that I've been waiting ever so patiently for, and it's all some clever ruse to extract my sad life story? Yeah, I don't think so."

"Okay, okay," she said, nodding in appreciation of my argument. "Fair enough. I owe you some answers. You're right. What do you want to know?"

"How about: Why did you attack me up there in the mountains? Why didn't you show up at Harold's when you said you would? And why do you look just like Ayva? For starters."

"See, this is where I'm having a hard time believing you, Denton."

"What do you mean?" I asked, growing impatient. "Why do you keep turning this back on me?"

"How do you know about Ayva?"

I shrugged. So much for getting my questions answered.

"I met her. We shared a moment. And then you threatened to kill me."

Raven shook her head, ignoring the last bit. "You met her, but you've never worked for the company? You're going to have to try harder than that."

I wasn't sure what answers she was looking for, nor what information I had to give. Was I supposed to go against the supposed common wisdom of not revealing anything about my tutorial?

What was the big deal, anyway? How could the events in my tutorial impact this world?

What advantage would she gain by knowing?

Screw it.

"I met Ayva inside my tutorial."

Raven squinted her eyes at me before asking, "What did she look like?"

"She had the same dark hair as you, beautiful green eyes, but she didn't wear a hood. She wore a white dress and her laugh was like music."

"Geez." She scoffed. "You sound like a love-sick teenager."

"What," I asked, dumbfounded. "No, I mean. What?"

She laughed it off and placed a hand on my knee for the briefest of moments.

"Don't worry about it. I was just teasing you. You're being serious, though? You really met her inside your tutorial?"

I nodded.

"If that's the case, and you aren't just lying to me about not working for the company... I think something might be wrong," she said. She sounded worried.

The sudden revelation took me aback, and I stared at her, unable to find words to express all the confusing thoughts running through my head. Finally, I stumbled on a phrase that seemed to fit.

"What do you mean? What's wrong?"

She reached backward, supporting her weight on her hands and allowing the hood of her cloak to shake free from her dark, glistening hair. The depths of her green eyes were bottomless, and a sudden familiarity struck me.

The similarity between the two women was uncanny.

She sighed. "Ayva shouldn't exist. It isn't possible. On top of that, she was never programmed to interact with Travelers."

I took another bite of the jerky and began to chew, then swallowed. "Well, I don't know what to tell you. She was there. She was in my tutorial. And I'm a Traveler, right? We definitely interacted with one another."

"Did you...?"

"Did I... what?"

"Did you kill her? As part of your tutorial, I mean."

"Now you're just being ridiculous," I said. "She was my... my spirit guide? My tutorial AI? I'm not sure what the term is, but no. We didn't fight."

Raven closed her eyes, took a breath, and then looked to the sky.

"To be honest," I continued, "I thought she was just another piece of software when I first met her. But by the end, well, I guess I felt like we shared some kind of connection. Not like it matters now. I don't think I'll ever see her again."

Raven remained silent for several minutes and the air seemed to grow heavy.

"Do you feel that way about me?"

"What do you mean?"

Raven turned to me. "Like we share a connection?"

"I realize you're not the same person," I answered, doing my best not to put myself in any more of an awkward position.

After a moment of silence, I continued. "But there are some uncanny similarities between the two of you. Especially since we've been off the mountain and I've had a chance to get to know you. That first part was a little intense."

Raven smiled and then looked back down at the people below. "I'm sorry about that," she said at last. "And I suppose I do still owe you some answers."

"Answers would be nice."

"First off," she looked me in the eye, "you shouldn't have spawned on top of the mountain like that. Most people enter EndWorld at a starter location. Like a small town. There are several around Fort Morrow. Some people even spawn here."

"What determines where you spawn?"

"It depends on the choices you make in your tutorial. Before I met you, I would have said that was how it worked for everyone. It's how the system was designed, anyway."

"And Ayva?"

"Ayva was modeled after me. Her code came from my scan. She was just a template. We used her for a pre-alpha software test back in the early days, before we went live."

"A template that shouldn't exist?" I asked, thinking through the logical explanation. "So, that means you deleted her, or someone did. Maybe someone reactivated her code?"

She nodded without looking up. "It shouldn't be possible, though. I deleted her myself."

"Backups?"

"I purged the backups, too," she answered.

"That's unnerving," I said, mentally running through all the possible implications.

"It's not that I was worried about the company owning a piece of me or anything, if that's what you're thinking," she said. "It's silly, I know, but my reasons are a little more personal. I thought I had it all figured out, but then you show up claiming this old scan is still in the system. And not just in the system, but in your tutorial no less. It doesn't make any sense. I don't know how it could be true.

"I'm not saying you're lying, it's just—"

"Just what?" I asked.

"I'm not sure what I'm supposed to believe."

"I guess when you put it like that, I can see how it would be weird having someone show up out of thin air claiming what I've claimed. I don't have any explanations, and I'm sorry if I freaked you out."

"No," she said. "That's not it. I get what you're saying. I don't know why, but you don't freak me out."

"Uh, thanks?"

"You know what I mean. I'm just saying that, and I know you didn't answer before, but I feel a strange connection with you, too. Though, you definitely weren't in my tutorial. It's all very strange."

"Yeah," I muttered. "There seems to be a whole lot of strange going on these days. Just look at all those people down there. I know

I'm new here, but I think there's even more than there were last night. Shouldn't they be out questing or grinding mobs by now?"

"A good number of them, yes," Raven noted. "Look over there."

She pointed to a shadowy area a ways outside the fort walls, somewhere beyond the Meadows. "There's a darkness emanating from Duskmorrow Swamp over there."

"What's out there?" I asked.

My mind wandered back to that moment on the trail the morning before. The pull toward the shadowy undergrowth.

Something was there.

Something evil.

Something that Truthseeker had been eager to face.

Was that possible?

Did weapons have a measure of will? Desires?

"Swamps. Moss. Creatures of ill-repute." Raven smiled. "It isn't the nicest of areas on a good day, but this shadowy cloud is new. And it seems to be growing. It's gotten much closer to us than it was just yesterday, when it first showed up."

"Death comes to Fort Morrow," I recited, reflecting on my dungeon encounter in Margaret's cellar. "That's what the Kobolds said last night. Do you think my quest line has something to do with it?"

"I wouldn't think so," she said. "Individual quests aren't designed to have such a wide area of impact until much higher levels."

"Hmm," I grunted.

"Then again, Ayva was supposed to be deleted. You were supposed to spawn in a starter city. And on top of that, what are the odds the two of us encountered one another so soon after you left your tutorial? There's a lot going on that doesn't make sense."

"Seems like a fair number of coincidences within a short period of time, doesn't it?"

"It does," she agreed. "Still, it's hard to believe that a low-level quest line would have this much impact so early on. Who knows? Maybe we'll find out tonight when we join up for that group quest of yours."

"Oh, yeah," I said, scratching at my growing stubble. "I suppose you're probably right. I've got a lot to do before then if I want to get geared up. These boots are amazing, by the way. Excellent call on taking me to see Jasper. I can't wait to see what a full kit looks like."

"It makes a big difference." She nodded. "Honestly, I can't believe you completed your first solo dungeon wearing those scraps. I'm still trying to decide whether doing so makes you more of a noob or less of one."

"Nope, I'm definitely a noob." I laughed. "But, hey, I'll take lucky over good any day of the week."

She paused, eyeing me thoughtfully.

"What is it?" I asked.

"Is that it? Are you lucky, Denton?"

"As much as anyone else, I reckon," I managed to say, still a little thrown off by her unexpected question.

"And yet, you say you didn't choose to be here," she said. "Was that good luck or bad?"

"I haven't decided yet," I answered. "Just a few days ago, I was back on Earth and dying of cancer. Today I find myself sitting atop a bell tower, having a friendly chat with a woman who threatened to kill me."

"Cancer?" she asked. "You said you didn't want to be here. You didn't work for the company and you weren't a paying customer. How does that work?"

"Right?" I laughed. "I didn't have that kind of money. Besides, I never really wanted anything to do with this computerized afterlife."

"Not much of a gamer?"

"I used to play games here and there," I said. "Before I got sick. It was more of a philosophical question for me. Stuff like: What is a soul? And, is a digitized mind the same as the real deal, or are people here nothing more than finely tailored strings of code?"

"I see," she said, considering my answer. "And what do you think now that you're here?"

I shrugged, then waved a hand in front of my face. "'What is real?' Isn't that one of Cyberternal's famous tag lines? For all I know, I could be a sophisticated program running on a computerized cube on someone's desk. It wouldn't be much of a stretch considering the tech I saw in the basement."

Raven blinked at me and shook her head. "What basement?"

"At the headquarters building in Dallas," I answered. "It's surprising the place has a basement to begin with. I didn't think it was possible to go that deep without running into issues, what with the clay and water table and all. Leave it to the magic of machines, right? 126 levels. I'm guessing it went deeper than that."

"126 levels..."

"I was supposed to be going in for treatment," I explained. "Some secret medical procedure, not that it matters now. That's the last thing I remember. I stepped into the medical pod, and then I felt the fiery burn of countless nano-doctors flowing through my bloodstream. It was agony."

"Then what happened?"

"I don't know. I guess that was it for me. I was told I lived for three months after the treatments and, when everything else failed to work, I somehow changed my mind about all of this."

Raven sat up and stared at me. "That can't be right..."

"And yet, here I am," I said, stretching my arms out wide. "After a few failed attempts, they apparently had to pull data from the original scan. Imagine my surprise when I opened my eyes and found myself standing on a tropical island."

There was a long, palpable silence as Raven digested my explanation.

"I'm really sorry about almost killing you after you spawned on the mountainside," she said after a long while. "I had no idea what you'd been through."

"Nothing you can do about that now, right? But you still haven't told me why. Is it really that bad in EndWorld?"

She lowered her gaze and took a deep breath before she spoke. "I was there for my quest. You know the dire wolf pups?"

I nodded. "How could I forget?"

"Well, I was supposed to be protecting them."

"Protecting them?" I asked. "I might be a noob, but it didn't sound like they needed much protecting. Especially not from someone like me."

"No. Not from someone like you. That was my mistake, and I failed the quest because of it." She shook her head and wiped away a budding tear.

"I don't understand," I said, unsure of how to respond.

It was clear that her quest had meant a lot to her, but there was so much I still didn't know. She seemed so tough, and yet the loss of her quest objective had obviously shaken her.

"You wanted to know why I didn't show up at Harold's."

I nodded.

"I doubled back to that spot on the mountain to check on the pack. I went to finish my quest. Then, when I was halfway there, I got the notification. Quest failed. It took some time to figure out what happened."

"What was it," I asked.

"Those three Travelers. Sven and Guilly and Ruby. They must have used their rabbits as bait, lured the smallest pup away from her mother, and then they took her."

"I thought they said they were headed to the arena?" I said in protest. In truth, I didn't want to believe the words I knew she would say next.

"They lied. EndWorld is a magical place, but it isn't some utopia. People do horrible things here. Things they might never have done when they were alive."

"Like Tommy and Fat Anthony," I said, recalling my first encounter upon entering the fort.

Raven looked at me questioningly.

I shook my head. "Don't worry about it."

She offered a faint smile and went back to staring at the shadow creeping over the horizon. "Anyway, I got another quest objective, the pup is still alive. As long as nothing happens to her..."

"Anything I can do to help?" I asked.

"I'm still waiting for my next prompt," she said with a faint smile.

"I finished up the last bit while you were having your shoes made. But if something comes up, I'll let you know."

"Sounds like a deal," I said, trying my best to offer an encouraging smile.

"And, hey. Who knows," she offered, sniffing and wiping at her eyes. "If that darkness over there really does have something to do with your quest, can you imagine what the loot would be like?"

"Not really." I shrugged. "Then again, I haven't gotten much of a feeling for what loot is normal and what is rare."

"Yeah? Give it time. Things will really start to click once you catch your stride. You're really not doing all that bad, as you said, all things considered."

"And here I was under the impression you thought I was a total noob." I chuckled, smiling at her compliment.

I was still smiling when she reached out and grabbed my hand.

Her touch was warm and her eyes sparkled mischievously before she pulled me off the tower wall.

35

Individual bricks of the tower wall faded into a blur of gray and the wind stole the scream from my chest as we fell. I started to struggle, but Raven held my hand tight.

The ground rushed toward us with dizzying speed.

Then, in an instant, the world disappeared, and I felt myself being enveloped in a sea of black. My senses revolted as the void took hold and then vanished as we emerged on the cobbled street.

"What was that?" I asked, dumbfounded and out of breath. "Can you give me a little warning next time?"

"And miss out on seeing that look on your face?" Raven laughed and gave my hand an extra squeeze.

"So happy I could be of some amusement." I spoke the words in jest, but the sentiment rang surprisingly true.

It felt good to see her smile.

"I'm really sorry, but I have to go," she said. "Something popped up with my quest. Can you manage the rest on your own?"

Still feeling off kilter, I rubbed at my eyes and shook my head. "I'll be fine," I said after regaining some composure. "Is it anything I can help with?"

"Just information gathering at this point," she answered. "My contact doesn't usually deal with Travelers who haven't built some reputation first. It's probably best if I do this one alone."

Nodding, I waved her on. "Go do what you've got to do."

"Thanks." She grinned. It was gentle, genuine, and warm. And it seemed in that moment as if we'd been friends for ages.

"I'll see you tonight at the guard tower?" I asked as she turned to leave.

"Be there or be square," she called back over her shoulder.

I leaned back against the tower and watched her go, thinking about the list of things I still needed to accomplish before the day was through.

Of course, there was more shopping to be done, but I also needed to make time to go see Margaret. And after that... What if she had another quest waiting for me?

I couldn't help but think about the quick profit I'd made from selling the bee stingers at the auction house. Then I wondered if there might be enough time to grind out a few more mobs in the Meadows before I had to meet up for the group quest.

It was already mid day, and I'd only managed to get a pair of boots and sell a few trade skill items. I was going to need to get a move on if I hoped to get everything done in time for my appointment with Captain Elsbaud and the others.

Opening my inventory, I stared long and hard at the list of items. Nothing really caught my eye. Amongst the drops I'd received in the dungeon there were several pieces of cloth armor scraps, a few pieces of rusty armor, and the odd trinket.

Most of the items looked like nothing more than vendor fodder, but I didn't know how I could be certain without examining each one individually.

I chuckled to myself as I thought, once again, about my encounter with young Zack, and how deftly the kid had used his menu. What if the kid was on to something? Perhaps there was more to the control system than I had first imagined.

Concentrating on my inventory window, I imagined opening a

new tab. To my surprise, a second window popped up next to the first. Now we were getting somewhere.

Within a few short minutes, I had all the new loot moved into the second tab and sorted by rarity. On the bottom, naturally, were the worthless trinkets and cloth scraps. Next was the rusty armor and a few low-grade weapons.

All of these items appeared to be fairly worthless. They would be easy to sell, but none of it seemed likely to bring in much coin.

At the top of the list were the more interesting items. There weren't as many as the others, but what I saw showed real promise.

I inspected each of them in turn.

Looter's Boots of Power.
[Feet] Defense: 3
Dexterity +2, Strength +3
Requirement: Level 3.
Quality: Average.
Rarity: Uncommon.
Armor Class: Medium.
Durability: 10/10.

These boots were nice compared to my old digs, but they were certainly no match for the pair Jasper had fashioned for me earlier that morning. While they weren't worth equipping, I was certain they might fetch a decent price, so I set them aside and moved on to the next item in the list.

Hempen Gloves of the Wizened Wizard.
[Hands] Defense: 2
Intellect +2, Spirit +1.
Requirement: Level 2.
Quality: Average.
Rarity: Uncommon.
Armor Class: Light.
Durability: 8/8.

Now that was more like it. They weren't the most fashionable things I'd ever seen, but the increase to my magic pool, another twenty points, would be significant.

I pulled off my old, leather half-gloves and equipped the new pair, feeling them bind to me as if by instinct. The drab green would take some getting used to, and I'd have to stow them while eating, but it was a minor inconvenience I could live with.

Falcon Orb of the Dying.
[Off-hand Talisman]
Agility +2, Stamina -3
Requirement: Level 2.
Quality: Average.
Rarity: Uncommon.
Durability: 10/10.

What a piece of junk. I couldn't imagine a situation I might find myself in where two points of agility would be worth 30 hit points. Definitely not with my build, and not to mention the cost of an off-hand slot.

With Truthseeker being a true hand-and-a-half weapon, my ability to wield the blade while holding the silly orb would be greatly diminished. Deciding to move on, I set it to the side with the boots and inspected the next item.

Margaret's Monocle.
Quest Item.
This item begins a quest.

New Quest Alert! *You've stumbled on a quest:*
The Missing Monocle.
You've found Margaret Wilson's missing monocle.
Return this item to Margaret Wilson to claim your reward.
Reward: *Unknown.*

Interesting. I silently kicked myself for not discovering the monocle the night before. Had I just looked at my inventory, I would have turned it in before leaving for Harold's.

Then again, I wondered if Harold's prompt to revisit Margaret today had a connection to the missing Monocle. If so, it seemed the system had been designed to keep wayward Travelers on track.

This made me think of Raven and the frequent errands she'd been getting. For the life of me, I couldn't even begin to comprehend why Sven, Guilly, and Ruby had interfered with her quest to protect the dire wolves.

And why had they lied about it?

The arena. What a load of crap.

Whatever they'd done with the pup, it certainly seemed to shake Raven pretty badly. I felt myself getting angry just thinking about it. And yet, it also seemed as if EndWorld was set on helping her correct course. I reflected on this for a moment before inspecting the last item in my list.

It was none other than the glowing blue gemstone the Kobold Boss had used to illuminate the dark cellar.

> ***Focused Sapphire of Illumination.***
> *EXCLUSIVE ITEM.*
> *This item cannot be sold or traded.*

Bummer. I pulled the gemstone from my inventory and held it in my hand. It glinted in the sunlight and I thought I caught the faintest sparkle flicker from somewhere deep within its depths.

"What could you be for?" I wondered aloud.

With a shrug, I placed it back in my inventory and struggled to stand. My muscles had grown stiff in the chilly afternoon breeze. After a few stretches I felt ready to head back to the market to sell my wares.

But first, I decided to make a quick stop to see a friend about my damaged blade.

~

THE BELL AFFIXED TO THE DOOR CLANGED, ANNOUNCING MY ARRIVAL with a ringing clatter. Jörgen looked up from his dealings and grinned.

"Denton," he said. "Good to see you. What? Level 3 already?"

In front of the counter stood a scantily clad blonde in black leather armor and a green cape that hung just above her waist. A long bow and a quiver full of arrows were slung across her back and she glanced in my direction dismissively before returning her attention to the deal.

"So, what do you say?" she cooed, stealing Jörgen's attention before I could return the greeting.

"You drive a hard bargain," he said, eyeing the goods she had laid out on the countertop. "Perhaps too hard a bargain, yes? I'm not sure how I could use these at that price and still earn an honest profit."

"You're certain you don't want them?"

Even from where I stood, I could tell she was putting every ounce of charm into her act.

"This is not a deal I can do," Jörgen said.

"You're going to miss out," she warned. "Haven't you heard? It's the next big gold rush. Black gold, they're calling it."

Jörgen laughed, slamming his hand down hard on the countertop. "I felt that, and it was very clever, but it won't work. I'm a Traveler, just like you, and from what I hear, obsidian is a horrible investment at the moment. No amount of charming skill will change that fact."

We both watched as she scraped the items into her inventory and left in a huff.

"Tough customer," I observed. "Did I hear that right, she tried to charm you?"

"She's the third one this week," he said, rubbing his temples.

"What do you mean?"

"Some idiot out there got it in his head that pretty women in tight armor and high charisma get better results when trying to sell overpriced items. I can't say this person is wrong, but I've still got a business to run."

"That's pretty ingenious." I laughed. "I mean, if it actually works."

"Oh, it works. Too well sometimes."

"What do you mean?" I asked.

"You remember Kenneth, don't you?"

"How could I forget?"

"It pays to keep an ear to the ground. To stay on top of the latest sales, yes? I hear he bought a bunch of very expensive obsidian shards from a Traveler just this morning. The way her gear was described to me, there was no way she was out swinging a pickaxe in the Frostwind Mountains. Even so, there isn't much local supply. This bunch likely came from outside the province. Rumor has it, the deal left him in quite a bind."

While it was true, there was no love lost between Kenneth and myself over my decision to keep Truthseeker and his subsequent blow up, I couldn't help but feel a little bad for the guy.

I remembered the crowd of Travelers gathered around him when we'd first met. It wasn't hard to see how such a setback would have a ripple effect throughout the market.

"But look at me going on like an old hen," Jörgen continued. "Something tells me you aren't here for market gossip, no? What can I do for you, friend?"

"I'm not sure you'd be interested, but I've got some low quality gear I need to sell. I also managed to ding up my sword pretty good in a dungeon last night. I was wondering if there was anything you could do?"

"A dungeon? Already?" Jörgen nodded his approval. "You are becoming quite the adventurer. I'll tell you what, I'm not in the market for cloth or leather at the moment. It's only good for padding in my line of business and I have enough. Crude armor or metal-based weapons, I will take. With a little work, I can break them down to their base components."

"You can really do that?" I asked, almost unable to contain my awe.

I'd seen this sort of thing before in other games I played throughout the years. It was hardly a new concept by any means, but I hadn't gotten even the slightest inclination it was possible from my crafting efforts within the tutorial.

"With enough skill, yes." Jörgen grinned. "You'd be surprised. Some of these items are worth far more when they're dismantled than they are at simple face value."

Reflecting on my adventures in the market and at the auction house that morning, I didn't doubt for a second that there was a whole world of profit-turning just waiting to be exposed. It was both a little daunting and incredibly exciting all at once.

"Let's see what you've got," he prompted.

I emptied my inventory of the crude shield and rusty dagger, placing them on the counter, and piled on an assortment of other bits I'd managed to retrieve from the Kobolds in the cellar.

After a few minutes of stacking everything I hoped to sell for scraps, I watched with intense interest as he sorted through the haphazard pile. He selected a fair number of the items and set them aside, then nodded.

"I'll give you 55 silver for this lot," he said. "And I have an additional 10 silver for that makeshift club you put up for consignment. It sold this morning, and I was told to pass you a message."

"Oh?" I asked, but before my mind could fill in the gap with crazy assumptions, Jörgen explained.

"The buyer would like five more if you can manage."

"Five more?" I asked, not sure of what to make of the unexpected opportunity. "At 10 silver apiece?"

"Whenever you get around to it," he said. "It isn't a rush order."

New Quest Alert! You've been offered a quest:
Fulfilling an Order.
Your Makeshift Club has left quite an impression.
A customer has put in an order for 5 more.
Reward: *10 silver each.*
Turn in completed items to Jörgen Olsen.

"I'll see what I can do," I said. "Thanks."

Jörgen smiled and slid a stack of coins to me before he began tossing the items he'd selected into a bin on the other side of the shop. "This should keep me busy a while. Honest work is good for the soul. Yes?"

"Sounds like good advice if I've ever heard any," I said, gathering the rejected armor scraps and dented weapons and placing them in my inventory.

Then I unsheathed Truthseeker and set it on the counter for inspection. The large chip in the edge of the blade made my heart sink and immediately drew Jörgen's gaze.

He paused mid-toss and the crude shield clanged to the floor. "What is this?"

"I chipped it," I answered, feeling all the more stupid for stating the obvious.

"It must have been quite the struggle," he said as he picked up the blade and balanced the cross-hilt on his palm. After carefully measuring the weight of it, he eyed the edge as it tilted first one way and then the other.

"It could use a good sharpening, and the balance is off," he grumbled. Then he gave it a test flick through the air before handing it back.

"Is there anything you can do for the chip?" I asked, still somewhat hopeful.

He scratched his head and shrugged. "I don't think so. Did you see the total durability? It's dropped from 15 points down to just 5. I can sharpen the edge and perform some minor repairs, but I'm afraid there's only so much I can do. You'll need a new weapon soon."

Swallowing hard, I inspected my sword.

Truthseeker
[Bastard Sword]
Damage: 10-15.
Strength + 1, Dexterity +1.
Quality: Poor.

Rarity: Rare.
Durability 2/5
Craftsman's Mark: Jörgen Olsen
Partially Bound.

Jörgen was right. The total durability had dropped from 15 down to just 5, and it looked like I'd barely managed to avoid a total break.

"What do you have in stock?" I asked.

He considered the options and shook his head. "Nothing that would compare to your blade's base damage, without a substantial level requirement, I'm afraid. You're already level 3, but you're still too low to equip them. The only other option would be to go to a sub-par weapon."

"Oh..."

"If you can hold off on buying a replacement a while, I could forge something a little more custom. Fair warning, though. It won't be cheap. Or..."

"Or what?" I asked, hopeful for a small bit of good news.

"Or you could try to hold out for a loot drop. You might get lucky."

My heart sank. While Jörgen was right, and there was always a random chance of getting a loot drop, my new boots reminded me of the value of custom-crafted gear.

I scratched my chin as I thought about the offer. "How much are we talking about?"

"10? 15 gold, perhaps? It's a lot of coin, but you'll have a weapon that's been crafted specifically to meet your needs. I can even balance the weight for your individual fighting style. It can make all the difference in a difficult fight."

When I hesitated, he quickly added, "It should last you several levels before you need an upgrade, and I'll guarantee a successful binding this time around."

"And how much to repair Truthseeker?"

"For a blade like this, and considering the amount of damage, I would have to charge 50 silver. You could continue to use it as is, but it could result in destroying the blade if you run out of durability points."

"50 silver?" I echoed.

He nodded. "The integrity of the blade has been badly compromised. I might be able to improve the max durability by a point or two. Though I can't make any promises. Even with a repair, I don't think it will last much longer at this rate."

"How long will the repairs take?" I asked. "I've got a group quest just after sundown. I'm guessing I'll probably need a decent weapon."

"Only a couple of hours," he answered with confidence. "It'll be done before your quest starts, or I'll do the repair for free and send you off with my best loaner." Then he stooped to retrieve the fallen shield and tossed it on the pile.

I passed him 50 silver across the counter and slid Truthseeker into its sheath before unbuckling the scabbard and handing it to the smith.

"You've got yourself a deal," I said. "And I think I'd like to go for the custom craft. I'll have to work on getting more coin, but I have a few ideas. Can you put me on the tentative schedule?"

"Put a gold piece as a deposit and I'll pencil you in." Jörgen laughed. "There are plenty of opportunities to make money if you're willing to put in the work. Not all of them require a sword."

"Like the order for the Makeshift Clubs," I observed.

"Yes, that's right."

I slid him a whole gold piece.

"Consider yourself on the schedule," he said. "And when you come back in a couple hours, I'll have your repair complete."

"Thanks, Jörgen."

The bell on the door clanged as it shut behind me and I immediately smelled the mouth-watering aroma of roasting food.

"Fresh Kabobs," a nearby street vendor shouted. "Get them while they're hot. Two for five, best deal in town."

My stomach grumbled.

"I'll take two," I called, pulling 5 silver from my inventory.

"Coming right up."

36

The sun had passed its zenith and the shadows in the street were growing noticeably longer by the time I finished my transaction with the food vendor. With kabobs in hand, I kept an eye on my compass and hurried across the fort toward Margaret's house.

Every turn resulted in a new bottleneck. Each opportunity to get ahead was a false start. Open pathways seemed to close immediately around me, boxing me in and further delaying my progress.

"Fresh mugwort, day-old parsley. Get your ingredients here," A vendor with a large wooden tray and bulging muscles stepped forward to block my path.

"Fresh roses, beautiful daisies. Impress the object of your affection with a fresh-picked flower. Only two silver," a woman with an ample bosom and a low-cut blouse called out, also stepping in front of me as she did.

I lifted the skewers high and spun out of the way, narrowly missing a collision with a kid wearing a pair of scrappy boots and an overwhelmed look of awe.

"Sorry," I muttered, tucking the kabobs closer to my chest and darting my gaze around the plaza as I searched for an alternate route.

At this rate, I wasn't sure how I was going to make it to Margaret's house with the food still warm and unmolested. After considering all available options, I made a calculated gamble and cut through a nearby alleyway.

It was a risk, especially without a weapon at my side, but there was still so much to do and I was quickly running out of daylight.

The air smelled damp in the forgotten space between the cramped, stone buildings, and the stench of rotten vegetables filled my nose. Rats scurried amongst the disheveled crates and screeched as they fought over whatever scraps the darkened shadows concealed.

The shortcut proved much faster than attempting to navigate the busy streets and I managed to weave the rest of the way without incident. Perhaps it was still too early in the day for an encounter with the shady types one might expect to find lurking in the shadows.

Or maybe I'd just gotten lucky.

Finding myself standing at the edge of the street, I was eager to step once more into the fading sunlight.

"You there," a deep, male voice shouted from somewhere in the shadows behind me. "What you doing in my alley? Think you can just go wherever you please without paying the toll?"

My back stiffened, and I froze in place. Then, finally making sense of the situation, I darted out into the anonymity of the street.

Unlike the encounter with the two miscreants outside the alchemical shop that morning, I now found myself weaponless and unsure of the actual implications of getting into a tussle within the fort walls.

Bodies mingled around me and I tried to catch my breath. Still, the man advanced, shouting all the way.

"I saw you," he called out. "Don't pretend you can't hear me. You think you're safe in a crowd, is that it? Turn and face me like a man, you freeloading coward. Or run. Go right ahead. Believe you me, I'll get my due."

Within twenty paces I found myself at Margaret's door. Knocking frantically, I turned to glance backwards, watching for any sign of hurried movement.

No one answered and a ragged-looking man wearing a torn shirt and what appeared to be an apron of vomit came careening into the walkway. He had matted gray hair and his head swung back and forth as he assessed the passersby.

"Where did he go?" he demanded, contemptuously eying anyone unfortunate enough to cross his path. Then, unsatisfied with those in the immediate area, he scanned further.

When he finally saw me, he pointed a gnarled finger in my direction. "Aye, you best have my toll ready. You don't go traipsing through my alley without paying in coin or blood."

I knocked on Margaret's door again, even more desperate to avoid an unarmed encounter or a possible run-in with the fort guards before my scheduled appointment with Captain Elsbaud.

Footsteps sounded from somewhere deep inside the house, drawing closer to the door as the man shoved his way through the crowd until, at once, they stopped.

"Who is it?" Margaret asked.

I tried my best to keep my voice low in case my pursuer was close enough to make out the answer. "It's me, Denton."

"Who?" she demanded, growing irritated.

"Get out of my way," the thug shouted. He pushed through the last remaining onlookers still gathered between us.

"It's me, Margaret," I said through clenched teeth. "Denton."

"Denton, is it? Why in EndWorld didn't you just say so?"

The lock mechanisms rattled, and the door swung open. Then Margaret's gentle smile faded as I darted inside, slamming the heavy, wooden door behind me with my back.

"What's all this?" she asked, concern evident in her eyes.

"Nothing," I said, trying to catch my breath. "I thought I'd take a shortcut through the alley, but I seem to have made an unexpected friend."

"You made a friend in the alley? There aren't usually many

friendly types hanging around in places like that," she admonished disapprovingly.

"Not exactly."

The door shook within its frame as the man pounded on the solid wooden surface with all his might.

Margaret's look of concern turned sour, reminding me of her mood when I first met her the night before. With a grim expression and strength that defied her small stature, she pushed me aside and opened the door.

"Wait." I gasped.

My mind struggled to comprehend the events unfolding before my eyes and time slowed to a crawl as I followed her out into the street. The man stood at her entryway and his eyes locked on mine before he turned his attention to the widow.

"What do we have here?" he asked. His voice now thick with greed. "Pray invite me in, Marm? Mayhap we can discuss my fee for the safe passage of your charge."

"Your fee? Margaret asked, her tone defiant. "For safe passage, is it?"

"Through my alley, Marm."

"Your alley?"

A flash of unrestrained confusion filled the man's eyes before he answered. "Yes, Marm. It's my alley," he said, choosing to double down as his confidence returned. "And he trespassed. Now he must pay the price."

"You mean the one behind my house?"

"That be the one, Marm. That and all those connected to it. Aye."

Margaret lifted a hand to her chin as if she were considering the man's claim.

"I see," she said after a moment of awkward silence. Then she turned and looked at me and the two kabobs I was still holding aloft.

Just as I started to wonder why I hadn't stowed them in my inventory in the first place, she turned to face the man once more.

"You dare try to lay claim to my property, accost my errand boy, and delay my supper?" she asked. "Are you so foolish that you don't know who I am?"

The man looked at me and then back at Margaret. He laughed. "Who you are makes no difference to me and, if it's all the same to you, I'll have my toll. Blood or coin. It's the way of things, you understand."

"I'm afraid not," she said.

"I ain't asking."

What came next was almost impossible to comprehend, and it took my mind a virtual eternity to make sense of it. I watched dumbfounded as the scene played out before my eyes.

In an instant, the man lunged forward and attempted to push past her, but Margaret's hands began to glow the faintest green.

I recognized the spell immediately. It was the same move I'd used against the Kobolds to great effect.

Tempest.

Margaret pivoted with blinding speed, matching the trajectory of my would-be attacker and grabbed him by the arm in one deft motion.

Just as the street thug began to realize he'd met his match, she unleashed dual blasts of fire and lightning at his unprotected chest.

A wave of heat exploded around us and the hapless criminal flew backwards, landing several feet away in a cloud of smoke and ash. Static electricity filled air, and I felt my hair standing on end.

I blinked, willing my mind to catch up.

Within seconds the guards were upon the ruin of a man. Two hoisted him to his feet while another prepared the shackles.

Margaret turned and smiled. "I do hope one of those kabobs is for me?"

I nodded, still dumbfounded by her unexpected display of power.

"Well? What are you waiting for?" she prompted, dusting off her hands and motioning me inside. "Let's get to the table before the food gets cold."

Completely at a loss for words, I followed Margaret back inside and watched as she fiddled with the locks. When she was satisfied the door wouldn't budge, she gave a curt nod and led me to the dining room before disappearing into the kitchen.

When she returned, she was holding two plates and corresponding sets of silverware.

"You're missing your sword," she observed as she arranged our places. It was almost as if the event on her doorstep had never happened.

Unsure of whether her nonchalance was genuine or some kind of test, I offered her the spare kabob and nodded. "It got pretty dinged up last night when I was fighting those Kobolds in your cellar. I guess I didn't realize how bad it was."

"I see," she said as she sat, motioning for me to do the same. "I suspect you've dropped it off for repairs somewhere, then. Is that it?"

"Right," I answered, taking my seat. "I've left it with Jörgen. He said he'll have it done tonight. It shouldn't take too long."

"That sounds quite reasonable," she mused, though it was clear it wasn't all she had to say on the matter. "Is that why you ran from that hooligan back there?"

Her question was stern and the look she gave me indicated she wouldn't tolerate anything but a straight answer.

"I'd be lying if I told you it wasn't at least part of the reason," I admitted. "Honestly, I didn't want to risk being late for a group quest I've got tonight."

"Go on."

"Well, what options did I have? A fight with an unknown assailant could have ended in any one of several different ways. Sure, I might have died and that would certainly hurt, but I'd just respawn at the home point here in town, right?"

Margaret shrugged.

"Or, I could have won, which has its obvious perks..."

"But?"

"I don't know. What if I found myself detained by the guards? I'm still learning the rules here. Is it okay to engage in open warfare in the streets just because some lunatic has it out for you? Are some of the guards on the back alley pay roll? Could I find myself rotting in a dungeon for fighting inside fort limits? And those are just the questions I came up with on the fly."

"I see."

I went on. "Without knowing how things work here, I figured it just wasn't worth the risk if I could avoid it."

"Fair enough," Margaret said, the hint of a smile playing about the corners of her lips and eyes.

I let out a sigh of relief and set my kabob on the plate in front of me.

"So, are you going to just sit there keeping an old gal waiting? Tell me about this group quest of yours."

"What's there to tell?" I shrugged. "All I know is that we're supposed to meet when the moon rises."

"Is that all?"

I checked my quest log and read it aloud.

"The Captain of the Guard has requested a party of able-bodied Travelers to assist with a special errand. Meet Captain Elsbaud tomorrow evening at the Northern Gatehouse when the moon rises. No reward."

"Very interesting. You received this quest last night, and from Harold I presume?"

I nodded.

"I think this calls for a drink," Margaret declared as she stood. When I went to stand as well, she waved me down.

"Sit. I can fetch refreshments on my own. What'll it be? Something warm? Something cold?" she asked as she disappeared into the kitchen.

"Uh, either is fine. I guess," I called after her. "Whatever's easiest."

"Whatever's easiest?" she asked from around the corner. "What kind of an answer is that? Since when is taking the easy option the best course of action?"

When she emerged, she held a dusty bottle, two fluted glasses, and a heavy frown upon her lips.

"I don't want to be a burden." I shrugged. "You've already had to deal with enough from my screw up in the alley. I don't want to be a bother, that's all."

"A bother, he says. Imagine that. Might want to leave it to me to determine the level of my own hospitality, if you know what's best for you." Margaret harrumphed, setting the glasses on the table.

"I'm sorry," I said. "I'm still trying to learn how things work here."

"We'll consider it a lesson learned, then."

She held the bottle aloft and, with a simple flick of her wrist, the cork popped into the air.

My eyes went wide as I watched her catch it in one smooth motion. Even without casting Tempest, her speed was unbelievably fast.

She began to pour the clear, bubbling liquid into the glasses before I snapped out of my trance-like daze.

"How did you do that just now? With the cork, I mean."

"Simple parlor magic is all," she answered, but then cocked her head. "Though, perhaps a good object lesson for a young, prospective Battle Mage such as yourself."

"Oh?"

Margaret took her seat.

I watched, waiting for her to explain as she picked up her kabob and began to dismantle the meat and vegetable arrangement.

When she was finished, her meal had been transformed from a simple, humble street kabob into a gourmet-looking dish. The ingredients were the same, and yet the food had been changed dramatically by her tinkering.

She gestured toward my plate. "Give it a try."

In an effort to get a reference for the task, I looked at her plate once more and set to work. One by one, I removed the roasted chunks of meat and vegetables from the wooden spit. The stack grew larger until, at last, I'd cleaned the whole kabob.

I set the stick aside and attempted to mimic her arrangement. The result wasn't nearly as elegant, but I was rewarded with an unexpected system message.

New Skill! *You've learned the skill:* **COOKING.**
You can now prepare an assortment of low-level foods.
Practice this skill often to increase the complexity of meals in your culinary repertoire.
Cooking *is a Basic Trade Skill.*

Margaret smiled her approval and sampled a sensible fork-full of her dish. "Well done, Denton," she said. "What a fine choice for an early evening meal."

Still astonished by the surprise skill gain, I asked, "How did I just learn Cooking? I didn't actually cook anything."

"Things don't always have to be as complex as we might expect," she explained. "Besides, when it comes to cooking, sometimes it's all in the presentation."

Even though I wasn't quite satisfied with the answer, I decided to let it go. There were more important things to get caught up on than a basic trade skill. Cooking would have its uses, but it was easy to see that dwelling on it now wouldn't do me much good.

"Well, thanks for the lesson," I said before taking a bite of my own. "Oh, that is good. Isn't it?"

"Quite delicious," she affirmed. Bringing her glass to her lips.

I raised my glass and took a gentle sniff. The subtle scent of strawberries and fresh spring flowers flooded my senses and tiny bubbles tickled my nose.

"Is this cordial?" I asked, taking a small sip.

"It is."

A ripple of pure delight washed over me and I could feel a rush of warmth blossom on my cheeks as the liquid went down. The sensation reminded me of Harold's raspberry cordial from the night before, but the comparison was incomplete.

There was something more to Margaret's concoction.

Glancing up at my status bar, I saw a flashing icon of a blue arrow pointing upwards and my assumption was confirmed. I focused on it and willed the user interface to reveal additional details for the temporary buff.

You are refreshed.
+1 Mana every 5 seconds.
Duration: 5 minutes remaining.

"Wow," I breathed. "This is really good, and it has mana recovery to boot?" I shook my head in disbelief. "What I wouldn't have given to have some of this during my encounter with that Kobold Boss in your cellar last night."

Margaret just smiled before taking another sip. "And yet you managed."

"I guess I did." I chuckled.

"A Battle Mage without mana, a Battle Mage without a sword," she intoned, staring through the sheer cloth curtains of the front window.

"Is this the object lesson?" I asked, taking another bite of my meal.

"Indeed, it is."

I considered her words for a time before breaking the silence. "You didn't use a sword against that man from the alley, but I recognized the spell you cast."

"Tempest," she said, turning her eyes toward me once more, but her gaze was somewhere far away. Then she focused and gave me a gentle, sad smile. "And I didn't have a corkscrew to open this bottle."

"But you managed," I said, completing her thought.

It was starting to make sense, this bit of wisdom she was trying to impart. No matter what situation I found myself in here in EndWorld, I had to use whatever resources I had available. I couldn't count on learning new spells in a clinch. Whether it was fighting without a sword or without mana, success would come from making the most of what I had at hand.

My items, my skills, my wit.

"I think I see what you're getting at," I said.

Margaret nodded. "Yes, I believe you do."

Then, after a pause, she added, "You know, Denton, I've been thinking about this group quest of yours..."

"What is it?" I asked, intrigued and eager for any advice the older woman might have to give.

She leaned back in her chair and seemed to mull over what she might say next. At last, the words came. "While I can't join you on your quest, there is a way I might be able to help. I could teach you the ways of the Battle Mage, if you're interested in learning from a crotchety old widow like me."

Her hands were shaking, and I sat in silence. I was eager to accept, but it was plain to see that this was a big event and she wasn't quite finished making her offer.

"I haven't taken an apprentice in many years," she explained. "At times, I've wondered if I just wasn't born with the disposition for it, but I know that isn't true. Ever since my late husband passed..."

No stranger to loss, I reached out and took her trembling hand.

She sniffed and continued. "At any rate, I'd be willing to make an exception and take up your training. If you'd be inclined to accept my offer, that is."

"Absolutely," I answered, unable to keep myself from smiling.

"It won't be easy," she said, growing stern. "Nor will your training be filled with quests of plucking tulips or swiping sugarplums. If that's what you're expecting, you might rid yourself of those fantasies right away," she warned.

"No plucking, and no swiping. Got it."

She picked up her glass, raising it up in a silent toast.

I lifted my own and gently clinked it against hers.

"To an incredible teacher," I intoned.

"To a Battle Mage Reborn."

Congratulations! *You've chosen a Class Trainer.*
Margaret Wilson has agreed to instruct you in the ways of the Battle Mage.

Your Class Trainer will provide you with class-specific training and quests.
Be sure to check in often to unlock new spells and abilities.

37

With all the excitement of my journey to Margaret's house and all the events that had unfolded since arriving, I'd nearly forgotten about the two items in my inventory. I was still in shock over the realization that I'd just met my Class Trainer.

Battle Mage. The title felt right, and it seemed I had finally earned it.

I glanced out the window and saw the first tint of orange from the setting sun. Time was growing scarce. I still had more shopping to do if I wanted to secure any other upgrades before retrieving my sword from Jörgen.

Unwilling to waste another moment, I reached into my inventory and pulled out the monocle I'd found in the cellar the night before. Then I silently offered it to Margaret.

She stared at it for a long time, disbelief plain in her wizened eyes. "How? Where?"

"I think I must have found it in your cellar when I was fighting the Kobolds," I answered. "I'm sorry I didn't return it sooner. I wasn't really checking my inventory at the time and then with all the excitement with that thug on your doorstep—"

"Say no more," she said, reaching out with trembling fingers to take the item from my hand.

Quest complete! You've completed a quest:
The Missing Monocle.
You receive 2,500 Experience Points.
Additional Reward: *+300 reputation with Margaret Wilson.*
50 silver.

Margaret stood without warning and walked around the table to where I was sitting. She placed a hand on my shoulder and I thought I saw the slightest pang of sadness before she spoke.

"This belonged to someone very dear to me. You've no idea how much it means to have it returned. Thank you, Denton Wade. You have done me a great service."

It was in moments like these, and during the encounter on her doorstep, that I couldn't help but wonder what Margaret might have been through in all her years of experience in EndWorld. Though it seemed she tried to hide it with her prickly demeanor, it was becoming apparent that there was a lot more to this unassuming widow than she cared to let on.

The thought struck me, and I quietly considered the implications. It hadn't really occurred to me before, but I didn't see the woman standing before me as just another bundle of code. She didn't seem like a cleverly programmed AI.

Not at all.

When I looked at Margaret, I saw something more. She was a widow who still mourned her late husband. She was a guide and a mentor; a powerful Battle Mage who didn't take any flack from anyone.

Moreover, she was as genuine as any person I'd ever met in the real world. It was almost funny how much she reminded me of my own grandmother. The feeling only seemed to grow with each simple interaction.

Was that a coincidence?

At last, she wiped the tears from her eyes and gave my shoulder a gentle squeeze before leveling her gaze on mine.

"There is one more reward I might offer you," she said. "Are you ready?"

"I think so."

"Then close your eyes."

The room went dark as I lowered my lids and then, all at once, I was filled with a strange sensation. Margaret's grip tightened and a flood of energy flowed from her hand.

New Spell Acquired! You've learned the spell: MANA SURGE: RANK 1.

*You can now cast **Mana Surge** on friendly targets.*
***Mana Surge** causes the target to recover mana over time.*
Spell Affinity: Arcane.
Rank 1: +3 Mana every 5 Seconds.
Mana cost: 30 MP.
Duration: 150 Seconds.

The feeling subsided, and I gasped, opening my eyes.

"Mana Surge," I said, rereading my log. "Thank you, Margaret. I'm sure this will be very useful."

I was already doing the math in my head. Rank 1 had a 30 mana cost upfront and provided 60 mana points for free over time. Not bad at all. But...

"You look confused," Margaret observed.

"I've never received this much information about a spell before," I explained. "It's refreshing to get so much detail, but why so much now? Everything else has been a whole lot of trial and error."

"I see." She laughed. "Call it one of the perks of being my student. Any spells you learn on your own or from other sources will probably be just as vague as you're currently used to. I expect it will remain so until your skill improves."

"I guess that makes sense."

She gave me a gentle pat on the head and returned to her seat, tucking the monocle into her inventory as she went.

"I can't stay too much longer," I said, watching her sit back in her chair. "I still need to pick up a few more pieces of gear and grab my sword before I meet up with the others."

Margaret nodded and picked up her fork. "I understand. As is the life of the busy Traveler, my dear, and the sun is getting low."

"Before I leave," I reached into my inventory and pulled out the elemental shard, "I was wondering if there was something you could tell me about this."

"Oh." She gasped. "Where did you find this?"

I hadn't expected such a direct question about the origin of the shard, and I wasn't quite sure how much EndWorlders knew about the places beyond this world. Thinking quick, I decided to play it safe.

"It was in another place, before I arrived at Fort Morrow. The strange thing is, it can't be sold or traded. And, unlike your monocle, there doesn't seem to be a quest associated with it."

"Would you mind?" Margaret held out her hand.

I offered the shard to her, but she recoiled in pain as soon as its crystalline surface touched her skin.

"Oh my," she exclaimed, but before I could ask if she was okay, she began to laugh.

"There is powerful magic in that shard of yours," she said between fits of laughter. "I should have known better than to touch such a thing."

I frowned and stowed the shard back in my inventory. It was beginning to look like answers weren't in my future.

"It's quite a specimen," Margaret said. "There are plenty of charlatans in the fort, and many more beyond, who would claim to know the answer you seek. Always for a price, you see. If you're looking for real answers, there is only one person I know of who might be able to help."

"Who?" I asked, barely able to contain my sudden excitement. The unexpected prospect was invigorating.

"Have you chanced upon an encounter with Beatrice Potts yet? She's quite the cartographer, and I hear she sells compasses to new Travelers at her shop here in Fort Morrow."

New Quest Alert! *You've been offered a quest:*
See a Woman about a Shard.
Show Beatrice Potts your *Elemental Shard.*
She may know what it can be used for, or she might be able to tell you who does.
Reward: Unknown.

"Actually, yes," I answered, accepting the quest.

I glanced out the window and my mind raced as I plotted a course through the market stalls, planning the best possible route. I still had to buy gear and pick up my sword, and I'd need to avoid the alleyways if I wanted to avoid any more chance encounters.

"It isn't as busy out there as when you first arrived," Margaret observed. "Seems as though we aren't the only ones who have settled for a meal. Go on, I know you're eager to be on your way. Just don't forget to come back and visit from time to time. You hear?"

"Thank you for everything," I said, flashing a smile as I started to stand. Then I stopped. "What should I do about—"

"Don't you worry about the dishes. I'll take care of them when you've gone. Come, I'll walk you out." She took my arm, and we walked toward the door.

When we stood on the threshold, she reached toward the locks and then turned to face me.

"Life in this place isn't just about fighting and surviving," she said. "As a Battle Mage, you will probably do much of both, but you will also learn to support those around you."

I considered this and nodded. Mana Surge was a prime example. It was an amazing spell by itself, but it would be far more effective when to bolster the mana pools of my party members as well.

"Do me a favor, would you?"

"Sure," I replied.

"You Travelers have had quite an impact on Fort Morrow as of late," she explained. "Some of it has been good, and some bad. What I'd like you to do is to keep an eye out for ways you can help others like myself, others who might have had a hard go of it. This isn't a quest, per se, but I'm sure you'll find even the slightest of good deeds bring their own rewards. Do you think you can do that for me?"

My mouth went dry, and I did my best to swallow my apprehension. Of all the possibilities to make a positive difference, my mind settled on one in particular.

Kenneth Johnson.

I let out a prolonged sigh. "I think so," I said. "Turns out I just heard mention of a merchant who might have found himself in just such a bind."

"Good." Margaret's eyes glinted as she unlocked the door and swung it open. "One more thing."

"Yes?"

"Do try to stop by Beatrice's shop before your quest if you have the time. I'll send one of these other Travelers her way to let her know you'll be by."

I glanced toward the sky and then surveyed the street. She was right. There was much less foot traffic than before.

"Okay," I said at last, flashing her a grin. "I'll do my best."

"If you're going to be my apprentice, only your best will do," Margaret said, returning my smile with one of her own. "That's all I'll ever ask."

I walked along the street in silence, pondering over Margaret's words and letting the chaos of the marketplace fade away. While I wasn't altogether pleased with the idea of helping Kenneth after our last interaction, I could see the sense in what she said.

Like me, other Travelers had flooded into the fort as of late, and it wasn't hard to see how the natural ecosystem would be thrown off balance by the sudden influx.

Kenneth was just one of the countless victims of the misdeeds and high jinks of Travelers throughout the fort. Something told me Fort Morrow probably wasn't unique in that regard, and I knew all too well what it felt like to be on the receiving end of such antics.

Stopping at an intersection, I glanced toward Beatrice's shop and thought of the dusty scrolls and maps that littered her counters. She was a nice woman, busy though, but my patience had been rewarded with a minor increase in reputation.

I looked once more to the sky. The sun was dipping faster now, and it was clear I was running out of time.

With grim determination, I turned and headed toward Kenneth's stall.

"Help a girl out, she says. Well, I'll help her out alright. I'll help her right out of my fort, that's what I'll do." The merchant stopped cold and threw his broom down in disgust when he saw me.

"Hello, Kenneth."

"Well, if it isn't my dear friend, Denton. I should have known you'd be the one to show up in my darkest hour. What do you want? The deal is off, I said. You blew your shot. Besides, as you could probably tell from your eavesdropping, I don't have the means to buy that blade of yours now even if I wanted to."

I grit my teeth and held my tongue, doing my best to avoid a confrontation. This was going to be harder than I thought.

"Actually, I heard you might have something I could use," I said, walking closer.

"Oh? Is that true?" he asked. His voice was still full of sarcasm. "And what would that be? You must be blind. Has someone cast a spell on you, a nasty curse maybe?"

I shook my head.

"Well then, what could you possibly want? You can see the extent of my inventory."

Glancing around his open-air shop, I noticed his shelves were empty.

"I don't understand," I said after a moment of awkward silence. "I was told you might have something I'd be interested in."

"Fat chance," he muttered. "I liquidated every last item to help that rotten Traveler out, and what's the return on my investment? I'll tell you. Obsidian up to my gills, an over-saturated market, and not a single loyal customer. Some thanks I get for trying to help the lot of you."

I let out a sigh and nodded. "Good. I was worried you might have tossed your inventory. I'm actually looking for some obsidian shards," I offered. "That's why I'm here."

"Very funny. Couldn't resist an opportunity to gloat, could you? You just had to come and prove how smart you are."

"Actually, no. Not at all," I answered, careful to keep my response calm despite Kenneth's increasingly bad attitude.

"What is it then? I don't have all night to play games with you Travelers."

"I really do want to buy a few pieces of your obsidian. I'm looking for a specific shape, though. Do you have any that look like long arrowheads or maybe claws?"

Kenneth considered me for a moment before speaking. When he finally did, it was through a nasty smile.

"You don't have your sword," he observed. "Are you looking to craft a pair of fist weapons like that ogre of a friend of yours? Is that it? Decide the blade was too much for you, as I warned? Perhaps my day is starting to look up after all."

"Not exactly," I said, still doing my best to keep my cool. "I'm getting a new edge on the blade, but you were right. I should have listened to you. Truthseeker and I weren't a good match."

"Hmph," Kenneth huffed, but then his tone softened slightly. "Yes, you should have listened to me in the first place."

"Anyway," I pressed, hoping to get the conversation back on topic so I could make it to Beatrice's shop before my quest. "I was thinking the shards might work as an upgrade for Ely."

"No," Kenneth said, waving me off. "Forget about it. I'm not doing business with that oaf, or with you for that matter. That's it. End of story."

"Oh." I shrugged. "That's okay, I guess. I just figured the durability of his claws couldn't be that great, what with the bone he's using. Obsidian would be a much better material, but I'm sure I can find another seller around here somewhere. I bet they'd even take some loot I found on consignment. You know, beef up their inventory a bit after a rough trade."

He watched in disbelief as I started to walk away. And, truth be told, I was okay with it. There was something satisfying in the look of dismay that flashed in his eyes and I knew I'd given it a good effort. Margaret couldn't fault me for that.

"Denton, wait. Perhaps I was a little hasty," he said, his voice suddenly soft and subdued. "How many pieces do you need?"

Ten minutes later I found myself standing back on the cobbled street. My reputation with Kenneth had increased by 1,000 points due to the transaction and I had several high-quality obsidian shards in my inventory. He'd even taken the loot Jörgen didn't want on consignment, with the promise of payment upon sale. Despite the initial discomfort and unpleasantries, the whole thing had been relatively painless.

In fact, it had been downright easy.

The thought struck me. Since when was anything in EndWorld easy? And then I had an idea.

It was a terrible, horrible idea.

But it was also brilliant.

I turned around and cleared my throat. "Hey, Kenneth?"

The merchant stopped adjusting the few wares on his shelves and tried in vain to hide the apprehension that was clear on his face.

"What is it? You haven't changed your mind, have you?"

After what must have felt like an eternity to us both, I looked at my remaining gold balance. Between the money drops from the Kobolds and selling my wares in the marketplace, I hadn't done too badly for myself. 3 gold, 55 silver.

Satisfied, I walked back into his stall. My hands trembled and my mouth went dry as I reconsidered the offer I was about to make.

"Is there anything else I can do for you, Denton?"

"I have a crazy idea," I blurted out before my nerves could get the better of me.

Kenneth looked puzzled, but it was clear his interest was piqued. "Go on."

"You have a lot of that obsidian, don't you? More than you showed me. Right?"

He nodded. "Of course. I only showed you the best specimens, but I have plenty more. More than I know what to do with, to be honest."

"Good." I nodded, staring off into the distance as I mentally connected the dots.

"What about it?" he asked. "Several other buyers in town are in the same boat. Like I said, it's a saturated market. I'm really not sure what I can do with it, and I can't imagine anyone will be buying obsidian in the foreseeable future."

"What if you bought the rest of the stock? Not all at once. Certainly not fast enough to raise suspicion. Could you do it?"

Kenneth laughed and picked up his broom, setting to the mundane task of cleaning his stall.

"Well?" I pressed.

He looked up. "That wasn't a joke?"

"No. It wasn't," I answered, keenly aware of the time I was losing.

"Oh." He scratched his head and then nodded. "I'd wager I could. Most of the merchants would probably be willing to sell at a significant loss just to be rid of the stuff. But you have to understand, it would take time and capital I don't have. A few gold at least. And even at that, it would take ages before I could move any of it at even a sight profit."

"A few gold?" I asked, feeling my heart quicken in my chest.

"Maybe 4 gold pieces, I'd say, given my current understanding of the situation. Could be more, maybe less, depending on how well I haggle."

Four gold. It was more than I had, but I'd just given Jörgen a deposit on a new sword. What if I got it back and delayed the custom build?

It might just work.

"I think I can swing that," I said. "It'll take your best haggling and a little work, but maybe we can turn this whole thing around. How would you like to be business partners?"

A wide grin blossomed on Kenneth's lips.

***Hidden Quest Complete!** You've completed:*
A Friend in Need.

You are now business partners with Kenneth Johnson.
***Reward:** 2,000 Experience Points.*
+1,000 Favor with Kenneth Johnson.

After handing Kenneth the rest of my coin and informing him of the gold piece I had on deposit with Jörgen, I bid him farewell and headed back toward Beatrice's shop.

Could I trust the man?

There was no way to know for sure, but I felt good about the transaction. I'd had an idea and, even though I was still fairly inexperienced when it came to the market in EndWorld, all the pieces seemed to fit. Even Kenneth liked the plan once I explained it.

Besides, it wasn't like I had nowhere to turn if things went south. Opportunities were everywhere if one were so inclined. For starters, I could deliver the order for makeshift clubs and try farming more intact stingers.

With any luck, I'd be able to recoup any losses with some hard work and maybe a few days' worth of grinding. Not to mention whatever drops the group quest had in store tonight.

The unexpected reminder of my final errand of the night caused my heart to quicken. With the looming deadline fresh on my mind, I hastened to pick up speed, winding through the crowd with newfound determination.

The compass painted on the wooden sign of Beatrice's cartography shop was illuminated by the flickering light of the first oil lamp lit on the street below. Meanwhile, merchants worked to pack up their wares, shutting down their stands or stalls until the first rays of the sun dawned on a new day.

Was I too late?

I looked in the window and a rush of relief washed over me.

Beatrice sat in the far corner of the shop, illuminated by the soft glow of her candle, and just as hard at work as she had been the day we'd first met.

I took a calming breath and stepped inside.

"Denton, is that you?" she called out, not bothering to look up from her delicate pen strokes on the yet unfinished map.

"Yes," I replied. "I'm so sorry I'm late. I tried to get here as fast as I could."

There was a brief pause as I carefully wove my way through the maze of dusty scrolls and overburdened shelves.

"No bother," she said at last, glancing upward long enough to squint in my direction. "Margaret sent word you'd be on your way. It was a very cryptic message, but I suppose it got the point across."

"Cryptic?" I asked. "You mean she didn't tell you why she sent me? That's strange."

"She told me enough, that much I can assure you. But you must understand, Denton, information is valuable around here."

"I keep hearing that."

"That's because it's true. Whoever you've been speaking with has given you a great insight. Whatever message Margaret intended on sending would be subject to the whims and curiosities of the Traveler through whom she sent it."

I considered my souvenir from the tutorial and couldn't think of a single reason Margaret might want to keep it secret.

"Take my shop, for instance," Beatrice went on. "What can you tell me about it?"

"Well, you gave me my compass," I said, feeling a bit sheepish as a result of being put on the spot.

"And?"

"And, from what I can tell, you make and sell maps."

"Is that all?" she pressed. "Surely, you must have seen more to it than that."

I looked around the shop once more, taking in the smallest details and cataloging everything I could find. Maps. Scrolls. Dust. Then, of course, there were the cabinets and tables lined with maps, scrolls, and dust.

I shrugged.

"This might look like a simple storefront for maps and scrolls," she intoned, "but I'm actually in the business of selling information."

"What kind of information?" I asked, suddenly intrigued.

Beatrice smiled. "I think that might be a conversation for another time."

"Oh, come on," I said, returning a grin of my own. "You can't be serious. That was an awfully big lead up just to leave me hanging like that."

"Level up and come back, we can discuss it then. For now, I've gotten the impression you have a certain artifact you'd like me to look at?"

I nodded and pulled the shard from my inventory. The notion that there was more to Beatrice's shop intrigued me.

Glancing around once more, I couldn't help but wonder what secrets the woman kept. And what was the nature of the information she bartered in? It all looked so benign. Level up and come back. I made a mental note to do just that.

The shard was still in my hand when I felt the weight of her piercing gaze. When I looked up, our eyes met.

"I don't usually do things like this for free, if at all. But since the moment you first stepped foot in here, I sensed there was something different about you," she explained. "I also owed Margaret a favor. You can let her know this makes us even."

Swallowing hard, I nodded and opened my hand, revealing the item I'd received from the golem.

"Is that what I think it is?" Beatrice asked, reaching for the shard and then stopping short. "May I?"

"Please do," I said. "Just... be careful. It gave Margaret quite a shock. She said it contained powerful magic."

Beatrice smiled and took the shard in her hands. It started to glow.

"It does," she said, losing herself in the crystalline depths. "Very powerful magic, indeed. But there's no need to worry, I've been well educated in artifact lore and the mysteries of the arcane. Margaret was very wise to have sent you here."

"What can you tell me about it?" I asked.

"It's most certainly an artifact, but..." She eyed me suspiciously. "I don't think it came from EndWorld. How did you happen to come into possession of such a rare specimen?"

"I killed a golem," I answered truthfully, hoping my omission of the tutorial would suffice.

"A golem, you say?" Beatrice pressed. "Last I checked, there wasn't much of a supply of golems in this neck of the woods. Such a journey would take a week or more, and that's once you've traversed the Frost-wind Mountains. That doesn't seem very likely for a level 3 Battle Mage, let alone the level 1 who walked into my shop to deliver a package not too long ago."

"I fought the golem in a place that exists outside of EndWorld," I explained. "It's sort of complicated."

She rewarded me with a knowing smile. "So much in this world is complicated, Denton. Lucky for you, the powers of this shard are relatively straightforward. Now, if only you had a length of chain."

"What for?" I asked, thinking back to the previous night. Hadn't Harold given me one? It was when I leveled up, the bonus reward for turning in the quest to help Margaret.

"I'll need a length of chain if I'm to finish the craft I have in mind. I suppose I could leave it unfinished—"

"Hold on." I checked my inventory. There it was, just as I'd remembered.

A length of Silver Chain.

"Would silver work?" I asked, producing the string of shiny metal links.

"That's perfect." Beatrice beamed with unrestrained eagerness as she snatched the chain from my outstretched hand.

I was still looking on in shocked amusement when she regained her composure.

"I'm sorry," she said, shrinking back into herself a little. "This is perfect for the craft I had in mind. Perhaps I got a little excited."

"I'm guessing silver is really good, then?" I asked, hoping to make sense of her uncontrolled burst of emotion.

"I should say so," she quipped. "Silver has long been known as a pure metal. By its very nature, it repels evil and can help ward off curses. Combined with the latent energies of your elemental shard, I should be able to craft a potent talisman of protection. Would you like me to try?"

I shifted uncomfortably. "Well, yes, but can I leave it with you? I still have to retrieve my sword from Jörgen and then I'm supposed to meet up with Captain Elsbaud for a quest. I'm sort of running out of time."

Beatrice nodded and flashed me a knowing smile. "No rest for a doer of deeds, as my father always used to say. Go. Get your sword from Jörgen and swing by on your way to your errand. I'll have your talisman done by then."

"I don't have any money right now," I added. "But I should be able to pay you for your work within a few days. I can come back then, if you'd like."

"No," she answered, her voice growing stern. "I don't need your coin. As I might have mentioned, the currency I choose to dabble in is that of information. Come back when you've gained a few levels and we'll find a mutually beneficial way you can repay my services."

New Quest Alert! You've been offered a quest:
Come Back When You're Stronger.
Beatrice Potts has made you an interesting offer.
Come back when you've gained a few levels.

Reward: _A Unique Quest._

I STEPPED OUTSIDE, STILL TRYING TO WRAP MY MIND AROUND THE unexpected quest, and gazed upon the endless line of oil lamps that had joined the first mesmerizing flame. Now the entire street was illuminated, each dancing orb of light joining forces to keep the encroaching darkness at bay.

A quick upward glance confirmed the moon had yet to rise, but I knew it wouldn't be long before the glowing lunar body met with the twinkling stars above.

Once again I wove my way through the mingling crowd as I retraced my steps. With each twist and turn, I increased my pace until I was nearly running down the cobbled street.

I was completely out of breath when I entered Jörgen's shop.

"There's the man of the hour," Jörgen exclaimed over the clanging bell affixed to the door. "I thought you might have stood me up to head out to face the denizens of the night without a proper weapon."

"No, not at all," I managed to say between breaths. "I'm sorry I kept you waiting. It's been a very busy night."

The hearty laughter that followed said it all.

I sighed and slumped against the counter. "You're not upset?"

Jörgen grinned. "It's been a long day for all of us, I think," he said. "But something tells me your night is just beginning."

He nodded out the front window and I followed his gaze.

"I haven't seen a night this dark since I arrived," he went on. Then he slid Truthseeker, safely tucked within its scabbard, towards me.

I unsheathed my sword. The weight of it was comforting. Like an old friend, the pommel rested against the inside of my wrist. If I listened hard enough, I was sure I could hear a distant hum coming from the blade. The edge glinted in the lamplight and I could feel a smile play about my lips.

"It should do for now." Jörgen's words cut through the magic of the moment. "I was able to restore a bit of the durability, but the blade won't last long. Lucky for you, I should be able to get started on that custom build within the next few days. Just try to hold out until then, eh?"

I frowned. "Actually," I said, feeling the pain of seeing the blacksmith's look of eager anticipation fade, "there's been a slight change of plans."

Without going into too much detail, I explained how I decided to help Kenneth in his time of need.

"That's a very noble gesture," Jörgen said at last, nodding slowly. "And one noble gesture deserves another, wouldn't you think? Tell you what, I'll hold your gold for Kenneth and I'll even keep you on the schedule. For now."

"Really?" I asked. "You'd do that?"

"If you can come up with the coin before I get to your order, we'll move ahead with the build," he offered. "Otherwise, I'm afraid I'll have to move on. I can't promise when I'll be able to get back to you. With more Travelers finding a home in Fort Morrow, I imagine there'll be more work than I know what to do with."

"Fair enough," I agreed.

Jörgen nodded toward the window once more. "It's getting late," he observed. "You'd probably best be going."

I agreed and shook the man's hand. His grip was firm and strong and there was no mistaking the kindness in his eyes.

"Thank you, Jörgen," I said as I opened the door. "I won't let you down."

"No," he said, "I don't think you will. I've got a good feeling about you, Denton."

I could still hear his deep chuckle as the door swung shut behind me and I began to weave my way back into the crowd.

Within minutes I was standing outside Beatrice's cartography shop, and once again found myself out of breath.

Which stat would I need to increase to improve my endurance?

I blinked and shook my head, looking down at my new boots. Had I really just now put the pieces together?

Stamina, strength, agility, intellect, dexterity, and more. Each point lined my stat page, but I hadn't put much thought into any of it until this very moment.

Intellect increased my mana pool, and stamina increased health. These had been my primary resource pools thus far and the concept had been fairly straightforward. How had I managed to miss all the other possibilities?

I chuckled and grabbed the doorknob in front of me. Sure, I was a noob. Just a few days prior, I'd had no intention of stepping foot into EndWorld. Some of these people had had months to research and prepare for their new lives inside this simulated existence.

All things considered, I reckoned I wasn't doing all that bad. I'd managed to complete a solo dungeon and slay a Kobold Boss. I'd made friends, found a mentor, and even engaged in a promising enterprise.

"Denton?" Beatrice called out.

"I'm here," I answered, stepping inside the shop.

"Do come in, will you?" she insisted. "The hour is growing late and we both have errands yet to run."

When I stepped to Beatrice's desk, I watched in awe as she put the final touches on the elemental talisman she had painstakingly created.

Silver swirls wrapped around the earthen shard, culminating at the top in a delicate loop.

"Don't allow the design to fool you," she said without looking up. "You'll find no craftsmanship its equal within a hundred kilometers. The clasp will hold or I'll eat..."

She looked me up and down, nodding with approval at my change in footwear before resting her eyes on my chest.

"Your shirt," she said, finishing her thought.

"You'll eat my shirt?"

"If my craftsmanship is lacking, yes. I'll eat your shirt."

"You've got yourself a deal," I replied, unable to resist a smile.

Beatrice handed me the pendant and chain and I held it in my palm in quiet reverence, staring deeply into the torrent of earth energy trapped within the shard.

Quest Complete! You've completed a quest:
See a Woman about a Shard.
*Reward: 1,000 EXP, an **Elemental Amulet**.*

"What do you think?" she asked, startling me from my unintentional meditation.

"It's amazing," I breathed.

"Come now," she chided. "You haven't even given it a decent look over."

She was right, of course. I'd been so entranced by the craftsmanship and intricacy of design that I hadn't even bothered to inspect the new piece of gear.

Elemental Amulet of Earthen Resolve.
[Amulet]
Strength +2, Stamina +3
Dark Resistance +10
When Equipped: Increases Potency of Earth Magic.
Requirement: Level 3
Quality: Exquisite
Rarity: Artifact

I took the silver chain in my fingers and placed it around my neck. Then I tucked the shard safely beneath my shirt. A sudden wave of power washed through my veins, reinvigorating my tired muscles. My health jumped 30 points and the increase in strength was a new sensation all on its own.

It felt amazing.

Noticing that she was still waiting for an answer, I cleared my throat. "This is amazing, Beatrice. I'll be honest, I never expected to get anything this nice at such an early level."

"I'll take that as a compliment," she replied with a pleased grin.

"Absolutely," I agreed. "I imagine it takes a great amount of skill to create an artifact with such a low level requirement."

"It does, but the quality of materials certainly helps," she explained, but the blush on her cheeks seemed to indicate the compliment had hit its mark.

"At any rate," she went on, "it would appear the moon has just about risen."

I glanced out the window and nodded. "You're right. I best be going. Do I owe you anything for this?"

Beatrice shook her head. "Margaret can consider her favor repaid. As for you, I'd only ask that you come back later, once you've gained a few levels. I might have some mutually beneficial errands for you then."

"Deal," I said, then turned for the door.

"One more thing," Beatrice called out, stopping me in my tracks.

I turned.

"Be careful tonight."

"Be careful?" I asked, unsure of what to make of her warning.

"Yes," she answered, looking once more out the window. "I fear the moon is a bad one this evening."

"A bad moon on the rise?" I muttered, recalling a song from another world and another time.

"Indeed."

39

The first hint of moonlight flirted with the horizon as I left Beatrice's shop. A cold mist had descended into the fort and I tried in vain to ward off a shiver, rubbing the warmth back into my arms while mentally pulling up my map.

The northern gatehouse was at the uppermost top of the fortified city, a good distance away from my current location. I appraised the first sliver of the golden, lunar orb through the fog and set my compass on my destination.

Thankfully, the trip was quick and uneventful.

When I entered the courtyard in front of the gatehouse, I saw a man with dark hair and a full but trimmed beard standing in full armor. He had piercing eyes that took in every detail and was equipped with both a sword and shield.

Despite an air of impatience, he betrayed no real emotion and was impossible to read. A quick inspection confirmed my suspicions.

This was Captain Elsbaud.

My friends stood in a group nearby. All of them wore concerned looks and shifted nervously until they saw me approach.

Captain Elsbaud cleared his throat as I neared.

"You must be Denton Wade. We've been waiting for you."

I looked at the faint aura of the moon, still a third hidden beneath the horizon and fog.

"Yes," the captain intoned. "It would appear you've just managed to make it on time. Even as the case may be, one should be wary of keeping important people waiting. You may find there are times here when on time is just a little too late."

I nodded, swallowing the urge to protest. There was more on the line than the small measure of pride I might hope to defend against a man who likely had a lot more to offer.

"Yes, sir, I understand," I answered. "My apologies."

Elsbaud grunted his approval. "Gather around."

Ely let out the breath he'd been holding and everyone seemed to relax. As one, we shuffled closer to the captain of the guard, eager to hear about whatever errand he had prepared.

"You sorry lot have been nominated by an esteemed citizen of Fort Morrow to provide a much-needed service. Before we proceed, I'll need you to confirm that you were promised no reward and that you are all here of your own free will. On your honor, do you attest to these words?"

"Yes, sir," we answered in unison.

"And you've the fortitude to see the task through?"

"Yes, sir," we chimed, though there was no way of knowing what we might be up against.

Elsbaud leaned back on his heels and appraised us each in turn. The silence stretched across endless seconds and I felt a heavy weight grow within my stomach.

Raven's eyes twinkled with determination in the moonlight. Pops stood a little taller. Ely clenched his fists, and even Attia seemed eager to get on with the task.

"Very well," he said at last. "There is but one problem."

"What is it?" Raven asked.

"Him." Elsbaud pointed an accusatory finger in my direction.

"Me?" I asked.

"Indeed."

All eyes shifted in my direction, but I still wasn't sure of what to make of the situation. What had I done wrong? I'd made it to the gatehouse on time, hadn't I?

I dreaded the thought of costing my friends such a great opportunity. Sure, we didn't know exactly what kind of rewards we'd find on the other side but, even if we didn't come across any loot, there was always the chance of increasing our reputation with the fort guard. Not to mention the chance at netting a good number of experience points.

That alone was worth seeing the task through.

"And what is it about Denton that you have a problem with?" Ely asked, taking a bold step forward. "Because if you have a problem with him, then you have a problem with all of us."

"That's right, sir," Raven added from the shadows of her hood. "After all, it was Denton who was given the quest. We're just here for the ride."

"Is that so?" Elsbaud pressed, pausing for effect. "And I take it you all feel this way?"

"I'm afraid so," Attia answered while Pops nodded his agreement.

"Even without hearing my objection?"

"What is it?" I asked, inserting myself into the conversation. "What did I do wrong? If it was something I did, I don't think my friends should have to suffer the consequences of my actions."

"What did you do wrong?" Elsbaud asked, his brow furrowing. Then he let out a deep laugh.

Unsure of how to respond, I waited for the man to continue.

"What did you do wrong?" he repeated, shaking his head. "Nothing, as far as I can tell. But you're only level 3. The task I have in mind is usually completed by Travelers no lower than level 5."

"Oh," I said, feeling the full weight of my shame.

If only I'd spent the day grinding mobs and running errands instead of shopping and zigzagging across the fort like an idiot. "So, you're saying my friends and I can't do your quest until I'm level 5?"

"No. I never said that," Elsbaud said, his voice growing stern. "Your friends can indeed complete my quest. If they have the mettle for it, that is."

"We do," Pops said as he placed a gentle, restraining hand on Ely's chest.

Captain Elsbaud rested his own hand on the pommel of his sword and grinned. "It would appear so," he said.

"What must we do?" Attia asked.

"If you insist upon taking up the challenge, you must do so on equal footing. And the task will be all the more difficult for it."

"What do you mean?" I asked.

"Experience is earned," Elsbaud replied, his words made all the more cryptic by the silence that followed.

"You're saying we'll suffer a level reduction while the quest is active?" Raven asked, looking perplexed.

"Precisely."

"And what is the quest?" Ely asked.

"A simple yes or no will suffice."

Attia stepped forward and removed her hood. Her dark eyes beamed with determination in the filtered atmospheric glow. "I will do it."

Ely chuckled. "As will I."

Pops looked at me and nodded. "You have my axe and all the strength of my runes."

I looked at Raven, but even from the depths of her cowl, I could tell her gaze was fixed firmly upon the captain.

"Our spells and abilities will be restricted to those requiring level 3 and below?" she asked.

The officer grinned and the first hint of mischief flashed briefly at the corners of his lips. "That's correct."

Raven studied the man for a moment longer and then turned to me. "This is very unusual," she said. "I don't know where this road goes, but I owe you. I'm in."

Satisfied with their answers, Captain Elsbaud unsheathed his sword and pointed it toward our group as he began to chant. None of the words coming from his mouth made much sense, but I could feel a cold sensation creep down my spine before a cloud of miasma formed around each of my friends.

Then, just as quickly as it had appeared, the dark haze dissipated into the swirling fog.

Elsbaud put away his sword and crossed his arms, resting them on his plated mail.

"Now, then," he said with a satisfied grin. "Your quest."

"You did say this was temporary, right?" Ely asked, looking at his hands and suddenly sounding a little unsure.

"The effect will only last until you've finished your task. It will be a challenge, I assure you, but I dare say it might be doable."

"And what is it you would have us do, sir?" Raven asked, tossing Ely a sideways glance.

"Ah, yes. I was just getting to that."

New Quest Alert! You've been offered a quest:
Clear the Sewers.
Captain Elsbaud has assigned you a task.
Your group has been instructed to clear the sewers.
Reward: *None.*
Sometimes service is its own reward.

Ely's eyes went wide in disbelief. "You want us to clean the sewers?"

Attia shook her head at him and turned back toward Captain Elsbaud. "It would be our pleasure, sir."

From in the distance, we heard the faint clamor of armor. The captain turned, and the sound grew louder. Whoever it was, they seemed to be approaching our group from the direction of the gatehouse.

Then a figure emerged from the mist, stepping toward Elsbaud as he did.

It was another guard. He was equipped with the same style of sword and shield, though the imprinted design on the crafted metal differed slight.

"You'll have to excuse me for a moment," Elsbaud said, turning away from our group with the other man. "It seems my lieutenant requires a word from me."

After taking a few steps away from us, the man leaned close and spoke. Even in the relative stillness of the empty courtyard, his words were too quiet to hear.

"I see," Elsbaud said, rubbing his chin.

He cast another look in our direction, but said nothing while the lieutenant went on with whatever report he had to deliver.

When the man finished, Elsbaud nodded. "You're certain of this?"

"Yes, sir," the lieutenant answered.

Elsbaud turned and addressed us directly. "Folks, it appears circumstances may have changed somewhat. My lieutenant has just informed me that there have been reports of undead creatures lurking about."

"Undead?" Raven asked, then glanced in the direction of the cloud she'd shown me earlier. It wasn't visible in the dark fog, but I, too, could feel its presence.

"That's right, Miss." Elsbaud replied. "We have patrols on route to confirm the reports. If you would rather hold off and allow a team of my soldiers to clear the sewers this night, I can arrange for you to come back next week. It should give your friend enough time to put on a few levels and there will be no need for your current handicap."

"If you don't mind me asking," Pops said, spreading his hands in front of him. "How does any of this change things?"

Cleaning the sewers didn't sound like a very glamorous task under normal circumstances, but undead? Something felt off. Could this event be a way for the system to correct itself, adjusting to make up for my lower level and the increased difficulty of the task? It could be our way out.

The thought of spending the next few days leveling up, improving my skills, and padding my now-empty wallet did sound appealing.

Or was this something more... A chance at more experience and better loot, perhaps? More difficulty, more reward.

Elsbaud considered the question for a moment before answering. "Operationally speaking, who knows. There's a good chance you'll just encounter the odd assortment of rats and slimes, but there's no guarantee that's all you'll face. If the undead attempt to breach our defenses, there is a chance they may come through the sewers. If that happens, you'll be on your own and there's no telling what you'll be up against."

"Whatever comes, we'll be there to face it," Ely said. His face was determined, and he pumped a balled fist into an open palm.

"I can't remove your level restriction if you choose to continue," the captain warned. "Your level will be tied to that of your companion's. It's a big decision. If you'd like, I can give you a minute to discuss and weigh the best course of action. But know this: There will be no penalty for putting the task off for another time."

Ely was about to answer when Attia took his hand. "Yes, Captain," she said. "A moment to discuss as a group would be most wise."

We all turned and walked a few paces into the mist while Captain Elsbaud resumed his conversation with the lieutenant.

When we stopped, it was Raven who broke the silence between us.

"I've never heard of anything like this," she said. "On one hand, we could attempt to complete the quest as it stands. Maybe we encounter some undead mobs, maybe we don't. But say we take the other option. We opt out of the group quest and come back when Denton hits level 5. Who's to say our choice won't have a profound impact on Fort Morrow or the people living here?"

"And what if we can't manage the task?" Pops chimed in. "We lose some experience points and maybe some durability on our gear. Big deal. We can always try again. Right?"

"It's a little more complicated than that," Attia said. Her concern was plain upon her face. "Dying is a horrible, painful experience. A skilled healer can mend your wounds, but what of curses and disease? At level 3, I only have access to the most basic spells. I am willing, but I am unsure to what degree I am able."

"I'll take the brunt of the damage," Pops said, giving her a gentle smile. "Just back me up in whatever way you can. That's all I ask."

Attia nodded, and we all looked to Ely, waiting for whatever response he might have.

After staring at the lot of us for an awkward moment, he shrugged. "It should be obvious, right? I'm in. I mean, this is it. This is Denton's level 5 quest. It's the climax to the beginning of his story. He's already completed a solo dungeon. Things only get better from here, right? How could any of us say no?"

Attia frowned. "That's not fair, Ely. Don't pressure him."

"Are you comfortable with this, Denton?" Raven asked, turning her attention back toward me.

In that moment, it seemed as if I were carrying the weight of the world upon my shoulders.

These people were my friends.

How could I say no, knowing that by doing so I might be denying them a very unique opportunity?

And yet, these people were my friends.

How could I possibly ask them to risk the pain of death to pursue a potentially dangerous errand with no guarantee of a reward?

"What do you say, Travelers?" Elsbaud called out. "Shall we call it a night? I can send a group of my best soldiers and we can all get out of this infernal, armor rusting fog and go back inside."

I looked at my friends and swallowed hard. It took a moment before I found my words.

"I don't know," I said at last. "I mean, I'm not especially skilled. Sure, I've killed some Kobolds, but that doesn't mean I know what I'm doing. I'm still just trying to figure all of this out."

"If you're not comfortable with this, we can wait," Raven said. Her words were smooth and gentle. "Don't worry about us. We're all adults and we've been this level before. We know full well what we might be getting ourselves into."

I looked at Pops and Attia, then Ely, and back to Raven, considering each of them in turn. Their expressions were steadfast and full of certainty. Their breaths were measured and calm. If only I could have felt the same.

"Captain Elsbaud?" I called back, walking to face the man. "The group has put it to me to answer and I think I've come to a decision."

Elsbaud remained in place, waiting for us to finish our approach before he spoke. "Will you put your quest on hold, then? Considering the circumstances, it's a very sound strategy."

He unsheathed his sword and prepared to remove the level restriction debuff from the rest of the group.

"We've discussed it," I replied, halting his ritual. "I believe I have the support of everyone here when I say, we've decided to proceed with the quest."

Elsbaud's brow furrowed, but he retained his calm veneer. "This man speaks for the lot of you?"

The rest of the group nodded and Elsbaud blinked in disbelief. Then he looked to his second in command. "You heard the Travelers, Lieutenant. It appears the fools are going in. Call off the contingent and redirect them back to the outer defenses."

"Yes, sir," the lieutenant replied, snapping a sharp salute. Then he was off, vanishing back into the mist from the direction in which he came.

40

We stood at the entrance to the sewer, each of us contemplating the adventure that awaited us on the other side of the wrought-iron gate. Meanwhile, swirls of putrid vapor enveloped us as the steam from below mixed with the mist at street level.

The foul stench clung to our skin and clothes like a specter, haunting each reluctant breath.

"This isn't going to be pleasant," Pops muttered while Attia held her nose.

"I called it, didn't I?" Ely said. "I just knew it was going to be latrine duty."

"It isn't exactly latrine duty, though, is it?" Raven countered, sounding irritated.

"Yeah, same difference," he pressed. "But worse. Look, all I'm saying is, I hope this turns out to be worth it."

The sudden change in tone was disconcerting, and I started to wonder if I hadn't made the wrong decision. Still, the location of the task hadn't changed. A sewer was a sewer.

"Let's just get it over with," Raven suggested.

I nodded and took a step toward the gate and then paused and turned to Ely.

"Before we go in," I said, mentally pulling up my inventory and initiating a trade window. "I have something for you."

"What is it?" he asked, looking confused.

Instead of answering, I dropped the obsidian shards into the window and prompted the trade.

He looked at them long and hard before accepting. The window closed, and the shards were gone.

"What are these for?" he asked.

I nodded toward his fist weapons. "I thought they might make good claws. I don't know how well they'll hold up, but I remember hearing that obsidian was used for arrowheads and primitive knives."

"What?" Ely drew the word out as he put the pieces together and an idea began forming in his head.

Taking a seat on the cobblestones, he pulled two smooth, wooden objects from his inventory. Makeshift tools and bits of leather came out next and he set to the task of affixing the shards.

"I found this wood today. I think it's ironwood. Really tough stuff."

"It looks nice," I said, giving him a nod.

"I spent a few hours carving and polishing it because I thought it'd make a good base. It took a lot longer than I would have thought, just because it's so strong. To be honest, I was planning on crafting a new set when I got access to better materials," he explained while he worked. "It looks like I might not have to wait as long as I thought."

Any complaint about the sewer or the task ahead of us had been forgotten. It looked tedious, but we all watched in silence, entranced by his singleminded focus.

At last, he was done.

Ely stood and tucked the tools into his inventory and then held his new weapons aloft. They were fearsome things, horrible implements of death, and it was clear he was quite happy with the upgrade.

He placed the claws on his hands and then his old weapons, too, disappeared into his inventory.

"Well," he said, grinning from ear to ear. "What are you all gawping at? Let's do this thing."

~

THE SMELL GOT WORSE AS WE DESCENDED THE STAIRS AND INCHED OUR way further into the depths of the sewer. Water sloshed around our legs as we went, the sound punctuated by the odd squeak of a rat that ventured too close to the bottom of a boot.

You have entered a low-level dungeon:
The Sewers of Fort Morrow.

"This is it," Pops said without missing a step. He held his makeshift torch aloft and nodded, ushering us ever forward and guiding us through the looming darkness. "Welcome to the sewers."

At times, we heard the sound of something moving somewhere in the distance. Growls and groans became more frequent, and then the sickening slurp of an oncoming mob signaled our first encounter.

A slime approached with mind-boggling speed, blubbing and blobbing as it raced toward the only source of light.

Pops was ready.

"Prepare yourself," he exclaimed.

In one fluid motion, he tossed the torch to Attia's outstretched hands and unslung his axe. The runes on his weapon glowed red, and he braced himself for the oncoming blow, then pivoted around the slime.

The move distanced him from the group, but exposed the creature's back to the rest of us.

Thin wisps of white light emanated from Attia's palm and she concentrated her focus on keeping Pops alive. Beads of sweat began forming on her brow as each successive blow whittled at his health.

"Any time now, folks," Pops grunted, deflecting one undulating strike while taking the full force of another to the leg.

A greasy, corrosive substance burned at what little armor he wore and blisters formed on his exposed flesh.

Ely leapt into action, slashing and kicking the back of the defenseless blob while I unsheathed Truthseeker and prepared to engage.

"Move to the side," Raven commanded, drawing her blades and readying an attack of her own.

Ely shuffled sideways, leaving the slime's back exposed to Raven, and plunged his fist deep into the gelatinous goo.

"Oh, gross," he said, tugging his hand free after struggling for several seconds.

Attia sent a wave of healing light toward the burns on his clawed fist and grit her teeth. "I'm already down a third of my mana," she warned.

*You cast **Mana Surge** on Attia.*
Attia is now refreshed.

"Thanks," she said, flashing me a welcome smile.

Raven refocused her attention on the mob and prepared a strike. I blinked as she disappeared into the shadows and then reemerged. Her daggers sunk into the slime and the creature arched up in pain, momentarily changing its aggro before redoubling its attack on Pops.

"Let me build hate first," Pops chuckled, red runes on his weapon burning like fire. "Just poke away at it for a little while longer. Then you can go all out."

Raven nodded.

*You cast **Mana Surge** on yourself.*
You are now refreshed.

Next, I readied Wind Blade, and began my own assault.

The glowing green orbs of energy swirling around my blade cast an eerie glow around us. It helped a little with visibility, but the length of my weapon made fighting in the cramped corridor difficult.

I cast a jealous glance toward Raven, envying her ample room at the back of the mob.

"Now's good," Pops said with a nod as he lodged a critical strike deep into the creature's rancid flesh.

Several of my strikes glanced off the slime's gelatinous skin. At most, the swipes resulted in 1 or 2 hit points of physical damage, but the added wind element on my attack made up the difference.

Blow after blow slid off the slime and my hands rang with pain as Truthseeker struck the stone bricks beneath the sewage.

Finally, in a moment of frustration, I let loose an Earthblast.

"What was that?" Attia asked through a frown of concentration.

"Earthblast?" I answered, readying another strike with my sword.

"Do that," she said. "Elemental attacks seem much more effective than physical for this thing."

"Indeed," Pops grunted, once again pulling the mob's attention back away from the group. "Give me another second or two and then hit it again."

Ely swiped at the slime, cutting a hunk of its flesh free. It fell into the sewage with a bubbling hiss and I prepared another cast.

"Now," Pops commanded.

Pulling deep, I harnessed the energy that flowed from somewhere inside, envisioning the stones beneath my feet and the larger connection to the surrounding earth.

*You cast **Earthblast**.*
***Critical Strike!** The Sewer Sludge takes 75 HP Earth damage.*

Pops spun, raising his axe above his head as he moved before bringing it down in a fiery blaze.

The slime recoiled in pain and then shrunk into itself, trembling in silence.

Further attacks proved ineffective while the creature seemed to boil from within.

"Defensive stance?" Ely asked.

We all shrugged, watching the bulbous mass quiver before us.

"That was some hit," Raven said, nodding toward Pops. "Does anyone have another earth-based attack?"

"I do," Ely answered. "I can use Knockout Punch. You want me to give it a shot?"

"Not yet. When Pops uses that fire strike again, wait a few seconds, and then chain your attack." She looked at me. "Once Ely lands his punch, wait a moment to see if the elements react and then cast your spell."

I nodded and raised my sword, eyeing the slime with suspicion. "I think something's wrong," I said.

It was getting smaller.

Just then, the slime erupted in a spinning torrent of burning goo, showering us with acid-like filth.

The Sewer Sludge uses **Fluid Strike.**
Fluid Strike *hits Pops for 15 HP.*
Critical Strike! **Fluid Strike** *hits Ely for 86 HP.*
Critical Strike! **Fluid Strike** *hits you for 92 HP.*
Critical Strike! **Fluid Strike** *hits Attia for 96 HP.*
Fluid Strike *hits Raven for 35 HP.*

All but Pops cried out in pain and surprise.

In the seconds that followed, Pops regained aggro and Attia channeled a group-healing spell as she desperately worked to attend our wounds without taking hate from the slime.

"Can I get another cast of Mana Surge?" she asked.

I obliged, then refreshed my own buff as well.

"Next time, we back up and get out of range if it does that again," Pops said.

"A sound suggestion," Raven agreed.

"How is your MP, Attia?" I asked, keeping my attention on the slime.

"A bit less than half," she answered. "Mana Surge really helps, thank you."

"We've only managed to take this thing down to about half," Ely grunted as he launched a kick at the slime.

"Just remember to chain your attacks like I told you," Raven said.

"Just tell me when," Ely replied, smiling in the low, green light.

"Almost there," Pops said. "I still have to build up a bit more energy."

I glanced at my health and mana. Even with the refreshing effect of Mana Surge, my MP was getting low. Each few seconds without a cast boosted my available points slightly, but it was clear we couldn't keep this up forever.

"You ready?" Pops asked as he parried a heavy attack.

"Go," Ely said, pulling back from the slime and centering his fists.

Pops unleashed his flaming axe strike, dropping another ten percent of the creature's hit points. Then Ely burst forward with blinding speed, connecting with the slime and sending it sliding in my direction.

I dodged the creature and watched with amazement as shards of crystalline rock formed within its gelatinous flesh, growing outward with each passing second.

"Now, Denton," Raven shouted. "Cast your spell before it's too late."

The crystals began receding, and the slime turned toward Ely as I let another Earthblast flow from my fingertips.

*You cast **Earthblast.***
***Elemental Chain Bonus!** The Sewer Sludge takes 274 HP Earth damage.*

You have defeated the Sewer Sludge.
You have gained 1,200 Experience Points.
*You have found a **Corroded Vial of Slime Ooze.***
*You have found a **Rotten Skull.***

"Wow," I breathed, looking on in a stupor as the slime bubbled and dissolved in the rancid sewer water at our feet.

"Elemental chain bonus," Raven said with a nod. "Coordinated attacks deal heavy bonus damage when coupled with a corresponding magic burst."

"Huh," Ely grunted, smiling his approval. "Why didn't we do that in the first place?"

"Slow down there, big guy," Pops interjected. "We did it, and that's good, but we can't just unload an attack like that at the beginning of a fight. We've got to set it up correctly or Denton here will take way more hate than I can control."

"Okay." Ely nodded. "So, you build up hate, say the word, and we'll do it again. If we time things right, the slime will die and we'll be good to go, yeah?"

"That's about the gist of it." Raven nodded.

"Did you guys get as much EXP as I did?" I asked, still staring at the remains of the creature in disbelief. "Twelve-hundred..."

They all nodded.

"These mobs are designed for a party of level 5's," Attia explained. "We're all synched to your level."

"Which explains why the fight was so hard," I muttered. "Still, that was a lot of experience."

"So worth it." Ely grinned.

"Let's not get cocky," Raven said, flashing Ely a warning glance. "Everyone rest up. There will be more of these and we need to be ready."

"Yes, Ma'am," Ely responded, returning her glance with a mischievous grin.

"Do you think there are other mobs in here?" Attia asked. "Besides possibly the undead, that is."

Raven was quiet while she considered the question. After a while, she answered, her words soft and etched with concern.

"I imagine so," she said. "And probably much worse than this slime. The good news is that we should level soon. That'll even the playing field a bit. Whatever lies ahead, we'll need to be prepared to face it."

"Together," Pops said, holding his hand in the air, palm down.

"Together," Attia replied, placing her hand on top of his.

"Together," Ely, Raven, and I said in unison, stacking our own hands in the mix.

Our words echoed down the stone corridor and then there was silence. Then the sound of a droplet of water falling into the standing sewage. And then the slurping sound of another slime as it descended upon our group.

41

The slime pushed a small wave of putrid water in front of it as it slid toward our group. We watched in silence as it advanced. Once again the runes on Pops' axe glowed red, and the mob responded.

"Remember the plan." Pops grunted. He blocked a strike from a protruding globule and, just like before, he moved the creature into position.

We each maneuvered into our places as if by instinct, preparing ourselves for the delicate dance we were about to perform.

Without being fully rested, our resource pools were even more limited than during our previous encounter. A fourth of my MP bar was missing and my health hadn't quite topped out yet.

I looked to Attia, but she shook her head.

"You first," she said. "Then me."

I was about to protest when the wisdom of her words struck me. By casting Mana Surge on myself first, I could recover enough mana over time to make the second cast. I could also monitor my buff and recast on us both once the spell fell off. This would save me the trouble of guessing or combing the logs to know when Attia's refresh effect had worn off.

*You cast **Mana Surge** on yourself.*
You are now refreshed.
*You cast **Wind Blade** on Truthseeker.*

I struck the slime twice before the recast timer on Mana Surge was up.

*You cast **Mana Surge** on Attia.*
Attia is now refreshed.

Things proceeded better than the first encounter, with each of us doing our best to balance the mob's aggro levels while we slowly brought down the creature's health.

At seventy percent, Pops spoke up. "I'll wait until we get to around sixty percent, then I'll use my Fire Spin attack. Are you two ready?"

"Ready and waiting." Ely grinned.

I nodded, sending an Earthblast toward the slime and shaving five percent of its hit points off its health bar. "Me too."

"What if Denton doesn't kill it?" Attia asked.

She made a good point. I was nowhere near the tank Pops was and something told me I wouldn't last long under a direct assault.

"Leave that to me," Raven said. "Just remember to back away if it recoils like the last one did."

"Don't have to tell me twice," Ely replied, causing us all to laugh.

It felt good. Laughing. The camaraderie in the face of pain and death. Just being with people I felt like I could understand.

If even for just this one dungeon, this one party, we were sharing a connection and doing something even Captain Elsbaud deemed foolish, if not completely impossible. Not only that, we were doing it in style.

"Now," Pops said, launching into his Fire Spin attack and hefting his weapon high overhead before bringing it down on the slime.

Ely followed suit, using his Knockout Punch as he had before. The resulting elemental chain struck the Sewer Sludge, turning its insides into crystalline shards just as before.

I focused on the crystals, measuring my breath and harnessing the power of earth. Time slowed, and I watched the slivers grow. Each second was like an eternity, but the power welled within me, raging at my fingertips.

When the moment was right, I unleashed the spell.

*You cast **Earthblast.***
***Elemental Chain Bonus!** The Sewer Sludge takes 312 HP Earth damage.*

The slime turned, directing its attention toward me before readying a counterattack.

"Denton," Attia cried out. "Help him. I'm almost out of MP."

"I'm trying," Pops grunted.

The slime swung a bulbous glob of flesh at my chest and then another at my leg.

Dodging the first blow, I brought Truthseeker down to block the second, but the slime's flesh flowed around my blade like water before my skin erupted in fiery pain.

"I've got this," Raven said, her voice trembling. And then she was gone.

Even as distracted as I was from trying to deflect another attack, I recognized her movements from our time at the tower. She'd entered the void.

Then, with an animal-like howl, she emerged. Her daggers glowed like the fangs of an enormous beast before they sank deep into the ooze.

Raven has defeated the Sewer Sludge.
You have gained 1,300 Experience Points.
*You have found a **Corroded Vial of Slime Ooze.***
*You have found a **Discarded Sandwich.***

"You did well, Denton," Pops said, clapping me on the shoulder. "That must have been a lot of pressure, but you didn't panic. That's good."

"It was close." I wiped the sweat from my brow and glanced at my HP bar. "I only had 24 hit points left. One more hit and I would have been walking back."

"I'm sorry," Attia said. She rested her back against the wall and let out a long breath. "We'd better rest before the next fight. I'm not sure how many more encounters like that I can handle. Not without access to some of my better spells."

"Good point," Pops muttered. "Let's keep it down so we don't draw any more attention."

"Did you see what it dropped?" Ely whispered. "A discarded sandwich. That's disgusting. What are we supposed to do with that?"

"Who knows? Hopefully those vials of slime ooze are worth something," Raven replied with an amused shrug.

We sat in silence for several minutes, idling away the time while our health and mana recovered. The sounds of the sewer echoed around us and we listened, intent on detecting an approaching threat before it got too near.

When our injuries were healed and our energy restored, we once again moved forward and I allowed my mind to wander as we went.

Both of our encounters so far had been against a single mob. Though we were caught unrested by the second slime, we'd managed to defeat it without loss with the use of our coordinated attacks and a little luck on my part.

Still, I shuddered to think how things might have gone down if we were forced to fight two slimes at once.

*You receive a **Corroded Vial of Slime Ooze**.*
*Ely receives a **Rotten Skull**.*

"Wait, how?" I started, but Attia turned and explained in hushed tones.

"It was the loot from the first slime," she whispered. "We can cast lots for each item, or just let the system distribute things as we go along. If something drops that you really want, you can always roll for it. Or if you don't want junk clogging your inventory, you can pass from the loot menu."

"I see," I whispered back.

Pops slowed and then came to a stop as he peered off into the distance. I listened to the echoes of water dripping into water, waiting for what might come next. At last, he turned.

"It looks like this waterway opens up not too much further."

"What do you think is up there?" Attia asked.

"I can't be certain but, if I had to guess, I'd say it looks like there might be a flow valve of some sort."

"How can you tell?" Ely asked. "I can't see a thing."

"There was a light source. It was dim, but it was there. Might have been the moon filtering in from a grate in an alleyway. Who knows?"

"And if this leads to an open room," Raven began.

"Then there's probably a group of mobs waiting for us inside," Pops finished. "We'll have to be careful. Does anyone have a ranged attack? We need someone to pull the mobs one by one so we can tackle them here in the waterway instead of fighting in the room."

"I'll do it," Raven said, standing a little taller.

"I-"

"No." She cut me off with a smile.

"But-"

"Earthblast will draw too much hate." Then she flashed her daggers in the crackling torchlight before they disappeared once again under the shadow of her cloak. "Don't worry about me. These aren't my only weapons."

I nodded begrudgingly and followed the others as we made our approach.

Taking a strip of what appeared to be heavy cloth from his inventory, Pops extinguished the torch.

"Denton," he whispered.

"Yes?"

"Can you cast that Wind Blade spell of yours? It's less light than the flame, but I'm hoping it might not attract as much attention."

I obliged, infusing Truthseeker with wind energy. Once again, the stone bricks around us glowed from the light of the pale, green orbs.

We inched our way toward the open area ahead and the walls began to narrow. Moonlight flitted in and out of view and, as we drew near, the sounds of slimes and other creatures filled our ears.

Finally, we stopped short, and I peered forward. A good twenty paces stood between us and a darkened void where the waterway ended and the room that housed the flow control valve began.

Raven stepped toward the front of the group as she prepared herself for the task at hand. Then she turned. "Everyone ready?"

"Ready," we whispered back as one.

As she was about to leave, Pops placed a tender hand on her shoulder.

"Be careful," he said. "Take your time."

"I know, I know," she whispered. "We don't want any links. I got it."

"Right, we don't want any links." He nodded, raising an eyebrow. "But, more importantly, we don't want anyone getting hurt."

"I'll be fine," she retorted, but she couldn't hide the hint of a shy smile that played about the corners of her lips.

We cleared the first three slimes in the room without any issues. Raven pulled them, one by one, into the waterway where we could fight unimpeded. Each elemental bonus chain was better than the last as we learned to gauge when to execute.

By the final slime, it had become almost second nature.

Three more vials of slime ooze filtered through the loot system as we fought, leaving only one in the queue. There were no more discarded sandwiches, but a handful of bones and rotten skulls joined the mix.

"You know," Ely said, examining his fist weapons. "Before tonight, I'd have been scrambling to get my hands on those bones. But these obsidian shards are top-notch."

I smiled. "I'm glad you like them."

Raven returned from the room looking confused and without a mob in tow.

"What is it?" Pops asked.

"I could have sworn there were at least two more slimes last time I pulled," she explained, "at least. But now it's empty."

"Empty?" Ely asked. "Are you sure?"

Raven rolled her eyes. "Yes. I'm sure. I don't know where they went, but they aren't there."

"Then what are we waiting for?" he returned. "Let's move up and take a look."

"Hold on—" Pops started, but Ely was already headed toward the darkened control room.

Moonlight was once again filtering down through a street grate when we stepped out of the waterway and into the chamber. Even upon first glance, it appeared that Pops had been right.

The room housed a number of large gears and gates designed to control the flow of incoming rain runoff and sewage.

"Huh," Ely said as he poked his head around the gears. "Looks like you were right. There are no mobs here. No slimes. Nothing. The other waterways are blocked off. Where do you think they went?"

"Told you," Raven said, but it was clear her thoughts were elsewhere.

"What's on your mind?" I asked.

"This light," she said, eyeing the grate above our heads. "Do you think it could have something to do with it?"

"You might be onto something," Attia said as she scanned the room. "That first slime didn't like the torch much."

Then she lit Pops' extinguished torch and held it aloft.

"It's possible," Pops said, "and it makes sense if you think about it. These creatures spend their time in the dark. Any source of light might cause them significant pain."

He paused for a moment, surveying the room and investigating the walls for any sign of an escape route. "The important question seems to be, where could they have gone? And, maybe even more important than that, will they come back?"

"What about this?" Ely asked, pointing to a small opening on the far wall near the ceiling.

The hole was just large enough for a small child to climb through, but rusty iron bars blocked any passage.

"They are slimes," Ely said as he walked across the room. "Who says they can't just slurp past those bars and wiggle their way to where ever this leads?"

When he reached the wall, he bent close and ran a finger through a thick trail of goo.

"Yep," he said as he inspected the filth on his fingertip. "They definitely went this way."

"Ely," Attia said, glancing from him to the grate and back again.

"Yeah?"

"Come back over here."

"Hold on," he said, grabbing the bars and hoisting himself upward. "I think I see—"

The light in the room faded as the moon slipped behind a curtain of clouds.

"Ely—"

"Just a second."

"Ely," Pops shouted. "Come back."

"Hold on. I think I see—"

Even from across the room I could hear the slurping sound that followed.

"Yeaargghh," Ely's muffled shout of pain echoed off the slimy, stone and brick walls as he fell backward in a shower of ooze.

42

We watched in stunned silence while Pops rushed forward. He traversed the space of the room with blinding speed, racing toward Ely and the coagulated slime.

"Hold on, you big idiot," he shouted, thrusting his arms into the goo. "Denton, I need your help."

Shaking myself from my shocked stupor, I sheathed Truthseeker and joined the old man. As soon as I slid to a halt, I sunk my hands deep into the gelatinous flesh that now towered above us.

It burned.

And the slime that had enveloped Ely was still growing.

"Pull," Pops yelled.

We tugged with all our might while Attia healed our wounds. Then Raven was beside us. She dug into the slime, fishing for Ely's leg.

"We have to get him out of there before it finishes forming," she said.

The thing was massive. Easily the size of four slimes put together.

And it was still growing.

"Denton, I need Mana Surge," Attia called, sounding conflicted.

She was running out of MP, struggling to keep us all alive while Ely was running out of air.

I looked back and thrust a slimy hand in her direction.

*You cast **Mana Surge** on Attia.*
Attia is now refreshed.

Ely's eyes widened, and he began to squirm, making it difficult to hold on through the grease and goo.

"He's suffocating," I shouted, panic welling in my chest. "Forget the slime. It'll finish forming no matter what we do. We have to get him out before he..."

"Before he drowns," Attia sobbed, finishing my thought.

I redoubled my grip on Ely's wrist and pulled, slipping on the greasy stones beneath my feet.

And yet we were making progress.

Inch by inch, he neared the surface. Then his fingers breached the stale air. Another heave and he collapsed on the floor in a spluttering mess.

He was still choking on the ground when the slime reared back and roared its sloppy challenge.

Pops raised his axe.

"Get back," Attia yelled.

Raven grabbed Ely's wrist and vanished into the shadows while Pops blocked an incoming blow.

"Go." He grunted, preparing himself for the next attack. "I'll hold it off while you guys get ready."

It took a second for his words to register in my mind. I couldn't take my eyes off the monstrous beast that now towered above us.

"Get a move on," Pops shouted as he blocked another blow.

I fumbled backwards, willing my feet to move despite the deep-rooted shock that held me in place.

By the time I reached the other three, I'd regained at least some of my wits. I glanced around and surveyed the situation.

Things were looking grim.

Ely was still balled up on the stone floor at the edge of the flow control room while Raven clenched her daggers, eyeing the slime's every move. Meanwhile, Attia channeled her healing spells with abandon.

Her mana was desperately low and her refresh buff was about to fall off.

*You cast **Mana Surge** on Attia.*
Attia is now refreshed.

"Thank you," she mumbled, not taking her eyes off Pops for even a second.

I grit my teeth and nodded, fully aware that her attention was elsewhere.

Pops shuffled backwards, dodging and parrying attacks with his axe as he made his way to our new camp.

Ely cast a startled glance upward and rolled to his side. He looked like death and his muscles trembled. He coughed up bits of rancid slime, but the spirit of battle still burned deep within his eyes.

"Not you," Raven said. "She can't keep both of you alive. Not now. Rest and make sure you don't take any hate before we get this under control."

"I'm... sorry," he said, choking over the words. "I—"

"Save it," she growled, cutting him off. Then she raised her daggers and prepared to launch her attack.

I unsheathed my sword and cast Mana Surge on myself, stepping into position as the renewed buff scrolled through my combat log. I cast Wind Blade and readied an attack of my own, but stopped short.

Remembering all my past mistakes, I quickly inspected the slime.

*You **Inspect** the Massive Sewer Slime.*
Level 10. Hit Points: 3,412.
The Massive Sewer Slime has a Defense Bonus.
*The Massive Sewer Slime is affected by **Hunger**.*
You have learned INSPECT: RANK 2.

You may occasionally uncover additional details when you inspect your target.

I swallowed hard and grit my teeth. This was going to be tough, but the room was much larger than the cramped waterway and I had a lot more space with which to maneuver.

Truthseeker sang as it whipped through the air, scoring the slime's putrid flesh with the imbued power of wind.

The damage was negligible.

I struck the beast again and again, burying my weapon as deep as I dared without fear of losing my momentum. Still, the slime's health bar didn't so much as budge.

I was frustrated and confused and on the verge of losing my breath from the prolonged exertion. But I wasn't out of options just yet.

*You cast **Earthblast**.*
Critical Strike! *The Massive Sewer Slime takes 12 HP Earth damage.*

"What's going on," I asked, unable to keep the sound of disbelief from my voice.

"I'm not sure," Raven replied. "My attacks aren't doing anything to it."

"Nor mine," Pops added. "Just keep going. It's much bigger than the other slimes and hits harder, but it's slower too. Keep your eyes open and watch for a weakness."

"Or special attacks," I grumbled.

"Right." Pops laughed, sounding sardonic as he deftly blocked another heavy blow. "And special attacks. We don't need a repeat of last time. Especially not at this scale."

We fought on for what felt like ages, barely scratching at the slime's HP and gradually draining our resources.

It was a battle of attrition.

And we were losing.

Raven ducked into the shadows and emerged mid-air, plunging to the ground with an attack that burned through the slime's outer flesh.

With a lurch, the creature began to ripple and churn.

"Heads up," Pops warned. "Something's happening."

"Should we back away?" Attia asked.

Without anyone speaking another word, we all began distancing ourselves from the slime.

Something was happening.

But whatever it was, it didn't appear to be the same as the attack we'd experienced before.

I looked at my companions, now clearly illuminated by the light of the moon streaming through the grate in the ceiling.

"It's the moonlight," Ely gasped, struggling to his feet. "I think we're supposed to attack now."

It made sense.

The rest of us exchanged glances before rushing back to the fight. Each of us thrust our weapons at the slime, scoring a precious few critical hits before the moonlight began to fade.

The slime burned red as the last of the light faded. Then its attack speed increased with sudden vigor and it pummeled Pops with blow after blow.

*The Massive Sewer Slime gains **Berserk**.*

"Don't let it hit you," Attia shouted. "I'm almost out of mana."

"I'm trying," Pops hollered back. He took another hit to the leg. "It's too fast when it's red like this."

Another strike flung the axe from his hands. It clanged against the far wall with a painful crash that echoed around the room like thunder.

Pops slumped to his knees, and the slime was upon him. Towering above his exhausted body, it prepared to swallow him whole.

"Watch out," Raven yelled, springing into action.

She raced forward, shoving Pops aside as she brandished the discarded sandwich.

Despite the buildup of hate, the slime seemed to forget about its prey and honed in on the moldy treat.

It thrust forward in an attempt to retrieve the prize, but Raven dodged backwards.

Several makeshift limbs sprang out, thrashing at Raven like tentacles as they beat the air.

My mind raced, and I struggled to keep up with the action.

As best as I could tell, she was shadow-tanking. Slipping in and out of the void fast enough to evade the attacks.

But how long could she keep it up?

Sooner or later her energy would run dry and she'd be just as vulnerable as the rest of us.

"Run," Ely shouted. "You can't sustain that in close combat forever. You have to kite it."

Raven took his advice. She slipped into and out of the void, distancing herself from the slime while it made a hasty pursuit.

Attia tossed the torch on the ground and brandished her staff. She rushed toward Pops while the flickering light cast eerie shadows as the flame spluttered in the darkness before regaining its strength.

I recast Mana Surge on her and stood by, helpless. My friends were suffering and there was nothing I could do but wait. What I wouldn't give for another spell. Something, anything, that I could use to help the team.

But Margaret was right. I couldn't count on learning new abilities on the fly. I had to make do with the tools I had at hand.

"Be patient," Ely whispered.

His hand clenched on my shoulder for support and comfort and I knew he was right.

Each of us had our own strengths. Together, we were a team, and together we could kill this thing. We just had to be patient. Wait for the right moment. And then strike.

"I'm almost out," Raven said before dodging another attack.

"Hold on," Attia pleaded. "Just a little longer."

"I'll do what I can."

Attia stood above Pops and raised her staff. "Everyone," she said, "come to me." Her voice was soft and her gaze far away as she began to chant sing-song words I couldn't understand.

A soft, white light emanated from the tip of her staff. It was small at first, but grew in intensity as she continued to chant.

Once again, the entire room was filled with a glowing brightness, but this time it wasn't from the moonlight filtering in from the street above.

The slime stopped and pivoted. It was no longer interested in the discarded sandwich Raven held aloft. Its tentacle-like arms waved like the severed heads of a hydra. More sprouted forth, and it set its sights on Attia.

"I need more time," I heard her plea between the foreign words that filled her chant.

I clenched Truthseeker with both hands and took up a defensive stance in front of our healer, refreshing my own Mana Surge and then using the last of my MP on Tempest.

My Wind Blade buff dropped, overwritten by the more powerful spell. Green wisps of wind enveloped me, adding to Attia's glow as Tempest surged through my body.

"Lighter than air. Faster than a hurricane," I whispered to myself, unable to resist the dark smile that played about my lips.

I knew then that there was no way I could take the creature on my own. But I could buy my friends more time.

Squaring off against the slime, I rushed forward, hacking and slashing as I went.

Just like Raven, I could take the heat from Attia and Pops for a while, and maybe... just maybe... we could get back on our feet and finish this thing.

Critical strike! You hit the Massive Sewer Slime for 18 HP + 45 Wind damage.

Critical strike! You hit the Massive Sewer Slime for 17 HP + 43 Wind damage.

Dodged! The Massive Sewer Slime misses its attack.
Dodged! The Massive Sewer Slime misses its attack.
You hit the Massive Sewer Slime for 8 HP + 20 Wind damage.

Adrenaline flooded through my veins and my arms trembled with excess energy I couldn't release quick enough.

I felt more than alive.

You've been hit! The Massive Sewer Slime hits you for 40 HP.
You've been hit! The Massive Sewer Slime hits you for 50 HP.

The feeling of soaring sank, replaced with an invisible fire that threatened to consume me as the slime's tentacles burned at my armor and struck my flesh.

Ely was beside me now. Sweat poured down his brow and his lips were twisted in a savage snarl. He punched and kicked with a fury, each strike taking away a sliver of the slime's health.

Just like the moon, the light from Attia's staff had exposed its weakness. Even non-elemental attacks were more effective.

*Attia casts **Moon's Blessing.***
Attia recovers 5 HP and 150 MP.
You recover 112 HP and 80 MP.
Ely recovers 250 HP and 25 Energy.
Raven recovers 50 HP and 125 Energy.
Pops recovers 350 HP and 3 Active Runes.

The slime burned red and focused its attack on our healer.

The Massive Sewer Slime hits Attia for 65 HP.
The Massive Sewer Slime hits Attia for 60 HP.

Attia cried out in pain. She clutched her staff thrusting it back and forth in a blind attempt to fend off the slime's blows.

Her health was dropping and nothing I did seemed to make a difference.

Raven dipped in and out of the void. When she emerged beside me, I saw she had brought Pops his great axe.

With a roar that seemed to shake the walls, Pops leapt into action. His runes burned brighter than I'd seen before.

He spun in midair, still yelling his battle cry as his axe ripped a flaming gash in the slime's backside.

Ely closed his eyes, meditating for just a moment before releasing his Knockout Punch.

The slime stuttered, seemingly confused by the massive shift in hate.

Then the crystals began to form deep within its hulking mass. The sound was like glass crunching beneath a heavy boot, muffled by countless layers of ooze.

There was no shouting or commands to attack. Each of us knew exactly what we were supposed to do.

I waited, listening to the crackling crescendo growing inside the slime until just the right moment.

*You cast **Earthblast**.*
***Elemental Chain Bonus!** The Massive Sewer Slime takes 1,253 HP Earth damage.*

The Massive Sewer Slime burbled out in pain and then hunkered down, folding into itself just as the first slime had in the waterway.

"Back up and spread out," Pops commanded. "It still has the berserk buff. If you get caught in the spread, you're as good as gone."

He treaded backwards, watching to make sure the slime stayed put as he went.

The light from Attia's staff faded, and we all looked on in silence as the disgusting pile of goo quivered and hunkered down in the shifting firelight.

*The Massive Sewer Slime uses **Fluid Strike**.*

The Massive Sewer Slime misses its attack.

I breathed a quick sigh of relief and waited for our foe to reengage. Even after the failed special attack, it still burned red.

"Give it the sandwich," Ely shouted.

The slime lurched forward, tearing toward me with uncanny speed.

"Why?" Raven asked.

"Just do it."

Raven tossed the discarded sandwich in front of me, but the slime didn't appear to notice. It kept coming, refusing to slow and enjoy the tasty treat.

Within seconds it was upon me, absorbing the bundle of moldy bread and its contents on the way.

Then it stopped short.

I stared into the bubbly goo in disbelief as it turned from red to a putrid green.

> *The Massive Sewer Slime enjoys the Discarded Sandwich.*
> *The Massive Sewer Slime is no longer affected by **Hunger**.*
> *The Massive Sewer Slime is no longer affected by **Berserk**.*

Despite the loss of the berserker buff, the slime had not lost its will to fight.

Tentacles once again protruded from its flesh, each swinging and slapping in a desperate attempt to dissolve anything they might come into contact with.

But Pops was there.

He raised his axe and growled, nearly knocking me over with the force of his protective fury.

I slipped to the side and stepped back in an effort to allow the aggro from my Earthblast to settle while Pops wrestled for the slime's attention.

"Good job," Raven said, smiling.

Her encouragement in the heat of battle felt surprisingly good, and I found myself laughing. I returned her smile with exhausted amusement and the gesture proved contagious.

Soon we were all laughing, brandishing our attacks on the unwitting creature as if our lives weren't in jeopardy.

"One more moon cycle and we might just be able to finish this thing off," Raven said between blows.

"I'm really sorry about aggroing this thing," Ely said. "This whole thing would have gone a lot better if we'd been ready."

"Don't worry about it," Raven replied. "Good idea about the sandwich, by the way. I'm sorry I yelled at you earlier."

"You too." He chuckled. "And I deserved to be yelled at, so don't sweat it."

"Eyes on the mob, folks," Pops interjected with a bit of good humor. "Let's get ready for the next phase."

I renewed Mana Surge on Attia and continued my slow and steady assault on the slime. Every slash was a delicate balance of mechanics: enough damage to whittle away at the creature's health while it was less vulnerable, but not enough to raise my aggro too much in case it survived our next coordinated attack.

At last, the cloud cover passed, showering the subterranean room with the moon's soft, blue light.

"There's no berserk buff on the slime, so let's make it count," Pops shouted as he initiated his flaming axe strike.

Ely followed suit, landing his Knockout Punch with determined force.

And I finished the chain.

*You cast **Earthblast.***

***Elemental Chain Bonus!** The Massive Sewer Slime takes 895 HP Earth damage.*

The slime shivered, bubbling and boiling as its flesh burned red. When it turned to face me, my stomach lurched high into my chest.

*The Massive Sewer Slime gains **Berserk.***

"Not this time, you slimy bastage," Raven shouted, pushing in front of me in a cloud of smoke and shadow.

The slime rose in the air, preparing to strike at me while she crouched low.

Unsure of what to expect, I raised my sword. A few more ticks of mana and I'd be able to recast Tempest.

Unfortunately, I was running out of time.

In a mind-numbing blur, Raven's daggers hummed with a surge of luminescent power as she leapt upward to meet her foe.

She popped in and out of the void, and streaks of blue light danced across my vision. Each successive strike seemed to increase in power until she landed the finishing blow.

*Raven uses **Bite of the Dire Wolf**.*
The Massive Sewer Slime takes 315 HP damage.
Raven has defeated the Massive Sewer Sludge.
You have gained 7,200 Experience Points.
*You have found an **Oversized Gem Setting**.*
*You have found a **Sword of the Forgotten Champion**.*
*You have found a **Rusty Key**.*
Congratulations, Traveler of EndWorld,
on reaching Level 4!

"Ding," we all exclaimed in unison. Then we laughed together in exhausted triumph.

Sitting in the bubbling remains of the slime was an old, wooden chest. A rusty lock hung from the clasp. It looked ancient, yet formidable.

"Slimy bastage, huh?" Ely asked, nodding to Raven with approval and chuckling to himself. "That's pretty good. I'm going to have to remember to use that one later."

Raven smiled and shrugged. "It was sort of in the heat of the moment. What can I say?"

I watched Attia with curiosity as she bent down and picked up the torch she had dropped during the fray.

Then she moved toward the wall. Once there, she walked the circumference of the room, touching the flame to one sconce after another.

The fire spread to the oiled cloth of the waiting torches, burning bright in the dark, wet space. Soon, the evenly spaced flames lit the room, extinguishing any lingering danger of attracting more slimes.

"You mean we could have just done that to begin with?" Ely asked. "Man, I feel like such a moron."

"Hey, at least we beat it. Right?" I offered, shaking my head in stubborn disbelief. "It could have gone a lot worse. And at least no one died."

Pops laughed, clapping me on the shoulder. "You doubted us?"

"Uh, yeah." I smiled. "Maybe once or twice."

We laughed again and Attia walked back to the group. She nodded toward the chest.

"What about this thing," she asked. "If we hadn't fought the slime, this chest wouldn't have dropped. Maybe there's something nice inside. Do you think that Rusty Key will fit the lock?"

"Probably," Ely said.

He crouched to take a closer look and flipped the heavy, metal lock with his fingers.

"Shouldn't Denton do the honors?" Raven asked, giving me a nod.

I shrugged and stepped forward, casting an uncontested lot roll on the key. It dropped from the loot table into my inventory and I held it in trembling, nervous anticipation.

The key was old and ornate and slid into the lock mechanism perfectly. Gears clicked their release as I turned it a full rotation clockwise.

And then the latch released.

43

A cloud of dust escaped the chest. It billowed into the firelight and we peered inside, each of us eager to see what treasures the box might hold.

"What is that," Attia asked, leaning forward to get a better look.

Nothing showed up in the log.

I furrowed my brow and inspected the rusty hunk of metal laying at the bottom of the box.

A Forgotten Lever.
Quality: Poor.

"Just a lever?" Ely scratched his head before retrieving the heavy item. "That's it?"

Raven turned and scanned the room. She eyed the walls and the floor and then focused her attention on the large gears.

"There," she said, pointing to a spot where the hunk of metal might fit.

She was right.

The lever was obviously meant to control the embedded contraption.

"What does it do," Attia asked, putting a voice to what the rest of us were quietly pondering. "Maybe we should wait a minute. At least until we decide what we're going to do with the other drops?"

"Good idea," Pops said, sitting on the stone bricks and kicking his feet out.

"Sword of the Forgotten Champion," he recited in awe, reading his log aloud. "It's a greatsword. And look at that. It even has good defensive stats and slots for runes."

He was practically beaming with delight.

"It's too big of a weapon for me," I said. "Would it satisfy the requirements for your level 5 quest line, you think? What was it again? Find a blade that's been forged in battle, isn't that what you said? I imagine a forgotten champion might have seen their fair share of battles."

He nodded. "I think it will do."

"Well," I said after a moment of thought. "I vote we let Pops have the sword and cast free lots on the gem setting."

Raven shook her head, quickly adding a verbal response to explain. "I don't have a problem with the blade. I don't have any intention of wielding a sword that size. That said, I don't even have an option to loot the setting."

"Me either," Ely confirmed, looking to Attia for her response.

"Nor I."

"I can't loot it," Pops said with a shrug.

"Are you sure it isn't part of your quest?" Raven asked.

After double-checking my logs, I shrugged. "It isn't. But if you all can't loot it, I guess I'll take it." I looked around at my friends once more before continuing. "No objections to Pops getting the sword? Last chance."

No one objected, so we cast our lots.

I received the setting, and the old man got the sword.

Pops stood and held his new weapon aloft in one hand while gripping his axe in the other.

The runes on his axe burned bright and then fizzled before vanishing in tendrils of smoke.

I watched in astonishment at what happened next.

As the runes burned away, the axe began to crumble.

Somehow Pops was unconcerned.

He focused his attention on the sword. After carefully appraising the keen edge with his now-free hand, he stared into the weapon's glinting reflection for what seemed like an abnormal length of time.

No one else in the party seemed to mind, so I stood quietly and watched as he finished the ritual.

I was about to ask the others what he was up to when I remembered my own haphazard binding with Truthseeker at Harold's Tavern.

That was it.

He was binding his new weapon.

It seemed like ages had passed since that night, and I looked at my sword with a sudden pang of sadness. It had taken a beating since I'd accepted it from Jörgen, even with the repair work, and I already had plans to replace it as soon as I could scrape together enough coin.

The thought made me sad, but Pops' sword was a keen reminder of how things changed in this world.

Change wasn't always bad.

I was about to do a mental inventory of all the things I could do to earn more money after recovering from the dungeon when Pops stirred, shaking me from my wandering chain of thought.

As if in a trance, the old man gently touched the tip of the blade to the ground, kneeled, and began reciting silent words that never left his lips.

Symbols burned the brightest red and, like molten metal, etched themselves into the polished steel. The light was so intense that all of us, save Pops, shielded our eyes.

At last, the rite of binding was complete.

"This was it," he said, nodding and eyeing us all with a look of unfathomable appreciation. "Thank you. This was the sword I needed to complete my quest. You all have no idea how much this means to me."

"You earned it." Attia smiled.

"So, that's it, then?" Ely asked. "You've finished your level 5 quest line?"

Pops nodded, affixing the now-sheathed greatsword onto his back. "I did. I got most of the rewards just now. All that's left is to visit my trainer and I should be done."

"And?" Ely pressed. "What happened? What did you get for finishing?"

"Besides the sword?"

"Yeah."

Pops grinned. "A few new skills, another quest to pick up a new rune, and a pretty nice piece of armor I can wear once I've shown my trainer my new weapon."

"Not bad." Ely nodded his approval. "I wonder what I'll get once I finish mine."

"Hard to say," Pops said. "If your rewards are anything like mine, I'm sure they will be good ones." Then he turned his attention toward the gears. "What are we going to do about this?"

I scratched my chin and appraised the old, worn machinery. It was clear we were meant to operate the contraption, and yet none of us knew how we were supposed to go about it.

Of course, the mechanism looked simple enough. There was an obvious spot where the lever fit. There was a cylindrical bar that fit in the center of the circular base and corresponding teeth that fit with the adjacent gears. But was it a distraction?

There was always the chance that the obvious solution was too easy.

It could be a trap.

"Do you think it's rigged," Ely asked, echoing my own thoughts.

"I don't see any other way to use the lever," Raven said. "It was in the chest, so I imagine we got it for a reason. There certainly doesn't seem to be a use for the gem setting just yet. It has to be for later. The question is, which way should we pull the lever once we install it?"

"Would a pull in one direction result in a different outcome than the other?" Attia posited.

Ely shrugged and hefted the hunk of metal, sliding it into place with a grunt of exertion.

"There," he said, appraising his work. "It's Denton's quest. Denton's call."

"Oh, come on," I protested. "It's not like my quest log tells me which way we should pull the darn thing."

All eyes were on me and no one seemed ready to interject an opinion.

"Fine," I said. "Let's push it away from us and toward that far wall."

I pressed all my weight into the lever, but it didn't budge. Pops, Raven, and then Attia joined in, adding their weight and force to my own.

Still, the machine held fast.

"I don't understand," Pops said. He rubbed his hands and stared at the gears. "These marks suggest the lever should turn that direction."

"Move aside," Ely commanded. He puffed out his chest and made a show of preparing to save the day, flexing his muscles with gusto.

He leaned forward, and the gear lurched backward a fraction of an inch before locking tight. After a few minutes of unproductive struggle, he gave up.

"Maybe we should try the other direction," he offered, trying his best not to look defeat in the eye.

With that, he gave the lever a firm tug, yanking it halfway to the floor with much more force than was required.

"What the... ?"

A loud groan sounded behind us and we turned.

A hidden gate to the waterway we'd entered from fell from the ceiling.

We were trapped.

"That's not awesome," Ely grumbled.

We stood in stunned silence, staring for a few long seconds at the grime-covered bricks that were painted orange by the surrounding firelight.

The only passageway into the room had been sealed. There was no other way out.

I turned and looked at the lever then slid it back to its original position.

Nothing happened.

"Try pushing it forward again," Raven suggested. "Maybe it will work now that the other passage is closed."

I shrugged. It was worth a shot.

I was just about to put my weight into it when Attia held up a hand. She clenched her fist and then brought a single finger to her lips.

I didn't hear it at first. The sound of crackling flames echoing around the chamber filled my senses.

Still, she called for silence.

Ely shifted.

I looked to Raven.

That's when I heard it.

A faint scratching sound was coming from behind the far wall.

"Another slime?" Ely asked.

Attia shook her head and motioned him to shush.

We each took a tentative step forward.

Then another.

The sound grew louder.

Dripping water. Fingernails on stone and the rattling of bamboo or bones.

And then the stench.

The air tasted of decay and death.

Panic rose in my chest and my nerves faltered.

Ely choked back a sudden urge to vomit.

Pops remained calm, turning to the rest of us.

"Go back," he whispered, unsheathing his large, new sword. "Push the lever as far as it will go and be ready to engage."

We did as he asked. This time the lever didn't catch. It moved. The gears squealed as we pushed and heaved. At last, it latched into place.

A loud thud sounded in the distance and we listened nervously to the far-removed clinking of chains.

Something was happening.

The wall in front of Pops began to ascend into the ceiling and a foul wind rushed into the chamber.

The scratching stopped.

It was replaced by the sound of a stuttered shuffling. And then a stampede.

The runes on Pops' sword burned brighter than the surrounding flames. He yelled something, but I couldn't make it out.

Countless decrepit bodies lunged forward to meet his blade.

And then we, too, rushed headlong into the fray.

Undead fingers grasped longingly, clawing from the darkness in an endless tide of hunger and rot and despair.

"What do you want us to do," Raven asked from Pops' flank.

She was as eager to join the fight as the rest of us, but the fiends fell like raindrops under the sweeping swipes of his runed greatsword.

"They're only level 2." Pops grunted, turning his blade to cut down the decayed bodies that climbed the growing pile of their fallen brethren.

"Don't overexert yourself," Attia warned. "Play it safe. There might be more waves yet. Really, we have no idea what's ahead of us."

"Seriously, old man," Ely added, "if you keep it up like that, we're going to have to dig our way out of here."

Pops obliged, stepping back from the chokepoint to allow the creatures to spill out into the open chamber so we could all engage.

He was right. Each new foe I inspected checked in at level 2. Easy prey.

You have defeated the Lost Soul.

You have gained 85 Experience Points.
You have defeated the Shattered Rambler.
You have gained 87 Experience Points.

It was a slaughter.

Wave after wave poured into the chamber, and each of us engaged in the melee. Even Attia wielded her staff against the fiends.

Bodies fell to the floor in scattered heaps and it seemed as if the endless incursion would never cease.

But then it did.

I surveyed the room in the eerie stillness that followed. The fallen remains of the undead were countless and the newly opened waterway was now quiet.

Nothing stirred.

Dripping water and the crackling of torches was all that could be heard over the sound of our heavy breathing.

Pops sheathed his sword and leaned forward, placing his hands on his knees.

"We can probably expect more undead from here on out," he said between breaths, nodding forward into the darkness.

"We knew this was coming." Raven's tone was even and unperturbed. In fact, she was smiling.

"What are you so happy about," Ely asked. "You have a thing for this sort of stuff?"

"It's my level 5 quest," she explained, shooting me a look that reminded me of our conversation at the top of the tower.

"You got a lead?" I asked, eager to know the details, but intent on giving her enough room to give only what she was comfortable sharing.

"I did. I have reason to believe that the undead have an interest in the dire wolf pup I need to save. The undead are here, so there's a chance she is as well."

"She?" Pops asked. "The dire wolf?"

"Hold up," Ely interrupted. "You're supposed to save a dire wolf?"

Raven nodded and I knew it was as much of an answer as the two were going to get.

"We'll help you find her," Attia said, placing a gentle hand on Raven's forearm. "We'll help you save the pup."

"The pup? You're talking about this thing like it's a cuddly puppy. It's a dire wolf," Ely pressed. "Those things are dangerous. They are not puppies."

"Ely."

"Attia?"

"We're going to help Raven, because that's what friends do. Besides, you had no problem offering your help when she offered you that cordial last night."

Ely looked to me for support.

"It's what friends do," I said, "and you did promise to help."

Then I grabbed a torch from a nearby sconce and stepped into the waterway without uttering another word.

The flame from my torch burned bright in the dark space and water once again sloshed at my feet, racing ever downward with the gradual slope. Before long, the rushing and gurgling and splashing was all that I could hear.

There was nothing to turn back to now, just an uphill climb, an empty chamber, and scattered corpses.

The current tugged at my feet and I plodded forward. Our objective was somewhere ahead of us and I felt even more determined to see it through knowing that Raven's quest might also hang in the balance.

I'd already cost her a chance at saving the pup once and I wasn't keen on doing it again. So, I put on a brave face and pressed onward. Deeper and deeper into the depths of the sewer.

The air was still bad, stale and reeking of mold, but it wasn't as rank with decay as before.

A cool mist billowed up from the water ahead and my torch flickered as the fire fought to stay alive in the damp air.

"Careful," Pops warned.

It was too late.

The tug at my boots suddenly became a strong pull as the grade of the slope increased and I felt myself slipping on the mossy, brick floor. My arms flailed of their own accord and I fought for purchase, but it was in vain.

In an instant, the current swept my feet out from under me. I fell backwards while sliding down the perilous decline, striking my head in an explosion of agony.

Stars burst in my vision and the torch went out. Darkness enveloped me. I was no longer in control.

Putrid water threatened to fill my lungs and my fingers scraped at the stone walls as I went. But the current was unwilling to let me go.

I lost all sense of direction as I slid down the dark and curving waterway. With each twist and turn I gained speed, and the rushing torrent pulled me deeper and deeper below the fort.

Somewhere in the echo-y space behind me, I could hear the calls and shouts of my companions. All the sounds mingled together. I couldn't make out words, but I could tell they weren't too far behind.

I pulled my hands in and folded them over my chest after bouncing between the walls in my miserable attempt to slow my descent.

There was no stopping the ride. I was sure of it now. Forward was the only direction and this was the only path. So, instead of fighting, I decided to embrace it.

Once I let go, I felt a sense of exhilaration begin to boil in my chest. I hadn't felt like this since I was a boy.

The dark, sloping waterway was just like a water slide I remembered from my youth. The black hole, we'd called it. I'd gone down that slide countless times. It had a blackout tube that plunged beneath the earth.

It was both amazing and terrifying.

Though I'd long forgotten those bygone summer days, I could remember it now like it was yesterday.

I could almost smell the delicious aromas of a family reunion potluck and the hint of chlorine.

Though I hadn't received any further system messages, I suspected this was a part of my quest.

It had to be.

Up to this point I'd been so focused on how out-of-place I felt and how I hadn't chosen this path. I hadn't taken the time to let go.

Sure, there was plenty of navel-gazing on my part along the way, but I hadn't even scratched the surface of really trying to live in this world. To be a part of a greater story. Everything I'd done so far, every accomplishment, I'd just been getting by.

No more.

I yelled out as loud as I could, letting loose a whoop and holler that my younger self would have been proud of.

The sound echoed off the walls and a piercing pain behind my eyes reminded me of the blow I suffered when I lost my balance.

Maybe I hit my head harder than I thought.

But, somehow, I knew in that moment that everything was about to change.

I could feel it.

My feet were swept upward, and I came to an abrupt halt in a large pool. Water rushed up my nose, burning my sinuses, and I scrambled in the darkness before finding my footing.

The pool wasn't as deep as I feared.

I stood and wiped the moisture from my brow and blinked away a dizzying sense of disbelief as my eyes adjusted to the light.

The cavernous stone hall was lined with bright, luminescent orbs of glowing light that pulsed with some strange, coordinated rhythm. It was soothing and hypnotic and I found myself entranced for just a moment before shaking myself from the stupor that had overtaken me.

After taking a few steps, I felt something crunch beneath the weight of my boot and then brush against my shin. Fearing the worst, but still intrigued enough to want to know, I slowly bent to pick it up.

My fingers touched what felt like a scrap of cloth and I pulled the heavy object into the light.

It took a moment for my mind to process what I was looking at. Bloated and decayed bits of rotten flesh hung from the bone of a discarded limb. A leg. A human leg. And I was holding the last bits of whatever armor remained.

I dry-heaved before involuntarily throwing my disgusting find back into the murky depths. Though the image of the waterlogged tissue and grayed skin stuck in my mind. Somehow, it was much worse than the animated corpses we'd just struck down.

The echo of the splash bounced off the cavernous walls and I listened intently. The sound of the current behind me dropped a few octaves.

I turned to look at the waterway I'd entered from. The water flowing into the pool slowed just a bit and then Pops careened through the air and landed with a splash that nearly bowled me over.

Ely followed soon after. Then Raven. And finally Attia.

With the discarded limb now mostly forgotten, we stood together in a wet huddle and assessed our new surroundings.

The water's edge was about twenty yards away and large grub-like creatures hung from the high ceiling by what looked to be strands of thick, woven webbing.

"Do you think they'll be a problem," Attia asked, her gaze fixed upward.

"Only one way to find out," Ely said.

Pops grabbed him by the arm as he passed. "Hold up. No need to go rushing into things. We've made a few mistakes, both of us, but we've managed to get this far. Let's finish this right."

"They're just wormy bugs," Ely protested, pulling his arm free. "It's not like the slime. Besides, the boss is probably on the far end of this area. I don't think we have much to worry about until we get further in."

Raven stepped between the two men. "We are further in. The undead mobs were cake, but let's not get overconfident. Remember the slime. Remember what happened when we got cocky."

I inspected one of the dangling creatures.

*You **Inspect** the Slumbering Corpse Eater.*
Level 11. Hit Points: 3,200.

*The Slumbering Corpse Eater is affected by **Slumber**.*

My eyes went wide in disbelief.

"Level II," I whispered, nodding toward the nearest grub. "Probably better to avoid fighting them if we can help it."

Ely squinted his eyes. "No defense bonus, though. They might not be too much harder than the first boss. If we can choose our fights and avoid being caught off-guard, we should be able to handle it. And look at that silk... it has to be worth a pretty penny."

Raven slicked back her wet hair before speaking up. "The real question is whether they are part of the quest."

"Huh?" Ely turned and scratched his head. "Why wouldn't they be?"

All eyes were on Raven as we waited for an explanation.

"Well," she started. "We're here to clean the sewers, right?"

"Right," I answered. That's what the quest text had said, after all.

"Slimes and undead," she continued, "that's a no-brainer. Those things have to go. But these corpse eaters seem to be a natural part of the ecosystem."

"A natural part of the eco-what? What makes you say that?" Ely countered. "They're massive, dangling grubs. They're practically begging to be slaughtered."

"That's just it. It's too easy to just engage." Raven pointed upwards. "Look at those glowing orbs on the rocks up there. What do you think those are?"

Ely shrugged. "Luminescent mushrooms?"

Attia stepped forward. "No. Not mushrooms. Those are eggs."

An involuntary shudder ran down the big man's spine. "Well, that's gross."

Pops nodded as he put the pieces together. "It explains why there are no undead in this area. They eat corpses and they're protecting their young. If I had to wager a guess, I'd say attacking one would probably wake the rest of them."

"Press on without engaging, then," I asked, looking at each of my companions and hoping for a consensus.

"I think that's our best option," Raven answered for the group. "But in case I'm wrong, let's keep our weapons drawn. And step lightly."

Ely didn't mask his displeasure, but he donned his fist weapons all the same.

Being low on coin myself, I could understand his frustration. The intact stingers I'd sold that morning resulted in a bounty of unexpected plentitude. Now my coin purse was empty and the corpse eater silk had to be even more rare.

But we weren't here for silk. We were here to clean the sewers, and to possibly find Raven's dire wolf. As far as I knew, Ely didn't have a quest to retrieve corpse eater silk, so it couldn't be one of our priorities.

"Everyone ready," Pops asked, drawing his blade from behind his back.

I unsheathed my sword and nodded. "Lead on."

When we all agreed, the old man pressed forward, making his way toward the edge of the pool with the rest of us following closely in his wake.

More bones littered the water's edge in scattered piles. There were easily enough remains to assemble over twenty full skeletons.

"This must be where those undead came from," Attia whispered. "I think the corpse eaters did this."

Pops nodded his agreement. "Makes sense. And the mob of level 2's we fought up there were the ones lucky enough to get away."

"At least until we came along." Ely flashed a dark grin.

It was clear he was still perturbed about our choice to bypass the potentially lucrative encounters with the corpse eaters. And the looming threat of encountering a dire wolf. But at least it seemed his sense of humor had returned.

We stepped around the bones and pressed onward, weaving our way down the packed-dirt path. We did our best to avoid the slumbering grubs and the random piles of bones as we went.

The deeper we got, the more strenuous it became to navigate undetected. The piles of discarded body parts devolved into scattered skeletal remains. Each bone was a crunchy threat just waiting for a clumsy footfall to awaken the dangling corpse eaters.

After a while, something changed.

Tiny strands of fine silk covered the floor and bones like a shroud. It wasn't as shiny and thick as the material suspending the grubs, and far too thin to collect, but it was sticky enough to be a nuisance.

Long, knotted clumps stuck to our boots and slowed our progress, but we pressed ever onward.

The end was in sight.

Ahead, a large wooden door emerged from the snow white silken landscape.

"Watch your step," Pops whispered, pointing to a writhing figure entombed in the web.

Several more wiggling blobs emerged. Each had the distinct shape and form of a trapped humanoid. There were probably over thirty of them between us and the door.

"Should we free them?" Attia asked. Her quiet tone was full of worry and trepidation.

Pops shook his head and took another step toward forward.

"But what if they're... people?"

Raven leaned in and put a comforting arm around our healer's shoulders before stopping in front of a wriggling blob.

She bent and flicked her dagger at the silk, exposing the grayed skin of something undead beneath the woven strands.

"See?"

The entrapped creature froze, then shifted as if to face the sound of her voice.

The thud of my pulse filled my ears, and I tightened my grip on Truthseeker as I glanced upward and then back to the unmoving web.

The small bit of exposed skin wasn't enough to use my inspect skill, but something told me this wasn't just some level 2 Zomb.

"Maybe that wasn't such a great idea," Raven whispered, backing away slowly before shifting course. "Let's keep moving."

She stepped clear of the creature and it struggled against the webbed binding before going still once more.

Attia swallowed hard and followed Raven's lead. She held her staff tight and navigated the narrow path that would take her away from the entrapped zombie and toward the door.

Her eyes were still focused on the huddled mass when a barely exposed rib bone crunched beneath her feet.

A loud screech sounded from somewhere above us. Then a looming corpse eater twitched and began to descend on its silken thread.

Clacking mandibles opened and closed with alarming speed and globs of nauseating saliva dripped from its maw.

Attia gasped and stepped backward, raising her staff to the grub before remembering the original threat.

But it was too late.

The remains of a partially armored warrior broke free from the weakened webbing.

There was no life in the creature's sunken eyes and its once pristine jaw dangled precariously from its socket. Stringy bits of hair fell to the floor in clumps with the sticky strands that had comprised its prison.

Now free, it wrapped its arms around Attia like a vise. Its jaw flapped ineffectually at her neck and a throaty groan added to the corpse eater's hungry squeals.

*You **Inspect** the Forgotten Guardsman.*
Level 9. Hit Points: 2,350.
*The Forgotten Guardsman is affected by **Single Focus**.*
*The Forgotten Guardsman is affected by **Champion's Fury**.*
Attack and movement speed are increased.

Attia did her best to hold in her scream until the undead guardsman's tongue dripped out onto her cheek, leaving a trail of rancid saliva in its wake.

Her shrill screech reverberated off the cavern walls.

Two more corpse eaters began their descent.

With seconds to spare before the first eyeless grub reached us, I raised Truthseeker, preparing to strike at the guardsman, but then stopped short.

What if I struck our healer by mistake?

"I can't taunt it," Pops said. "The single focus buff is too strong."

The runes on his sword glowed red, but nothing happened. Several squirming webs stood between him and Attia. There was no way he could get to her in time.

"What do we do?" I shouted.

Raven closed her eyes and vanished into the void and then Ely was there.

"Eeyaaargh!"

Fists flew like I'd never seen before, landing blows on the zombie that shook the air between us.

I watched, dumbfounded as fragments of shadow enveloped him.

"Ely," I exclaimed, "you have to move."

The shadow darkened and Ely growled.

He was oblivious and either shrugging off my command or too enraged to hear it.

I had no other choice.

Using what little time that remained, I dropped my sword and flung myself at my friend.

The blow knocked him backwards and his eyes burned with blind hatred as the shadowy wisps coalesced in the space he'd occupied only moments before.

Raven reemerged from the void and stuck her daggers into the guardsman's spine.

Ely's hard elbow caught me on the cheek and I tumbled backward into another web, freeing a second guardsman before I slid to a stop.

With the first corpse eater now on the ground and two more descending, it was beginning to look as if our jaunt in the sewer would come to an untimely end.

Stars still filled my vision, and I looked toward the door.

It was fifteen paces away.

We'd almost made it.

> *You **Inspect** the Forgotten Guardsman.*
> *Level 9. Hit Points: 2,340.*
> *The Forgotten Guardsman is affected by **Single Focus**.*
> *The Forgotten Guardsman is affected by **Champion's Fury**.*
> *Attack and movement speed are increased.*

There was no way we could win against five level 9 mobs, let alone two level 9's and three level 13's.

We were screwed.

Pain thrummed behind my eyes, and I struggled against the matted webbing while boney fingertips dug at the flesh on my leg.

Truthseeker was now too far to reach, and I cursed myself for dropping my weapon when I'd moved to save Ely from Raven's attack.

Frustrated, I kicked at the guardsman, doing my best to distance myself from the threat of being devoured alive.

In that moment, a morbid part of my mind casually wondered what would happen to a Traveler if their body was consumed.

My boot struck at clenching teeth, and I fought to break free from the guardsman's powerful bite.

Would I find myself back at my spawn point if I was eaten, healthy, whole, and unscarred? Or would there be some kind of spawn penalty? A debuff or a mandatory respawn timer, perhaps?

The jagged, rotted teeth let go of my boot and sank into the flesh of my other calf.

You've been hit! The Forgotten Guardsman hits you for 43 HP.

And then Pops was there, standing above me like a hero amongst men. He raised his rune-laden sword and swung down hard.

The guardsman's grip loosened for just a moment. And then I felt the bite of its teeth once more.

You've been hit! The Forgotten Guardsman hits you for 45 HP.

My vision blurred, and I kicked as hard as I could, renewing my effort to get away.

It was no use. No amount of taunting could change the guardsman's focus.

"Go help the others with those corpse eaters," I yelled, unable to disguise the panic in my voice. "Just toss me my sword."

Pops nodded and complied, halting his attack long enough to lob Truthseeker in my direction before directing his attention toward the oncoming corpse eaters.

My blade clattered against the stone floor of the cavern, bouncing and sliding as it went. After what felt like an eternity, it finally came to a rest in a clump of matted silk, now mere inches away.

So close.

But not close enough.

*You cast **Earthblast.***
***Partial Resist!** The Forgotten Guardsman takes 20 HP Earth damage.*

My elemental attack was useless.

I kicked again and stole a look at Attia's mana pool. She was running low. Like me, every fiber in her being was intently focused on staying alive.

The rest of us were on our own.

I was on my own.

*You cast **Mana Surge** on Attia.*
Attia is now refreshed.

Kicking at the guardsman, I hefted myself forward. It worked, but the distance I gained was only a fraction of what remained.

I had to get to my sword.

With every ounce of my remaining strength, I fought against the weight of the undead creature, pulling us both toward my goal.

Each centimeter was agony.

My fingers were raw from my frantic clawing at the earth. Strands of silk webbing covered my face and arms. Grit crunched between my teeth.

Finally. I reached my blade.

*You cast **Tempest** on yourself.*
You are now infused with the power of wind.
Attack Speed and Dodge are increased.

A quick glance at my health bar was all it took to drive home just how dire things had become. Time slowed to a crawl, and I quickly surveyed the haphazard battle field.

Attia was on her knees now, dragged down by the weight of the first guardsman while Ely and Raven pummeled it with blows.

The glowing light of her heals created a constant pulse of white, but it wasn't enough. Her health was dropping faster than it could recover.

Pops stood in front of them now, sword at the ready and runes burning brightly. He taunted the three corpse eaters.

Their course changed and clacking mandibles flexed open and closed. The clacking echoed off the walls, and the guardsmen seemed to halt their onslaught for the briefest of moments.

The clacking stopped, and the struggle continued.

I had to get up. I had to get away from this fiend somehow. I had to help my friends. I had to...

Groaning, I returned my focus toward my attacker.

Blood oozed from the guardsman's mouth and gushed from the wounds on my legs. The hot, slippery liquid had drenched my pants and splattered nearby clumps of silk.

But maybe this was a good thing.

Along with the speed increase from Tempest, the slickness caused by my wounds was all the advantage I needed in order to break free from the guardsman's grasp.

It was morbid and yet surprisingly effective.

Our chances of survival were still ridiculously and impossibly slim. Still, I felt a sudden wave of giddy pride knowing that we wouldn't go down without a fight.

A mad grin twisted my lips, and a surge of adrenaline rushed over me. But the guardsman wasn't yet ready to let go of its wounded prey.

It lunged forward, tearing at my legs with insane desperation.

My wind-infused blade whipped through the air, striking the prone guardsman in the head and shoulders before batting away a groping arm.

Critical strike! You hit the Forgotten Guardsman for 25 HP + 35 Wind damage.
You hit the Forgotten Guardsman for 15 HP + 21 Wind damage.
Critical strike! You hit the Forgotten Guardsman for 27 HP + 37 Wind damage.

Each strike took but a sliver from the mob's health pool. At this rate, I'd sooner die from blood loss than whittle it down.

"We're missing something," Raven shouted as she pulled her daggers free from the animated corpse and prepared another attack.

"You mean like the rest of the mobs in this cavern," Ely shouted back, his words drenched in sarcasm. "You're right. Let's just pull them all while we're at it."

"Very funny."

Now that I was up on my feet, I finally had enough maneuverability to distance myself from my foe and rejoin the group.

Ely tossed me a nod and quickly averted his gaze.

It was good to see he had regained at least some of his senses after launching into his full-on berserker attack but, all joking aside, Raven made a good point.

I felt it too.

We were missing something.

Something silly and stupid and right in front of our faces.

I slashed four quick strikes against the exposed flank of the undead creature that was attacking Attia with similarly disappointing results.

If only we could set up an elemental chain like we had with the slimes.

"I don't think we can hold out much longer," Pops yelled as he parried incoming blows from the two nearest corpse eaters.

A flash of movement in the upper corner of my field of vision caught my eye. The Tempest icon glowed bright and then dim in my status bar, indicating the buff was about to drop.

Pops was right. With the Forgotten Guardsman now trailing close behind and a bleed effect slowly draining my HP, I didn't know how much longer I could keep this up.

The third corpse eater closed in, brushing past Pops' defenses.

"Watch out," Ely exclaimed as he pushed around both Attia and Raven and squared off to face the oncoming grub.

"No. Wait," Raven said. She squinted at the monstrous fiend and then looked at the guardsman and back again.

*You **Inspect** the Devouring Corpse Eater.*
Level 11. Hit Points: 3,250.
*The Devouring Corpse Eater is affected by **Hunger**.*

We exchanged glances for the briefest of moments before she nodded and slipped into the void.

Everything moved so slowly. I wasn't sure if it was the last bit of Tempest coursing through my body or the sheer, unadulterated shock of what came next.

Raven reappeared behind the Forgotten Guardsman that held our healer. She wrapped her arms around the decayed flesh of its abdomen, and then the two of them slipped back into the shadows.

I blinked in disbelief. I'd experienced her shadow dance firsthand, but I'd never considered the possibility that she could carry a mob with her into the void.

When they re-emerged, they were directly in front of the pulsating maw of the maggot-like creature.

"What do you think you're doing," Ely shouted. "It's going to swallow you whole."

Raven danced backward and swung a powerful roundhouse kick into the guardsman's jawless face.

Teeth fragments skittered across the floor and the fiend stumbled a few paces before recovering from the blow.

A deep, throaty howl escaped what remained of its windpipe.

Then, with a speed that was hard to comprehend, the Devouring Corpse Eater lunged forward, tearing the guardsman in half with its razor-sharp mandibles.

I stood in awe as I watched the creature feast on the rancid entrails of the undead mob.

"Denton," Attia shouted. "Watch out!"

Our healer was now standing upright and glowing with healing energy. Wisps of white light swirled around her and I felt the pain in my legs begin to subside.

My health bar began to fill and my fatigue lessened, but even still, her face showed genuine and growing concern for my wellbeing.

I was about to thank her for the much-needed heal when I suddenly understood.

The other Fallen Guardsman had freed itself from the last remains of tangled webbing and had taken full advantage of my distraction.

I felt its teeth sink into the flesh of my right shoulder and I grimaced in pain. Then the clang and clamor of Truthseeker falling to the cavern floor shook me from my paralyzing shock.

The nearest maggot was now fully immersed in the act of devouring its rotten meal. While conveniently located, I already knew it wouldn't make a move on the remaining zombie.

It had to be one of the other two.

Two corpse eaters, one zombie.

Two corpse eaters, one zombie.

The thought played over and over again in my mind. With one last ounce of effort, I lunged forward in a dogged attempt to close the distance between myself and my disgusting, potential saviors.

If only I could shadow dance like Raven.

In the next moment, she was beside me. She stared into my eyes in a way that felt as if she could see the very essence of my soul.

With a lurch, all three of us dipped into the heart of nothingness. I could feel her presence, but the sticky stench of the guardsman was overpowering.

I closed my eyes and tried to tell myself it would be just like the leap up the tower earlier that afternoon.

Only, it wasn't.

This time, we didn't immediately emerge from whatever shadow realm Raven moved through.

The guardsman wailed and screamed, and its voice sounded almost human.

"Let me go," it pleaded, writhing around me in the darkness as if it were on fire.

Still, we did not emerge.

"My vigil has been long. Give my weary soul respite," it demanded. I felt the heat of the once-alive guard's breath on my neck. The voice imparting those words sounded even more human somehow.

Then it moved to plead its case to Raven.

When neither of us gave a response, the creature grew more agitated. It bellowed and howled, thrashing about in the sightless void like a rabid beast.

My lungs felt heavy. Every fiber of my being cried out for breath. But, unlike the frantic guardsman, I was unable to move, unable to breathe, unable to do anything but wish we would once again return to the underground cavern from the world of shadows.

And then we did.

I felt my body slam into the earthen floor and wisps of silk caught in my throat, sucked in as a result of my ragged inhale.

"Raven, Denton," Pops bellowed. "You've got to move."

The guardsman's jaw clenched tighter on the flesh of my shoulder and I cried out in pain, chancing a look upward as I fought to free myself from its unrelenting grasp.

Dripping mandibles clacked and shuddered and the nearest corpse eater quivered with delight at the sight of its delivered meal.

Heeding Pops' warning, I looked to Raven. Blood was trickling out her nose and her eyes were wide. She seemed dazed, and I thought of the tremendous strain her shadow dance must have put on her body and mind.

The corpse eater lunged.

Forcing myself into action, I rolled sideways toward Raven, pushing her out of the way while fighting the weight of the guard on my back.

The corpse eater's mandibles struck the stone, and it reeled back in pain before refocusing its attack.

There was only one problem.

The guardsman thrashed beneath me and I stared into the maggot's open maw.

This plan was about to backfire if I didn't do something quick.

At the very last second, I felt Ely's strong hands grip my ankles. Then the world lurched as I was unceremoniously hefted through the air with such force that the guardsman was left squirming on the ground with nothing but a torn shred of my armor between its rotten teeth.

By the time I landed with a thud several feet away, the corpse eater had set itself on the all-it-could-eat undead buffet.

Stumbling to my feet, I tried to blink the blur from my eyes. My shoulder felt as if it were on fire, and I was still dazed.

Despite my rapid blinking, I was unable to get a firm bearing on where I was. Pain throbbed throughout my body, and my vision went dark.

The fight wasn't over yet.

"We need one more," I shouted to the group as I did my best not to falter. I was still unsure if I was even facing the right direction.

"One more what?" Ely shouted back from somewhere behind me.

I turned and yelled my answer, "Two corpse eaters, one guardsman."

"What?"

"We need another guardsman."

My vision was just beginning to clear when I saw the result of my command.

Ely started to protest.

He was undoubtedly eager to engage the last corpse eater, but we were in no condition to keep fighting. I could almost hear the fleeting hope in his voice as he grasped at the possibility that we might still be able to score a rare silk drop.

"Denton's right," Pops yelled. "We need another guardsman to distract this last maggot."

But it was too late.

Attia, now fully recovered, dashed toward the nearest writhing mass of webbing.

Seeing my expression, Ely turned. "No, wait. Let me do it."

Our healer's staff swung through the air and the blow rang hard and true, cutting through the silken mass like a hot knife.

A level II Forgotten Guardsman emerged and let loose a horrible, shrill cry that left my ears ringing.

Raven was the nearest party member, but she was in no shape to intervene. Pops and Ely were too far to get to Attia in time.

What had I done?

I tried to will my muscles into action.

It was no use.

But Attia was not afraid. The white gem affixed to the top of her staff burned with a furious, piercing white light. She thrust it forward, striking the guardsman's chest before firing a holy missile from the palm of her other hand.

I stumbled forward until I found myself standing by Pops and Ely. There we watched in stunned silence.

When Ely came to his senses, he started moving forward. But Pops put a gentle hand on his shoulder.

"This is something she needs to do on her own, son."

I struggled with those words.

Attia was our healer. We were supposed to protect her. Weren't we? And yet our tank was telling us to stand down.

Why?

Foot by foot, the guardsman lost ground. The holy damage burned at its skin and it howled with tortured rage.

And yet, Attia pressed her attack. Her staff cut through the air and missile after missile burst on the undead creature's chest. Gradually, she herded it toward the salivating corpse eater.

At last, the oversized maggot joined the fray. With its mandibles spread wide, it lunged forward, swallowing the guardsman whole.

"Atta-girl, Attia," Pops cheered, thrusting his sword high above his head.

The sound echoed off the cavern walls and Attia turned to face the group.

She was smiling.

"I guess I did it, didn't I?"

The others started moving toward the door at the end of the cavernous chamber and Raven took my offered hand, pulling herself to her feet.

"You sure did," she said. She gave Attia a warm smile before her knees buckled.

I caught her just in time, maneuvering to drape her arm around my shoulder so I could better support her weight.

Once she was stable, we carefully moved to join the others.

This was it.

This was the moment we'd been working for.

We were all so exhausted, but the door was before us. It was the only thing standing between us and the end of the dungeon. Whatever lurked behind its massive frame would be our final test.

I could feel it.

We all could.

Ely grabbed the large brass handle and gave it a strong tug.

The door didn't budge.

He pushed on it, thrusting all his weight against the ornately carved mahogany.

The result was the same.

"Huh." He shook his head and sat with his back against his quarry.

"It's probably for the best." Pops chuckled. "We aren't exactly in fighting shape, are we? And who knows what's waiting for us on the other side of that door. Break the seal and we might be forced to engage straight away."

"Pops is right," Raven muttered. "I need a few minutes to recover before we barge in with guns blazing."

Having helped Raven to a sitting position, I stepped closer and ran my fingers along the smooth, carved designs.

"Strange place for a wooden door," Attia observed.

I turned. "What do you mean?"

"My grandfather used to build high-end cabinets. Real wood, never any filler. That was his slogan." Her ebon fingers caressed the mahogany grain. "It's far too damp in a place like this. In the real world, this door would have warped and split and cracked. Galvanized steel would have been a better choice."

"Welcome to the magic of EndWorld Everlasting." Raven cast a genuine smile.

My hand moved of its own accord, tracing the carvings with mindless abandon.

Then my fingers alighted on something strange. A tarnished brass medallion a bit larger than my hand was affixed in the center of the door.

I tapped it with my fingernail and it gave slightly.

Intrigued, Attia reached over and swiveled the plate upwards, revealing the geared heart of the door's embedded machinery.

"How strange," she whispered.

47

Everyone took to their feet and examined the hole the circular plate had revealed. There were gears inside, but it was obvious to all of us that something was missing.

"What do you think is supposed to go there?" Ely wondered aloud.

No one had to say anything else.

I knew.

Pulling the Oversized Gem Setting from my inventory, I gently placed it into the mechanism.

"It looks like it's still missing something," Attia observed. She looked back over her shoulder at the jagged path we'd traversed and shuddered.

"We got the setting, but we didn't get a gemstone," Ely said. His longing gaze lingered on the last of the corpse eaters still devouring its meal.

Raven shook her head.

"I don't think that's it," she said. "The corpse eaters helped us defeat the guardsmen. It doesn't make sense that we'd have to kill them."

"Where else are we going to get a gem?" Ely shot back.

I cleared my throat.

All eyes were on me as I reached into my inventory.

There.

I held the Focused Sapphire of Illumination I'd looted from the Kobold Boss in the palm of my hand. The gentle glow seemed to resonate with that of the corpse eater eggs on the ceiling far above.

"Where did you find that," Ely asked, his eyes glistening in the pale, blue light.

"In the cellar dungeon," I answered without taking my gaze off the gem.

"It's beautiful," Attia whispered.

I looked back at the door.

"Whatever's behind that lock, the Kobolds were afraid of it. I imagine the fight isn't going to be pleasant. Not if what the Kobolds said was true."

"You told us at Harold's, right?" Raven touched a finger to the sapphire and quickly pulled back.

I nodded.

"What did they say," Pops asked.

"They said Death was coming to Fort Morrow, and that darkness would take us."

"Darkness will take us." Ely laughed, but his merriment didn't last and the reverberating sound of his voice faded as the weight of the situation started sinking in.

"Wait a second," he said after a long silence. "Are you saying that Fort Morrow is doomed if we fail this quest?"

I shrugged. "I'm kinda new here. I'm still trying to figure all of this stuff out. Maybe. Maybe not? I don't know."

Raven frowned and looked from the gem to the door and back again.

"I can't imagine the price of failure at this level would be so steep," she said. "But even so, we should be prepared for the worst when we open that door."

Pops stretched his back and popped his neck.

"We've made it this far," he said. "And that's no small feat. But I think you might have hit it right on the head, Raven. We open that door and there's no turning back."

"We've got this," Ely said, cutting in.

He was so eager to share his excitement with the rest of the group, but he was only slightly successful.

It was hard to fight the overwhelming sense of dread that seemed to emanate from the rich wooden tones of the portal that blocked our path.

It really was a beautiful door.

With our health and energy finally restored, it was time to press forward.

Each of us, in turn, mourned our brief reprieve in our own way. Even Ely stepped slowly forward as I raised the glowing sapphire to the setting.

As if by magic, the mechanism sprang to life. Gears whirred and churned. Subtle vibrations shook the earth beneath our feet.

And then it stopped.

We held our breath and watched, waiting for some concrete indicator of change, exchanging furtive glances, and then inching closer.

The door opened slightly.

Then a little more.

A gentle breeze flowed through the tiny gap and the hinges creaked as the gap widened.

Attia reached out a hand and grasped the red-hued wood before looking back at the rest of us.

"No turning back," she said, speaking ever so softly.

"No turning back," the rest of us whispered in reply.

48

The old, mahogany door creaked open, and Attia stepped aside, waiting for our tank to lead the way into the darkened chamber.

Acknowledging his role, Pops stepped forward and then stopped suddenly, blocking the way for the rest of us.

His spine stiffened. Then, without a word, he turned to face us. His eyes and expression were filled with confusion and concern.

"Denton?" he asked, giving me a quizzical look.

"Let's do this." I responded with a nod.

But it wasn't the response he was looking for.

"What is it?" I asked.

Everything about the moment felt wrong.

It was in the darkness on the other side of the threshold. It was in the look Pops was giving me. I could almost taste the palpable tension. The air felt heavy in my lungs, and I looked to the rest of the party for some clue as to what had changed.

"Something feels different," Raven observed. "Did you get a quest update?" She was looking at me.

"An update?" I asked. "No. Nothing since we got our assignment from Captain Elsbaud. Why?"

Pops sighed deep and hung his head.

After a moment he spoke. "I did. I got the quest update. It was just as I was about to enter the next room. I'm so sorry, Denton."

"What are you sorry for?" I asked.

"It's okay," Raven said, nodding slowly. "It's fine, Pops. It's okay, really. Anyone else get a quest update?"

Attia and Ely both shook their heads.

"What aren't you guys telling me?" I asked.

"I don't know for certain," Raven admitted. "I can only guess. If your original quest hasn't changed, we just have to clear the sewers to meet the original objective. But..."

"But what?" I insisted.

She looked to Pops. "What can you tell us?"

Pops unsheathed his massive greatsword and held it in his strong, calloused hands.

The blade trembled.

"My quest update says that I have to earn my sword," Pops explained, looking at me with sorrow in his eyes once more.

"Okay. So we help you earn the blade, right?" I asked. "I don't see why that would be a problem. Why apologize?"

"The focus of the dungeon has shifted," Raven explained. "If Pops received a quest update when we were about to enter the threshold..."

I was beginning to catch on. "Then it must mean the boss is meant for him."

The words sounded hollow as they fell from my mouth. It was as if someone else was speaking my thoughts and I was barely hearing the echo as my mind raced to catch up.

Pops nodded, again sorrow filled his eyes.

"This was supposed to be your quest, Denton. I'm so sorry."

Ely shook his head in disbelief. "Wait a second. You mean you somehow hijacked his quest? That's unbelievable—"

Raven shot him a scathing look and cut in. "Pops didn't hijack anything, Ely. Chances are, the outcome would have been the same no matter what."

Ely smirked. "Are you trying to tell me that Denton went to all the trouble of getting that gem to open this door so Pops could keep a sword he didn't even have yet?" He motioned toward the door and the glowing sapphire to punctuate his point.

"It does seem odd, doesn't it?" Raven mumbled. "But there's no way to hijack a quest. It isn't possible. The system is far too complex for something like that."

"It isn't possible," Ely shot back, his voice filled with sarcasm. "Like you would know."

Except Raven would know. It's exactly the kind of thing she'd have intimate knowledge of from her time spent working to build EndWorld Everlasting.

She knew it.

I knew it.

And yet it wasn't my secret to tell.

Pops remained silent, staring down at his blade with heavy eyes.

"Are you saying you think I'm wrong, that Pops really did somehow game the system to steal the end quest for the dungeon?" Raven pressed, eyebrows raised.

Ely looked at Pops and his shoulders slumped.

After a moment, he sighed.

"No."

"I think I'm just as confused as Denton," Attia said, chiming in on the discussion. "What's so significant about Pops getting a new quest for his sword? How does it change things?"

Silence followed.

But I was glad for the question.

It didn't bother me that we needed to help Pops defend his claim on the blade. We'd all seen his axe crumble away when he removed the runes.

Without the sword, he was weaponless.

I knew what that felt like.

It was a feeling I wouldn't wish on anyone undeserving of it.

And Pops didn't deserve it.

In EndWorld, a weapon was like an extension of one's self. Not having a weapon was like losing a limb.

Knowing this, we had no choice but to help.

It's not just something friends would do for one another.

It was what we would hope others would do for us.

Still, the question remained.

What was the significance of a quest prompt at this particular juncture? Like Attia, I didn't understand how this impacted me, in particular. All of us, as a group, that was something I could understand.

We would risk life and limb for Pops, as I was sure he would for us. So what was all this drama about?

I heard myself ask the question before I realized I was speaking.

"How does your quest prompt change things?"

Attia and I shared glances.

I looked at Pops.

He didn't avert his gaze, but there were no answers in his eyes.

Then I looked at Raven.

Finally, she spoke.

"When Pops got the quest, the focus of the dungeon changed. That can only mean one thing."

"What's that?" I asked, unsure if I was ready for the answer, but unwilling to go another minute without one.

"Whatever we find beyond this door, whatever boss we have to face off against, it isn't for you."

I didn't know what to say. Why was that significant? None of this was making much sense.

Raven went on. "This isn't your level 5 quest, Denton."

Her words hit me like a ton of bricks and my world turned on end.

Not my level 5 quest?

"Well, that's all right," Attia said cheerfully. "Whatever happens, when you do get your quest, you can count on us to be there."

Pops nodded.

As did Raven and Ely.

I let out a held breath.

That was it, then?

While the shock had gotten to me at first, now it didn't feel like such a big deal.

I mean, it wasn't like I was in a hurry to level up and obtain new skills. Sure. It would be nice. But there was still so much about my new life I didn't yet know.

I had a few orders of clubs to make for Jörgen's customers, a new sword to commission, and a budding obsidian enterprise to foster.

And like Attia said, when the time came, I had a great group of friends I knew I could count on.

I shrugged my shoulders and smiled.

"It's no big deal," I said, offering my hand first to Pops and then to the others.

Pops stood tall and a big smile blossomed on his lips.

"I'll give you my share of whatever loot drops," he offered.

I waved him off. "Don't worry about it. EndWorld will sort itself out. Friendship comes first."

Raven gave me an approving look and then smiled at Ely.

"Friendship comes first," she said.

Ely flashed her an awkward grin and nodded. "You're right. You're right," he said, scratching at a tuft of hair. "Friendship comes first."

I considered my friends for a moment before nodding toward the dark unknown.

"What do you say we do this?" I asked. "No turning back?"

"No turning back," they exclaimed.

Their voices rang loud and true, echoing off the cavern walls in surround.

Then something inside the darkened chamber stirred.

In the uneasy seconds that followed, a grating sound echoed in the darkness. It was the sound of something heavy being dragged, scraping unceremoniously across the stone floor as it neared our position at the edge of the room.

Death hung on the stale air and our fingers tightened on our weapons as we prepared to face off against the unknown foe.

Then the movement stopped.

A set of armor shifted in the mysterious, black shadows before us.

The soft clinks and clanks reminded me of the Travelers I'd seen milling about the marketplace, searching for something, but unsure of what they were looking for or where it might be.

All of us, save Pops, exchanged nervous glances. Meanwhile, Pops stared forward, reading the text of a new prompt.

Looking down at his new sword, he nodded. Then silently activated one of his abilities.

Thoughts swirled in my mind. Images of what might be lurking just out of sight teased my nerve, and I wondered what sort of information our tank had received.

The grim expression on his face didn't bode well.

Then the creature turned and began dragging its burden further into the depths.

I let out a breath I hadn't realized I was holding and my mind naturally started filling in the blanks.

It wasn't a slime. That much was obvious.

And it wasn't mechanical like the inanimate contraptions we'd encountered so far. Sluice gates and a magical lock embedded in a wooden door were one thing, but whatever this was... it had to be something else. There were no sounds of gears, and the gait was too irregular. The movements were too chaotic.

Corpse eaters didn't wear armor.

Unless maybe it was dragging the shambling remains of a humanoid.

With the smell of death on the air, my mind stopped on the guardsmen. It was possible the boss was a souped-up version of the steel-willed creeps we'd barely managed to defeat, and only with the aid of the corpse eaters at that.

An involuntary shudder ran down my spine.

The way it was pathing.

It was looking for something.

Was it us? The sword?

Whatever it was, it was a sign of intelligence.

Desire.

Unfinished business that required bloodshed.

The noises stopped.

"What do you think," Ely whispered as he looked to Pops to fill in the blanks. "Is it just the one, or are the more of them lurking in the shadows."

I blinked away my disbelief and the unexpected question even gave Pops a moment of pause.

It wasn't the question itself. The inquiry itself was logical.

No. That wasn't it.

It was the source.

We all looked at our impetuous friend. His question was so uncharacteristic, so cautious.Its mere utterance leant a measure of credence to the gravity of our situation. A level of gravity that felt all the more heavy because of it.

We were in for a fight.

And this time we were all on the same page.

"It's just the one," Pops replied. Then he continued, "I can't get a good read on it. That can only mean one thing."

"What?" Ely asked.

"It's powerful. Probably the toughest thing any of us have encountered in EndWorld this far."

Ely grunted. "Hmm. I'd hope so. I mean, anything less would be a disappointment."

Pops nodded and flashed the rest of us an uneasy smile. "I guess he's right."

"Of course I'm right." Ely laughed loudly, slapping our tank on the shoulder. "But at least you don't have to do it alone, ya old geezer. Am I ri—"

The silence in the room was shattered, and hard footfalls echoed off the walls, nearly drowned out by the dragging sound we'd somehow grown accustomed to. Armor clinked with a rising crescendo, and we all watched the darkness in a daze as our foe drew near.

Ely winced.

"Sorry," he muttered, but it was too late.

The boss was upon us.

49

A huge, rusty hammer struck the ground at our feet, sending a shockwave of unbelievable force in our direction.

The sensation of flying was almost euphoric.

My mind went blank, and I closed my eyes. I remembered my time inside the forgotten void. The time before the tutorial. Before EndWorld.

The waiting.

The thought of another Denton living and dying inside of those months shook me to my core and ripped me from the quiet darkness.

And then I struck the ground with alarming force.

Truthseeker clanged off into the distance.

I was weaponless. Again.

Weaponless and tired of these stupid knockback attacks.

Weaponless and alone.

Weaponless and afraid.

I didn't know why, but I couldn't stop trembling.

A quick look at my status bar revealed I was under the effect of some kind of debuff. A horrible screeching sound tore my focus back to my immediate field of vision. The details of the effect would have to wait.

The boss rushed forward, ripping the mahogany door from its frame with a single hand as he entered the chamber.

Debris showered around the champion's massive frame, and I felt myself tremble. Before me stood a hulking undead fiend, defiantly scanning the area from the cloud of dust that was just beginning to settle.

For a moment, it was all I could make out in the muffled glow from the sapphire.

Why was I feeling so frightened?

Then he stepped into the light of the egg-lined chamber.

It was just a man.

Or, rather, the forgotten corpse of a man long dead. A champion. With pieces of armor that hung loose on his emaciated frame.

Not a guardsman.

Something more.

Higher rank. Higher station. Chiseled cheekbones barely visible under a dented helm that was once pristine. Not even death could take the soldier's nobility.

He was nearly seven feet tall, with an aura of despair that threatened to overwhelm my senses.

Empty eye sockets scanned the area.

I reached for Truthseeker. It was too far.

No one else stirred.

The champion approached, hammer raised.

Attia was nearest.

Her chest rose and fell in shallow breaths.

Strong, skeletal hands prepared to strike. The hammer drew higher.

Raven twitched.

Forcing myself to stand, I activated Tempest and lunged toward my sword. With my blade clenched tight, I rounded to face our enemy.

*You cast **Earthblast**.*
Resist! The Forgotten Champion takes 3 HP Earth damage.

I was disappointed in the damage, but it didn't matter. I had to do something to get the champion's attention.

Shouting my defiance, I rushed forward.

*You cast **Earthblast**.*
***Resist!** The Forgotten Champion takes 2 HP Earth damage.*

The champion was not fazed.

His hammer fell and Attia, now awake, screamed.

There was no time to stop the powerful strike. And from my encounter with the Kobold Boss and his pickaxe, I knew my sword couldn't withstand the weight of a direct blow from such a heavy weapon.

The hammer would strike anyway, destroying my blade in the process.

There was only one solution. I didn't like it, but there was nothing else.

Without Attia, our group was doomed.

I knew what had to be done.

The crushing blow of the champion's hammer struck hard and true. I felt the weight of it immediately and something inside me crunched.

***Critical Strike!** The Forgotten Champion hits you for 132 HP.*

My knees buckled, and the world began to spin.

Even before I hit the ground, I realized I was losing consciousness. It took every ounce of my willpower to hold on.

I tried to fight for control. I gave it everything I had.

Another blow would come.

I had to be ready. Maybe this time I could manage to deflect.

I couldn't lift my sword.

My arms were too heavy. It was useless.

Attia was still screaming in horror.

I could hear Pops calling my name.

Ely stumbled to his feet and looked on, helpless as the champion raised his hammer a second time.

Then Raven's hands were on my shoulders.

We slipped into the now-familiar nothingness of her shadow dance. My ears were still ringing when we emerged.

Despite my best efforts, I lost control.

Everything faded to black.

THE SOUNDS OF A SCUFFLE PULLED ME BACK FROM THE BRINK. I TRIED to ignore the din and clamor. It was no use, and I felt perturbed.

The interruption threatened to dismantle the quiet respite of my being.

I wasn't dead.

But I didn't feel like I was alive either.

The closest approximation I could grasp was nothingness. And I wanted nothing more than to let that nothingness envelop me like a shroud.

Instead, the surrounding noise was something. That something pulled me from the nothingness, though I tried so hard to remain.

It felt like my bones were filled with ants.

Then my body, too, became aware of the world and the pains of wakefulness. A dull energy thrummed to life inside of me, and jagged spikes of pain tore through my head with the rhythmic pounding of my pulse.

My breath caught in my chest.

Everything hurt.

I wanted to cling to sleep. I wanted to let the troubles of EndWorld wash away. I didn't want to open my eyes. I didn't want to fight.

I wanted rest.

Then, unexpectedly, a touch of light took root inside of me. It was small at first.

Fragile.

I would have snuffed it out, but it was so beautiful. It wasn't harsh or glaring. It cut through the fear and the cold and the darkness I'd held so close.

I had to protect it.

Slowly, it began to glow. Dim at first. And then brighter. Ever brighter.

The ants receded.

The pounding in my head diminished.

Ely was yelling something and Pops responded.

Their voices were strained. I couldn't quite make out the words, but the tone and cadence of their shouts were desperate.

Raven's soft whisper sounded at my cheek.

I wanted to listen. I wanted to hear her out. But the light. I had to protect the light.

Hot tears struck my cheek.

They weren't mine.

"Come back to us." Raven's words joined the gentle glow, and the two became one.

I groaned.

"He's coming around, Attia. Keep it up."

Our healer was close. I could hear her now.

"I don't know how much longer I can manage," she warned. Then added, "Pops, are you okay?"

"For now," the old man answered. He didn't sound hopeful.

That was all I needed.

My friends were counting on me.

They were covering for me.

I opened my eyes and struggled to my feet.

A quick glance at my status bar revealed a list of icons that indicated I was suffering from Crushing, Bleed, and Horror effects.

The Horror icon began blinking.

Then it faded.

I was still injured, but most of my hit points had recovered from our healer's focused efforts. I could only imagine the strain it must have put on her, healing through the crushing blow and blood loss.

*You cast **Mana Surge** on Attia.*
Attia is now refreshed.

Raven pressed the hilt of my sword into my hand and smiled. Her expression was so sad and grateful and determined.

"Hello," I mumbled, instantly feeling dull at my inability to pull off a timely, witty phrase.

"Welcome back," she replied. "You should probably try to keep a better hold on your weapon. I think you're probably going to need it."

I returned her smile and gripped the hilt tighter as I looked at Pops and Ely squaring off against the champion.

It wasn't going well.

With a flash of anger, I cast Mana Surge and Tempest on myself. Then I prepared to engage as the world slowed and the power of an angry storm coursed through my veins.

Truthseeker glowed green, hewing at the champion with each strike, empowered with the imbued strength of wind.

Critical strike! You hit the Forgotten Champion for 25 HP + 22 Wind damage.
Critical strike! You hit the Forgotten Champion for 30 HP + 22 Wind damage.
Dodged! The Forgotten Champion misses his attack.
You hit the Forgotten Champion for 15 HP + 20 Wind damage.

"Watch those random attacks of his," Pops warned. "This guy seems a little more intelligent than your average mob. I can hold hate for the most part, but he certainly has a mind of his own."

I gave our tank a quick nod and resumed my attack. Meanwhile, Raven took her place at the champion's back and prepared to strike.

"Wind seems to do boosted damage, but my Earthblast didn't faze him," I said between blows.

"There goes our coordinated attack and elemental damage bonus," Raven acknowledged. "Unless you have a direct wind attack?"

"Nope," I said, striking at the champion and then ducking as his hammer flew mere inches from my head. "Just the weapon enhancement."

"Bummer," Ely grunted. "This is going to take a while, then."

I looked at the champion's health bar. Ely was right. Despite the potency of my added wind damage, we'd barely managed to put a dent in his health pool.

What's more, the mechanics of the fight almost seemed too easy.

My Tempest buff was still going strong, but something wasn't right. The champion almost seemed clumsy now compared to the way he'd barged through the doorway and set upon our group.

Was he gauging us? Learning our attack patterns and how we reacted to his momentary shifts in aggro?

*You **Inspect** the Forgotten Champion.*
Level 13. Hit Points: 4,400.
Dark Paladin
*The Forgotten Champion is affected by **Horror Aura**.*

A Dark Paladin? Before I could voice my growing concern, the champion shifted. He lowered his hammer to the ground with a thud. Then lunged toward Ely.

"What?" Ely gasped.

He was jolted upwards like a rag doll.

And then the champion threw him.

I couldn't help but watch as my friend flew through the air and then crashed into a writhing mass of silk.

A guardsman.

"Oh, no you don't," Pops shouted.

He jumped forward, blocking the boss's path to Ely and the now-emerging decayed corpse of his minion. The runes on the old man's sword burned bright, and the champion staggered back a few paces.

Though the champion's skin was stretched tight and his eyes had long rotted from his skull, there was no mistaking the expression. Recognition.

It was clear he had an intimate knowledge of the weapon Pops now brandished against him. The scream that ripped through the remains of his throat was horrifying.

It was echoed by a gnarled moan that tore through the guardsman's rotten maw.

"Go help Ely," Pops managed to get out before the champion lunged forward.

"Are you sure?" Raven asked.

Pops whipped his blade up against the haft of the champion's hammer and then rolled it down to one side, expertly deflecting an oncoming blow.

"I've got this," he grunted, preparing for the next attack. "Now go."

50

Ely was still struggling to wrest himself free of the guardsman's iron grip when Raven and I managed to make our way through the silken maze.

Luckily, we were facing off against just one this time. But something was different about the way this guardsman moved. Not like the ones before. Less primal. More intelligent.

Bony fingers ripped at Ely's flesh, but this time the guardsman wasn't single-mindedly focused like the others had been.

It blocked and parried our strikes, traded blows, and positioned itself so we had to work for any kind of leverage on the field of battle.

Bit by bit we whittled away at its health pool.

But the progress came at a cost.

We were now several feet away from our initial point of conflict.

Further from the boss.

Further from Pops and Attia.

I parried a blow, then lashed out with a flurry of attacks. The guardsman danced backwards and avoided my advances.

The exchange drew us even further away.

I looked back at the rest of our party.

Pops and Attia were keeping the Champion busy but, despite how much progress we'd made on the additional mob, I couldn't help but feel uneasy.

It was the distance.

There was no way it wasn't tactical.

A quick glance at Raven was all the confirmation I needed. She, too, looked apprehensive over our current state of battle.

*You **Inspect** the Forgotten Guardsman.*
Level 9. Hit Points: 1,346 / 2,240.
*The Forgotten Guardsman is affected by **Champion's Command.***
*The Forgotten Guardsman is affected by **Champion's Fury.***
This unit is under the command of the Forgotten Champion.
Attack and movement speed are increased.

What was this?

The Forgotten Guardsman was under the command of the Champion.

No wonder.

I looked back at Pops.

The old man was still trading blows with the boss while Attia stood by, healing his wounds. Despite the distance between us, our group seemed to be doing well.

I refreshed Mana Surge on myself and then on our healer before reengaging our foe. Still, I couldn't get the thought out of my mind. If the Forgotten Champion was in control of the guardsman, then that meant...

Another screech echoed off the cavern walls and a second guardsman joined the fray.

Then another.

And another.

Where did they come from?

There were now four minions on the field along with the vengeful boss, and the champion seemed to be keen on the idea of playing with his prey.

"The corpse eaters," Ely shouted, looking down the length of the cavern in desperation as the new creeps descended on Pops and Attia.

Before either of us could interject, Ely was picking up silk-covered bones and tossing them at the nearest dangling maggots.

"Come on, you mealy worms," he shouted, egging them on. "Come and get your dinner."

"Ely, wait," Raven started.

It was too late.

The corpse eaters descended, rearing up and clacking their mandibles as they sensed the rotting flesh of their prey.

It didn't take long for them to devour the adds, but then the boss changed his focus. With alarming speed, the champion charged the four gorged corpse eaters.

We looked on in abject horror as our strange heroes were smashed into pieces by the weight of the hammer.

Bits of flesh and decayed matter splattered the silken carpet of the cavern floor, adding a fresh element of morbidity to the lingering stench.

I watched Ely take in the results of his actions. Sorrow filled his eyes and his bottom lip trembled slightly before curling into an angry grimace.

This was wrong. Dealing with the additional guardsmen like that was too easy.

The cost was too great.

"That's what he wants," Raven growled, giving Ely a harsh glare.

"Sorry," Ely mumbled. He looked at us and then the boss and shrugged. "I had to do something. What else were we supposed to do?"

"I don't know," Raven shot back, but then her glare softened. "I'm sorry, Ely. You're right. We need to think about this. All of us. You couldn't have known, but there has to be a reason the boss wants us to call the corpse eaters."

"He obviously wants to kill them," Ely answered.

"That seems to be it." Raven nodded, surveying the pulverized remains of the corpse eaters. "But why?"

"Hey, you lot," Pops shouted, interrupting the exchange. "If you aren't too busy standing around and going on about the weather like a bunch of old men, we could use some help over here."

He was right. The champion had redirected his attention toward Attia and it was everything the old man could do to shield her from the onslaught.

The three of us raced back toward our friends, carefully avoiding the wriggling masses of the yet-uncovered guardsmen as we went.

By the time we arrived, Pops had once again established control. But seeing him up close was unnerving. He was drenched in sweat and his movements were slower and pained. It was apparent he'd taken quite the beating while the rest of us had been preoccupied.

"What took you so long," he grumbled.

"Sorry," I answered, refreshing Tempest. "We were talking about the corpse eaters. There has to be a reason..."

Critical strike! You hit the Forgotten Champion for 26 HP + 22 Wind damage.
You hit the Forgotten Champion for 14 HP + 19 Wind damage.
Critical strike! You hit the Forgotten Champion for 29 HP + 22 Wind damage.
Dodged! The Forgotten Champion misses his attack.

Before I could continue my thought, the champion feigned a strike at Pops, but pivoted away from me mid-blow.
What was this?

Critical Strike! The Forgotten Champion hits you for 119 HP.

My landing was cushioned by the silk-covered mass of another guardsman several yards away. It wriggled and writhed, and I rolled to my knees in an effort to distance myself from the fiend.

We both groaned in unison. The guardsman from its unsated hunger. Me from the pain of the hammer strike and my subsequent crash landing.

Somehow, I'd managed to keep a tight grip on Truthseeker despite the strength of the blow. My head was still spinning, but I had to engage.

I held the point aloft and prepared to strike.

"Don't fight it there," Raven yelled. "Bring it back to us."

My mind caught up in an instant, and I immediately began limping my way to the group.

The guardsman followed.

White streams of magic channeled from Attia's staff, filling my body with a soothing rush of healing. Minor wounds vanished before my eyes and my gait steadied as the pain receded.

So many thoughts raced through my mind as I neared the rest of my party. The runes on Pops' sword were burning bright and Ely's fists moved so fast they were a blur. Raven danced in and out of the shadows, wielding her daggers with deadly precision. And I was so thankful for every ounce of effort Attia put into mending my wounds.

Now back at the group's position, I turned and faced off against my pursuer.

Ely and Raven joined in.

Even Attia raised her staff against the lone guardsman.

The champion howled his fury when his minion fell. The sound of it rang off the cavern walls, and it seemed even the corpse eaters took note of the growing danger.

An eerie silence followed, and the champion made no move to reengage. But the fight wasn't over.

The boss still had around eighty percent of his hit points remaining.

Pops raised his sword and swung hard at an unarmored section of the champion's chest.

The strike never met its mark.

The champion, somehow taking control of the blade, slowed and then halted the attack.

An unnaturally dark fire burned in the empty sockets and his withered jaw locked firm with the effort.

Pops struggled to maintain control. His muscles trembled and beads of sweat dripped down his brow. Then, one by one, the runes on the blade turned to ash.

With a fierce battle cry, our tank pushed forward, tearing the blade free from whatever magic the champion wielded.

But before he could strike...

The champion summoned a torrent of black energy that tore through the surrounding air like a tsunami of death.

> *The Forgotten Champion uses **Shadow Nova**.*
> ***Shadow Nova** hits Pops for 45 HP.*
> ***Shadow Nova** hits Ely for 54 HP.*
> ***Resist! Shadow Nova** hits you for 12 HP.*
> ***Critical Strike! Shadow Nova** hits Attia for 72 HP.*
> ***Shadow Nova** hits Raven for 55 HP.*

The ring of despair struck me in the chest.

Even though I partially resisted the spell, I felt the nauseating drain on my life force before I even realized what had happened.

Given the reaction of the rest of the party, there was clearly a knockback effect to the attack that I'd somehow managed to evade.

I blinked away the darkness that clawed at my vision and surveyed my surroundings.

Pops was lying on his back, shielding his eyes from the impossible purple flames that had engulfed our foe like unholy armor.

Attia, too, lay stunned.

The hammer rose.

But this time the boss did not prepare to strike.

Instead, the champion stowed his weapon on his back and reached for Pops' sword.

"No." The word tore itself from my throat and I lunged forward, facing off against the boss with a strength I didn't know I possessed.

The formidable undead champion stood almost a foot taller than me and, though he had suffered the ravages of death, had a significant advantage in both strength and weight.

Still, I held my own.

I didn't know if it was the added buffs of Tempest, or if it was something else. Something primal inside of me.

What I did know was that I couldn't allow this fiend to take control of the weapon we had fought for and that Pops had claimed as his own.

I couldn't allow him to reclaim a blade that would increase his power, a power used to inflict horror and death.

And although I didn't know how I would do it, I knew I couldn't allow him to continue hurting my friends.

That was my purpose.

It was my truth.

Truthseeker began to hum. And then, slowly, the sound became something more.

I could hear the sweet melody of an ancient song. It was soft at first, timeless and seemingly coming from nowhere and everywhere all at once, but it grew louder until it filled my soul and every fiber of my being.

A surge of strength that rivaled the rush of Tempest coursed through my veins as Truthseeker's blade began to glow with holy magic.

The Forgotten Champion reeled backward, shielding his eyes from the bright white light.

From somewhere deep inside, I heard the blade's voice once more.

At long last, you have found Truth.
You are worthy.

Congratulations!
You have successfully bound a weapon.
Truthseeker's stats have increased.

Truthseeker
[Bastard Sword]
Damage: 17-22.

Strength + 4, Dexterity +3.
Holy damage randomly added to attacks.
Quality: Fair.
Rarity: Rare.
Durability 3/7
Craftsman's Mark: Jörgen Olsen
Soulbound.

I didn't have time to read the log or think about the implications of what had just happened. The champion thrust a palm forward and a pillar of shadowy flames rained down upon me.

*The Forgotten Champion uses **Dark Smite.***
***Resist! Dark Smite** hits you for 52 HP.*

The dark fire burned my skin and a growing sense of dread washed over me. Even still, Truthseeker continued to glow bright, ebbing away at the encroaching darkness. Quelling my fears.

Then I saw it.

Another light in the darkness.

How could I have forgotten?

Still affixed to the splintered debris of the mahogany door was my glowing sapphire. The pale, blue light glowed from beneath the ruin.

It reminded me of the Kobold's curse.

Darkness take you.

Not today, Kobold...

"Not today, you fiend," I shouted, brandishing Truthseeker against the champion.

The holy light infused into the cold steel of my blade cut through his dark armor.

Then Attia joined the fray, doing significant damage with her holy magic. Together, we lashed out, alternating our attacks with blinding bursts of white that challenged the oppressive shadows the champion had wielded against us.

After meditating over his greatsword, Pops was back on his feet. A thin line of blood trickled from his nose from the effort, but the runes were once again etched into the steel of his blade.

The others, too, had regained their composure.

We attacked as one and the boss stumbled backward, distancing himself from our onslaught and retrieving his hammer once more.

Sixty.

Fifty.

Forty percent of his hit points remained.

The air grew heavy as he let out the most horrible battle cry.

It hurt my ears and tore at my will to fight. Terrible echoes bounced off the cavern walls, compounding the initial demoralizing debuff.

Loud groans followed.

Many of them.

Far too many.

I turned and felt my jaw tighten.

Ten. Fifteen. Twenty guardsmen were shrugging off their silken confines, tearing at the air and gnashing their teeth.

It was too much.

I looked at Attia, but she shook her head. Then she mouthed the words, "I'm out."

Mana...

In my haste to deal as much damage to the boss as I could, I'd forgotten to renew her buff.

*You cast **Mana Surge** on Attia.*
Attia is now refreshed.

Giving Attia the mana refresh buff now seemed like a pointless gesture in a way. But even though there was no way we could fight off so many mobs at once, I wasn't ready to give up just yet.

We had to try. Even if the end turned out the same.

We had to fight.

Or did we...? The guardsmen weren't advancing.

Instead, I watched in disbelief. One by one, they shifted their attention toward the other end of the chamber.

"Look at that," I breathed, giving voice to my observation.

Ely turned away from the boss long enough to contemplate the scene of the retreating guardsmen.

"Maybe they're headed back the way we came?" he asked, returning his attention to the champion. "If so, the joke's on them. They'll never get past the gear room. It was shut off from the front entrance the moment we pulled that lever."

I shook my head. "No. That's not it. They aren't trying to make it to the fort. I think they're going to kill the rest of the corpse eaters."

"We have to do something," Raven said, her words sounding both irritated and a little desperate. "With a mob like that, they'll tear through the corpse eaters like they're nothing."

"But if we do something, they'll tear through us like we're nothing," Ely retorted. "Look, I don't like it either, but what can we do?"

He dodged an incoming hammer strike before continuing. "I think our only hope is to kill this guy first. Maybe then we can pick them off."

"It can't be that simple," Raven said. "There's a trick here. If the boss wants these creatures dead so badly, there has to be a reason."

"What if the reason is to distract us from actually trying to put him down?" Ely shot back.

Raven remained silent as she processed the possibility that we were being played, choosing instead to focus her efforts into her dagger strikes while she pondered.

I looked at the cavern walls and then at the glowing blue gem that was still trapped within the door's locking mechanism.

"Unless..." I said, looking back at the glowing orbs attached to the cavern walls. That blue light. It couldn't be a coincidence. Could it?

Pops deflected an oncoming blow before giving me a look that suggested he was eager for options. "What's on your mind, Denton?"

Without saying a word, I dashed toward the mangled remains of the mahogany door. The wood was splintered and the exposed metal gears were bent and off-kilter.

But it was too low to the ground, and the gem was too far to reach.

If I could manage to get under it somehow... Knocking a few loose boulders off the pile, I gripped the edge and began to lift.

It was heavy.

My muscles burned as I tried to free the door from the pile of fallen debris. I only needed to reach the gemstone, but large rocks barred any progress.

I pushed and shoved. It was no use. I felt my footing give way in the fine grit and stone that littered the cavern floor.

Then Ely was beside me. He braced his shoulder against the wood and groaned.

This time the door shifted, lurching upward a few precious inches. Rocks and bricks tumbled down the debris pile and the load got lighter.

Inch by inch, the door rose from the ground until, at last, there was enough room for me to climb underneath.

"Go," Ely breathed. The muscles in his arms and legs quivered from exertion and his jaw was clenched tight from the effort. "Get the stone."

"You sure you've got it on your own?" I asked.

"I've got it. Just... hurry."

Scrambling beneath the door, I reached for the gem. Several jagged splinters found their mark before I finally felt the cold, hard surface of the faceted stone.

"I've got it," I shouted, but no sooner had the words left my mouth than I discovered another problem. "Wait. Hold on."

"What's wrong?" Ely asked, his voice strained.

"It's stuck," I answered while working the stinging fingers of one hand into the mechanism. "But if I can just—"

Click.

The gem fell into my palm, and I quickly pulled my digits free from the tension lock that had held it in place. It snapped shut.

"Come on," Ely pleaded. "I can't hold it much longer."

As soon as I rolled free of the door, his grip gave way. Debris and wood crashed down in a heap once more, sending a cloud of dust high into the air.

We both turned.

The boss was gaining ground on the rest of our group and the guardsmen had made it halfway across the large chamber.

"Now what?" Ely asked. "What's the plan?"

I looked down at the glowing gem, staring into its depths in search of an answer. In truth, I didn't really know.

"Denton?"

I let out the breath I'd been holding and shrugged. "I guess I'm going to try to get his attention."

"Wait. You guess?"

I didn't answer. Instead, I ran back toward the champion, brandishing Truthseeker in one hand and the sapphire in the other.

The Kobolds had revered this strange, glowing gem. More than that, they'd trusted it to keep the darkness at bay.

Now it was time to put that trust to the test against a real darkness, a Dark Paladin that stood between us and the end of a very long dungeon.

51

The champion shielded the shadows of his eyes against the growing light of the sapphire, temporarily leaving himself vulnerable to attack, but the reprieve from his onslaught didn't last long.

He struck out with his hammer in a blind attempt to snuff out the source of the light.

I dodged with ease, but then the hammer struck again. It was an attack much like the one that had destroyed the mahogany door, but much weaker this time.

"It must be the stone," Raven said, plunging her daggers into the champion's exposed back. "He's losing strength."

"And if the gem can weaken him," Attia added, "then what about the light from the eggs? It's much brighter."

"It's worth a shot," I said, dancing away from another blow. "But how do we get him there?"

"Sounds like a game of keep-away to me," Ely said, laughing.

It was such a hearty and pleasant sound that it struck a stark contrast with our gloomy surroundings. I couldn't help but return his wide grin as he opened his palms.

The champion's hammer swung wide.

Pops flinched, suffering a glancing strike to the side and groaning as he tried to recover.

"Whatever we're going to do," he said, firming up his stance, "let's do it. I don't know how much more of this I can take."

I tossed Ely the gem and the champion instantly shifted, pursuing the source of the light.

Raven was next and then Pops and finally Attia.

The champion followed, and I positioned myself for the next toss.

I caught the large gem and turned to gain some distance before the next handoff.

Further back in the cavernous chamber, the guardsmen had engaged their opponents. The cries of the enraged corpse eaters were horrifying. But, despite their will to fight, they were grossly outnumbered by the wave of undead soldiers.

"What happens if they don't make it?" Ely shouted.

I stopped and faced our oncoming foe, ducking a hammer strike and lobbing the gem to Ely at the very last moment.

"I don't know," I said, once again establishing some distance from the boss. "But I'd prefer not to find out."

Everything about the plan was going smoothly. We'd managed to lure the boss out of the easy shadows and into the brighter part of the open chamber.

There was still a ways to go before we reached the eggs, but the champion's movements seemed to be weighed down in the growing light.

"We're almost there," Raven said, catching the stone after Ely's toss. "Just a little bit further."

The boss stopped, halting his pursuit.

He stared at us with his empty sockets and didn't bother to shield his eyes from the growing light. Then he glared with palpable hatred at our retreating Shadowdancer.

Sensing the shift, Raven stopped and turned to face the Dark Paladin.

"What's wrong, Ugly?" She shouted. "Have you had enough? Are you too tired to fight, or are you just too slow?"

The boss roared his defiance and lurched forward, gaining several paces before Raven could react.

She turned toward Pops and prepared to toss the gemstone, but it was too late.

The hammer left the champion's hands and swung forward, hurtling through the air like a freight train.

It struck Raven before she could react, knocking the sapphire from her grasp as she fell backward and slammed to the ground.

But the champion did not follow. Instead, he lunged toward Pops.

Within the blink of an eye, he was upon the old man, grabbing him by the neck and hoisting him into the air like a broken doll.

Attia raised her staff. Holy light filled her eyes, and a bolt of magic sprang forth from her palm.

The champion was ready.

He swung Pops around like a shield, blocking the magic attack with his body. Then he tossed our tank to the silk-covered ground and pried the greatsword from his grasp.

Boney fingers wrapped around the hilt of Pops' blade and black fire enveloped the steel. It burned with a shadowy intensity that swallowed the light of the eggs.

Through the growing darkness, I watched as Pops' runes turned to ash once more.

The Dark Paladin stood taller, cracking the bones in his back before giving the blade a few test swings. The smile that followed filled my stomach with revulsion.

We had won a small battle in getting the boss this far into the light, but now we were on the verge of losing the war.

Our overconfidence had been our undoing.

I looked behind me and quickly surveyed the battlefield.

The guardsmen had continued their rampage and the corpse eaters suffered several losses. The skirmish had pushed back until both groups were nearly at the water's edge, at the point where we'd slid down from the upper chamber.

We didn't have much time before the last of their ranks were diminished. And then the guardsmen would return, bringing the wave of destruction with them.

But worst of all, the Dark Paladin had been reunited with his fabled weapon. And the bond between the sword and the champion was strong.

Coming to, Pops groped for his missing blade. He tore at the strands of silk until his fingers grasped the nearest object.

A bone.

By the looks of it, he'd grabbed the femur of some unfortunate soul who hadn't made it out of the depths of the dungeon. Upon realizing what he'd latched on to, Pops dropped the object and groaned.

The Dark Paladin shook with morbid laughter and the black flames surrounding him burned darker. They swallowed the light and spread shadows like a disease.

He raised his reclaimed blade and prepared to strike.

"Denton," Raven exclaimed, tossing the sapphire toward me.

I barely had time to appraise the damage the hammer had inflicted before the stone tumbled into my outstretched fingers.

Despite the blue glow, all I could see was red.

Blood matted Raven's dark hair and covered the silk she'd crawled through to retrieve the gem.

I turned in time to see the champion begin his downward strike at our disabled tank. If he landed the deathblow, Pops would have no choice but to return to the Home Point far above the depths of the dungeon.

But the champion no longer had his hammer. And Truthseeker was much better suited to deflect an attack from a heavy sword such as his.

With a quick nod to Ely, I raced forward, tossing the gem toward the boss as I went. The dark flames swallowed its light until it was gone, passing over the champion's shoulder and disappearing into the blackness beyond.

I could only hope Ely had understood.

Either way, the immediate action of throwing the gemstone had the desired effect.

It gave me enough time to span the gap.

The sound of metal on metal rang in my ears as our swords met. The dark flames of his blade against the holy light of my own. Then I twisted my hilt, deflecting the weight of his blow and dancing to the side.

With a growl, he lashed out once more.

I stepped out of the strike, swinging Truthseeker through the air and harnessing the weight of the heavier blade to propel it in a circle. First down and then upward in a quick revolution.

Though I'd hoped to disarm my stronger opponent, his death-like grip on the hilt of the greatsword held firm.

Still, his recovery had come at a cost. In an attempt to regain his footing, the boss took a step backward.

And that's when he found Ely crouched low behind his knees.

Skeletal arms flailed as the champion tried to maintain his balance, but it was too late. Gravity had already taken hold.

He toppled to the ground, landing with the clattering sound of his armor and the greatsword bouncing off the hard earth.

Like a wrestler, Ely was quick to take advantage of the opportunity. He wrapped himself around the champion's core, expertly pinning the boss's limbs in his weakened state.

"Do it," Ely grunted, struggling to muscle through the fight. "Put this monster down."

White light emanated from Attia's staff, infusing Pops with healing magic as I raised my sword.

"Wait," Pops groaned. "Toss me the stone. There's something I need to do."

Attia bent down and picked the large sapphire from a mass of silk and walked forward, handing it to the old man.

Pops glared at the champion and stepped closer before standing in silence for a moment as he finished reading an update to his quest.

When he spoke, his words were chilling.

"Paladin, you were charged with the task of protecting Fort Morrow, but you turned against the city that placed its trust in you.

And in your hubris you turned the men under your command into monsters."

The champion reeled with fire and hatred at the accusations, but Ely's grip held firm.

"No more," Pops shouted. "Your reign of terror has come to an end. No more will you lurk in the shadows. No more will you gather lost souls and lead good men astray."

With that, Pops slammed the blue sapphire downward, lodging it in the champion's empty eye socket where it gathered and amplified the light from the eggs.

The boss roared in agony and began to thrash.

The struggle was too great and Ely lost his grip as the champion tore free. But our foe was no longer interested in a fight.

Instead, he tore at his face in an attempt to dislodge the gem from his eye.

The stone held firm. Its light shining ever brighter in the fading shadows.

With our window of opportunity quickly coming to a close, Ely and I both prepared to strike.

But Attia's voice halted our advance.

"No, wait," she shouted. "Watch." Then she took in a shocked breath and began to read something the rest of us couldn't see.

Silently obeying her command, we looked on as the champion, blinded, continued to thrash his way toward the cavern wall where the large, glowing eggs awaited him.

I cringed as he smashed one after another in his desperate fervor to extinguish any source of light.

I couldn't force myself to look away.

Not until I heard the groans of dismay from the other end of the chamber.

The corpse eaters.

Though it was impossible to believe they could see what was happening, they wailed and screamed at the loss of the eggs.

The guardsmen fought on, seizing the opportunity to inflict heavy damage on the dwindling number of their foes.

Then my stomach lurched into my throat as I watched something else join the fray. It looked like a bus and it screamed its rage at the wave of guardsmen before exacting its vengeance.

And what bloody vengeance it was.

"What the..." Ely gasped.

"Those are the eggs of a lunar moth," Attia explained, pointing toward the glowing orbs the boss was so intent on smashing.

"Was that your quest update?" I asked. "A Lunar moth... why is that important?"

"You'll just have to wait and see."

"And that thing?" Ely asked, pointing toward the monstrously large creature.

She shrugged. "It must be their big brother. Those ones, the ones we encountered earlier, they're just babies. Actually, corpse eaters are more like caterpillars than maggots."

"Just babies..." Ely echoed, unable to keep the twang of fear from his voice.

My eyes focused on what details I could make out in the flurry of action. Attia was right. The creature was none other than a giant corpse eater.

And it was angry.

Black mandibles that glinted like glass in the light of the eggs tore through guardsman after guardsman while the other, smaller corpse eaters quivered, laying their heads low to the ground.

Once the army had been sufficiently devoured, the monstrosity turned its attention toward our location and screamed once more.

Wrinkled flesh creased and jiggled as it raced across the silk-covered earth. It was much faster than I'd anticipated, and I took an involuntary step backward.

In an instant it was upon us, wreaking of death and filling my bones with despair. It was nearly three times the size of the champion and at least five feet wide.

"Don't tell me we have to fight this thing, too," Ely muttered in awe.

"Don't move," our healer whispered. "No matter what."

Ely and I exchanged confused looks, but we did as Attia commanded. We watched in silence as the giant corpse eater clacked its obsidian mandibles and screeched in fury at the Dark Paladin.

Finally, sensing the creature's presence, the boss halted his attack on the glowing eggs.

He turned.

And spoke.

"Dhu hrath isk tahl."

The silk-covered bones at our feet began to tremble and quake, but the corpse eater only drew nearer to its prey.

It rose up until it was at full height and stared down at the champion, oblivious to the new army being formed all around us.

*You **Inspect** the Forgotten Champion.*
Level 13. Hit Points: 1,156 / 4,400.
Dark Paladin
*The Forgotten Champion is affected by **Command Undead**.*

Despite all our efforts, the boss still had about a fourth of his hit points remaining. And with the addition of these new minions… Things were not looking good.

"Dhu hrath isk tahl."

The first of the skeletal warriors raced forward, attacking the large corpse eater in a blind rage.

Then another joined in.

And another.

The boss must have pieced together every last corpse in the entire chamber. Before I realized what was happening, there were too many to count.

And yet the corpse eater remained motionless as the minions tore at its flesh.

Pops slowly started to reach for the blade the champion had abandoned while there was still an opportunity to act, but Attia gave him a quick, sharp shake of the head.

And then, without warning, the corpse eater lurched into action.

It slammed its belly downward and began thrashing with wild abandon. Fragments of bones and strings of mucky silk stuck to its torn flesh as the army of makeshift warriors were pulverized in its wake.

When it finished the rampage, the corpse eater looked like an undead aberration. Like armor, every inch of it was covered in shattered bone and matted silk.

And only the Forgotten Champion remained on the field of battle. But the boss took the defeat in stride, thrusting a hand forward and calling for his blade.

"Dhu thist ahk mreh."

The greatsword began sliding toward the champion's outstretched hand and a twisted grin curled the remains of his leathery maw.

That's when the corpse eater struck.

My eyes struggled to make sense of the speed of its attack. Before I even realized what had happened, the fight was done.

His arm, still reaching for the weapon as it struck the ground, was the only evidence that the boss had even existed.

His fingers twitched for the last time and the sword slid to a stop.

The spell was broken.

The Mature Corpse Eater has defeated the Forgotten Champion.
You have gained 12,500 Experience Points.

I stared at my log, not wanting to believe what I'd just seen. But it was true. The corpse eater had finished the boss. Not just that. It had eaten him nearly whole.

My mind stumbled over the question of what would come next. Were we now supposed to face off against this beast instead?

As if in answer to my silent question, the Mature Corpse Eater gave our group an appraising look, clacking its mandibles in a slow, rhythmic fashion.

It began scrunching into itself, shivering in a way that made my skin crawl, before it began making a sound that felt distinctly familiar.

Where had I heard it before?

It sounded like a cat.

Like a cat that was about to—

WERRIGHHK. WERRIGHHK. WERRAAUUUGHHK.

Mucous-covered objects tumbled from the creature's mouth and onto the cavern floor.

The smell.

I covered my nose and mouth with a hand and struggled against the urge to revisit the kabob I'd eaten earlier that evening.

Ely wasn't as successful with his own inner conflict. "Sorry," he muttered, wiping his mouth on his sleeve.

But all eyes were on the corpse eater.

It turned to face the remaining eggs and let out a long, low hum that was heavy with sadness.

The smaller corpse eaters inched closer, surrounding their larger, bone-covered brother.

One by one they added their chorus to the mournful dirge.

And then the singing stopped.

The smaller corpse eaters flattened themselves on the ground and clacked their mandibles while the larger one began climbing the wall.

Once it had reached the cavernous ceiling, the Mature Corpse Eater slowed and came to a stop above our group.

It dangled there for a moment.

And then the transformation began.

Using the caked blood and silk and crushed bone, it tugged and pulled at its skin until it had formed a perfect chrysalis.

"Sleep well, friend," Attia whispered. "You earned it. And when you finally emerge from your cocoon, you'll be the most beautiful lunar moth EndWorld has ever seen."

52

The rest of the corpse eaters retreated back to their silken webs near the newly formed chrysalis, leaving us alone with the mucous-covered pile of loot.

Pops was the first to move. He bent down and retrieved his greatsword, sliding it into the sheath on his back without bothering to replace the runes.

Ely stepped forward, eyeing the loot pile but shying away from moving any closer to the foul-smelling bile that covered it.

Raven wasn't quite as bothered.

"There's no getting around it," she said, plunging her hands into the smelly goo. "Loot is loot, after all."

Item after item was tossed over her shoulder until the pile was exhausted of useable gear and salvageable materials.

Once she finished, I carefully inspected the haul.

Hardened Leather Gloves of the Runemaster
[Hands] Defense: 6
Strength +3, Stamina +4.
Requirement: Level 5.

Quality: Superior.
Rarity: Rare.
Armor Class: Medium.
Durability: 17/20.

Pugilist's Boots of Fortitude

[Feet] Defense: 4
Strength +1, Stamina +6.
Requirement: Level 5.
Quality: Superior.
Rarity: Rare.
Armor Class: Medium.
Durability: 17/20.

Modest Sitabaki

[Legs] Defense: 5
Strength +2, Stamina +6.
Requirement: Level 5.
Quality: Superior.
Rarity: Rare.
Armor Class: Medium.
Durability: 17/20.

Lunarfang

[Dagger]
Damage: 13-19.
Agility +4, Dexterity +4
Quality: Superior.
Rarity: Rare.
Durability 17/20

Naevelda's Spire

[Divine Staff]
Damage: 9-14.

Mind +3, Spirit +8
Quality: Superior.
Rarity: Rare.
Durability 17/20

Chipped Sapphire of Illumination
Loot Restriction: Denton Wade

62 Grimy Cotton Cloth Scraps
6 Gold. 75 Silver.

Ely leaned back and planted his fists firmly on his hips. "That's some haul," he said, nodding his approval.

"Some haul, indeed," Attia whispered.

Her earnest excitement over the prospect of getting a new staff was heartening. She'd worked so hard to keep us all alive, and it was clear to everyone in the group that she'd earned it.

"The coin is easy," Raven said, dispensing a share to each of us. "Roughly one gold and 68 silver each, give or take a copper or two."

"Anyone want to call dibs on anything in particular?" Pops asked. He, too, was excited, but the exhaustion in his voice was unmistakable.

When no one responded right away, he added, "I'd like to get my hands on those gloves, if no one else is interested."

"No pun intended?" I asked, flashing the old man a smile.

He chuckled. "No, I guess not. Not intended, but it is a good pun, isn't it?"

I looked at the stats on the gloves again. Then inspected the boots and pants.

None of the gear had Intellect, which was a crucial stat for my mana pool and, if my suspicions were correct, the stat probably boosted my spell damage as well.

Nothing in the pile of loot was of particular interest to me. Nothing except...

"I'll take the chipped sapphire," I said, bending down to claim the one piece of loot that was inarguably mine.

"Can I get the legs and the feet?" Ely added. "They go with my build really well, and I'd love to get out of this stupid subligar."

"I thought you liked that thing." I laughed and the others quickly followed suit.

"Sure, it's good enough for a few laughs around the tavern, but it's probably as uncomfortable as that boss must be in the belly of the corpse eater."

We all chuckled and, with no objections, Ely retrieved his new gear, tossing Pops the pair of gloves he'd asked for in the process.

"Would you mind if I get changed here?" Ely asked. "The last time I was in a situation like this... Well, you know. That's how I ended up wearing a subligar."

After having another good laugh, we all turned around so our brawler could get changed.

"I would like the staff, please," Attia said once Ely was finished.

"And the dagger for you, Raven?" I asked.

She nodded. "Yes, please," she said, reaching down for the blade and balancing it lightly in one hand before tossing Attia the staff. "This would certainly be a good upgrade compared to what I have now."

All eyes lingered on me.

"What?" I asked.

There was a long, awkward pause.

"I think we all feel a little bad, Denton," Raven answered, speaking for the rest of the group.

My heart grew a little heavy, and I knew what was about to come next.

"This was supposed to be your dungeon," Attia added.

"And you didn't even get any real loot," Ely said, chiming in. "Just a chipped sapphire. What about the champion's hammer? If we find it, maybe you can sell it."

Raven looked around, rummaging through the silk and bones in the area where she'd been struck.

"It's gone," she said. "It'll probably be a part of the next iteration of the dungeon."

Attia frowned. "You mean it could be a reward for the next group who comes to slay an epically difficult boss here?"

Raven shrugged. "Maybe. But more importantly, it isn't here for Denton to claim."

"It's okay," I said, doing my best to brush off their concerns.

Speaking up for the first time since donning his new gloves, Pops interjected. "No, Denton, it's not okay. We're going to make this up to you. When you get your level 5 quest—"

"Listen," I said, cutting him off. "It's okay. Really. Right now all I care about is making it back to Harold's and getting some sleep."

"It has been a long night," Attia admitted, letting out a long sigh.

I nodded, then continued. "Honestly, I should have known this twist was coming. Margaret told me I needed to start looking out for the non-Travelers of EndWorld. Maybe this dungeon has something to do with that advice. Maybe forming up a party and helping Captain Elsbaud with this run was exactly what I was supposed to do. Besides, we don't know the significance of the sapphire."

Raven smiled, but her enthusiasm didn't come across as genuine as she might have hoped.

"You're probably right," she said. "That gem could easily be the most valuable item here."

"Wait," Ely interjected. "Who is Margaret again?"

"She's my class trainer," I answered. "Anyway, all this probably happened for a reason, right? I'm sure I'll find out why soon enough. But not tonight. We all just need some sleep."

When I got nothing but silence in response, I pressed my point. "Raven might have gotten a new blade, but she didn't exactly find what she was looking for either. Has anyone seen any sign of a wayward dire wolf pup?"

"That's true," Raven replied. Her shoulders slumped a little at the mention of her failed quest line.

"We still want to help," Pops countered.

It was clear my older friend wasn't going to let it go. I had no choice but to acquiesce.

"I'm not mad, and I'm not saying you can't help, but it's been a really long day. Let's finish up and head back. We can figure out the rest once we've had a chance to sleep."

Raven shifted on her feet, but gave a slow nod.

While I still wasn't clear on why this wolf pup meant so much to her, I'd really grown to like Raven over the course of our misadventures. I could almost feel her pain. It wasn't just some quest.

Raven was just as exhausted as the rest of us, and yet something told me there would be no sleep for her once we reached the streets of Fort Morrow.

"We best be heading out," she said. "Does anyone have a spare torch? It's going to get dark once we move away from the light of these eggs."

Pops pulled a spare torch from his inventory and set flint to steel to spark a flame.

"Ready when you are," he said, pausing for a moment before leading the way back toward the broken door.

WE WALKED IN SILENCE, NAVIGATING OUR WAY THROUGH THE MAZE OF silk. With care, we climbed over the debris and rubble and left the remnants of the mahogany door in our wake.

The chamber beyond was unnaturally dark, and the air was cold. Though he was gone, the champion's presence lingered.

I could still feel the weight of his hatred. But aside from the aura of hate and fear, nothing else remained.

The boss's chamber was barren in the flickering torchlight.

"Too bad there isn't another chest," Ely said.

"Wouldn't that be nice?" Attia replied, agreeing with his disappointment. "I would have liked a nice surprise for Denton."

"Not this again," I groaned before forcing a chuckle. "Sleep is all the reward I need right now."

At the other end of the small chamber was a pathway that disappeared into a darkened recess.

"That must be it," Pops said.

He lifted his torch and nodded.

The echo of our footsteps filled the space left by our withered conversation and we set our path up the slight incline of the passage.

A light draft pushed at us from behind. It was gentle at first, but strengthened as the walls narrowed.

Little things skittered overhead, fleeing from the transitory disturbance of our trespass.

Despite the refreshing breeze behind us, the air was dank and smelled of mildew. The walls grew closer and the wet touch of moss was all that greeted fingers in search of a stable handhold in the cavelike surround.

My eyelids grew heavy in the low light. Still, we plodded onward. Upward. The path steepened and began to curve, building into a wide, invisible spiral as we ascended toward the streets above.

Our adventure was nearly over. Soon we would find ourselves back in Fort Morrow proper, turning in our quest and parting for what little remained of the night.

I couldn't help but reflect on just how much we'd accomplished. How much I had accomplished. And none of it had been easy.

Pops came to an abrupt stop, sending the rest of us crashing forward like dominoes in reverse.

He cocked his head.

All I could hear was the crackling pop of the flames from the torch before the faintest of sounds reached my ears.

It sounded like chaos.

Deep voices clashed in the undertones. None of it intelligible from where we stood. But one thing was unmistakable.

The urgency of it all.

"What do you think—" Ely started.

"Shh," Raven hissed, cutting him off before she inched forward and quietly activated one of her abilities.

After an endless, anxious silence, she turned. Her face was ashen white and her eyes wide. When she whispered, it took my tired mind a moment to process what she'd said. When the pieces came together, I felt a weight in my chest.

It gripped my heart with the icy fingers of fear.

"The undead are attacking."

53

The scene on the streets of Fort Morrow was just as I'd feared. Soldiers, citizens, and Travelers alike moved with purpose in the crowded, torch-lit square. Warning bells sounded the alarm from every tower top while guards marched with shield and spear to shore up defenses at the nearest exit.

Above the clamor and commotion, one familiar voice stood out above the rest. It barked orders with authority, commanding all those nearby into swift action.

The crowd thinned, if only for a moment, revealing the stoic form of Captain Elsbaud. Despite the chaos, he spotted our group and beckoned us forward.

"Travelers, status report. I see you're not dead and I could use some good news. How fared your excursion into the sewers?"

He was looking at me, his eyes probing in an effort to gauge the final outcome.

"We've finished your errand," I said, and it felt good to say those words.

"The sewers are clear?"

"Yes, the sewers are clear."

"And?" He waited impatiently for me to continue. "What, pray tell, did you encounter? It's important."

"Slimes and the undead, sir. Guardsmen mostly, and then the Forgotten Champion," I explained.

Elsbaud's eyes narrowed in disbelief, but then he caught a glimpse of the hilt of the greatsword sheathed on Pop's back.

"The Blade of the Forgotten Champion," he breathed, his tone filled with awe and respect. "So it's true. And it appears the weapon has chosen its new master."

"It wasn't easy," Pops said.

"No, I don't imagine it was." Elsbaud gave our tank a knowing nod and then addressed the rest of us.

"The Champion of Fort Morrow died long before the first Traveler entered our world, and his is a cautionary tale for another time."

He paused briefly, then added, "I know you have fought hard this night and I know you are weary. But if I could, I would ask that you hold strong and help me rout the vile threat to our home and people."

Quest complete! You've completed a quest:
Clear the Sewers.
You've received: 1,000 Experience Points.
+500 Favor with Captain Elsbaud.
+500 Favor with the Morrow Watch.

Before we could answer, the lieutenant from earlier that evening rushed forward. He stopped short of bowling into our party and gave a sharp salute.

"What is it?" Elsbaud asked after returning the courtesy.

"Sir, we have reports of an incursion at Bailey's Farm."

"More undead?"

"No, sir. It seems a group of bandits have taken advantage of the ensuing chaos. I'm afraid our ranks are too thin to divert forces without weakening our defenses here," the lieutenant responded.

When Elsbaud remained silent, the lieutenant shifted and then finally prompted a reply. "What are your orders, sir?"

The captain turned his attention back in our direction. "Friends, what say you? Can I count on your fortitude in this dark hour?"

We all looked at one another before answering as one. "Yes, sir."

"Sir," the lieutenant added before we could receive a quest prompt, giving us all a saddened glance. "I'm sorry, but there's more."

"More?" Elsbaud prompted. His expression grew perturbed. "Don't let the words get stuck in that maw of yours, Lieutenant. Let's hear it."

"Yes, sir," the lieutenant stammered. "Scouts have reported three travelers and a dire wolf pup headed toward the source of the darkness."

Elsbaud rubbed the stubble on his chin and frowned. "Where were they last sighted?"

"North, near the Kingsroad, sir. A party might be able to cut them off if they traveled the Eastern path. They would need to be fleet of foot, with the wind at their back. Even then, they might not make it in time."

"That does complicate matters, doesn't it?" he asked.

After a moment of deliberation, he looked back at our group. "Friends, the lieutenant is right. Your fellow Travelers and the citizens of Fort Morrow alike have been mobilized to the fullest extent. Our forces are already spread too thin, but these events cannot go unanswered.

"I'm afraid I'm going to have to ask you to split your party as well. I know you must be tired, yet this our only hope to rout the remaining threat."

Pops looked at Raven and nodded.

"We understand," he said to Elsbaud. "Our Shadowdancer has unfinished business with the pup. I volunteer to help rout the incursion at Bailey's Farm. I am familiar with the location and the Baileys have been kind to me."

"Very well," Elsbaud returned and pointed to Attia and Ely. "You two go with him. Denton, I see you've got Tempest. You will need to make haste. Go with your shadowy friend and head off the Travelers before they reach the swamp if possible."

"And if it's not possible," Raven asked, her eyes alight with anger.

"If not. Well, I'll leave that to you. But be careful, both of you. We don't know what you will encounter out there. None of our scouts who have ventured into the swamp have returned."

New Quest Alert! You've received your Level 5 Quest:
Face the Darkness.
A scout of the Morrow Watch has spotted 3 Travelers headed toward Duskmorrow Swamp with a dire wolf pup in tow.
Stop the Travelers from entering the swamp or deal with the consequences before the threat grows.
Reward: *Unknown.*

"Yes, sir," I answered, giving my friend a gentle smile. "You can count on us."

"Wait a second." Ely frowned. "That was your level 5 quest, wasn't it?"

I nodded.

"Oh, come on," he said in protest before turning to Pops. "We've got to take out those bandits fast and meet them at the swamp."

Pops frowned.

I wasn't sure where the farm was, but I was pretty certain our tank was calculating the distance. His pained expression communicated both his desire to help and his uncertainty over whether they could make it in time.

"We'll make it happen," Ely promised. "Won't we, Pops?"

But Elsbaud wasn't having any more of the conversation.

"We have no time for this," the captain shouted. "I would keep you all together if I could, but in times such as these we don't have that luxury. Please, friends. You must go. Each to your own errand. And may the light be with you all."

54

My heart thumped within my chest, filling my ears with the rhythmic drumming of excitement. Adrenaline surged through my veins and all traces of fatigue washed away as Raven and I raced toward the fort's Eastern gate.

I felt alert. I felt alive. Even Truthseeker yearned to uncover the dark mystery hidden within the swamp. The sword pulled me forward with an invisible force I didn't yet understand. Obediently, I followed.

Cobbled streets gave way to the Eastern path and our footsteps quieted. The packed earth was much softer under foot. After the long hours spent underground, we had no need for torches. And yet, a thick mist rose from the depths of the forest. So much so that we nearly missed the fork that would take us deep into Duskmorrow Swamp. The fork that had called to me after my encounter with the rabbit.

I found it difficult to keep up with Raven's Shadowdance ability and had to stop, refreshing Tempest and Mana Surge before I followed her further down the darkened trail.

The smell was the first indication of the change in terrain. A pervasive, foul odor filled my nostrils, and I felt my breath stutter and then catch within my chest. Rancid water and decay hung on the air like a wet rag. At last, we had neared the edge of the swamp. I covered my mouth and nose with the back of my hand and stared out into darkness before us.

Large balls of green light danced between the trees, glowing and thrumming before fading back into the shadows. Only to reemerge a little further away, pulsing with a hypnotizing sort of magic.

"Fireflies?" I asked, still in awe of the spectacle after minutes of watching the enchanting dance of the luminescent orbs.

Raven shook her head beside me.

"No," she answered. "Not fireflies. They call them ghost lights. They're known for drawing any who would follow to their deaths. Always beckoning. Always just out of reach."

"Should we avoid them, then?"

Again, she shook her head. "Usually, yes. But not tonight. Tonight they will lead us where we want to go."

Without further hesitation, Raven took off along the path. She slipped in and out of the void, leaving me to catch up.

Racing forward, I forced a breath. Then another. And then the path softened. Packed earth was replaced by the soft give of wet moss beneath my boots. A sudden splash up ahead broke my stride, and I struggled to stop on the slick material covering the pathway. Each of my movements were exaggerated by the speed boost I received from Tempest.

I flailed my arms in a vain attempt to salvage my sense of balance. The effort only made it worse. Instead of falling backwards with the force of my initial momentum, I landed face first in the slimy muck.

Pulling myself from the mud with a squelch, I swiped the stomach-wrenching goo from my eyes and tried to locate the source of the original sound. Raven was nearly fifty paces ahead. I watched in confused shock as she continued to fight for purchase in the knee-deep water that had swallowed the path.

My first thought was that a mob had caught her beneath the surface of the muck and mire. I searched for any sign of a creature or undead fiend that might have caught wind of potential prey.

Nothing.

"Are you okay?" I shouted. My hand instinctively grabbed at Truthseeker's hilt, which was now covered in the foul, slimy mud.

"Be careful," Raven yelled back. "It drops off pretty quick."

"Does something have you? Are— Are you being attacked?"

She regained her footing and stood.

"No and no," she answered with an embarrassed laugh. "I came out of the void in a bad spot. I didn't realize it dropped off right there. I guess fast travel isn't much of an option from here on out."

Then she looked at me.

"What happened to you," she asked, now unable to stop her laughter.

"Yeah, yeah," I said. "Laugh it up. You scared the crap out of me."

"Not literally, I hope?" Her voice was playful.

I frowned and sploshed my way to the water's edge, gently easing myself into the thigh-high bog.

"No, not literally."

She waited while I made my way to her position. Then we both sploshed in silence for a time. The water and moss posed a heavy barrier to our progress, and it wasn't long before we were both breathing hard from the exertion.

"Why do you think they're bringing the dire wolf here," I asked between breaths.

Raven remained silent for a moment. When she spoke, her voice was uncertain. "I don't know. But if it has something to do with the undead incursion, I think we can be sure it isn't good."

She stopped walking and turned to face me.

"Denton, we have to stop them."

I nodded. There it was, that strong-willed determination. I could see it in her eyes. Failure was no longer an option.

"It isn't just a dire wolf, is it," I asked. "There's more to this, right?"

Raven took a deep breath and continued trudging through the mire.

"EndWorld Everlasting was designed to be an afterlife of sorts, right?" Her words were gentle and even, despite her continued exertion.

"Right," I agreed.

"Well, a good portion of us have a certain kind of baggage we carry with us. Memories, injuries, doubts, and insecurities, that sort of thing," she explained.

"Unfinished business."

Her gaze met mine, and she nodded. "Unfinished business. This world was designed to help people get over the pain and sorrow of their past. But each of us have different needs, different requirements to get us back to a position of being whole."

"And that's where the quests come in?"

"Some of them, yes," she answered. "Sometimes the system is a bit more subtle. And it's always up to the individual to choose their path."

"The dire wolf pup is—"

"Personal," she said, cutting off any further questions on the subject.

I was beginning to understand. This was why people didn't often talk about their tutorials. This was why some people were a little more cagey about who they were and where they came from, and while not a justification for their actions, this might be why people like Fat Anthony and Tommy Lewis took advantage of new Travelers. Perhaps they weren't ready to face their own unfinished business.

Raven stopped walking and turned to face me, tearing me from my train of thought.

"What is it," I asked.

"When we find them, there's a good chance we may have to fight," she explained. "There are three of them and two of us. We already know their specializations. They probably leveled up and their specializations could have changed in the past couple of days. It isn't unheard of, but it's very unlikely."

"Range, close combat, and a healer," I said, hoping to score a few points.

"Right. So there's no need to inspect them," she asserted.

"I understand what you're saying." I laughed, thinking about that first night at Harold's Tavern. "Some people can tell when you inspect them. I learned that thanks to Ely. And we don't want to tip them off before we're ready to make a move. I got it."

Raven smiled. "Good."

I climbed over an ancient, downed tree. The remaining branches were covered in dry moss and hung in the air like the ribs of a giant beast. Raven followed.

"There's one more thing," she said.

I stopped and turned.

"I may have to leave you and attend to the pup. I'll be as quick as I can, but I can't promise that I can get back to you before—"

"Before they kill me?"

She closed her eyes and nodded. I waited for her to look at me again before I shrugged, sparking an expression of confusion.

"You're not the only one with a quest," I reminded her. "If my unfinished business is to sacrifice myself for someone I care about... well, it wouldn't be the first time."

I tried to keep the sorrow from my voice, but it crept in despite my effort. Memories of Helen and the kids flooded my mind. The flashback of getting the terrible news. Cancer. Helen was supposed to be there that day, but there was an accident involving the light rail. I was alone in the doctor's office when he told me the results of the tests. It was terminal. That's when I decided to keep my illness a secret. To leave and give Helen a chance to let go before it was too late.

When I got home, I told her it was a false alarm, that I wanted something else. It was the hardest thing I've ever done. And for months I wondered if it was the right choice, secretly wishing I could undo my horrible mistake. Then she met Roger.

"What's wrong," Raven asked, putting a gentle hand on my arm. "Are you okay?"

"No," I answered truthfully, and it was the first time I'd been truly honest with myself since that day.

The choice was stupid and cowardly and selfish. I'd been so afraid... But worst of all, I'd thought the decision was somehow noble. Raven frowned and wrapped her arms around me. Then she let go and looked me in the eye.

"Are you sure you're up for this?"

I gave her a sad smile. "It's just a little unfinished business. That's all."

WE HEARD THE SOUNDS OF A STRUGGLE BEFORE WE SAW THE TRAVELERS we were after. Sven, Guilly, and Ruby tugged at the thick leather leashes tethered to a harness. A harness that had been mercilessly tightened around the dire wolf pup's muscular frame.

The oversized pup whimpered and growled, snapping her jaws in vain at the three Travelers as they dragged her through the mud. Each of them kept at a distance from the others, their leashes taught and the leather creaking from the constant strain.

Raven unsheathed her daggers and prepared to engage, but I grabbed her arm and shook my head. Her white-hot glare nearly made me reconsider.

Something didn't feel right.

Even in this late hour, there was an almost magical and palpable darkness about the swamp air in the clearing. The more I thought about it, the more I realized it wasn't unlike the dark aura of the champion we'd faced off against below the fort.

Whatever the wolfling sensed nearby, it was enough to cause her to quake in fear. And if this thing was bad enough to strike fear into a feral dire wolf, even a pup, it was worth waiting to see what we were up against.

"Come on, you stupid beast," Sven yelled, tugging hard against the tether. "The sooner we can be done with you, the sooner we can get out of this wretched swamp."

The muscles in Raven's arm tightened.

"Wait," I whispered, pointing toward a new source of movement barely visible in the shadows. "Look there. I think something's coming."

A cloaked figure stepped into the small clearing. It wore a dark, hooded cloak with wispy trails of fabric that flowed unnaturally on the air as it approached. Necrotic fingers gripped a gnarled staff, and when the being spoke, I felt my blood run cold.

"At last," the raspy voice intoned, "you have brought me the beast."

The dire wolf growled and her hackles stood on end, but Sven stepped forward.

"We have done as you commanded," he said, offering his tether to the cloaked figure. "There was trouble along the way, a Shadowdancer."

"There was no mention of outside interference when you gave us the job," Ruby added. "It only seems fair that the reward for our efforts should reflect the difficulty of the quest—"

"Silence," the figure shouted. "I grow impatient and you shall have your reward."

A smug smile played about Ruby's lips and she cast a knowing look toward Guilly before her expression suddenly changed.

"What's this?" Sven cried out and Ruby let out a yelp of pain.

Skeletal hands reached from the wet earth, gripping the three Travelers and holding them in place. Then heads and torsos emerged from the depths of the swamp. The undead gripped and groped and pulled their prey downward, forming a tight, grotesque prison around each of them.

Ruby tried to cast a spell, but her magic was silenced by a simple gesture from the fiend. He cackled his pleasure at their inability to resist the significance of his power.

"Weaklings. Fools," he taunted.

"I told you we never should have trusted a Necromancer," Guilly shouted. And then to Ruby, "You've killed us all."

"No." The Necromancer laughed again. "Not all of you. I need only one. An echo for my charm."

I watched, dumbfounded as he raised his staff and cast a mesmerizing spell on the wolf. Her hackles fell, and she slumped down, whining but fully hypnotized by his dark machinations. Beside me,

Raven's breath stuttered. Her dagger glinted in a flitter of the pale moonlight that had momentarily escaped the rolling cloud cover.

"Wait," I whispered again. "We can't take all of them on our own. If he kills one, it'll be one less for us to take on. The other two might even join us. Then we just need to stall until the others get here."

It felt like a solid plan. Ely would come and he would bring Attia and Pops with him.

The Necromancer stepped forward and tore at the wolf's bindings. His movements were strong but subtle, and he ripped through the leather like it was nothing more than paper. The pup struggled to stand and a low growl escaped her throat.

"Enough," he commanded.

The wolf slumped down once more. Her growl faded to silence.

"Please," Guilly pleaded. "Let us go. You can keep the dire wolf. We don't need a reward."

The creature returned his attention to the three. "Oh, but you do. And I shall deliver in spades."

My heart quickened as the monster once again approached the Travelers who had been the first to show me kindness, to offer me their hospitality and a seat at their fire. Despite their ultimate trickery, they had been nice to me. Kind. They had shared their food and their company on my first night in this strange world. It seemed so long ago. Now one of them would die.

I thought of the pain I'd felt at the end of my ill-fated fight with the Meadows Rabbit and was overcome with sympathy, but then there was Raven. How much pain had they caused her with their selfish actions? And who else had they hurt?

"You," the Necromancer hissed, pointing a crooked finger and drawing ever closer to his mark.

I couldn't make out who he was pointing to from our angle, and I felt myself lean forward. My chest ached with morbid anticipation.

Closer. Ever closer.

"No," Sven shouted and strained against his restraints. "No. Take me instead."

The Necromancer did not listen.

The staff slipped back into his inventory, replaced by a large glass container. It was about a foot tall and ornate, triangular shapes adorned its faceted surface. Wrought iron bands wrapped its circumference, ensuring whatever contents it might contain would never escape. Moreover, the object emanated strange, dark vibes like an evil talisman. Then a curved, wavy blade of steel glinted in the Necromancer's other hand. Before I realized what had happened, the deed was done.

I stared in stunned silence, replaying it over and over again in my mind. Ruby's scream caught in her throat and then there was silence.

"Shhhh," he soothed like a mother comforting a sick child as he plunged the ornate kris deeper.

Guilly struggled at first, but then his body went limp and he slumped on the blade. It was over. The jovial Berserker would have no choice but to release and go back to whatever home point he'd last bound himself to. Probably Fort Morrow.

His body did not disappear.

I looked at Raven, my eyes wide in horror. Then a new source of movement drew my attention back to the gruesome scene.

Blue light traveled in wisps from the hilt of the blade to the crystalline container, filling it with some kind of mercurial liquid that splashed and bubbled with a life of its own.

"You monster. What have you done?" Sven cried. "Guilly, let go. You have to release."

"Yes," the Necromancer cooed. "Release. Let go. The echo of your soul now belongs to me."

One word escaped Raven's lips in that moment of despair. Her whisper was filled with shock and dread. It was a word that would haunt me for the rest of my life.

"Perma-death."

55

A million fractured thoughts raced through my mind. None of it made any sense. Guilly Ortega was dead. For real. Perma-death. There would be no respawn. No returning to the home point. No more everlasting adventures in EndWorld.

How was that possible? Could a Traveler really die forever? Everything I'd been led to believe up to this point now stood in direct conflict with what I'd just witnessed.

The dark wizard withdrew his curved blade and took a step backward while eyeing his prize. And that's when I recognized it for what it was. This container of bubbling liquid wasn't just an ornate glass jar. It was a phylactery, a special kind of prison. Magical. Mysterious. And costly.

It was a prison for souls. For Guilly's soul.

What did the Necromancer say he needed it for? An echo for his charm? The words were cryptic, but just recalling them caused a deep feeling of anger to rise in my chest. The makeshift walls of undead withdrew back into the swamp as the Necromancer held the phylactery high and began to mutter the incomprehensible words of another spell.

Meanwhile, Guilly's unresponsive corpse collapsed into the mud and began to sink, becoming one with the legion of the lost at the bottom of the mire. Ruby's sobs returned as she looked on, but Sven was silent. His eyes were locked on the body of his dead friend. There were no words for his utter defeat. Neither of them moved when the fiend stopped his enchantment and withdrew the spell that had held them in place.

There was no fight left. No anger. Just despair. I felt it too. It took root in the deepest part of me, but there was something else. Something that burned with the heat of a thousand suns. It wasn't just anger. It was an unbridled rage that threatened to tear me apart from the inside. This... thing. This monster. This lich or Necromancer, whatever it was, it had the power to take life. To steal a soul.

Raven touched my hand, and I had to force myself to peel my glare from the fiend.

"Go back," she whispered.

I heard my response escape my lips before I realized what she'd said.

"No."

"We can't fight," she returned. "Our best chance is to warn the others and spread word around Fort Morrow."

"What about you?" I asked without taking my eyes off our foe.

She didn't reply right away, and it was enough for me to read her intentions.

"You'd really send me back to town while you try to save your wolf on your own? After everything we've just seen?"

A tear trickled down her cheek.

"I can't leave her."

"And I can't leave you," I shot back. Then I glanced toward the Travelers and the dark wizard.

Sven and Ruby stood, transfixed by the monster's actions. He was standing over the pup now, the glass jar with the glowing liquid held aloft while he chanted words I couldn't understand.

*You **Inspect** UNKNOWN.*
Level 19. Necromancer. Data Unintelligible.

Error.
Object cannot be identified.

As soon as I'd done it, I knew I had made a grave mistake. The Necromancer stopped chanting and stowed the phylactery. And then the kris.

Without looking at Sven or Ruby, he equipped his staff and shouted, "Fly away my little birds, while you still can."

The words were like venom. As if everything before this moment had been nothing more than a perverse game. The gloves were off.

The fiend turned to face our position. I could barely hear the echoes of their footsteps over the drumming of my heart.

"I'm sorry," I said to Raven as I frantically attempted to free Truth-seeker from the scabbard at my side. "I didn't know."

She looked at me in stunned silence and then at the pallid glow emanating from my blade. Fear filled her eyes, and she glanced back at the approaching lich as he renewed his enchantment and commanded the wolf to rise.

"What didn't you know?" she asked, no longer bothering to keep her voice low now that the lich was aware of our presence. "What did you do?"

I was still numb with disbelief when Raven repeated her questions. But what was I supposed to say? The creature that now approached our position was something more. Something less. Something horribly in between. I didn't know if the error I'd received was due to a lack of skill on my part. Or perhaps it might have been a trick, a clever ploy to hide his information. There was one thing I did know, and the implications were more horrifying than anything else I could come up with.

"I inspected him."

Raven's brow furrowed. "You— you inspected the Necromancer? That's how he knew?"

I nodded, and she looked back at our approaching foe.

"This isn't good," she muttered and gripped her daggers tighter. "None of this should be possible."

Any further thoughts were cut off by a wall of moans rising from the mud behind us. There was no escape.

"What have we here?" He asked the dire wolf in a pensive tone, then offered an answer to his own query. "Unexpected guests. Very unexpected."

The wolf's hackles rose and a deep, throaty growl escaped her curled lips and gnashing fangs.

"Can you break the spell?" I asked without taking my eyes from the oncoming threat.

"I think so," Raven answered, "but I'll need some time."

I nodded and activated Mana Surge and Tempest. Then, without saying a word, I advanced.

"Denton, wait," she said.

I turned to face her, but there wasn't much time before the Necromancer closed the gap. The expression in her eyes was conflicted.

"Are you sure about this?"

All around us, an undead wall of corpses encroached. My heart was racing in my chest and the rush of adrenaline compounded with Tempest surging through my veins. It was almost too much.

"The only way out is to go through. Besides," I answered, "we don't have to win. We just need to survive."

SOFTLY GLOWING MIRE LIGHTS FLOATED LIKE GHOSTS ON THE SWAMPY air in the small clearing. The orbs weaved and bobbed hypnotically, seemingly drawn to the scene of violence and despair.

Truthseeker thrummed in my hands with a strange sort of energy, as if the blade itself were trying to warn me of the danger we faced, but I already knew. Everything was on the line. Life. Death. It all hung in the balance. What else was there to know in a place like this? Against a foe who could inflict perma-death?

At last, we squared off. The Necromancer with his staff. Me with my sword.

He didn't move.He didn't advance. No words of incantation

escaped his frail lips. He merely stood, watching and studying me for what felt like an eternity. Every lack of action was a silent confirmation that he had us dead to rights, caught alone and virtually defenseless in his domain.

When he spoke, his words cut me deeper than any sword could.

"So conflicted. Such turmoil. I can see it. How you abandoned your family and your beliefs. And yet you stand here before me like a hero. Would you seek to vanquish one such as I? You are too weak."

Anger welled up inside my chest as the foul sorcerer retrieved the phylactery from his robes. Before he could act, before he could equip the curved kris, I swung my blade with every ounce of strength I could summon. The glass container fell to the ground while the Necromancer recoiled from the unexpected strike. Dark red blood oozed from the wound on his forearm and he stared at me with venom and hatred and something else. Admiration?

It didn't matter. This was my chance.

I scooped up the phylactery and stashed it in my inventory before continuing my onslaught, but this time he was ready.

I cried out in pain and stumbled backward as a burst of purple flames struck my chest. It wasn't enough to kill me, but it hurt more than anything else I'd ever experienced. Fear and pain clawed at my mind. I was alone. I'd somehow managed to destroy every meaningful relationship I'd ever had. My wife. My kids. No friends. Just this. Always just this. This moment. This despair. No hope.

Just let go.

"Denton," Raven yelled. "Look out."

Her voice brought me back from the edge. It was just a spell. Those dark thoughts. They had almost been too much. If it hadn't been for Raven...

Another burst of purple escaped the Necromancer's open palm. This time I was ready. I jumped backward and to the side, narrowly avoiding the dark bolt as I harnessed every ounce of speed from Tempest. The effort was exhausting, but effective.

With the distance between us, I took the chance to check on Raven's status with the wolf. Neither had joined the fray. Both stood facing one another. The dire wolf bared her teeth and crouched low to the ground while Raven held her hand aloft and stared into the beast's eyes.

Growling in annoyance, the Necromancer advanced once again, but then stopped short. He looked at me and then slowly turned. The laugh that followed nearly made my blood boil with rage. He was mocking us and our pathetic attempts to defy his power, and he had no feelings for the wolf.

With a single, guttural word, he commanded her to attack.

Raven danced backward. She was barely fast enough to avoid the dire wolf's sharp fangs, but the pup did not relent. Nothing about this encounter was going to be easy.

Satisfied that my companion was sufficiently occupied with saving her own life, the Necromancer turned his attention back to me. Fingers of bloated flesh wrapped themselves around my calves and clawed at the wetness of my armor.

I struck out at the undead limbs with my sword, careful not to cut myself in the process, but it was no use. The effort to free myself was in vain.

With the squelching sound of footprints in mud, the Necromancer drew ever closer until I could hold my breath no more and the smell of decay filled my nostrils. In one last-ditch effort to escape, I retrieved the chipped sapphire from my inventory and thrust it toward the fiend. He merely swatted my hand away, and the sapphire plopped into the bog somewhere near my feet.

Then he spoke.

"Pitiful. So naïve. A true spark will ignite a fire that will ravage the lands of EndWorld. Just as the echo shall become the source, so shall your soul be mine. I will rise to power and the whole world will tremble."

I tried to lift Truthseeker. To strike at the too-powerful foe. Instead, his open palm slapped my cheek and bright bursts of light filled my vision.

The sapphire was gone. Rotten, bloated body parts wrapped around my own, holding me in place. I couldn't defend myself. Even without the phylactery, the Necromancer reached for his blade. Was this really the end?

The kris emerged from his robes, but then Raven was there. Standing behind him with the wolf hot on her trail. With a quick nod in my direction, she wrapped her arms around our foe. Then they both disappeared into the shadows of the void.

Everything went deathly quiet.

The limbs holding me prisoner went limp and the dire wolf whimpered, looking around the clearing in a confused daze. Our eyes locked, and she bowed her head.

Raven and the Necromancer did not emerge.

The sinking feeling inside my stomach began to grow as I recalled our encounter with the guardsman. Of slipping into the void and feeling the weight of the lost soul's thoughts, its demands to be set free. The force of its blows in the world between worlds.

The wolfling sniffed the air and let out a desperate whine. Poor creature, she was just as scared as I was. I clapped my hand on my thigh, calling her toward me without knowing whether her feral mind would understand the gesture. After a pause, she hesitantly made her way through the mud, stopped short, and then nuzzled my outstretched hand.

Had I not been so worried about Raven, I might have marveled at the wonders of petting such a ferocious creature. Both our minds were elsewhere. How long would they remain trapped inside the void? Long minutes passed, but still nothing happened.

When the two did finally re-emerge from the world of shadows, the Necromancer held Raven by her neck. Her feet dangled and kicked and her eyes were wide with a look of pure mortification and fear. Then, with inhuman strength, he threw her against an exposed tree trunk and raised his staff.

Raven was dazed by the blow, and when she looked up she wasn't looking at the dark sorcerer. Nor at the wolf. Instead, her eyes were locked on me.

The dire wolf pup growled and bared her teeth. Her hackles rose once more, but this time was different. The Necromancer's spell was broken, and I knew at once what had happened. Like my encounter with Truthseeker, she had made a pact. She had chosen Raven as her companion. As had I.

We both rushed forward. The wolf with her fangs and me with my blade. My Tempest buff was nearly gone, but I made the most of what I had, covering the distance faster than I'd ever gone before.

The tip of the Necromancer's staff arced downward, filling the air with a darkness that threatened to swallow every possible source of light. Using the momentum from the burst of speed, I slid through the muck with my sword raised. The staff connected with Truthseeker's steel and a loud crack and twang rang in my ears.

The weight in my hand was lighter and my mind struggled to fathom the cost of my heroic deed. Truthseeker had shattered at half-length and the Necromancer was smiling. He swatted the wolf away with his undamaged staff and then slipped the weapon back into his inventory.

The kris emerged from his robes and he grabbed me by my neck, hoisting me effortlessly from the ground. I watched in muted horror as, once again, the curved blade of the long, ceremonial kris flashed in the eerie glow of the swamp.

"Go," I croaked at Raven. "Take the wolf and—"

The strained words died as the Necromancer gripped my throat tighter and plunged his weapon deep into my chest. Raven let out an anguished cry and my lungs caught fire as my mind caught up with the overwhelming pain.

In a desperate attempt to relieve even an ounce of pressure from the weight of my body pressing down on the blade, I gripped his skeletal arm with what was left of my strength. It was no use. A wave of panic began to take hold of my senses. Wisps of energy surged from somewhere inside of me and out through the cold steel.

There was no phylactery. Nothing to contain my soul. Nothing but the Necromancer himself. The fiend began to cackle, and I slammed a fist into his chest. Then the other. Each blow weaker than the one before it.

"That's right, frail hero," he whispered. "Struggle. Fight to hold on to the pathetic life you once thought to throw away. Your efforts will only speed your end and fuel my rise to power."

Then he cocked his head.

"Or do not. It makes no difference now, and I revel in your anguish."

"Run," I croaked again. The sound was heavy with spluttering crimson.

I knew it then. Everything became clear to me. I could see my final moments playing out in high-fidelity in my mind. Soon I would drown in my own blood and, with the essence of my soul devoured, there would be no more respawns. Like Guilly, my adventures in EndWorld Everlasting were coming to a gruesome end.

As the last of my consciousness slipped away, I tried to ignore the final words of the monster. To focus instead on the serenity that was stealing my will fight. It was all for naught.

"So long have I awaited this night." He laughed. "So very long. And I will be denied no longer."

56

I blinked and shaded my eyes from the sudden influx of light. I was no longer in the swamp. No longer skewered on the Necromancer's curved blade. No longer in the familiar lands near Fort Morrow. No longer—

Orange-red hues filled the sky, filtered only by wisps of clouds that rolled across the horizon without rush or anything close to a sense of urgency.

I blinked again. Tufts of grass swayed in the gentle, salty breeze and the sweet smell of tropical flowers caught my attention. The scent was much more pleasant than that of the murky swamp water that I'd just started to get used to.

This place was familiar. Where had I seen— My tutorial.

I looked down, expecting the same toga I was wearing when I'd arrived on the island the first time. When Roger had explained how I died months after leaving the pod. Months that this version of my consciousness never got to experience.

But I wasn't wearing the toga. I was wearing my clothes from EndWorld. Still-wet blood stained my brown shirt and mud caked my gloves, pants, and boots. How did I get here?

"Daddy?"

I recognized the voice at once and turned to face my daughter. "Eliza?"

Tears filled my daughter's eyes, and she rushed forward, embracing me and holding me tight.

Ayva reached out and touched my shoulder, giving me a sad, knowing smile. I wrapped my arms around my eldest child and felt hot tears running down my cheeks. Terrible sobs wracked my chest and the pain from the injury inflicted by the Necromancer's kris burned anew.

Eliza took a step back, and I touched a hand to my in-game wound. My shirt wasn't just wet. I was still bleeding, and now the crimson stain had spread to Eliza's clothes as well.

Looking to Ayva for answers, I tried to form the words but failed.

"We don't have much time," she said, her tone apologetic. "You're dying and what's left of this world cannot last."

Unable to process what was happening, I took a step backward, shaking my head. "What? Why? I don't understand. Does this mean... Is Guilly back in his tutorial, too?"

Ayva closed her eyes and let out a gentle sigh before speaking. "I'm sorry, Denton. I'm afraid Guilly is gone."

"Gone? But..."

"Daddy, listen," Eliza cut in. "We don't have much time. Ayva is right. You're dying and you can't stay here. You have to go back to EndWorld."

"No." My reply was firm. "No, I don't think so. I think maybe I'll stay here while I can. With you."

The words felt heavy as soon as they left my mouth and my knees buckled. Before I realized what had happened, I found myself crouched on the warm, sun kissed earth.

The pain in my chest was like a loose thread, threatening to unravel what was left of me. Elisa was quickly at my side, one hand on my shoulder and the other braced upon my arm.

"Are you dead, too?" I asked through the pain, though I was immediately afraid of the possible answer.

She sniffed. "No, Daddy. I'm not dead."

"Then why are you here?"

"I'm here for you." She flashed me a sad smile.

It was then that I looked at her more closely.

She was wearing business dress. The now-stained outfit looked much more expensive than a paycheck an intern position at a firm like Cyberternal would cover. And she wasn't wearing a badge.

Did that mean she had an embedded chip like Krysta, the woman who had introduced me to the pod and the microscopic nano-doctors? Like Roger? There was something else. Something my mind almost refused to register. Eliza's cheekbones were slightly narrower, her eyes a little sharper, and her hair had grown at least five inches since we said goodbye and my adventure inside the game began. Yet it had only been a few days inside EndWorld.

Impossible.

"You didn't enter EndWorld until just recently," Ayva explained, once again reading my mind. "Your assumptions are correct. The time between worlds isn't always linear. It is for some, but not you. We don't have time for a full explanation, but it's been almost two years since you passed through that door."

Still kneeling, I glanced over my shoulder and watched as the door to EndWorld appeared once more.

But I lacked the strength to stand.

Every second stole a little more of me. Soon I feared there would be nothing left.

Ayva stepped forward and crouched down, then held out her palm. Slowly, an object began taking shape, floating above her hand like an illusion.

My eyes grew wide in horror as recognition set in. It was different than the one I'd seen in the swamp.

Instead of harsh lines and iron braces, hers was a bumpy but smooth crystal forged of raw power. Silver bands wove around it like delicate ribbons.

"Yes, it is as you suspect," Ayva explained, her voice sounding small and sad. "But this one is not for you."

"Then who?" I looked up, noting the tears in her eyes.

She didn't respond, but my instincts told me there was only one possible answer.

"Raven?"

She nodded and the phylactery slowly began to fill with the same type of mercurial, dancing liquid as I'd seen flow from the Necromancer's blade.

Blue wisps of energy traveled from her arm to the glass. The phylactery began to fill and tremors shook the island. Chunks of rock sheared from the cliff-face and tumbled into the ocean far below.

It was then that I realized that Ayva and my tutorial world had been intertwined from the very beginning.

"It was you, wasn't it?" I asked. "You sent me to the mountain so I would meet Raven. That's why I didn't spawn in a starter town like everyone else."

Again, she nodded, but this time it was slower, pained, weaker than before.

Eliza's hand moved to my shoulder.

"Daddy, I need you to listen to me," she said. "This is important. Are you listening?"

I looked at her and smiled. "I am, Eliza bug."

"Ayva needs you. And Raven needs you, too. I wish we could stay here forever just like this, but we can't. My mind isn't strong enough to withstand the strain of this place and if you stay here much longer, you'll die."

I looked to Ayva. "What do you need me to do?"

"You must take this phylactery back to EndWorld and keep it safe. Keep it hidden," she answered. "You must go back to EndWorld and face your demons."

"My demons?"

With her free hand, she pointed at my wound.

"I can't beat him," I shouted. "Even if he didn't have his cursed blade lodged in my chest, he's too strong. Besides, I have no weapon. Truthseeker has been shattered and my sapphire is gone."

"You have had everything you required since the moment you left this place," she countered, her words cryptic but full of promise.

Another tremor shook the island, and I looked to Eliza for answers that Raven's doppelgänger could not or would not provide.

"I have to go soon," she said, glancing toward Ayva before continuing. "There's a problem in EndWorld. I know you didn't choose this, but it seems that this fate has chosen you. That's why you're here, Daddy. You can put a stop to it."

"You must restore the balance, Denton," Ayva added.

"I can't," I said. "I don't know what you're talking about, let alone what I would do to restore any sort of balance in that world."

Ayva wordlessly thrust her free palm to the side, opening a portal for my daughter to leave.

"Wait," I yelled in protest. "Just wait. Tell me what I need to do."

"Take my phylactery," Ayva countered, ignoring my plea. "Hold on to it until the moment is right."

Then she kissed me. It was gentle and pure and sweet. I wanted to hold on, to kiss her back, to make the moment somehow last.

But I couldn't. Our lips parted, signaling the moment was gone.

She looked at me for the briefest of seconds before refocusing her efforts on filling the phylactery.

"What do you mean, 'when the moment is right?'" I asked.

"You'll know when the time comes. Until then, keep it safe and tell no one. Not even her."

The light traveling into the phylactery slowed and grew dim before it stopped altogether.

The last of Ayva's soul had been captured within the glass chamber. She smiled at me one last time before crumbling into tiny particles of dust that scattered in the ocean-bound breeze.

I picked up the phylactery and placed it in my inventory. The act felt mechanical in the face of what I'd just witnessed. Ayva was gone. She was gone, and I was now in possession of her soul? To hold for Raven until the time was right?

None of this made any sense. I was still trying to comprehend the magnitude of loss I'd just witnessed when my daughter moved beside me, tearing me out of my state of shock. Before I had a chance to grieve, I felt Eliza pulling at my arm and lifting me from the shaking ground. The entire island was in a state of upheaval. Still, she ushered me back toward the door to EndWorld. Large cracks and fissures formed at our feet as the island began to crumble, and I could see we were both running out of time.

"No," I asserted. "Stop, Eliza. You don't have time to get me to the door and get back to the portal. You have to leave me or you won't make it."

She looked at me in protest, but I doubled down.

"I can do this, Eliza. I can get where I need to go from here. I'll do what you asked. I promise."

She hesitated a moment before giving me a quick nod.

"Remember what Ayva told you," she said. "You won't have much time when you get back, but you already have everything you need."

Though I still didn't know what those words were supposed to mean, I gave her my best confident smile. I spoke the words I had tried to say the last time we parted.

"I love you."

Her eyes welled up with tears and she hugged me tight.

"I love you, too, Dad."

She let me go and raced toward the portal that would take her consciousness back into the real world. I continued watching for a moment longer and then turned. With my hand firmly on the doorknob, I cast one last look backward. Eliza met my gaze, and we both nodded at one another before stepping toward our separate destinies.

57

The bleak void that greeted me on the other side of the door to EndWorld pulled at every fiber of my being, threatening to tear me apart. The space was neither EndWorld nor my tutorial, but I could feel the Necromancer's presence growing. Doubts and insecurities flooded my mind. The pain was overwhelming.

I was back in the swamp. The kris was still lodged in my chest, the Necromancer's grip was like a vice around my neck, and blood filled my lungs like a rising tide. I tried to fight. It was no use. I fervently wished I could do more. To stop him. To break free. To end his reign of terror once and for all. No more victims. No more souls lost.

I had everything I needed to defeat him. That's what Ayva had said. It wasn't a delusion. It wasn't a passing flicker of my mind before I died. Or was it? Had the whole thing been a lie?

I redoubled my efforts, thumping my fist frantically against the Necromancer's arm. But it was too late. I was out of time. The last ribbons of blue light traveled through the hilt of the blade, leaving my body nothing more than an empty husk.

You have died.
You have lost Experience Points.

Return to home point?
Yes. | No.

Critical Error.
Data Corrupt. Object Unknown.
...
Runtime Ejection Initiated.

Everything went black. There was no more swamp. No more EndWorld. No more pain or fear. No more Necromancer. No more me. My entire concept of time and space began to unravel. My sense of self was gone. Thoughts and memories disintegrated. Did Guilly go through this before the end?

Before I knew it, even that concern faded away and was no more. So this was what it meant to die. To really die. To be no more.

A Hidden Trait has activated.
*You have used: **Second Chance.***

WARNING:
*You will no longer benefit from the Hidden Trait: **Second Chance.***

That laugh. That horrible, morose laugh. It filled my ears and mind, but the world was still dark. Empty. And then the laughter stopped.

"What is this?" the Necromancer cried out in disbelief.

I opened my eyes to see the wisps of blue light pulling back through the hilt of the dagger. Back into my chest where the weapon still held fast. The Necromancer saw it, too. Then we locked eyes. Mine burned hot with hatred, his were suddenly consumed with fear. Not of me. Not of something so insignificant, but of losing the prize he had thought was his.

My health and mana bars both filled, but then started ticking downward rapidly. The kris. It would continue to cause damage, and without a healer, there was no way to stop myself from succumbing to the mortal wound once again. What good was a second chance if I was doomed to die?

The Necromancer pulled at the blade and thrust the hand holding my neck out as far as it would stretch. It was no use. My soul continued to return, but I immediately knew the truth. When I was fully restored, the feedback would end, and my soul would travel back to the Necromancer once more.

There would be no more chances. This was it. My timing had to be perfect. The mire lights descended. Gathering together to create a shroud of eerie light as they fed on the palpable feelings of despair. And then the dire wolf attacked, sinking her sharp teeth into the Necromancer's leg.

He howled with laughter, and I could see that he had alighted upon the same assumption as I had only moments before. All he had to do was wait. I was powerless to defend myself against a Traveler of his strength and level. Even the dire wolf pup was no match. Her bite too weak to do significant damage to someone so strong.

Then the words came back. Ayva's words.

Eliza's reminder.

"Remember what Ayva told you," she had said. *"You won't have much time when you get back, but you already have everything you need."*

What did it mean? A *Second Chance.* Another opportunity to right the wrong and overcome the hand I'd been dealt. To avoid permadeath. To defeat this monster and free myself from the nothing he would condemn me to for the rest of eternity.

Something was missing. What was it? What else had I received from my tutorial?

A broken hilt of a crude blade: a hilt now in Jörgen's possession back in Fort Morrow. It was useless, nothing but a part of a relic I would never see if I didn't make it out of this swamp alive. That couldn't be it.

My health dipped down to fifty percent and a cruel smile curled the Necromancer's lips. If only Attia were here. But even then... what good would it do without the other piece to the puzzle? What was I missing?

The blue light began to slow. Soon it would reverse paths. I had to think of something before it was too late. That's when I felt it. A subtle reminder. A simple weight on a silver chain. A four inch crystal of earthen power.

I reached for the **Elemental Amulet of Earthen Resolve** that Beatrice had crafted from the shard I received upon defeating the golem. Could this be it?

I closed my eyes and willed the power of the shard to spring forth, to strike at the Necromancer and propel me backwards, freeing me from his grip and the dangers of the blade in the process. Nothing happened.

I clenched the four inch crystal shard tighter and used the last of my draining mana to strike at my foe.

*You cast **Earthblast**.*
Error.
Object cannot be identified.
***Full Resist!** UNKNOWN takes 0 HP Earth damage.*

Despite the blood once again filling my lungs, I grit my teeth and let loose all my anger and frustration in a fearsome howl that rang in the swampy air. Nothing was working, and I was running out of time. The last blue light of my soul traveled through the hilt of the blade and into my chest.

The Necromancer laughed once more. It was a horrible, greedy laughter that was heavy with the knowledge of the inevitability of my death. He knew it. I knew it. Raven knew it...

Raven.

She appeared behind the fiend, blood trickling down her brow from her last attempt at tangling with our foe. She raised her daggers as if to plunge them in his back, but even her last-ditch effort was in vain.

The Necromancer released his grip on my neck, allowing me to slump downward into the murky water of the swamp. Then he used his free hand to grab Raven and toss her through the air.

She was too late. The blue light reversed course and flowed back down through the ceremonial kris. Fear pulled at my mind and I felt panic set in. There was nothing left. No answers. I had failed and the cost would be an eternity of nothingness.

Unless. Unless there was something. Something I was missing. Like turning the page at the end of a story, only to find a few more pages waiting to be read. Hidden, but always there. Always waiting in plain sight.

It had to be something I'd received in the tutorial, but what hadn't I tried? In a move of pure desperation, I snapped the chain that held the crystalline amulet and then plunged the golem's elemental shard deep into the Necromancer's neck.

He stumbled backwards, crushing the crystal with one hand. Brown-gray lines flowed from the shattered fragments in his neck, spreading like an avalanche down his chest and arm.

"What is this?" he demanded, his eyes growing wide in disbelief. "What have you done? What is this trickery?"

The earthen magic continued flowing downward, slowing and then paralyzing the Necromancer as it went.

"You will pay for your insolent treachery," he spat, though it was clear he knew he had been bested.

In the background I could hear Raven shouting, but I couldn't make sense of her words. Something was wrong. Couldn't she see we had won? Then I saw it, too.

The petrification of the Necromancer's flesh had begun to spread down the other arm. The arm that held the hilt of the kris that was still embedded in my chest. The Necromancer sneered. With his chest fully turned to stone, he was unable to laugh. I felt grateful for it, but I could see the truth in his eyes.

We would share the same fate.

I had no mana and my hit points were desperately low. I had used the shard, but I was still running out of time. The cold steel of the Necromancer's kris began turning to stone, traveling steadily toward my wound. I pushed myself backwards, desperate to free myself from the blade. I only managed a few inches. Inches that were quickly losing ground to the advancing stone.

With one last slip into the void, Raven closed the gap and threw her dagger. It spun and whirred through the air until it struck the kris. Both blades exploded in a shower of stone and earth and I felt myself slump to the ground.

One last look at the Necromancer was enough to bring an exhausted smile to my lips. Nothing remained but a gruesome statue, a horrible stone wizard staring into eternity with unsatisfied hatred, forever knowing he had been denied his dark purpose.

You have defeated UNKNOWN.
Error.
Object cannot be identified.
You have gained 21,999 Experience Points.

Congratulations, Traveler of EndWorld,
on reaching Level 5!

Quest Complete! *You've completed:*
Face the Darkness.
Reward: *5,000 EXP, Increased reputation with the denizens of Fort Morrow and surrounding territories, 1 Gold, A shattered Death Blade.*

*You have learned **EARTHBLAST: RANK 2.***

Raven appeared beside me. Tears coursed down her soft cheeks and her wolf pup nuzzled my arm.

"Ding," I whispered, doing my best to smile.

My health and mana had once again restored, but the remnants of the cursed blade were still lodged within my chest. And without a conduit with which to syphon my soul, the damage ticked much quicker.

I closed my eyes. So tired. So very tired.

"Don't you leave me, Denton," Raven sobbed. "Don't you dare leave."

I didn't want to close my eyes. I didn't want to give up on EndWorld and the friends I had made, but I didn't know how much longer I could fight. I felt my eyelids flicker. Each breath was a little shallower than the last.

Raven cradled my head in her arms and her tears flowed unchecked. Somewhere far above, the moon broke free from the thick cloud of darkness and showered us in light. Still, I felt my consciousness slipping. My grip on this reality began to fade.

I imagined my friends gathering around me. I could almost hear their voices. Strange synapses fired in my brain. It was curious and confusing, but I wanted to believe they were all here with me in the end. It was a pleasant dream, and I was glad for it.

I tried to speak, to tell Raven of the phylactery Ayva had given me. There would be no other time to divulge the secret, but I lacked the energy to move or talk.

*Attia casts **Moon's Blessing**.*
Attia recovers 0 HP and 0 MP.
You recover 260 HP and 220 MP.
Ely recovers 0 HP and 95 Energy.
Raven recovers 100 HP and 85 Energy.
Pops recovers 0 HP and 2 Active Runes.

I couldn't help but smile. It was like we were in the sewers all over again, fighting as one against an unexpected, massive slime.

"Help me," Raven shouted, choking on her sobs. "He'll die if we don't get it out."

I opened my eyes. Who was she talking to?

Ely looked from me to the statue and back again and I felt his eyes rest upon the wound in my chest. He dropped to the ground beside me and tore open my blood-soaked shirt.

"We need to get Jörgen," he breathed, then stood and backed away before disappearing from my field of vision.

"It's a vivid dream," I croaked to Raven through parched lips.

"Stay with us, Denton," she responded. "You don't have to go."

"Keep those heals steady, Attia," Pops said. "We need to get that weapon out of his chest. I'm sorry, Denton. This is going to hurt."

Then the burly man hoisted me up and slung me over his shoulder. Pain tore through my chest, but the healing magic from Attia's palms was soft and soothing.

"Be careful not to let the blade prick you," Raven warned. "It's been made with a foul sort of magic."

"Understood," Pops grunted.

My head lulled to the side, and I felt the world slip away as my grip on consciousness finally gave out.

I awoke to warmth and the sounds of a crackling fire, but I did not open my eyes. Instead, I reveled in the moment. In the utter peace of not having to fight for my life.

I was no longer in the swamp. Instead, the air smelled toasty with hints of smoke that had escaped the hearth. Soft blankets and furs covered me. Beneath my weary body, I felt the embrace of a cozy bed. A mattress that reminded me of my room at Harold's tavern, but there was also something else. Someone else. A familiar presence lurked somewhere nearby.

I wasn't dead. My aching body was proof enough of that, though my heart felt heavy. My fingers reached toward the wound in my chest and felt the bands of tightly wrapped cloth. A dull pain seemed to blossom where the blade of the kris had been. It reached deep into my core and a foreboding sense of dread settled in.

Perma-death. Second chances... Why me?

And that was just the beginning. I had so many questions. So many doubts. About who I was, why I was here, and why Ayva had chosen me to deliver her gift.

I pushed the questions aside and pulled the warm furs down a few inches, peeking at my silent guardian. Raven sat nearby, staring bleakly into the flames that danced within the glowing hearth. I immediately felt torn. I wanted to speak, to tell her how much she meant to me, what a good friend she had been. To thank her for not giving up in the swamp.

I also wanted to stay in this moment a little while longer, watching her like this. A protector. My silent sentinel vigilantly keeping the darkness at bay. Then I noticed we were not alone. Raven's dire wolf was resting at her feet, enjoying the warmth of the flames. It surprised me how tame she appeared. How serene. She was acting nothing like the feral beast we first encountered under the Necromancer's spell.

Raven reached up and wiped a tear from her cheek. She sniffed and then blew her nose into a silken cloth. The wolf pup looked briefly and then rested her head on her paws once more.

The dire wolf was right. Raven wouldn't want me to see her like this. So vulnerable and sad. I pulled the covers up and then cleared my throat, tossing and turning a few times despite the pain.

Raven was at my bedside in an instant, but she didn't speak. She didn't say a single word. Was this how it had been? How long had I been asleep, tossing and turning, grumbling and fighting off the night terrors that plagued my mind even now?

When I didn't respond, she turned and started to walk back toward her chair by the fire. This wasn't the end, there was still more to my story. Suddenly my mouth felt dry. My words came out like a hoarse whisper.

"Wait," I said. "You don't have to go."

CHAPTER 58

Raven stayed by my bedside for what felt like hours. I listened as she recounted the events in the swamp. How Pops had carried me toward the fort while Attia kept me alive. How Ely had raced ahead to summon Jörgen to my aid.

"The Necromancer's blade?" I asked, once again touching a hand to my wound.

"A cursed thing," she spat. "Jörgen was able to extract it, but it wasn't easy. Such a weapon shouldn't exist in EndWorld. I made him promise to smelt it down."

"I feel like a part of me is missing," I said, admitting the sinking feeling that had plagued me since I first awoke in the bed.

"You're lucky to be alive."

It was more than that, though. More than life and death. I no longer felt whole. And the secret I'd been made to keep felt heavy in my heart.

"Speaking of weapons," Raven said, standing and walking back toward the fire.

When she returned, she held out a small scabbard. Then she unsheathed the broken remains of my sword.

"I know it isn't quite what it was," she said, responding to my sullen gaze. "But Jörgen did his best to salvage what he could. At least it will make a functional weapon until you get something else."

I took the shortened blade in my hand and felt my heart sink as I examined it.

Seeker
[Weighted Short Sword]
Damage: 12-19.
Strength + 2, Dexterity +1.
Quality: Average.
Rarity: Rare.
Durability 8/8.
Craftsman's Mark: Jörgen Olsen
Soulbound.

The tip of the sword didn't meet in the middle at a defined point, but was a jagged cut. It was sharp like the edge of a razor, and I knew that was where the Necromancer's staff had struck with its imbued darkness.

Was it a functional weapon? Yes. But it was not the sword I had come to trust. Not the weapon I had learned to depend on.

How fitting. A broken blade for a broken man.

I wanted to reach out to the sword, to hear it sing, as Truthseeker had in the sewers, but I couldn't bring myself to do it. What kind of voice would belong to a broken blade?

I cleared my throat and shook the thought from my head.

"Are you feeling well enough to go for a walk?" Raven asked, eyebrows raised. "It might do you some good to get a bit of fresh air."

"How long have I been asleep?"

"It's been a week. The first few days were rough. You had a fever and suffered from terribly bad dreams. We weren't sure you were going to pull through. None of Margaret's tonics seemed to be working," Raven's voice was soft and wistful.

"Then the fever broke," she added. "The nightmares didn't stop, but your body seemed to be recovering."

I stretched and then turned, placing my feet on the warm floor-boards. A whole week and I still felt the pain from my injury. Such a thing would have been expected back in the real world, but this was EndWorld. This place was supposed to be different.

The dire wolf looked at me. Her eyes were knowing and pensive. Almost human in their depth of thought.

"What about her?" I asked. "Is she coming, too?"

Raven got up and stroked the dire wolf's head, stopping to scratch behind one ear and then the other.

"Aavra will be fine here," she said. "We go out at night. Mostly. It's been a week, but the people of Fort Morrow still aren't used to seeing a creature like her roaming within their walls."

She tossed me some clean clothes.

"Get dressed. I'll be just outside the door when you're ready."

I nodded and watched her go before changing into the new linens and pulling on my boots. They had been cleaned since our excursion into the swamp and felt as good as new. The leather was still soft, and the fit was perfect. I strung the new scabbard on my belt and placed my hand on the once-familiar hilt.

It felt different. Like a stranger. It was a weapon that was filled with hurt, and anger and pain, and something else. A raging desire for something unknown. It wasn't truth, that much I knew. Was it revenge? Fate? Destiny? Something else?

I forced the thoughts from my mind. Though I had just awoken, I felt exhausted under the weight of it all. The sword could wait. All I wanted at the moment was to see my friends and enjoy one of Harold's piping hot meals while we caught up on everything I'd missed.

My stomach grumbled, echoing the sentiments of hunger. After I tentatively extended the palm of my hand, Aavra leaned forward and allowed me to touch her head.

"Thanks for taking care of her," I whispered to the wolf, then opened the door and stepped outside.

The corridor was empty, save for Raven, but one thing stuck out in my mind. This wasn't my room. I furrowed my brow and looked to Raven for an answer.

"No use burning rent in a room of your own," she answered. "Besides, someone had to... keep you company."

There was a hint of something meaningful in her words. As if I needed protecting in my sleep. It gnawed at me for a moment, but then she smiled and linked her arm in mine.

"Let me help you down the stairs," she offered.

When we got down to the tavern proper, Harold greeted us from behind the counter.

"Well, now," he said. "If it isn't Denton Wade. As I live and breathe. Glad to see you back amongst the living."

Raven flashed him a dark look, but then smiled. "How about something to eat, Harold?"

"Just the two of you?" he asked.

I looked around the mostly empty space. There was no sign of Ely, Pops, or Attia. "Where is everyone else?"

Raven shrugged and shook her head.

"Off to finish a few quests," Harold answered with a shrug of his own. "I suspect they'll be back some time before dark."

Raven took the lead and pulled up a seat at the bar. After a moment, I did the same.

Harold put down the glasswork he was drying and flipped his towel onto his shoulder.

"So," he said, rubbing his hands together in anticipation. "I imagine the hero of Fort Morrow has got to be famished after a week of nothing but warm broth. What can I get for you this morning? It's on me."

"The hero of Fort Morrow, eh?" I laughed. But Harold's eager expression didn't change.

I smiled and leaned back in my chair before answering. "Chef's choice."

Harold's eyes twinkled, and he gave us both a sharp nod. "Aye, an excellent decision," he said. "You won't be disappointed."

And disappointed we were not. There were tender potato-like

roots, roasted to perfection with sprigs of rosemary, sautéed onions and mushrooms, a side of eggs, and heaps of bacon.

"Slow down," Raven urged with concern in her eyes. "You heard the man, you've had nothing but broth for days. You'll make yourself sick with all that fat and grease."

I smiled and finished off another piece of bacon.

"This is so good," I managed to say at last. "I feel like I could eat another plate full."

"Something tells me that isn't such a good idea," she warned. "Besides, do you just want to sit here eating all day?"

"Hmmm." I pondered. "That doesn't sound like such a bad idea."

"Well," she countered. "I was thinking you might enjoy something else."

"Oh? Like what?"

Within minutes, I found myself thanking Harold and following Raven out into the cold and busy streets. Strangers mingled in the market stalls and lingered to discuss deals as they had done in the days before. Although, now there were fewer bodies crowding the cobbled byways as there had been on the day we'd entered the sewers.

I looked to the sky and my eyes traveled toward the swamp. The lurking darkness had gone.

"Many of the Travelers vacated Fort Morrow soon after the threat of danger receded," Raven explained. "I hear it's been much quieter since then."

I nodded silently and followed as she stepped into the street toward some unknown destination. We walked along in silence, weaving our way through the light crowds as we went. Until, at last, we came to Kenneth's place of business.

I stopped short and bowed my head, refusing to approach the merchant's stand until I had formulated some sort of a plan. What was I supposed to say? I had all but left the poor man with nothing but a fort-load of obsidian without so much as an explanation. It was too late for that now.

"Denton, my boy," Kenneth shouted, eagerly rushing forward to shake my hand and usher me back toward his stall of wares.

What was this? My jaw went slack as I recognized one of the weapons on his shelves. Tightly bound leather gloves with obsidian claws, much like the ones Ely had crafted at the entrance to the sewers. There was more. Clubs with obsidian studs. Obsidian-tipped arrows. Nasty looking daggers with razor-sharp obsidian blades. Even a horrendously gruesome battleaxe.

It looked as if business was booming. That's when I felt Raven's hand interlock with mine.

"We all pitched in," she explained. "It was Ely's idea."

"And I couldn't be happier," Kenneth announced. "Our shop has become the talk of the region. We've got the best obsidian wares this side of Castle Harrund."

Our shop?

Kenneth noticed my quizzical look and was quick to explain.

"Jörgen told me everything. How you nearly succumbed to a mortal wound when you faced the monstrosity in the swamp. Naturally, I wanted to help, but there was nothing I could do. And with all that obsidian on my hands. Well, that's when I told young Elyograg Nightly of our arrangement."

"Jörgen told Ely you might be trying to corner a saturated market," Raven added. "And that's when Ely offered to make another pair of his hand-to-hand weapons."

"They've sold quite well." Kenneth rubbed his hands together. "Ten pairs in the last three days alone. But don't worry, I've secured your share of the profits. Some of it has gone to pay for the potions and elixirs you required, but there's still a few gold left."

I nodded to the man and walked into the center of his stall. Swords, belts, metal knives, and a wide assortment of other non-obsidian merchandise lined the walls. He had done quite well while I'd been unconscious. I turned and offered my hand, which Kenneth eagerly shook.

"If you would like, I could cash out your initial investment now," he said. "Or we could continue our partnership, if you feel so inclined."

I let his words sink in, considering the original advice from Margaret for a moment before giving my answer.

"If it pleases you, Kenneth, I would very much like to remain business partners."

"Indeed," the merchant exclaimed. "Yes, that would be most advantageous for us both, I'd wager."

"Very well," I agreed. "Can you tell me where we stand with all of this?"

Kenneth was more than happy to oblige.

"We still have quite the supply of obsidian. But enough of the other vendors still have a foul taste for the stuff. We should be able to work through our stores without much competition. Now, as you can see, I've started trading with other Travelers and have amassed quite a selection of random, high-quality goods. The real question is, where do we go from here?"

"I think I might have a few ideas." I chuckled. "What can you tell me about Intact Bee Stingers?"

"They are incredibly hard to find," Kenneth answered, his interest clearly piqued. "The Meadows is the only place in the entire region where they can be found, but their acquisition is... tricky."

This was good news.

"How do you feel about giving quests?" I asked, leaning into the subject. "And I don't mean offers to buy goods or weapons, per se. But the kind of quests where a Traveler might go out and spend an entire day killing oversized bees?"

"Well, I don't see why I couldn't," Kenneth answered, looking puzzled. "But I've never seen the sense in it."

Over the next few minutes, I detailed my plan to amass a fair number of the intact stingers I'd managed to farm out in the Meadows. In return, Kenneth would offer new Travelers a fair, but modest reward for the repeatable quest.

"You want to imbue some of our weapons with toxins from the intact stingers?" Kenneth asked, rubbing his chin in thought.

"Worst case, we control a large portion of the market for pristine specimens," I offered. "We could always sell to other merchants and crafters at a reasonable markup. As for the weapons, I'll admit there's still a lot I don't know about crafting in this world. Maybe it isn't possible?"

"No, no, no," Kenneth exclaimed. "It's a brilliant idea. And if none of your friends have the Alchemy skill, I know the perfect alchemist for the job. She might even be willing to take on an apprentice."

At this, he looked to Raven and raised an eyebrow. She read the invisible quest text, then smiled and offered her hand.

"You have yourself a deal," she said as she shook hands and accepted his quest.

Things were really starting to come together, and I was glad I chose to listen to Margaret's advice.

After a few more pleasantries, we departed from Kenneth's stall, and Raven led me further through the city. Past the open courtyard. Past Jörgen's shop. Further and further until we finally approached the southern gate. The place where I'd first entered the city of Fort Morrow.

"Stay here," she said, giving my hand another gentle squeeze.

"What's going on?" I asked.

"Just stay here and watch," she whispered.

She slipped into the slowly moving crowd, drifting further away but always staying within my line of sight. I couldn't understand what all of this was about.

Raven walked toward Fat Anthony's cart just as another Traveler threw a tainted cake to the ground, cursing and spitting bits of tainted food from his mouth. The fat man's laughter filled the street, and the unfortunate mark looked back in disgust.

That had been me not too long ago, and I couldn't help but sympathize with the poor guy. Something had to be done. I gripped the hilt of my shortsword and started to advance, but then stopped short as Raven slipped into the void. She emerged behind Fat Anthony for a brief moment and then disappeared once more.

"Stop," Fat Anthony yelled. "Thief. Guards, there's a thief in the fort."

Two burly guards rushed forward and grabbed the man by the arms while a third walked slowly toward the scene.

"What's the meaning of this," Fat Anthony shouted. "Unhand me this instant or there will be hell to pay."

The approaching guard showed no concern toward the idle threats. Instead, he unrolled a parchment and began to read.

"Citizens of Fort Morrow, Travelers, and visitors from both near and far, hear me now. This man, commonly known as Fat Anthony, has peddled stolen goods and preyed upon those who would visit our fair city for far too long."

He addressed Fat Anthony in the same official tone.

"By decree of Captain Elsbaud, and as agreed upon by the Council of Five, you are hereby sentenced to five days' imprisonment within the dungeons of Fort Morrow.

"Following your sentence, you will have the opportunity to serve the citizens of our city by endeavoring to clean the sewers. For this task, you may enlist the aid of any who would choose to accompany you."

The guard standing to the right of Fat Anthony laughed. "I hope you managed to make a few friends while you were making mischief. Now get moving."

The guard on the other side shoved the vile breadslinger forward, chiming in. "Don't worry. There will be plenty to eat while you're serving your time. There's a whole cart filled with your not-so-tasty treats. Isn't that right?"

Fat Anthony wailed, struggling in vain to break free while the men hauled him away. Meanwhile, the remaining guard rummaged through his cart for the rest of the tainted biscuits and quickly followed in pursuit.

EndWorlders and Travelers alike cheered, and I felt a wide grin tug at the corners of my lips. Then Raven was beside me once more.

"Did you know the guards were coming?" I asked.

She nodded and flashed me a mischievous grin. "I might have heard something along those lines."

"Then what was all that about?" I pressed. "Did you steal from him? You could have been caught."

Instead of answering my protest, she reached into her inventory and produced another small scroll.

"It seems your friend managed to piss off the wrong people," she explained. "I was only fulfilling my part of a quest to retrieve some stolen goods."

She put away her scroll and produced a piece of folded paper, offering it to me with eyebrows raised.

"What's this?" I asked.

"Open it."

New Quest Alert! You've been offered a quest:
Return the Stolen Candelabrum.
Margaret Wilson is missing a cherished family heirloom.

Hint: Return Margaret Wilson's missing candelabrum to receive your reward.
Reward: 1,500 Experience Points, 20 Silver, and Improved Favor with Margaret Wilson.
Bonus Reward: *Unknown.*

"Well," Raven said, holding out the stolen candelabrum. "What are you waiting for?"

I took the tarnished silver candle holder in my hand and buffed a section of the metal with the sleeve of my shirt. There was no mistaking it, the object was a perfect match to Margaret's set.

Raven squeezed my hand and smiled. "Would you like me to join you?"

I shook my head. "No, it's all right. I think I can make it there on my own. Margaret can be a little... untrusting."

When her eyes filled with concern, I pressed my reassurances. "I'll be fine. I promise."

Then I stowed the candelabrum into my inventory and gave her hand a return squeeze. "I'll see you back at Harold's as soon as I'm done."

～

WHEN I KNOCKED ON THE WIDOW'S DOOR, I WASN'T GREETED BY THE harsh tones of the highly suspicious woman I'd come to know. Instead, the bolts unlocked with relative haste and the door swung open. Standing before me was Margaret, dressed in full battle regalia, complete with a jewel-pommeled sword inside its ornate scabbard at her side.

"Come in, Denton," she exclaimed. "Come in."

I stared in awe for a moment before complying with her request.

"What's all this?" I asked. "Are you heading off to battle?"

Margaret only smiled and shut the door behind me before leading me toward the parlor. When we reached the familiar table, she pointed toward the nearest chair and then took a seat nearby.

"I see you are awake, young man," she said at last, then nodded toward the wound in my chest. "Nasty business, that."

My fingers followed her gaze, and I touched the tender wound, filling my mind with flashbacks of that terrible night.

An overwhelming rush of darkness and dread washed over me, and I could almost hear the Necromancer's harsh laughter. It sent a powerful shiver down my spine, and the pain began to spread.

Margaret's hand gripped mine. When I opened my eyes, she gave me a sad, knowing smile. Seizing the moment for a worthy distraction from the pain, I retrieved the forked candelabrum from my inventory and placed it on the table.

"What is this?" Margaret asked, taking the object gently in her trembling hands. "It's my missing silver. Where did you find it?"

Quest Complete! You've completed:
Return the Stolen Candelabrum.

You've received: 1,500 Experience Points, 20 Silver, and Improved Favor
with Margaret Wilson.
Bonus Reward: *A Sealed Letter.*
Hint: *This letter is for your eyes only.*
Open it only when you're sure you are alone.

"Unfortunately, I believe it might have been taken from you by one of the Travelers you may have sent on an errand," I answered. "From there it found its way into the hands of Fat Anthony. He's been spending his time harassing other Travelers near the southern gate."

"And what of this Fat Anthony character, then?" she pressed. "Is he still harassing Travelers and receiving stolen goods?"

"No," I answered with a dark smile. "The guards are taking him to the dungeons as we speak."

"Well," she huffed. "Good riddance. He'll likely rat on his contacts, mark my words. Most do, you know. A few nights in a cold dungeon and those wayward Travelers usually crack. And that is when real justice will be served."

"And the ones who don't?" I asked. "That don't crack, I mean."

"They usually get bored with places like this," she replied, her tone matter-of-fact. "They move on to other areas, or risk facing the ire of those they have injured in their sport."

"I see," I said, taking a moment to think about the bigger world I'd yet to see.

If EndWorld Everlasting was as big as I'd been led to believe, then the number of possible adventures seemed nearly limitless. The mere thought of it conjured images of far-off lands and fantastical wonders.

"And you?" Margaret prompted. "Do you intend to stay in Fort Morrow, Denton?"

Her question caught me off guard, and I struggled to find an answer. Margaret only laughed.

"It's natural to move on, and in time you will. As for now, I suspect there are things on your mind you wish to discuss?"

"The Necromancer in the swamp." I said the words without thinking, blurting them out as if I'd been holding them in since the moment I awoke in Harold's Tavern.

"Yes," she said, nodding in understanding.

It was a prompt for me to continue, to explain the unexplainable. To share the very heart of my fear.

"The Necromancer wasn't a boss. Not like any I've encountered, anyway. Is it possible for Travelers to be bosses?"

"That I do not know," she said, her expression growing concerned. "What leads you to believe he was a Traveler?"

"I can't really explain it, but I inspected him," I answered. "That's when he saw me. And there was something else. The data I got back was all jumbled. As if the world itself didn't know what he was."

"Strange, indeed," Margaret admitted.

"I got lucky out there, Margaret."

"There's nothing wrong with a little luck now and then."

"But I shouldn't be alive," I protested, giving voice to the words I'd been afraid to admit. "I shouldn't be here, but I am. What do I do with that? Where do I go from here? I'm only level 5, but I feel like I've got the weight of the entire world on my shoulders."

"Yes. The darkness of his magic was stronger," she said. "And yet, you were able to overcome. There will be many struggles for you in this world. I, too, can sense that much. But you should never forget..."

I looked her in the eyes and searched for the answer. "What shouldn't I forget?"

"You prevailed, my young apprentice."

I felt the hot sting of tears in my eyes and wiped them away with my sleeve before responding.

"A part of me doesn't feel like I won," I mumbled. "In fact, it seems I may have lost a part of myself that night, and if it hadn't been for—"

"Yes," she cut in. "If it hadn't been for those closest to you, you truly would not have survived. Second chances are very rare in this life. Even still, you bear the burden of the Necromancer's mark. It is a growing darkness that may threaten to destroy everything you hold dear."

"That sounds ominous," I said, offering my best attempt at a joking smile. The expression felt awkward and out of place.

I shifted my gaze downward and focused my attention on the thin, lacy table covering. The craftsmanship was exquisite, the pattern beautiful. And the material, it reminded me of the corpse eater silk we'd seen far below the fort in the furthest reaches of the sewers.

"Ominous, indeed," Margaret said. "But you need not face what lies ahead alone." Her words were gentle and reassuring. Her touch on my hand motherly and warm.

"There are times when one must depend on the strength of those around him if he truly wishes to regain the parts of him that have been lost."

I looked up and smiled. The old woman, for all her early rancor, was my greatest teacher.

"What do I do now?" I asked. "How do I repair the damage that was done?"

She was quiet for a long moment, and when she spoke her words were filled with purpose.

"If you wish to walk the path to recovering what was taken from you, you must first travel to the peaks of the Frostwind Mountains. There you will find the icy snowthistle. But beware the cost of death, for you bear the Necromancer's dark mark and your soul has not yet been renewed."

New Quest Alert! You've been offered a quest:
Snow-Covered Snowthistles.
Margaret Wilson has offered you a quest.
Collect 20 Pristine Snowthistles from the peaks of the Frostwind Mountains.

Hint: Beware the cost of death. Your soul has not yet recovered from the wound you sustained from the Necromancer's blade.
Reward: 11,500 Experience Points, 75 Silver, an Elixir of Souls, and Improved Favor with Margaret Wilson.

Bonus Reward: *Unknown.*

I nodded and accepted the quest.

So this was it. I'd already made up my mind. Soon I would head to the Frostwind Mountains to regain that which I had lost.

THE END.

(Keep reading for a special Bonus Chapter.)

AUTHOR NOTES

Greetings Travelers! First of all, I want to thank you for joining Denton on the first steps of his unexpected journey in EndWorld Everlasting.

If you've read this far, it means you stuck with Denton through his doubts and his struggles. You know his greatest fear isn't just about being inside a game, but what it means for his soul. The journey isn't quite over yet, however. Keep reading for a special bonus chapter, and then continue on with the next book: The Broken Blade. (www.rbradyfrost.com/thebrokenblade)

EndWorld Everlasting is a place of many faiths. Of gods known and unknown, and of no god at all if you choose not to believe. It is a place for the sword and the shield, magic and might. The bow, and the axe, and other blades. Or perhaps none if you prefer the rake or hoe or coin.

It is a place where soulbinding your weapon means receiving its approval. Truthseeker isn't special in this regard. It partially refused Denton because he wasn't ready. By now, you might have realized that Jörgen's gift certainly came at a cost.

EndWorld Everlasting is a place for all of us, but it is seldom what we expected. That's because every Traveler in the game is the chosen one: the unlikely hero of their own story.

It is an afterlife, where quests are designed to help deal with unfinished business. You can always walk away, but the lesson will come back around in another form, and it won't always be quite so pleasant.

This might make you wonder about that quest Denton received to collect high-quality hare meat. What was he supposed to learn? What lesson could have been in store? Perhaps he needed to learn about death.

I hope you enjoyed Second Chance as much as I enjoyed writing it. The road was long for me, and I certainly faced many doubts along the way.

Could I do this? Should I? Would people enjoy the story I wanted to write? Shouldn't I finish my other book first? The one I had spent years refining?

In the end, I persevered. I stayed true to *this* path. And I'm glad I did. But how did the journey start?

I listened to an audiobook for Ready Player One back in 2017, which opened my mind to the idea of a world where books and video games became one. This wasn't entirely new. In fact, I remembered that even Ender in Ender's Game had spent some of his time messing around inside a digital world. Once I started thinking about it, I jumped down a rabbit hole that had been right there the whole time. I listened to Russian LitRPG courtesy of Hoopla and my Kindle Paperwhite took me on even more interesting adventures.

There were so many stories. So many books. They scratched an itch that video games hadn't in years.

I still had the urge to play games, but I usually spent my time messing around on the auction house, making gil or gold — depending on the game I felt most drawn to at the time. I had months of play time stored up in WoW tokens and stockpiles of gil in both FFXI and FFXIV.

Unfortunately, logging in was becoming a chore. Reading became more and more of a draw. My mind went back to my early MMO days when I first logged in to Final Fantasy XI. It was like a dream.

After my PS2 beta copy got delivered to the wrong address and lost in 2003, my wife got me the PC version for Christmas. I recall going through each of the job descriptions at the character creation screen. I liked the idea of playing a Black Mage, but I decided to start out as a Red Mage instead. With the ability to fight and heal and cast damaging spells, it seemed like the best choice for me.

I logged in.

I walked around Windurst for the first time. I felt so lost, and yet amazed at how big the city was. I tried talking to people. No one would talk back, and I was so frustrated when those first attempts were fruitless. No one seemed very interested in conversing with a total noob…

I also remember how embarrassed I felt when I discovered I had been talking to NPCs instead of other players. NPCs who couldn't read my chat and had no way to respond unless I used the system-recognized commands.

With my frustration mounting, my jaunt around the town was short lived. There had to be monsters I could fight.

My wife was sitting next to me, watching as I experienced this new world called Vana'diel . I was aching for adventure and she was eager to see how her gift had turned out.

After running around looking for an exit for what seemed like ages, I stepped outside. There it was: a zone called West Sarutabaruta. Blades of digital grass swayed in a breeze I couldn't feel. Other adventures engaged in combat.

I targeted the nearest unclaimed creature, and drew my weapon.

It was a Savanna Rarab, a cute little rabbit creature with beady, black eyes and long, straight ears tipped with white at the ends.

The next few seconds played out pretty much like Denton's encounter with the Meadows Rabbit. I died in just a few quick hits. It was devastating, but I was hooked.

I've had much of the same feelings while writing Second Chance. While the going hasn't always been easy, the journey has been worth it. Progress was slow at times, but I've always done my best to keep the story moving despite everything else. A super huge help in this regard was my coworker, Stephen.

It was amazing finding someone who I could talk about this stuff with. Someone who understood the whole 'it's-a-book-about-a-game-world' thing.

I have big plans for Denton and even further plans for EndWorld

Everlasting. More than anything, I would love to have you along for the ride!

I've also been working on an EndWorld Everlasting co-writing project with my son. You've met his character, Zachary Smith, briefly in Second Chance, and I think you'll enjoy where his story is headed. As of this writing, Gryphon's book is done and will soon go up for preorder.

The title for his book is 'The Weakest Frost Mage'. Don't worry, while Zack didn't expect to die so young, he's very excited to be a part of EndWorld Everlasting... even if things don't really work out in his favor at first.

Please join my mailing list and follow me on Amazon to get the latest updates on my releases. The newsletter is very important. If you want special content, advanced notice of releases, and more, this is where you'll get that info. RBradyFrost.com/ABMR-Newsletter

As for Denton, he has a hard road ahead of him. There are so many questions left to be answered, and I'm sure he'll uncover even more along the way. Dark times are ahead. Not just for Denton, but for the entirety of EndWorld Everlasting.

Thank you, again, for joining me on this journey.

I sincerely hope your time in EndWorld Everlasting was memorable. There are a lot of great options out there, so many game worlds filled with imagination and magic by authors who really care about their creations.

If you enjoyed this book, please leave a review and recommend it to other fans of GameLit and soft LitRPG.

I can't stress how important your review is for a new author like me. Your reviews and ratings on Goodreads help other readers decide which worlds they will visit, and which books they don't have time to explore.

If you are interested in reaching out, you can find my contact details by clicking on the icons below, or you can email me directly at:

brady@rbradyfrost.com

I hope to see you again in the next installment of A Battle Mage Reborn: The Broken Blade. Denton will reconnect with old friends and meet a few new ones.

Again, for the latest updates on books within EndWorld Everlasting, you can join my newsletter at:
RBradyFrost.com/ABMR-Newsletter

Be sure to stay tuned for news about upcoming releases by joining my newsletter, and don't forget to turn the page.

facebook.com/RBradyFrost
twitter.com/BradyFrost
instagram.com/r.bradyfrost
amazon.com/author/rbradyfrost

[…]

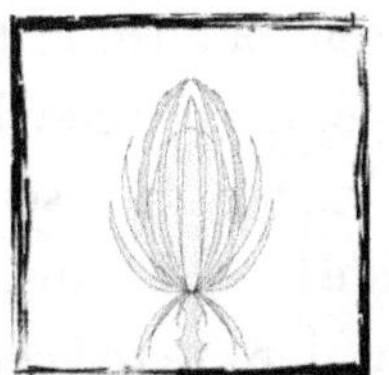

Harold's was as busy as ever. Even as I walked down the hall from our room, I could hear the familiar sounds of dinnertime in the Tavern. Old and new Travelers alike sat around crowded tables. The tempo of conversation ranged from idle chitchat to animated arguments, but the spirit of the place hadn't changed. Not a bit. The cordial flowed with toasts to health and boasts of contests won or to comfort those who had lost.

All of that commotion wasn't for me. I'd had my fill of wide-eyed would-be heroes. They all seemed to want me to regale them with the tale of our battle with the Necromancer, or give them details of the location in Duskmorrow Swamp.

Raven and I knew the truth. I was no hero, and the Necromancer wasn't truly dead. Not like Guilly, anyway. To tell the tale was to risk other lives.

There was no knowing when the fiend might break free. Until we better understood the forces we were up against, everyone was in danger. Real danger. The sooner we left Fort Morrow and set out for the Frostwind Mountains, the better.

The delicious aroma of food wafted up the steps as I made my way down the stairs, with Raven by my side.

"Harold has set the table for us down in the cellar," she said, flashing me a smile. "We'll be away from all of that."

"Is that where Aavra is?" I asked.

The Direwolf pup had not been in the room when Raven had come to fetch me for our meal.

She nodded. "I took her down while you were sleeping. I figured it would be best to do it before the main crowd arrived."

She was right. Aavra wasn't just some dog, and many of our fellow Travelers had a difficult time adjusting to her presence at Raven's side. Some were far too eager to pet her, while others seemed agitated simply by her existence. Neither of these reactions sat well with the wolfling, and both had made for a few awkward encounters.

We descended the final steps to the cellar, and I found the rest of my friends waiting, just as Raven had promised. They all looked at me with kindness and respect, and I did my best to return their smiles.

What they didn't know was that I was intending to leave them soon, to make my way alone toward the Frostwind Mountains. It was there that I would find the Snow-Covered Snowthistles that Margaret had tasked me to gather for the Elixir of Souls. And, while I was certain that each of them would accompany me on my journey, this was something I needed to do on my own.

In some way, I hoped that taking this task on by myself would prove to the others that I was worthy of the second chance I'd been given. Besting the Necromancer hadn't been due to my bravery or skill, and I knew he was strong enough to kill us all if he had the chance. If he managed to break free from his earthen prison, at least I would know that my friends would be safe from the fury of his wrath.

"Hey, man," Ely called out. "How are you feeling?"

"Much better," I lied, forcing a smile.

In truth, the wound in my chest had darkened and grown, and I felt a budding anger taking shape in the heart of my being. It was a feeling I couldn't quite explain. The emotions that poured through me at times felt foreign and had no real cause or cure. It was just an ebb and flow of something I couldn't quite control. A side effect of being wounded by the Necromancer's dark blade, I supposed.

"That's good, man," he said. "Really good."

"Let me take a look," Attia said as she approached.

Her hand brushed across my chest as I tried to step away. Pain shot through my core like lightning, but I did my best not to let it show.

"No, I'm good," I said, smiling. "You healed me earlier, remember? Go on, inspect me. My HP is fine."

This part wasn't a lie. As far as my Health Points were concerned, I was perfectly fine. According to Margaret, it was my soul that had sustained the lasting injury.

We all sat and enjoyed our meal in silence for several minutes before Pops spoke.

"So." He cleared his throat. "We've been waiting for you to start feeling better. Now that you're up and about, it's probably time to discuss what's next."

"Yeah, about that," I said, looking up from my meal. "Margaret gave me a quest."

"Oh? What is it?" Pops asked, and the others looked on with rapt interest.

"She has tasked me with finding twenty Pristine Snow-Covered Snow Thistles in the Frostwind Mountains. I know you all want to come along, but this is something I have to do on my own," I said. "At least to begin with."

"I don't understand," Attia breathed. "You're much too weak for that. Why would Margaret have you leave us, especially now, so soon after what happened?"

I didn't want to lie to my friends. I knew that if I continued down that road now, the lies would never stop. It felt just like hiding my cancer all over again. I was falling into the same old patterns, and I hated myself for it. Still, I couldn't shake the feeling that this was something I had to do by myself.

I had never felt more helpless than I had when I was at the mercy of that heartless monster with his blade of death. It was a feeling I never wanted to experience again. This was the only way to prove to myself that I was stronger than that.

"It wasn't Margaret," I admitted, feeling a wave of both relief and fear. "This is something I have to do. For me."

A heavy silence filled the air. It remained for several long seconds before Pops spoke.

"The Frostwind Mountains, you say?"

I nodded.

"I see," the old man mused. "Those are the snow-capped mountains to the northwest of here. If you leave here in the morning and stick to the lowlands, heading in a straight line, you should be able to reach Rosie's Respite by late afternoon. I'd advise you to stay away from Cave Trolls, though. That means no caverns or caves. They're some real nasty creatures, and that's with an entire party at your back."

"You aren't seriously entertaining this?" Attia shot back. "No. No way. You can't go out there on your own, Denton. Not now. Not after everything you've been through."

"That's precisely why I have to go on my own," I said. "I'll be fine. I promise. I'll avoid the Cave Trolls like Pops said. I'm just going to pick a few flowers. That's all."

"Hmmm," Ely grunted. "Sounds cold. You're probably going to want to get yourself a better jacket."

Raven had remained silent up until this point. Now it was her turn to weigh in.

"We can meet you at Rosie's," she said. "Just as long as you promise that you really are okay."

I had to choose my words carefully. The last thing I wanted to do was to continue to lie. If they knew the whole truth, however, I was certain that none of them would leave my side. That wouldn't work for any of us. We needed to get stronger before the Necromancer returned. That wouldn't happen if we were all trapped, hiding within the Fort walls.

"See for yourself," I said, making a show of flexing my muscles. A twang of pain pierced my chest, and I winced involuntarily.

"Yeah. See?" Attia exclaimed.

"Okay, you got me," I said, smiling at my friends. "I'm still pretty sore. That's easy enough to deal with, though. Right? I'll just avoid getting into any unnecessary fights. No grinding mobs for experience points or loot. I swear."

Attia frowned, but the rest of the group begrudgingly accepted my request. Within a few brief minutes, we made plans to meet up at Rosie's Respite. Pops even took time to show me the general location on my map. He was right. While the path was relatively short, the mountainous terrain was sure to make for a lengthy journey.

"Remember," he said. "Keep to the lowlands, avoid the Mountain Hares and Cave Trolls, and if you see a group of Travelers with a Berserker named Bruce, avoid them at all costs."

"At all costs?" Attia asked, raising an eyebrow.

"Okay, okay," Pops said, holding up his hands in defense. "Not at all cost, but you know what I meant."

"Are you sure you don't want at least one of us to go?" Attia pressed. "It would be safer that way."

Ely said nothing, but I noticed a sudden flash of excitement in his eyes. Even Aavra seemed to take notice, and her tail thwumped against the hard floor near Raven's feet.

"I know you'd all volunteer to go," I said, smiling. "But this really is something I need to do on my own. I'll be safe. You have my word."

"When do you plan on leaving?" Raven asked.

"First thing in the morning," I said. "Maybe I'll stop by and talk to Kenneth before I go. I could probably use a new jerkin."

"That might be a good idea, man." Ely laughed. "You're still wearing the shirt you made in your tutorial. Aren't you?"

I looked down at the doublet I'd crafted during my time in the tutorial and smiled. It had certainly taken me much further than I could have imagined.

"Sure am," I said. "It's probably time for an upgrade."

We ate the rest of our meal, recounting the highlights of our adventures in the Sewers of Fort Morrow. There was no mention of the swamp or the Necromancer, and I was grateful for it. While we might one day face that horrible threat, I could only hope that day wouldn't be soon.

At long last, we retired to our rooms. Tomorrow would be a new day and a new adventure. I would set out alone for the Frostwind Mountains. I would look for the Pristine Snow-Covered Snowthistles, and then I would meet my friends at Rosie's Respite. For tonight, however, I was happy to find myself in the company of such great friends.

ABOUT THE AUTHOR

R. Brady Frost is an author from Northern Utah. Brady spent his early years on the family's four acres surrounded by tomatoes, giant zucchini, and countless animals and critters.

As the years wore on, Brady discovered an innate love for technology. He was caught sticking a magnet into an electrical outlet at his preschool on Hill Air Force Base and, while he didn't gain super powers, he soon began dismantling the family's broken electronics. In time this behavior spread to taking apart functioning appliances. Before anyone could stop him, he was piecing together his Frankenstein robot army, which resulted in more than a few popped fuses but, according to official records, caused no lasting damage.

Brady writes engaging, character-driven stories where his words bring life to the worlds you'll want to visit again and again.

Sign up for Brady's newsletter for the latest book release news and updates about your favorite stories.

https://rbradyfrost.com/ABMR-newsletter

GET THE NEXT BOOK, THE BROKEN BLADE!

How do you fight the darkness that grows within?

Beware the cost of death.

After surviving the call to Duskmorrow Swamp, Denton Wade finds himself burdened with the weight of a dark mark and a broken blade. Sent to the Frostwind Mountains by his Battle Mage mentor, there is but one hope: an Elixir of Souls that can only be crafted after successfully harvesting 20 rare thistles hidden amongst the frigid mountain slopes.

In an afterlife world of quests and magic, Denton must make a difficult choice. Faced with two competing quest lines and a broken blade with a growing lust for battle, he discovers the right answer isn't always the obvious one. Will he answer the call to purge the darkness now plaguing the Frostwind Mountains, or will he fulfill his promise to a dying man?

The Broken Blade is the second book in the series: A Battle Mage Reborn, and is a GameLit Fantasy Adventure with soft LitRPG elements set in the digital world of EndWorld Everlasting.

The Broken Blade - Book 2 of A Battle Mage Reborn

https://rbradyfrost.com/TheBrokenBladeLink

COMING SOON: THE WEAKEST FROST MAGE

Zachary Smith plays a powerful Barbarian in the world of Kingdoms
Unbound.

Killing bosses and scoring loot isn't just a fun pastime. For Zack and his
party, it's a way of life. It's how they make their living. Before he can log in,
however, one thing stands in his way.

Homework. *Yuck.*

While working on his assignment, he learns about a magical place.
EndWorld Everlasting, a game world afterlife with monsters and quests and
loot. Even though Zack has no plans of dying any time soon, it sounds like

heaven on Earth, and it's just what he needs to finish his assignment and log into the game. His party is already waiting for him in Kingdoms Unbound.

Zack doesn't plan on dying, but when he does, he finds himself awakening to the world of his dreams. EndWorld Everlasting, a game for the dead.

And yet, something is wrong. He no longer feels like the powerful avatar he played in Kingdoms Unbound. Instead, he finds himself just as he is. A kid. Lost and alone... and weak.

Now he must choose his weapon and walk a new path. His eyes linger on the mighty battleaxe, but he knows he lacks the strength to wield it. When he chooses the staff, he unwittingly begins his journey as The Weakest Frost Mage.

Written by Gryphon Frost and R. Brady Frost, The Weakest Frost Mage is the first book in the series: Magus Rising, and is a GameLit Dark Fantasy Adventure with soft LitRPG elements set in the digital world of EndWorld Everlasting.

JOIN THE FAN GROUP!

Did you love this book? Join the fan group!
https://www.facebook.com/groups/travelersofendworldeverlasting

Would you like to be an ARC Reader?
Apply today at:
https://www.permafrostpress.com/arcteam-application/

You can also find me on Ream!
reamstories.com/rbradyfrost